DALE MAYER

A Psychic Visions Novel

INTO THE ABYSS

Books in This Series:

Tuesday's Child

Hide 'n Go Seek

Maddy's Floor

Garden of Sorrow

Knock Knock…

Rare Find

Eyes to the Soul

Now You See Her

Shattered

Into the Abyss

Seeds of Malice

Eye of the Falcon

Itsy-Bitsy Spider

Unmasked

Deep Beneath

From the Ashes

Stroke of Death

Ice Maiden

Snap, Crackle…

What If…

Talking Bones

String of Tears

Inked Forever

Insanity

Soul Legacy

Coveted

Boxed Sets and Bundles

https://geni.us/Bundlepage

About This Book

When she was a child, Tavika's family was taken from her by a serial killer who was never caught. As an adult, she puts on the appearance of normalcy, while burying herself in law enforcement as a detective. All her private energy is spent trying to find answers to what happened to her family … and to prepare herself for the day she intends to exact revenge from the culprit.

Jericho is just as much of a predator as Tavika is. He's caught the scent of old prey—a serial killer, the Ghost, one he's been a step behind all along. Discovering who the next victim is surprises him. Tavika is clearly a detective who gets her man—every time. The tug-of-war is on. She wants nothing to do with Jericho; all he can think about is her. She doesn't want or need his protection; he can't leave her alone to save his life. Sparks fly between them the first time they meet, the last, and all the times in between.

Two hunters converge, set to follow their prey into the abyss if need be—right where the Ghost can take out two enemies for the price of one.

He's cleaning up. Turning a new leaf. And wants no one left alive who can stop him …

Sign up to be notified of all Dale's releases here!
https://geni.us/DaleNews

CHAPTER 1

TAVIKA BANTRELL OPENED the door to the police station and stopped in the doorway. Her nerves cramped at the laughter inside. It always did when she was forced to return here. She belonged on the streets, not at a desk.

She understood the streets. But the computers, databases, and reports sucked the life out of her. As she entered, she slowly rotated her neck. The tension had balled up under the atlas bone and would hang there, until she could pound it out. Such a thing wasn't on her agenda anytime soon.

It was determined to sit there, like an irritated gnome, and to make her life miserable.

And she'd had enough of that today. Yet something stirred in her world. She didn't like it. It brought back memories she had worked so hard to keep hidden. Forced her to burn more energy and roughed up her senses.

"Hey, Tavika. Nice job on that drunk in the tank." Peters smirked.

"Yeah, Stoner has a thing for you," Mark added.

The sniggers started at her left and worked around the office. She did her best to ignore them. It was hard when she knew her shirt was ripped off at the lower right-hand side, showing her abs. Of course she wore a series of scratches and colorful bruises instead. Compliments of the six-foot-tall brute in the tank.

She'd gone out to walk the streets right afterward. Her way of working out the tension. She loved Portland. It was seriously beautiful, but it was just another big city in so many ways.

The homeless problem had hit an all-new high. The geese had returned and were shitting all over the place. And the heat, late for this time of year, made everyone crabby.

Including her.

"Nice job, Tavika." Lawrence smacked her lightly on her shoulder, as he walked past. "You know anyone else would have gone home and changed."

She snorted. "Like I'm anyone else."

"True enough." He motioned at her desk in the back of the crowded, noisy room. "Someone to see you."

She locked her gaze on her visitor's face. Her heart stilled, … then raced ahead. She tried for a deep calming breath. "I'm not expecting anyone."

Lawrence's voice lowered, as he nodded once more to where her desk sat in the corner. "This guy doesn't look like he marches to anyone's orders but his own."

Damn. This was not what she needed.

Giving Lawrence a curt nod of thanks, she stopped at the coffee station and poured a cup of black sludge. Sour, burned tasting, and hot. It was perfect. Fortified, she headed to her desk, determined to get rid of the visitor as fast as possible. If he was a snitch? Good. He could dump all over her, then hit the skids. She was so done with people today.

His aftershave hit her as she approached. She wanted to wrinkle up her nose in disgust; in fact, she started to, but something about the scent had her closing her eyes in appreciation instead. Her damn feet slowed too. Mentally she jerked hard on her errant body and slammed down her coffee cup atop her desk. She fell into her chair and lifted her scarred boots to rest beside her coffee, as she eyed the stranger over the top of her steepled fingers.

"You wanted to see me?" she asked, proud her voice was solid. She was solid. No flights of fancy in her world. She was a black-and-white, by-the-book cop.

But, right now, … at this moment, she wanted to jump this man's bones.

She clamped down on her jaw and stared at him suspiciously. She was pretty damn sure it was illegal for anyone to be this pretty.

He studied her, a secretive smile playing at the corner of his mouth. "I do." He lifted that gaze of his and locked it on hers. Shivers started to quake her insides.

Dear God, his eyes. … They were silver. As in molten mercury. They shifted with the same glimmering light too.

She swallowed and struggled to remain in control. "What can I help you with?"

"It's more what I can help you with."

Like she hadn't heard that before. "Oh, and what's that?"

"I want to report a murder, … if it's not too much trouble," he murmured, the wisp of humor obvious in his voice.

Her boots hit the floor, and she straightened up. All business now. "Who? Where? When?" She barked out the questions in rapid-fire fashion. This was her domain. Where she excelled. She hated to say it, but she loved a good old-fashioned murder.

"I can't say I have all the information you need," he replied, a note of apology in his voice, "but I can tell you the name of the victim."

"That's a start." She grabbed a pad of paper and pulled it

toward her. "What's your name?"

"Jericho. Jericho Sands."

She frowned, but inside she sent a mental high five to Jericho's mother. It was a freakin' perfect name.

"Who has been murdered?"

"Her name is Tavika Bantrell. Detective Tavika Bantrell."

She threw down her pen and leaned back in her chair, glaring at him. "That's hardly a joke," she snapped. "You're wasting precious police resources here."

"My apologies."

"No, you're not sorry," she declared in an accusing voice. "That's my name, as you perfectly well know, if you came here asking specifically for me." She threw her arms open wide and added, "As you can see, I'm fine."

Lord, she hated cases like this. Someone needed to escort this guy away from her desk and out of the station, where he could blend into the landscape. Silvery eyes or not, she wasn't into loony tunes.

"I meant no disrespect," he said. "It's just that I know this killer, and he knows you. Worse, he's about to make you one of his next victims."

She slammed her hands down on her desk and glared at him. "And you know this how?"

The silver in his eyes shimmered at her. She swallowed, struggling to not get lost in the potency of that gaze.

"The same way you knew I was here, before you entered the building. The same way I knew when you arrived. The same way I know your body is aching to be mine. ... I'm a psychic."

Her body shivered. She locked down her hormones and stared at him, trying to hide her deep unease. This was so not good. Could he know? How? No one knew. She'd made sure of it. She had worked hard to keep that part of her life hidden, buried so far below the surface that no one would ever know. Particularly the one person hunting her. Who had always been hunting her.

Instinctively she jacked up her energy shield. Her head boomed. She took a shaky breath. *Don't panic. You are safe. You'd stay safe.*

Then he lowered his voice and leaned closer, that mercury-colored gaze holding her captive. "A psychic, my dear Tavika, like you."

Her safely contained world buckled.

Ripples slid through her aura, shaking the pillars of her soul. This was so not good.

And no way in hell would she let him know. She gave a loud snort and sat back, crossing her arms over her chest and sneered. "The circus came into town two days ago. I suggest you go apply for a job."

He smiled.

That deep intoxicating movement of his lips made her heart thump against her chest. At the same time she wanted to rip out his heart and toss it across the floor.

"I understand you're afraid …"

She leaned forward and hissed, "I am *not* afraid." She waved her hand around the room. "Do you see this? This is a cop shop. This is where we actually work at catching criminals. This is not where we sit and pay five dollars for palm readings."

At that, he laughed.

A full-on belly laugh, completely amused at her response. Damn. His silvery eyes glistened with all things unknown. She'd seen other eyes like that. They saw past the barriers, slid under one's defenses, and ripped open your secrets.

Her mother had been like that. She'd never let Tavika have secrets. Or privacy. According to her mother, it was too dangerous. Tavika had no protection against her mother's pushiness. Yet, of course, her mother had secrets of her own. Like, about her first marriage and the firstborn son she hated to talk about. Tavika could count on one hand the number of times her half brother was brought up in conversations and never in a good way.

Jericho stood up in a smooth and elegant movement that she instantly hated.

If she even tried to act half as suave, she'd trip over her size ten boots. Still, she rose too, not to let this irritating man seemingly lord over her, if only via sheer physical positioning.

"Only time will tell." With a quick flick of his wrist, he pulled something from his pocket.

She automatically tensed. She'd been on the streets too long. She'd expected a gun, not the business card he tossed on her desk. She picked it up and gave a hard laugh. "A private investigator?" Deliberately she ramped up the scorn in her voice. "I should have known."

"That's okay. I love you too." With a wink and a sexy smile he turned and strode from the room.

As the door closed behind him, silence descended in the bullpen. She plunked her ass back down on her chair and glared at those few hapless detectives who still looked in her direction. "What's the matter? Don't you have any work to do?"

Lawrence, who sat at the desk closest to her, but still a half dozen feet away, replied, "Part of our job is to observe people. And that was one of the most interesting interactions I've seen in a long time." He gave her a toothy white smile that shone brightly against his black skin. The color of dark ebony, Lawrence was a good guy. A solid cop.

With a wave of her hand she dismissed her visitor. "He's definitely loony tunes' material."

"Intriguing," Mark teased. "I didn't know you went for the crazies." With a half whistle Mark sauntered off to the coffeepot.

Damn. Had her attraction to Jericho been that noticeable? Inside, her system was still absorbing the shocks. How had that asshole found her? And what did he really want?

And how would she shake him off her tail?

JERICHO STOOD OUTSIDE the station, staring at the drizzling rain. "Well, that went well."

In fact, it had gone better than he'd expected. He'd done his research, before walking in. He knew so much about her and yet understood so little.

He'd only confronted her now because time was short. The killer had moved up his agenda, and her name was rising up the list. She could be a hard-ass all she wanted. Jericho would still keep her safe. He knew full well she was psychic. Yet that was no guarantee of staying alive, especially if the Ghost wanted her dead. Ghost was the code name for the serial killer. A prolific sadist, who liked torturing his victims first. As Tavika well knew.

She was also a survivor. She'd been traumatized by her encounter with the Ghost, when she was much younger. From what Jericho could discern from the energy waves around her system, she was stronger than ever.

And, if he were honest, not only did he want to keep her safe but he also wanted to utilize her abilities to catch this killer, once and for all.

All he had to do was get her on his side. Easy, right?

Knowing his phone would ring, he pulled it out and held it to his ear, before the chime went off. He smiled like he always did at the ring tone. It was a few stanzas of music from the movie *Halloween*. Jericho walked in the shadows himself. Nothing like a good horror movie to make him laugh.

Reality offered more than movies ever could.

He lived it. He watched other people do the same, and, as far as he was concerned, it was his job to take down the assholes who created horror.

He acknowledged his caller. "Stefan, I got nowhere. You were right. She won't admit to that side of her personality."

"And yet she's very talented and uses those abilities for her own purposes," Stefan argued, fatigue creeping through his voice.

Jericho understood. Stefan saw too much. Heard too much. Understood even more. The one thing they could always count on were the horrors people inflicted on each other. Like Jericho, Stefan had no choice but to help.

"She shut me down." Jericho laughed. "She wanted me gone and fast."

"She is no ordinary woman."

"She might be no ordinary psychic, but I don't think she has any clue," Jericho corrected. "However, she's one hell of a woman."

"I wouldn't push that right now," Stefan warned.

"No worries," Jericho replied comfortably. "Plenty of time to rock her bones later." Stefan's sigh made Jericho laugh out loud. "Okay, I won't push it. At least not right now."

"She's likely to rock your bones and not in a good way. She is tough. Sharp. And has honed her psychic skills like no one else I've seen. She also has an energy shield that …"

"That's killing her," Jericho butted in. "She ramped it up while I was sitting there. The minute I mentioned the word *psychic*, her system went into overdrive. And she got hit with a hell of a headache. I watched her cringe, as the energy slammed into her head."

"The more she denies it, the more she locks that down, the worse the pain will get." Stefan's voice faded slightly.

"You and I both know that's just the beginning of it. If Tavika doesn't take better care of herself, her energy systems will kill her."

He lounged against the outside wall of the police station, under the eaves to keep the rain mostly off him, and was completely ignored by the world around him. He loved that about the city. No one noticed anybody because they were so busy trying to mind their own business, as they traveled from point A to point B. "Did you pick up anything more on the Ghost?" Jericho asked, as he turned to study the busy street.

"Not yet. He's in Portland, but I haven't narrowed down the location any better."

Jericho waited a minute to see if Stefan had anything more to add, then asked, "Anything new and ugly appearing now that he's in town?"

An odd pause followed.

"Stefan?" Jericho nudged him.

"Not sure yet. Drew is on it."

Drew was a cold case detective, not of the psychic variety. And engaged to Dr. Maddy, a friend of theirs. Only

Drew's department had no budgetary money for this case, unless they came up with solid proof that the Ghost had resurfaced. Drew had been keeping track of Jericho's progress on the case for years. That the killer had appeared to sleep for the last five years had been both a relief and a concern—if he had now resurfaced.

And he had. Jericho knew it. So did Stefan. Tavika too, regardless of what she'd let anyone else believe.

And no way the Ghost would disappear again. Drew was just as adamant to find him. Drew had eleven cold cases, all with the Ghost's name attached as a prime suspect. Files that, even with Dr. Maddy's and Stefan's help, the department hadn't gotten far on.

Jericho shook his head, wondering what it would be like for Drew, a humble human, to have an energy worker extraordinaire like Dr. Maddy in his life. But Jericho was also ornery and apparently contrary as well in his taste for women—because all he could think about now was having one very irritating, very female detective under him. He didn't think Tavika would go down easy. Surrender was foreign to her. But, when they got there, he knew they'd burn down the house.

He couldn't wait.

HE STOOD AND stared out the front window of the police station. Coming here today hadn't been part of his plan, but life was like that. And sometimes there was a damn good reason for it. Like maybe right now.

His mind was consumed with what he'd just heard. Surely the water-cooler gossip had been wrong. But the station buzzed with overheard tidbits of Tavika's visitor.

Something about the psychic calling Tavika the same. Hell, everyone for miles had heard by now. And that was wrong. No way she was. And gossip like that was a career killer. She'd never do anything to jeopardize that.

But, … if she were psychic? That was bad news. He'd saved her once. No way he'd do that again.

Love made one do stupid things, and he was no more immune than anyone else. Still, if she were one of those, he wasn't sure anything or anyone could save her this time—and why should he?

If she were one of those evil psychics, she needed to die—just like the rest of her family had.

CHAPTER 2

T AVIKA LOOKED AT her watch. Had she waited long enough? Would Jericho be long gone, or would he be haunting the front door of the station still? It wasn't like her to ditch the office so soon, unless Dispatch sent her elsewhere. But mistakes at this stage would be fatal. She packed up her desk, locked her drawers, and shut down her computer. Paranoid much? Yeah, but she had her reasons. She strode out of the bullpen without saying a word to anyone.

And met Henry in the hallway. She touched her old friend and mentor on the shoulder. Currently in a police liaison position, he'd been one hell of a detective in his time. She knew he wasn't solely responsible for her rescue all those years ago. Yet, every time she saw him, she thought of that.

And he'd stuck around since then to help her find normalcy in a world gone crazy.

He narrowed his gaze. "What's going on?" he quietly asked, checking his watch.

"Nothing. It's all good." She gave him a smile. "It's nice to see you."

He studied her for a long moment, then nodded. He slipped his hand into his jacket pocket and pulled out a small envelope, holding it out to her with a self-conscious smile. "We finally set a date. You're invited."

He turned and walked away, and she grinned, as she

watched him disappear down the hallway, figuring she knew what the invitation was all about. At least she hoped so. She stuffed it into her pocket, unopened. He'd been with his partner for as long as Tavika could remember. Originally he'd been a friend of her mother's and, as such, knew Tavika better than most. Yet still, he didn't *know* her—*no one* did.

She kept herself locked down inside. Always wary and detached. There was life before *the Event* and life after it. She'd changed afterward. Had disconnected from the world, her surroundings, even herself. It was easier. Then she'd been to hell and back. So who could blame her for holding herself apart from the rest of the world? And, if they did, tough shit.

Heading around to the rear exit of the station and into the back parking lot, she hopped on her Harley. She kick-started the engine and pulled the bike out into traffic. She had no idea where she was going, just knew she had to get the hell away. She pulled onto the highway and hit the gas.

Maybe she'd known she would need this mini-escape today. She usually brought her truck and left her bike for weekends. Today, this suited her mood. Only she had no jacket, and the chilly wind slashed at her bare stomach under her damaged shirt.

Going faster than she should, taking more risks, she navigated the roughly eighty miles in about one hour, and headed down the coast, trying to blow the stress and the fear from her soul.

When she finally pulled off on the side of the road and stared at the water pounding down on the surf below, she realized she'd gone far enough. She sat back on her bike to study her trembling hands. Tavika had let Jericho get to her. Her sister would have a heyday if she knew. And so would her twin, Travis. Her mother? ... She'd be scornful and derisive. As always.

Her phone in her left pocket rang. Of course Travis would be calling now. He always knew, but then twins were like that.

She pulled his phone from her pocket and waited for the words she already expected.

"Still running away?" Travis asked her. "You knew that Jericho was coming and that the Ghost was coming. Even after all this time, you're surprised when you're right?"

She ignored him. One couldn't argue with the truth.

"You could try," he noted comfortably, easily reading her mind, "but it would be a waste of your energy—something you can't afford right now."

Speaking under her breath, a quick glance around to make sure she was alone, she asked, "What difference does it make? You'd torment me either way."

He snorted. "Only because I love you."

She didn't bother to answer that. She wrapped her arm around her chest, shocked at the chill to her skin from her fingers. "You're right though. I did run."

His voice softened, as he added, "That's okay. You can't be strong all the time."

Like hell. She *had* to be strong all the time. She had no other option. She had cultivated her abrasive hard outside to stop people from getting too close. That was the last thing she wanted. Everyone who got close died. The only ones left in her personal world were Henry and his partner, Charles. And she let them only so close. She owed Henry. He'd been instrumental in getting her on the force and had helped her make detective. Maybe he did so out of guilt that they couldn't solve her family's murder case. It didn't matter why. She was grateful. Now to get rid of that pesky Jericho.

"He's right too, you know?" Travis's voice deepened. "The Ghost's hunting you again."

She ignored that. "I'm no one to him. And Jericho isn't right," she snapped. "He knows nothing. I'm no one to the Ghost."

"You're important. I don't know why," Travis argued. "Something about you makes him uncomfortable now. Jericho is looking down the road to the future. To when the Ghost comes after you."

"I know," she admitted softly. She'd asked her mom and her sister many times about the identity of their killer, but they went blank and disappeared when she tried to bring it up. Maybe not an unnatural response to a devastating event but frustrating as hell for Tavika.

She had no intention of being found by the Ghost again. Once had been more than enough. She'd come out the winner that time, if anyone could win a deadly game like that. Only the killer had escaped and had gone underground after her family had been exterminated. Hell, he'd slept erratically for years. Coming out to cause mayhem, then to disappear again after he got his fix. Who knew how many people he'd killed in total?

Why the hell would she want to revisit that? Still, she'd never been able to leave it alone. She was always on the lookout for him. No one could ever forget the Ghost.

"Hiding the truth from yourself, that's one thing. But if you think you can hide it from me, not happening. You knew Jericho was coming. And you know the killer is too." On that note Travis's voice disappeared.

Great. Now she'd pissed him off too. She was batting one thousand today. Still, edginess shimmered inside her system, stopping her from finding a level of comfort with her day. Is that what Jericho had intended? To throw her off balance and to keep her there by bringing up painful memories?

No way he could know she was psychic. That was *not* how it worked. She'd heard of a couple specialists in the field who were capable of assessing other individuals for psychic abilities, and, of course, there were the media-hound psychics, looking to drum up business, who often told desperate tales about dead loved ones.

Still, a few good ones were out there. According to everything she'd heard, Stefan was one. Dr. Maddy another, although she was better known for her healing abilities. Tavika had heard cops for miles around sing Stefan's praises. They used to sing her mother's. Her mother's reputation was always there in the background, terrifying Tavika of being found out. Knowing people looked at her sideways, wondering if she had abilities of her own.

Her phone in her right-hand pocket rang. She glared at it. And saw Dispatch on the caller ID.

"Reports of a deceased male. On 984 Hollard Street. Two blocks back from Kinsman Park."

"Kinsman Park?" Her heart stalled, then it picked up and raced forward.

"Yes. Two units on the way."

She was eighty miles away. Shit. Why had she gone so far out of town, when she was on duty? Murder didn't stop just because she needed to clear her head. She turned her bike in the direction of home and gunned it.

Kinsman Park area. Interesting location. Every time she heard that name, it brought ugly memories back. Two blocks from that very same park was where she'd been held prisoner for one week.

She slammed the memory back down into the black hole, where it belonged, to focus on the business of getting home again. When she pulled up outside the correct address about an hour later, she found the place already taped off and multiple black-and-white cars everywhere. She pulled her keys from the bike, pocketed them, and strode to the front door. No one said a word. Then again they already knew her.

And she knew them—in ways they wouldn't understand.

JERICHO WAITED IN Kinsman Park for Tavika to show, taking a seat on a nearby park bench, having a good view of the scene of the crime. He'd seen her take off from the station, flying down the highway as if the devil were after her. And he was. The devil called the Ghost. She just didn't seem to care. Of course she'd met the Ghost once already and had survived. Did she really think she'd do it again?

Details on her abilities were sketchy. Stefan had told Jericho a little, but no one knew anything for sure.

Every time Jericho tried to read Tavika, the dominant impression he picked up was confusion. He knew she had an energy barrier up. Was that showing up as confusion? Or were her thoughts behind it confused?

Her barrier was so slick and almost electrified that it was damn-near impossible to read the truth behind it. That she could even keep up such a defensive wall revealed much about her power and inherent abilities.

If she ever learned to direct that power, the world could be in trouble.

Nothing in her file said she was unstable or dangerous to the public. As he'd been collecting this data, he knew a lot about her already. He was a precog, so he saw things before they happened. And when the visions came in as strongly as they had been lately? They were scarily right. No matter what he did, he couldn't seem to change the outcome of what he saw. But that didn't mean he always understood his visions. And, if he were right, Tavika would not survive her argument with the devil a second time.

Focusing on his surroundings now, the energy of this neighborhood swelled around him. He closed his eyes and let the music dance. He was one of the few psychics with more than a single ability. And when energy spoke to him, it came in many forms.

Sometimes in color. Sometimes through music. Really no way to know how a message would manifest. If they couldn't get it to him one way, then they would through another.

Now if only he understood what they were trying to tell him.

In his mind's eye, he saw energy approaching the house, going around to the back, before sneaking into the open patio doors. He'd seen the original vision yesterday—and had recognized it for what it was. The Ghost's latest victim.

The old man had fallen asleep in front of the television. His death quick and easy. Not this killer's normal MO. The cops would never consider the Ghost for this job. It wasn't his style. A single knife slice across the throat wouldn't have given him anywhere near enough fun. But it was fast, efficient, and, in this case, expedited a problem.

At least that was Jericho's impression of the scene.

Jericho didn't understand what the Ghost was up to; Jericho just knew the asshole had to be stopped. So Jericho had waited in the park for several hours, awaiting Tavika's appearance. And then he sent her a message. He opened a spirit corridor, walked the short distance, and knocked on the door to Tavika's mind. When it opened, he delivered his message. *Come talk to me,* he said. *You know you want to.*

He almost laughed at her shocked response, followed by her epithet. The door slammed in his face. He could send as many messages as he wanted to hereafter, but she was no longer receiving.

And that was not what he wanted. If he couldn't tell when she was in trouble, how was he supposed to help when she really needed it?

I told you to watch it with her, Stefan warned Jericho in his head. *I don't know how much she believes in all this or whether she's just a loner who needs to keep her own counsel.*

"That will get her killed," Jericho stated out loud, looking around to confirm that he was alone and that no one heard him talking to himself. "I'm trying to keep her alive."

Then I suggest you use a little of that finesse you're well-known for, not a battering ram.

This time Jericho did laugh—the sound ringing out across the park. "I figured she needed the battering ram. That's the only way anyone will get through those defenses of hers."

As he stood to leave the park, he froze.

Tavika stood ten feet from him, a frown on her face and accusation in her voice as she asked, "Did you kill him?"

THAT DIDN'T TAKE them long. He frowned; it was too fast actually. He hadn't been watching from his window in the last few hours to see if anyone had traipsed in there, but surely the old man should have gone unnoticed for a day or two. He'd counted on it.

Every time something happened out of schedule, it bugged him. He liked things to be perfectly lined up.

And, when they weren't, he wanted to know why.

It was his fault that he hadn't already been watching the old man's house before now, and that bugged him. He didn't make many mistakes, but he'd assumed the old man was alone. And no one would know for days.

But someone had.

Another black-and-white unit pulled up to the house.

He shrugged. Oh well, time to make the best of it.

He walked back to the kitchen, hoping there was still a pack of popcorn. He'd planned to shop for more but thought he had time.

There was one left. Chortling, he popped it in the microwave. Who needed television? He had his own real life crime drama show to watch.

CHAPTER 3

TAVIKA RESTED HER hands on her hips and glared at the cocky ass in front of her.

Until he comprehended her question, then his cockiness fled to be replaced by an anger like she rarely saw. He bolted toward her. She narrowed her gaze at him and braced herself.

"You really think I killed that old man?" he asked in a low but harsh voice.

She studied the look in his eyes but saw the truth in his energy, regardless of his words.

"No, I don't." She took one step closer and widened her stance, as her own anger grew. Then again, anybody who'd seen what she had just found would be angry too. "It was just an old man, watching TV."

"And he's connected."

Her eyebrows shot up. That wasn't what she expected to hear. "Connected?" Was he telling the truth? What did Jericho know? Psychics were invariably unsure of the black-and-white answers when pressed. "Connected to whom?"

It was his turn to look at her in surprise. "You can't tell?" He took several steps on the path away from her. "Have you really distanced yourself so far from what happened before that you can't recognize the same energy of the man who preyed on you and your family as being the same one who preyed on that old man?"

She shook her head. "That makes no sense." Hell, it had better not make any. She looked at the ground uncertainly. She wasn't sure she could recognize the Ghost's energy. She could tell when someone was lying but hadn't considered energy recognition. Were the energies of people all unique? Like DNA or signatures or fingerprints? She didn't remember hearing anything like that, but what if such a thing were possible?

He waved a hand around. "Sometimes you have to step outside the rules."

"It's a different MO," she replied abruptly. She didn't mention that the Ghost had been known to change his methodology when it suited him.

"Sure, and that's not his regular target. But, for whatever reason, something in his world has changed. It's up to you and me to find out why." And this time he turned and walked away. When he was about ten feet from her, he called back, "Thanks for answering my request."

She didn't want to ask, but her curiosity got the better of her. "What request?"

His laughter resounded throughout the park, bouncing off the trees and rippling through the leaves, and then he was gone.

"Hell, that was no request. That was a fucking order," she muttered. She spun around to stare toward the house. Could Jericho be right? She studied the pattern of leaves on the grass, her mind assessing what she'd seen versus what she knew.

What possible motive could the Ghost have for killing an old man watching TV? The cops hadn't as yet ascertained whether anything was missing. The place hadn't been disturbed in any other way, except what was required to take a few steps into the room, slice a man's throat, then step back out.

The killer hadn't even stepped in the blood. And there had been a lot of it.

The cops would work the crime scene, but they already knew they'd find little. She snorted. That was actually the best reason to consider the Ghost yet.

The Ghost never left evidence behind. And yet he was thought to have committed eleven murders by her count. It could be much more. She'd often wondered if he'd traveled to other states, when she had deemed him as simply "asleep."

The evening air produced a cold bite by the time she returned to the crime scene.

Two of her colleagues, Mark and Lawrence, looked at her, eyebrows raised. "Sorry I'm late." She didn't add to that. She made a point to give very little in the way of explanation.

One of the beat cops, Calvin, turned to face her. "None of the neighbors heard or saw anything. We are still out canvassing."

"Of course."

She walked through the rest of the house, noting the sparse furnishings, living one step above poverty level, the lack of food in the kitchen cupboards, and the lean, frail body of the man who'd met an early demise. His life hadn't been easy, and he certainly didn't deserve to die like this.

"What do we know about the victim?" She placed her hands in her pockets, as she listened to the recital.

"Seventy years old, his name was Connor Breaker, a re-tired electrician, still did odd jobs for friends for a little bit of pocket change. He was on a pension and not much of that. A widower. His wife passed on some twenty odd years ago."

"So he lived alone. Are we thinking he's the victim of a

random act of violence?"

The cops nodded.

She shook her head. "I'm not buying it. Whoever killed him had to come around the back of the house and into the yard to do so. Had to know the old man lived here. And that he lived alone. That meant someone who knew him—or of him. Let's find out why. Maybe then we'll find a motive."

She stepped back, as the coroner arrived. Tavika didn't need to know time of death or how Breaker died. She'd get those soon enough. What she needed to know was why, and the medical team wouldn't be any help there. "I'll need the tox screen results as soon as you have them, Shelby."

Shelby was a fifty-something gray-haired, grizzled woman, who had no use for anybody. But, as such, Tavika understood her well.

"You'll get them as soon as I know something." Shelby stood and stared down at the old man. Then she shook her head. "What is the world coming to? We can't even have a cuppa tea and watch our favorite show anymore."

Tavika spun slightly and stared at the tea. "I wonder if that was drugged. It might make it easier to do this job."

"It wouldn't have taken anything to slice his throat. He'd likely been asleep at the time anyway." Shelby lifted her gaze to Tavika. "We'll test the tea anyway. I see no defensive wounds and no blood on his hands. He went down without a struggle."

"Which supports sleeping and/or drugged." Tavika thought about that. If she were sound asleep, and somebody slit her throat, she'd still reach up in a jerking reaction. But that didn't mean the slice wasn't deep or fast enough that Breaker couldn't do anything about it. Blood was all over the man's chest, with an arterial spray to the left. So the killer stood behind him, grabbed the man's head, and sliced to the right. The old man didn't have a chance.

She made one more walk-through of the small house, before stepping outside into the clean air. Nothing like the smell of fresh blood. It wasn't something she'd ever get used to. In her case it was the stuff of nightmares.

She walked over to her bike, keys in hand, and one of the cops called out to her, "Do you want a lift back to the station?"

She shook her head and waved. "I'll be fine, thanks." She gunned the bike and took off down the street. At the first corner she leaned into the curve and whipped around the block. She wasn't going back to the office. She was going hunting.

NOW WHAT THE hell was she up to? Jericho stopped in the middle of the sidewalk. In his mind's eye he saw her rip down the street on the bike. She'd just left the crime scene, so what the hell was she doing now? He watched her slowly turn the corner, heading into a shady area. Even in his vision, the neighborhood appeared run-down and seedy.

An area he recognized.

He frowned. Now why would she want to go back there?

Unfortunately, just because he saw bits and pieces of visions, it didn't tell him motivations or what the person was doing outside of his particular view. Right now he really could use that information. When he saw her park the bike and hop off, he swore. An old couple passing by him shot him a dirty look. He gave them a half smile and stepped off the pathway.

He'd planned to check out this recent crime scene, after

the cops were done, so he'd been hanging out in the park. But, at this point—after all these hours, after his confrontation with Tavika—Jericho's presence would be noticed. His phone rang, and he checked the text messages coming in. Hunter was out on a different job, trying to find a child who'd been kidnapped. Hunter was just that. A hunter of bad people and a psychic too.

Jericho kept catching little bits and pieces of Hunter's case but nothing big enough to help. Jericho's own skills were growing and improving, but it was a process—not one he could hurry. And he couldn't dredge information out of thin air. If visions didn't come, then they didn't come.

Hunter was looking to see if Jericho had more. *Anything?*

He responded in the negative. Maybe if he could solve one of these cases, the other would get more attention. Right now he felt splintered—his visions going in both directions, with neither case getting the full benefit.

Tavika wasn't exactly a case, but neither was she somebody he could ignore. He knew perfectly well the Ghost was involved. He'd been hunting this asshole for way too long to let the opportunity slip through his fingers. If Tavika didn't like Jericho getting involved, well, that was just too damn bad.

In his head he saw her reach for the doorknob, and, in spite of himself, knowing she couldn't hear him, he cried out, "No, don't."

Where was her instinct here? Something was wrong there.

A second later, he closed his eyes, focused his will, and blasted her the same message but ten times harder. *Don't open that door.*

Not waiting, he bolted for his truck. This would not end

well.

In his mind's eye, he watched her hesitate. Then she lifted her middle finger in his direction—a sure sign that she'd heard him—and pushed open the door anyway.

Shit.

AH, HAPPY DAY. He was getting to watch a double feature. He loved the view out his front window.

The popcorn was long gone. He'd been glued to the window. He did like to see Tavika so tormented.

"You're welcome," he said, with a sneer to the empty room, as she entered the destroyed house. It had once been a nice neighborhood but had long since fallen on hard times. Hell, the streets and those around it were the poorest of the poor now. When she'd lived there, it had been a nice middle-class area. Now vagrants lived wherever the hell they wanted. Most houses were otherwise empty and slated for destruction.

The whole street was supposed to come down with a new multifamily complex going up in its place, but the financing had fallen through.

He grinned. It was probably because the place was haunted.

He should know. He was the one who sent those freaks into hell where they belonged.

The youngest one was still on his list. Would he let her live? Was she a threat to him? At the moment he felt generous. After all, a man in love was entitled to some feel-good moments. He'd been alone for a long time. He was making a lot of changes for the love of his life. Major decisions to clean up his act.

He watched Tavika hesitate, then lift a middle finger to someone watching.

Shocked, he leaned forward. No one was around her.

What the hell? Who was she flipping off?

That her reaction was perfect timing to his thoughts sent a chill through his body.

Was that directed at him? Surely not.

He slowly walked closer and pressed his nose against the window. But she didn't come back out of the house.

If that middle-finger salute had been directed at him, then that would mean she'd seen him. … In which case, … he'd have to do something about her.

How to know for sure?

CHAPTER 4

TAVIKA DIDN'T KNOW why she insisted on coming here on a regular basis. The place held nothing but pain and torment for her, but knowing her family had died here gave her a connection. One she couldn't leave alone.

Or they couldn't.

Their spirits resided here. Even though she'd done her damnedest to help them move on—or at least move them to a nicer place—they had stayed tied resolutely to their violent ends. It was why Tavika had contacted Stefan years ago, to see if he could help her send their souls home. But Stefan had told her that she could easily do it herself. She'd hung up on him at that point. She could do a lot of things, but that didn't mean she was up to doing them.

For that reason she visited. As if somehow their existence would be a little easier by having her around.

Like hell.

The place looked the same as the last time she had been here. The city had planned multiple times to raze the property to the ground, but, of course, they never did. The land wasn't worth much. The neighborhood was a drug haven. Outside of a few homeless people who moved into the building every once in a while, Tavika usually found the place empty. Even the homeless moved out quickly. The house was haunted after all.

She applauded her sister's and her mother's efforts to amuse themselves, when, in a cop's reality, what they did may inadvertently save someone else from dying as they had. She didn't know if the Ghost returned here or to the scenes of his other crimes, but it was a common theme among killers. She'd questioned the neighbors every once in a while to see if anyone came by regularly. The neighbors changed with the seasons, but the message was always the same. Besides a few vagrants, no one came here but her.

Still, she wished her family would find a way to cross over. According to them, they weren't leaving her alone until their killer was dead too.

Which meant Tavika would die first.

And soon—if her mother's visions were correct. Tavika had had a few visions herself, but they were hit or miss. She didn't know if she could trust what she saw. And none were anything she wanted to come to pass.

Her phone jingled in her left-hand pocket. "I told you that it doesn't have to end this way," her twin brother, Travis, said, without preamble.

"You've told me lots. That doesn't mean fate will be changed just on your say-so," she replied, as she turned in exasperation.

"You changed your fate once. You were supposed to die with everyone else. That you haven't is already a change. You don't have to die this next time either. With the life you lead, you could have gotten shot any number of times, but you changed the course of life, extending yours much longer. That can happen again. The Ghost is out there. Yes, he's watching you. Yes, he might get you. But you also have the ability to take out *him* this time. Just think. You could put a stop to this, once and for all."

"Now if only that were true," she muttered. She tried to keep those words quiet but knew Travis would pick up on it. He always knew what she was thinking.

She walked through the desolate bungalow. She felt an edge to the air today. She stopped in the center of the living room and turned around slowly. What was different?

The *energy* was different.

Then she got it. With a wolfish smile she studied the energy around her. She saw … something. Something … familiar. He'd been here. The Ghost had actually been here. When? Had he done anything while he was here?

She closed her eyes and let the wisps drift through her mind.

She'd imagined him so many times. Squatting down, almost at the exact place where she stood now. A smile on his face as he relived the moments when he had wiped out her family. *Asshole.* She couldn't stop the stabs of hate darting through her. She'd always known he would kill her one day. As long as she took him out too, she didn't care.

The whispers of energy disappeared, and she was left alone, once again, inside this cold and empty place. As she studied the room, she caught a glimmer of something in the corner of her eye and slowly straightened. In a soft gentle voice she whispered, "Hello, Bellamy."

Her sister's spirit drifted closer. In a weird echoey voice her sister responded, *You know you shouldn't be here, Tavika.*

"But you're here." It was the same irrefutable answer she gave every time. Her mother and her sister didn't want her to continuously come, but, as long as they were here, Tavika felt compelled to visit.

"He was here, wasn't he?" She waited for the answer, watching her sister hesitate. "Bellamy, tell me the truth."

Instead of speaking, her sister nodded. Then, in a voice barely above the breeze dancing on the flowers outside she said, *Yesterday. He was here yesterday.*

Shut up, her mother ordered.

Instantly Bellamy disappeared, even now compliant under her mother's orders.

Tavika froze. "What?" She spun around, her heart slamming against her ribs. "He's back. Oh my God, he's really back."

Her mother's voice slammed through her consciousness. *You will not pursue him.*

Tavika straightened and turned to face the dominant presence in the room. Unlike Bellamy, who drifted in and out of existence, her mother's ghost was angry, vengeful.

Even in spirit form, she was hard to deal with. Tavika faced her. "I will do everything I have to do to bring him down."

And if it kills you? If he kills you? What then?

Tavika whisked the tears from her eyes. "Then we will be a family again."

Determined to not listen to the pleas of those long gone before her, Tavika turned and strode to the front door. Standing in the doorway, she caught a whisper of something else. Slowly, her heart in her throat, she turned.

And saw a beautiful little blue ball. A child spirit. Tavika shook her head. In a soft voice she whispered, "Who are you, and why are you here?" No answer came. As Tavika watched, the child's spirit blinked out of existence. "Bellamy? Mom? Who is this new spirit?"

As Bellamy tried to answer, her mother's voice cut through with displeasure. *Forget about her. You can't help her now. Besides, she's been here forever. How typical that you didn't see her until now.*

Unfortunately that was quite possible. Tavika couldn't see everything. And what she did note, she couldn't trust. Some truths were just too painful. Sadly Tavika whispered, "If you're right, there was never anything I could do to help anyway."

And she strode out into the sunshine.

Then froze. She took a hard gasping breath of the fresh air and slowly turned back to the dilapidated hovel.

What if her mother was wrong? Or just being spiteful—as she'd been so often in real life? What if the child was a new spirit? If she was, that meant a new murder. And in this location? That meant the Ghost had not only returned but he'd gone back to his old habits—murder. Only this time he was killing children.

JERICHO DIDN'T NEED to be psychic to see the shock in Tavika's rigid spine, the shaky hand she stuffed in her pocket. He was across the road, leaning against a tree. Following her around seemed to be his life at the moment. But it wasn't much fun when pain radiated from her very soul. He shouldn't have come. It hurt to watch her torment herself.

But, of course, she was not only a cop but someone who was dedicated to hunting down the Ghost. ... Well, he understood that part.

Although not the cop part. He'd spent his life avoiding them. Not his favorite people.

Other psychics made it their life's quest to help the police.

Jericho went the opposite direction. He bypassed the

cops and went after the killers himself.

He could play the authority game, if he had to, but he had no tolerance for it. Some things were much more fun, and sticking it to the establishment was one of those things. He hadn't always been that way. At one time he'd believed in the same rosy view so many other people did—that the cops were there for you. They would help when you ran into a calamity. But, when his life had been split wide open, and disaster had hit in a big terrorizing way, the cops hadn't been there for him.

It had been a problem so big that, of course, he'd turned to the cops for help. Because who else did one turn to? There were no other options back then. No powerful psychics like Stefan. Or maybe there were, but Jericho hadn't known about them. At the time it never occurred to him there was help in other quarters.

And maybe he would not have listened then. He'd been all about following the rules. And that meant calling law enforcement for help. Only the cops had failed. Even worse, after months of terror and paralyzing fear, he had found out the culprit had been a cop himself.

Walking away had been an easy decision. Staying out of mainstream politics and enforcement even easier. Hunter had found Jericho soon afterward. They'd been as close to being partners as two loners could stand to be. Jericho had always known he was "different" in an esoteric way, but he'd never looked at his visions as anything other than useless.

Until then.

The only reason he had walked into that police station this morning—his first in over ten years—was for Tavika. It really pissed him off that the first woman to set his body on fire—and to make his lungs hurt with an aching, throbbing need to breathe in her scent, to mate with her in the most primal way he'd ever imagined—was a fucking cop.

And not just a cop, but one through and through, a dyed-in-the-wool believer of justice and all the bullshit it meant.

Yet he couldn't take his eyes off her, as she stood in the doorway of her family's home and their murder crime scene, as if having just learned something horrific. It made him wonder. What had she found out?

She stood so still, having absorbed a blow in a way so few could, and still she didn't go down. What would it take for her to drop in defeat?

Death. Her own. Nothing short of her last day on this planet, from what Jericho saw.

And damn if he didn't want her even more.

SHE DIDN'T LIKE what she'd seen. Look at her. Even at this distance he saw her shaky hands, the pallor on her face. Interesting. He'd been by there yesterday. But no one could have seen him. He considered it, then shook his head. No, not possible. So what had freaked her out?

He lowered his binoculars.

Unless it was just old memories.

He kinda liked that idea.

He'd saved her life back then, as a gift. Who knew she'd provide so much entertainment over the years?

She was a gift that kept giving.

At least to him.

CHAPTER 5

T AVIKA SHOVED OPEN the door to her small apartment and walked inside. She knew she should eat something. She had a lot of work to do. But everything inside her had shut down. She was ready to drop.

It would take several hours to recover. A side effect of ending up in such a state meant it took all her energy to keep functioning.

What she really needed to do was crash. When she didn't listen to her body, her system had been known to take over and to make that happen, regardless of her wishes.

Today's multiple shocks had been so horrific …

When she found Jericho at her desk, waiting for her, that had been one, but seeing him in the park and listening to his hypothesis of the murder of the old man, … that had been yet another. The final and most debilitating shock had been entering that damn hovel of a house and finding the energy of yet another victim of the Ghost.

Tavika had waited for this moment for a hell of a long time. She wanted that revenge so badly that it was the sustenance that kept her going throughout each and every day. Hate was like that.

Now she had proof of her nemesis. She almost laughed at that. Not anything she could show anyone else though. Except maybe Jericho.

But he already knew. He'd tried to tell her. But she hadn't been willing to listen to him. She couldn't ignore it anymore. The Ghost was back.

Her initial euphoria was gone, leaving desolation in its wake.

She collapsed to sit on the side of her bed, staring at her hands. She could already see the Ghost's blood drop from her fingers. How was it that, as a cop, all she could think about was taking the man's neck in her hands and ripping out his throat?

Tremors racked her spine. She flopped backward onto the bed, and that's where Solomon found her a few minutes later. The huge Maine coon with the missing tail and half an ear hopped up beside her and lay down on her belly. He stretched from her pelvis to her breasts. And there he'd stay, until she awoke, guarding her from intruders—on both sides of the ghostly divide.

She closed her eyes and slept.

Disoriented and icy cold, she jerked awake, pulling out from the sleepy slumber she'd been in.

And cried out in distress. A gray, foggy world surrounded her, blocking her sight and cloaking her senses. Absent of sound, smell, and other sensations, she reached out and pinched her cheek.

And felt nothing.

She screamed, loud and hard, her mind hearing the noise, her ears registering nothing. As she knew they wouldn't.

Not here. Nothing was good about this place, except if you wanted to hide. Yet, because she couldn't see anything anywhere, she'd always been terrified the Ghost was there, like he had been before—standing just outside the fog, knowing full well she was inside the cloudy bubble—toying with her.

This was a place where nightmares were created.

And she had had enough of those fucking things.

She closed her eyes and willed herself to stay in control. She was no longer twelve years old. She was no longer a prisoner in her childhood home, with the bodies of her dead family strewn around her.

No, she was a survivor, with one goal left in life. That one burning light that kept her moving forward day by day—to avenge her family's slaughter and to kill the bastard who had destroyed Tavika's world.

Her childhood fear had brought her here. To this nightmare fog. And that same fear was keeping her here.

She just had to remember who she was. And who the Ghost was.

When she woke up a second time, it was all she could do to not cry. But, right now, the relief of having returned to the normal world and to not be stuck in that horror show brought tears welling up from deep inside, so hot and acidic they burned at the corners of her eyes.

Like hell. … She scrubbed her face. Hard. She had to hold it together. The only way she knew how was to stuff everything that bothered her deep inside. Those upsets had destroyed her. Had drained her of energy. It had to stop.

Jericho. It had started with his visit. And the sexual energy that had instinctively flowed through her. She couldn't afford the distraction. To have her energy split. It was too dangerous. *He* was dangerous. He also represented something she couldn't have. Not now. Maybe not ever. No matter how much she wanted him.

She had only one option. She closed her eyes and pulled

and pushed the frazzled energy, the sexual energy, the confusion, and stomped it all deep inside.

The same place she'd shoved the other nightmares. Taking a bullet was easier than being in that nightmare. And, because her subconscious accessed them without her permission, that lack of control gave them more power. She hated to think that this shit happened when she was at her weakest. That she had no way to guard against what came from inside her.

Hence the lack of sleep in her life. If she couldn't trust the very hours when she was out of control, how did she ever let go enough to get any sleep?

Dry-eyed again, she tried to roll over only to find she couldn't.

"Solomon, get your fat ass off me." She glared at the supersize feline, who gazed back calmly. He wouldn't give an inch until she calmed down. She'd had this out with him before. And somehow he always won. If she had believed in witches or vampires, then she'd have understood Solomon's role in Tavika's life was really that of a familiar. But, as she didn't know, not for sure, … that left Tavika with one cranky and very lazy pet.

With a tightening of her abs, she sat up, forcing Solomon to grab on or to slide down. Thankfully he chose the latter. Her skin had already taken a beating today. But the one her soul had taken was way worse.

Still, now that all the emotions were shoved down in the heart chakra where they belonged, she felt a lot better.

After a hot shower, she made her way to the kitchen. Her stomach had begun screaming at her as soon as she'd stepped under the water, looking for her to take care of its needs too.

Except her kitchen was empty. Her fridge was bare, and the garbage was ready to walk out on its own.

Shit. She grabbed the menu from the Red Dragon, a small take-out place right around the corner. A Chinese couple ran the small hole in the wall, offering the best soups in town. Within seconds she had a double-size bowl ordered for her dinner.

"You need more than soup," Vitus suggested.

"No, soup will be fine." She went through this conversation every time. She could just go downstairs and sit in the small restaurant, but that was the last thing she wanted to do. This was her best option.

The doorbell rang moments later, the sound louder than the dying gasps from her coffeemaker, as a fresh pot dripped. Walking to her front door, hand on her weapon—old habits died hard, after all—she looked through the peephole. Vitus was on the other side.

She opened her door with a smile and stared at the over-ly large container. "I said soup was fine."

He shook his head. "You must eat." He shoved the bag of food into her hands and walked away.

Rapidly, as he did everything in his world. She could appreciate efficiency, but he forgot to ask for payment—again. "Hey, you didn't ask for money again."

"No money—not from you." And he disappeared around the corner.

So what if she'd saved his restaurant from being robbed. Besides she'd only stopped a robbery in progress once. He would drive the place under if he didn't charge her.

Frowning at the man's generosity and feeling like a fraud for accepting the food, she carried it into the kitchen. With a sweep of her arm, she dumped the pizza boxes to the floor to clear a place.

A housekeeper she was not. The aroma wafted from the open bag, as she rummaged for a clean bowl. Not finding one, she gave up, grabbed a spoon, and returned to eat out of the containers. She heard her mother scream at her lack of manners.

Opening the first box, she found it full of noodles, mixed with vegetables. She liked veggies just fine, but Vitus seemed to think she never ate any, as he was forever adding them to her orders against her wishes. If she wanted veggies, she would have ordered some.

Still, they did look good. She picked out a chunk of broccoli and ate it. Lord, that was yummy. Before she knew it, she'd polished off half the dish, without even looking at the rest of the food. The good thing was, she had enough food here for several days. She could push her shopping off, yet again.

Solomon hopped up on the chair beside her and stared at her in that serious unblinking way of his.

"Don't even think about it," she warned him.

That gaze locked on her face, compelling her to feed him.

"Fine, but, if it gives you a bellyache, I don't want to hear about it." She fished out a chunk of chicken and placed it on the table.

He started to eat it, then stopped, and his ears went back.

She bolted from the table and grabbed her weapon again.

If there was one thing Tavika knew, Solomon's instincts were dead-on.

THE GHOST WATCHED as the Chinese deliveryman re-turned to the small restaurant beside Tavika's building. Poor child. She really hadn't done well for herself after all. He'd kept tabs on her throughout the years. For all of five minutes the thought of her in law enforcement had sent a chill down to his soul, but he got over it quickly. Still, it was a credit to the rotten salary she collected that she lived in this shack of a building.

Her mother and sister had both been stunners, with Ta-vika taking the ugly duckling position of the family. Apparently she hadn't even managed to catch a man and to move up in life that way. Why anybody would want to spend their lifetime hunting down bad guys was beyond him. Such a boring occupation.

So much more fun to be one of the bad guys and to out-smart the cops. Although that was getting to be a tad too easy as well. Still, it was her passion for take-out food that made it easier to pinpoint where she was. That and the fact he'd managed to hack into the system to get information on her.

And access her own laptop from her office log-in.

So simple when you knew what you were doing.

Plus, it was damn-near impossible for anyone to hide in the days of the internet. Except him. But hiding in plain sight was always a much better idea.

He strolled around to the corner of the restaurant and let himself in. It was so small. It was almost painfully poor. He knew they barely made the rent every month. He could buy this place out in a heartbeat. Hell, he could buy the entire block. Wouldn't that be fun? He could actually own the apartment where his victim hid. At that, his face broke into a smile. The lady at the front counter asked, "May I help you?"

Too bad he was working hard at turning over a new leaf. He'd like to cut those yellow teeth right out of her mouth. Instead, he gave her a pleasant smile and ordered. "I'll have a double bowl of wonton soup to-go, please."

He paid for the order, while her husband, who apparently was also the deliveryman—how cliché was that—made up his order. When it was ready, she handed it to him. Back outside he really didn't want soup. Pondering his next move, he walked across the street and studied the apartment where she lived. He had two categories of victims. Those who were decided on ahead of time and the ones who were more spur-of-the-moment. He liked to be methodical, even with those.

The planned ones he researched until he knew them inside out. The others? Well, … they were like his ice cream, a daily dose-of-cheer victims. But he was weaning himself off these, or trying. Part of his turning over a new leaf. As for his planned victims, he had his list and was going down it, marking them off—one way or the other. These were the loose threads he couldn't leave alone, just in case they unraveled and did him damage in the nice rosy future he had planned. He'd taken out two in this last week alone. Not that anyone would know. Tavika was there on his list, but she was number seven.

He was methodical. And refused to move up his agenda. But he'd have to make a decision about her soon.

JERICHO PACED HIS hotel room. Why was Tavika so damn stubborn? She didn't need to go inside that house.

No one had forced her to go in there.

If she'd listened to him, she'd be doing a lot better tonight. He knew she was a psychic of some kind and had to know it—at least somewhat. And, therefore, she should've picked up the energy of the Ghost at his latest victim's crime scene. And that would just trigger bad memories for her too.

Stubborn. She was just so damn stubborn. The phone rang beside him. He stared at it. It was the hotel phone, not his cell. Snatching it up, he said, "Hello?"

"We have a delivery for you. It's here at the front counter."

He sucked in his breath in complete shock. "What kind of delivery?"

"Chinese food from a local restaurant."

He straightened, his gaze swinging to the window. "It must be a mistake. I didn't order any Chinese food."

"No mistake. The delivery is for Jericho Sands."

Damn.

"Do you want us to send it up, or are you coming to pick it up?"

The last thing he wanted was to have the package up here. His mind was already sorting through potential donors to see who might've sent this. None of the answers that came up were good. Whoever sent it knew he was here. And that meant his position had been compromised.

Double damn. "Leave it there. I'll be checking out in a few minutes, and I'll collect it then."

As she protested his sudden checkout decision, he hung up and glanced around the room. He was packed and walking downstairs to the front desk within minutes. Sure enough, the take-out Chinese food bag sat on the counter. An itemized receipt and the name of the restaurant were stapled to the top of the plastic bag. Without touching the offending item, he read the name of the restaurant and took note of its address—on the same street where Tavika lived.

He smiled. Had she sent him dinner? As he paid for his room, pocketed the hotel receipt and the rest of his cash, he studied the contents listed on the take-out receipt once again. Should he take it with him?

"Don't forget to take your dinner. The man was quite insistent." The receptionist smiled up at Jericho.

"Man?" he asked cautiously.

The receptionist nodded. "Yes, a slightly older man, well-dressed, in a three-piece suit. He wanted to make sure you got it for your dinner. He said that you were hungry after all the hunting and searching you had to do. As a friend he wanted to make sure you looked after yourself."

Jericho's face hardened. Bastard. In a smooth move he picked up the Chinese food, walked it over to the closest garbage can, and dumped the entire bag. "Thanks. If you see him again, let him know what I did with it. Then call the police to report a murderer."

And he turned and walked out into the night.

CHAPTER 6

WHEN THE DOORBELL rang, Tavika froze, gun in hand. Who was out there? It rang again. Then Jericho called out, "Tavika, let me in. I have developments."

She frowned and stared down at the weapon in her hand. "So what if you have a development? What does that have to do with me?"

"I'm not telling you while I stand out in the hallway," he snapped in exasperation. "Let me in."

More a demand than a request but compelling nonetheless. She quickly released the deadbolts—all three of them—and opened the door. She studied the man, who was still too well-dressed for her liking. How the hell did he pull off that suave, debonair look, even when carrying an overnight travel bag, yet also the right size to be a weapon's case? She nodded at the bag and asked, "Going somewhere?"

He snorted and brushed past her. "Finding a new place to stay apparently."

She slammed the door shut and turned to face him. "Don't get any ideas that you're staying here."

"Oh, I got it. You don't like visitors. And you sure as hell don't like strangers."

His assessment was cold, cutting, and very true. Anger radiated from him.

Tough shit. She wasn't happy either. She walked to the

kitchen and poured herself a cup of coffee, before sitting down at the table. Chinese food was still everywhere.

He reached out for the delivery bag and read the label. "Red Dragon?" He sat down heavily on the chair. "Son of a bitch."

In spite of herself she was curious. "What's the matter?"

"I received a delivery tonight, from somebody who said he understood how hard I was hunting and needed to make sure I ate well. It was a bowl of wonton soup from this restaurant. Only my hotel is several blocks away."

She studied his face, her mind going *click, click, click.* Still she had no intention of jumping to conclusions. In a neutral tone she replied, "So? It's good Chinese food."

"No matter how good the Chinese food is, the chances of it being well-known blocks away from here is not likely."

She shrugged. "If I lived several blocks away, I'd still order."

"That doesn't say much about your taste buds."

She slammed down her coffee cup and glared at him. "If you just came here to insult me and my food choices, get the hell out."

He leaned forward. "You're missing the point. I know exactly who sent the delivery, and he sent it from your favorite restaurant to me." He snorted. "Chances are, it's also your favorite dish."

Their gazes clashed, hot and heated, both of them trying to ignore the pulsing primal urge that wafted through the air. Like an elastic band that had been pulled too far, both sat back and broke eye contact. Tavika picked up her coffee and took a big gulp. After a moment, when she felt able to trust her voice, she asked, "You think it was him?"

"I *know* it was."

Very gently she set her cup on the table. She really wanted to throw it against the wall and to scream and to kick something. Preferably Jericho. "You're telling me that he was in your hotel, yet you didn't see him? And you didn't go after him?"

"No, he was at the reception desk of the hotel, while I was in my room. I did not see him. And it would be very nice to go after him, but there's a reason why he's called the Ghost. Remember?"

Of course she remembered. Because he left no tracks and used multiple disguises. The end result was law enforcement had nothing to go on. Even if they confiscated the hotel's video cameras, if there were any, the Ghost would no longer look the way he had in the video.

"He's been watching you."

Her gaze flew back up to Jericho's in shock. Slowly she shook her head.

He nodded. When she shook her head again, he jumped to his feet and paced the small room. "Why is it you insist on being thickheaded and stubborn?"

"*I'm* thickheaded and stubborn?" she asked. "You storm into my life today, with a bogus story and a crazy attitude. I have never seen you before. I don't know you. I don't trust you. And now you come here tonight, telling me a serial killer people have been hunting for close to twenty years is now watching me." She snorted. "Why don't you just crawl back into whatever hole you crawled out from and go find yourself a different hobby? Because you really suck at this one."

He glared at her. Then smiled.

One that made her spine shiver. She studied him warily. "I don't like the look of that smile."

"Too bad. If you won't listen to me, and my duty is to keep you safe, then I'll stay here tonight. I need a place anyway." He walked over to the couch, bounced on it a couple times, nodded, and stretched out. "This will do just fine."

She gasped in outrage. "Get out of my apartment."

"No." He laughed. "What will you do about it? Call the police?" He reached forward, grabbed the remote, and turned on the TV. "I could use a good game."

She stood, fuming, at the end of the couch. He was right. What would she do? Call the cops? Hell no. Besides, he'd just tell them a story like he told her. It would be all over the precinct tomorrow. That was the last thing she needed.

"Okay, fine. I believe you. I'll take care. I'll ensure I'm not being followed." She added the last in a sarcastic tone of voice. But he wasn't even looking at her. "Hey, did you hear me?"

"I heard you." He flicked through the channels. Just when she was ready to scream in frustration or to pick up something to toss at him, Solomon strolled off her bed and walked over between them. He sat down in front of Jericho and leveled that golden gaze at him. Jericho immediately sat up. "Holy shit."

Interesting reaction. She watched carefully as the two made eye contact. She'd never seen Solomon act this way. Then again she didn't bring visitors home. She had the occasional relationship, a hot and heavy weekend that never made it past the tangled-sheet stage. And that was definitely not the relationship she had in mind for Jericho. No, ruthlessly she shoved the energy back down. Dear God, he was potent.

"His name is Solomon," she noted grudgingly. Jericho's mouth opened and then snapped shut. She wasn't sure whether he was shocked at the size of Solomon or if something else were going on. She walked around the two of them to check out Jericho's energy. He kept a tight rein on it, holding it close against his body, like so many other psychics she knew. Hers was no different. It was dangerous to be open and friendly. She kept hers locked down tighter than most.

Solomon's energy was exactly the same. But Tavika caught a crackle in the air, as if Solomon and Jericho were actually having a conversation. Curious and a little mystified, she sat down at the end of the couch. "Solomon?"

The cat broke the intense connection and turned his golden eyes on her. Then he walked closer and landed in her lap, put his head up on her chest, and his engine kicked in. She could do nothing else but wrap her arms around him and hold on tight.

Jericho looked at her and then his gaze slipped to Solomon and back up to her. "How long have you had him?"

"Why?" She refused to answer his question. "Now that you know Solomon lives here, would you please just leave?"

That look in his eyes softened. "I wish I could. I really do. But now that I know the Ghost has found where you live and has studied your habits, where you shop, where you eat …" He shook his head. "No way I can do that."

"You think you're guarding me? Protecting me?"

His grin flashed, sending little electric jolts into her nerve endings. "I know you're tough, sweetheart, but I can still beat you after three rounds."

Immediately her feistiness surged to the surface. "You're on."

He laughed. "You're so easy to manipulate."

"No, I'm not." Inside, she was ashamed. He was right. He hadn't had to do very much, and she was already jumping at him.

Her work cell phone went off then. She stood, still holding Solomon in her arms, and walked across to pick it up from the table.

Dispatch answered, "Detective Bantrell, a second body has been found at the same crime scene you were at earlier today."

The dispatcher rattled off the same address. Tavika slowly hung up the phone, questions running through her mind in an endless loop. "What the hell?" she whispered.

She automatically put the phone in her pocket and reached for her holster. Once that was strapped on, she donned a jacket. She was dressed for work, her jacket now hiding her hardware. This was who she was. She turned back to Jericho. Solomon jumped out of her arms to pad over to his food dish.

"I'll be gone for two maybe three hours, could be longer. Be gone when I get back," she ordered.

"What did Dispatch say?"

"None of your business." She walked to her front door.

"Wait," he said urgently. "This is what he wants."

"What do you expect me to do?" she scoffed. "Hide away until he comes after me? I have a job to do and a big bad world out there that needs protecting. I can't do anything huddled inside. If he comes after me, all the better."

"Except for one thing. You don't have a clue what he looks like. How the hell can you protect yourself against someone you won't recognize?"

She shot him a look and opened her door. Just as she

went to close it behind her, she reminded him, "Don't forget he staked out this apartment. Watch *your* back."

She disappeared into the stairwell to race down the three flights. As she stepped out into the night, she automatically slid to the left, slightly behind the big column in front, and paused.

Instinctively she lifted her nose to the air, searching, probing the evil that prowled the streets.

And found nothing. Satisfied, she headed off to the crime scene.

JERICHO WAITED ALL of two minutes for her to leave, then he muttered, "Hold down the fort."

Solomon settled on the couch, as if listening to Jericho's orders.

In another deliberate ploy, Jericho left his bag behind.

By the time he made it to the street level, she was long gone, but her energy hung in the air. He'd seen lots of people in his lifetime. He'd learned to read a lot more energies. But hers was unique. It shifted and moved, as if a lot of other peoples' energies were in her space. He'd yet to decide if she were the aggressive, uncaring person she projected to the world or if she presented that persona on the outside, while on the inside she cared too much.

But the thing about collecting energy was one didn't always know whose energy they carried. Some of them were more leech than friend and caused people all kinds of hell. He didn't think Tavika had many friends. He knew she had almost no family—if any. So who the hell were all these little bits and pieces of people clinging to her, and did she know they were there?

He assumed she must know some of it. Like so many psychics though, she probably had some knowledge but not all of it, working almost blind by not knowing what part of their education was lacking. There was no valid psychic network to check to see if all skills were mastered.

Not that Jericho was a master either, but he'd been honing his skills for the last twelve years. That gave him a slight advantage over somebody like her. Except that same raw power gave her a huge advantage over everyone. Now if only she understood just what she was doing. Keeping that guard up was blinding her to other dangers. She could only do so much without draining her energy system. The effort to hold inside all that energy and to keep the world out was an enormous drain on her reserves.

Her energy shield was stronger, her energy edgier, more distant. He didn't like it.

He understood her need for self-protection, but did she realize that, by burning through the energy required to keep her psychic powers inside, she was actually attracting the same unnatural element she was trying to protect herself from?

She was one hell of a cop. He'd read up on the commendations she'd received. The number of cases she closed was impressive, so much so that he knew she had to be using some of her abilities to solve them. He was all for crime fighting. Even more so for psychics to be the ones doing it. But he wondered whether the rest of her fellow detectives held her in high regard or just dismissed her as an oddball?

It could go both ways. Being abrasive could be just a cover, or, as Jericho suspected, it could be her way of keeping everyone else at bay. He walked out the front doors of her apartment building, noted the energy that hung heavy on the side, and followed her up the street. He didn't know if she had driven another vehicle or taken her bike, but her energy revealed she was walking. How would that work?

It was a balmy night but still not efficient to walk to get to where you're going. He hadn't picked up anything local happening, and, from the little bit he'd gathered, she was heading back to the same crime scene beside Kinsman Park. He hopped in his vehicle that he'd parked around the corner and drove slowly in the direction she'd gone. She would be livid when she saw him.

He smirked. That just meant he had to make sure he wasn't seen. Something he had in common with the Ghost.

After he locked his vehicle, he slowly crossed the grassy field of Kinsman Park. He hadn't taken a dozen steps when his phone rang. He checked the time and realized only one person would call at this hour. "Hello, Stefan."

"What's going on?" Stefan asked, his tone more agitated than neutral. That in itself was unusual. It took a lot to rattle Stefan's cage and explained why the phone call and not via telepathic communication.

"I'm not sure. I'm following Tavika as she returns to the crime scene from earlier today. Apparently a second body was found."

"Has the Ghost ever reused the same crime scene?"

"I don't know. However, as his MO has changed with the previous murder, now it's hard to say what it is at the moment."

He crossed the street, noting how dead the traffic was at this hour. It was just before ten o'clock; surely people would still be out and about. "What did you call for?"

There was a short, intense silence. And Jericho knew something was wrong. "Stefan, talk to me." He approached the house and walked past quietly, as if uninterested.

"I'm getting some weird readings from Tavika."

"Weird readings? What does that mean?"

Stefan yawned.

"Stefan, have you been painting the future again?"

"Just a little bit."

"Just a little bit about the future? Or just a little bit of painting?" Jericho asked in a wry tone. He'd been dealing with Stefan for a long time. They had an interesting relationship. Being dominant males and yet having very serious abilities, it was almost as if they were brothers.

"Both. But the images are very distorted still. So far they appear to be crime scene images. One of a teenager, an old man, and a young man in coveralls."

"Three different paintings or all the same?" Jericho frowned. He didn't paint, but he understood some of what Stefan went through.

"Three separate paintings but with a slash of red going from the left side of the first painting to the right of the last. A continuous wave of bloodshed."

"Great." Jericho turned to study the house behind him. "Did you call so I could have an art lesson, or was there a message behind this?"

"There is a message." Stefan fell silent. Just when Jericho was going to push for more, Stefan added, "Watch your back. This wave continues for a lot more paintings."

"What does that have to do with me?"

"Because, in the very last painting, the wave circles Tavika many times around. It'll impact everybody within her world. Including you."

THE NIGHT AIR was cool and moist, the light rain petering out. He smiled at the old metal-and-wood bench he sat on, across from Tavika's apartment and the Chinese food place. The streets were mostly empty. He could sit here in peace and enjoy his success. His plan had worked better than expected. He hadn't known Jericho would head to Tavika, like a homing pigeon.

It was just a bowl of soup, after all. Nothing worth sending him into a panic. He smiled. Or was it? Interesting that Jericho ran to Tavika. As if she hadn't had a hard-enough day, looking after his latest victim. She should have her dinner, then sleep. She would need it. He planned to be very active in the next week, all in preparation of his new life.

One he was looking forward to.

Just then Tavika walked out of her apartment.

He straightened. *Interesting.*

Where the hell was she going now? He watched her stand on the corner, then hop on a bus. Strange.

But even more strange was to see Jericho leave a few moments later.

What the hell? Something was up.

And he wanted to know what it was.

CHAPTER 7

TAVIKA APPROACHED THE same crime scene for Breaker's body, her cold hands shoved into her jacket pockets, as she strode along the road. She'd taken the bus, as something inside her needed to be on the streets at the level of the rest of her people. The crime scene wasn't very far away, and it was a no-stop ride, so, in theory, it was faster than driving. As she approached the same house for the second time, she studied the area. It was a small brown bungalow, one of a dozen just like it.

So many were here that it was hard to pick out the problematic one, as they looked like a cookie-cutter set. Except for one thing—the crime scene tape. She walked around to the back. This was the same pathway the killer must have taken.

Why? Why would he have returned to this same house? It made no sense.

If this was a drug house or a known gang hangout, then she could understand people coming back and forth, but the dead old man found earlier today didn't appear to have connections to anything like that. He played bingo at the seniors' hall on Friday nights, and that was all she'd found so far. And that had come from the neighbors.

Everyone they'd spoken to so far stated he was harmless.

But somebody had gone here specifically to kill him.

Then come back with a second body? Shaking her head at the craziness of a killer's mind, she stepped into the kitchen to join the others already here and froze. Her heart came to a shuddering halt, before picking up and racing again. A teenage girl's body had been sprawled at the center of the kitchen floor. Tavika bowed her head, her fists clenching as she absorbed the blow.

Some things were just too much to bear. That killers would go after someone so young and innocent was heartbreaking.

She pulled hard on her control, when all she wanted was to kick, scream, and pound on the walls in frustration and anger. She'd rather stomp the killer into the floor, but he wasn't here.

The atmosphere was somber. Not a person in that room spoke.

When faced with the atrocities of what people did to each other, Tavika reacted as she always did.

She pulled on her mantle of professionalism and pulled out a pair of gloves.

This young girl had fought her last fight.

Now the battle was in Tavika's court, and she had no intention of losing. This girl's death would not become another cold case.

Her heart welled with pity for the victim. The teenager lay with her arms and legs outstretched. Had she been lying on her back, she'd look like she were making snow angels. Instead, she lay on her stomach, and her head had been twisted around to face the ceiling. A travesty that was hard to look at.

It was also a macabre twist. And not something … She frowned, her mind darting through the cases she knew but couldn't think of one that was similar.

Shelby, the coroner, was on her way. She might have seen this before.

Tavika rocked back on her heels and looked around the kitchen. From her initial examination, Tavika considered the girl's broken neck the cause of death, but the coroner would do a full autopsy. Tavika wanted to know if any drugs were involved. The child looked peaceful.

Too peaceful.

Tavika saw no blood or other visible signs of trauma. She lifted one of the girl's hands and checked out her fingernails. They were clean, so she didn't fight her attacker. Tavika also noted no scratching or bruising on her palms, fingers, or arms. She wore running shoes and had a bright red band in her hair. She looked to be about fourteen.

Peters, another of her team, squatted opposite the victim. The look on the detective's face was one she'd seen before. They were all bleeding hearts when it came to children. Adding to the pain, Peters had twin girls a couple years younger than this one. "Who the hell would do something like this?"

"You know that we have no shortage of volunteers to step into that category," she murmured. "More to the point, do you have a missing person report for this girl?"

"No, we're checking for one now."

Tavika stood and walked to stand by the girl's feet. "She's well-dressed, in good health. She looks to have been well cared for."

Peters straightened and pulled out a notepad. "All that says is she could be anyone's kid."

"Which means she probably hasn't been chained up in some godforsaken basement for the last six months, like some of the others we've found."

Tavika turned her attention to the kitchen, trying to forget the case she'd inadvertently brought back to the surface. That case had taken months to solve, and, in the meantime, two more kids had been kidnapped and chained up. Thankfully none of the children had died, but they would need counseling, likely for the rest of their lives.

They, at least, had a chance to recover. This girl would never see another day.

When she'd done all she could with her small notebook in hand, Tavika decided to return to the office. Given the lateness of the hour she could have just gone home, but she had to find that connection between the old man and the girl. Tavika needed it. The first twenty-four hours after a murder were the most important. After that it was far too easy for witnesses to forget or to embellish their stories and the killers to take flight.

It was also easy for the horror of the initial visual of a crime scene to fade. She didn't want that to happen. Everyone deserved better than that, but, in this case, that girl deserved a whole lot more. Tavika snapped a few more pictures, then took another walk-through the house for the second time that day. She saw no visible difference.

Outside, she stood in the backyard. In her head she knew logically it had to be the same killer. No reason for two people to come through this old house on separate missions, one to kill an old man and another to drop off his recent kill. She wondered if the killer, having taken care of the old man, then went for his fresh victim and needed a place to dump her, so he decided to put them together. It was lame, but she'd seen worse reasons in her line of work.

Of course, when the killer returned with the second victim, he'd have seen the crime scene tape and would have known the cops had found the old man. So why risk leaving the child?

The fresh air helped clear her mind. Her soul was achy. But she fanned the anger inside. She needed something to drive her forward.

This time she caught a ride back with one of her team. At the office she sat back down at her desk and logged into her computer.

"I tried to log in to your computer today," Mark admitted in front of her. "It wouldn't let me."

Slowly she raised her head to study him. "Why would you try?"

He sat down in the spare chair across from her desk. "Mine wouldn't even turn on. But I had a lot of work to do, so I thought I could use yours by logging in with my own password. That way I'd get the bulk of the stupid reports done." He slapped the stack of paperwork on her desk.

"Why is it, if your computer wasn't working, you thought mine would?" She was no more a computer tech than anybody else in here. She was fair to average, maybe even slightly better when it came to research, but she didn't do forensic or cybercrimes, as she didn't have the knack for it. She did, however, understand how to keep her computer log-in safe.

He gave a snort. "Well, yours *is* working, so you get to do the reports."

"Like hell. Move them, or I'll dump them on the floor." She didn't even bother looking up.

He stormed to his feet. "Goddamn it." He snatched up the reports and returned to his desk.

"Besides, you probably haven't even tried to turn on

your computer again since we got back."

"Did you check out what time it is?" he protested. "We've logged in our hours for the day already."

"So? I've still got some work." She didn't bother cutting back her biting tone. All she was concerned about was that he did his job and maybe a little bit more, so they could clear the backlog of cases and actually put these criminals behind bars.

Sure she had a stronger record for solving cases than most of the other guys in the unit, but she swore that was because she put in the time and the effort to get the job done. And maybe because she had a slight advantage.

Not that the other guys cared. And that was because they had a life.

She lived for her work. That meant it became her life. She turned her focus back to the computer. There had to be a connection somehow between the two recent deaths.

WHAT A WAY to spend most of the night. Damn it. Jericho wanted to walk through the house, when it was empty of cops. He'd waited all afternoon in the park. Now that there was a second crime scene in the same house, he really wanted to take a look. He got as close to the damn place as he could, without his presence being suspicious. He was pretty sure several of the neighbors standing around in a group, watching as the ambulance arrived, were looking at him suspiciously though. He had ID if he needed, but it wouldn't be good if the neighbors called him in. With a last glance he disappeared into the crowd of EMTs and walked back to the park.

Besides, he needed to talk to Tavika about this.

Earlier he'd stepped into the house in spirit form, but it was hard to see much with everyone in there. He'd heard the cops talk though. Not a lot but enough.

Why a teenager? And why leave her body here?

He couldn't help but think that, in some way, it was an offering. And, if that didn't sound bizarre, nothing did. His inner sensor went off. His phone vibrated soon afterward. *Hunter.*

"What's this about a child?" Hunter snapped.

"Not the one you're looking for." Jericho studied the darkened sky around him. "A teenage girl found dead in the same house as the old man."

"Odd. Grandfather and granddaughter?"

Jericho shook his head, even though Hunter couldn't see the motion. "No, I don't think so."

"End of life, start of life?"

Interesting Hunter was picking up a theme. "Not that I'm seeing, but we will certainly check out that angle."

"If they are not family, then the connection'll be somebody who knows both of them." Hunter rang off.

Jericho stared down at the phone. That would make sense. Both victims had known the killer. So what kind of a killer spent time with an old man and a young girl?

There had been something peaceful about the girl's face. She hadn't died in terror. Neither had the old man. That brought Jericho's mind circling back to *Why?* They could have been asleep when attacked or more likely given a drug to render them unconscious. That would explain the lack of expressions.

As soon as Jericho had understood a teenage girl was dead in the house, he'd picked up his phone and started his own research. No recent missing person's reports matched the girl's description. According to the glimpses he'd caught, the girl was thin but cared for. It was possible she either hadn't been missed as yet or hadn't been with her captor a long time. But then why kill her? Questions just ran around in circles, but there were no answers.

Hell, in cases like these, none of the answers ever made sense anyway.

Jericho slowly turned and walked back to his truck, parked a couple blocks away. He'd left his bag at Tavika's on purpose. But he also figured she'd do her damnedest to stay at work overnight. That way she could avoid him.

Halfway there he lifted his head and took a sniff. The air was muggy, the scent of perfume heavy from small floral gardens close by. His senses picked up something else odd. An aroma he couldn't place. He frowned and kept walking, opening up his senses wider.

He was alone in the park. For many people that was a recipe for disaster. For him, not so much. He deliberately slowed his pace, so, if somebody wanted to come up and attack him, they could. He always felt it better to fight frontal hand-to-hand combat than to wait until somebody shot him in the back. Footsteps then fell in behind him.

He smiled and kept on walking. Every once in a while his energy attracted young males. He used power like every young man around wanted to. It was what they all sought.

But only those who had strong abilities to understand that came after him. He stepped up to a small footbridge, crossed the little creek, and stopped. Sure enough, the person slid behind a bush. It wasn't particularly late, just past ten o'clock. So the age of his follower could be all across the board.

Jericho noted no malevolence in the energy. Mostly curiosity and envy.

He understood the envy. He waited a few minutes and then called out softly, "Show yourself. I won't hurt you." He sensed rather than saw the person stiffen.

And then a young boy stepped forward. He stared at Jericho, with eyes very similar to his own. Almost a liquid silver rippling in the moonlight. Stunningly attractive, the boy also looked vaguely familiar. "Who are you, and why are you following me?"

"I'm not following you."

The child said nothing more but stared at him, an unnerving depth to that gaze. Jericho had no doubt the boy was one of power. And maybe even more developed than he could imagine. For that reason alone, he reminded Jericho of Tavika.

"Good. It seemed like you're either following or hiding from me." He smiled, knowing that would prick the young man's temper. If these young men had anything, it was ego and pride. One couldn't play without taking on the other. Both were a dangerous game. But, at this age group, it shouldn't be too bad.

Sure enough, the boy puffed up in anger. "I wasn't hiding."

"Okay. Are you waiting to see where I was going?" He kept his tone mocking and light, as if to say, "Hey, kid. It's okay. Back off now, and we will all be fine."

"Why are you following my sister?" Then the boy took several steps back, and Jericho realized he saw right through him. "Just stop it. Leave her alone." And he took off.

Following his sister? Who the hell was his sister?

NOW WHAT THE hell was going on? He sat in his fancy silk smoking jacket, twiddling with his police scanner. Nothing made sense. They'd found another body? At his crime scene?

Was someone following him? Imitating him? That thought curdled his stomach.

But why dump a body with the old man?

Did nothing make sense anymore? It should. It had to.

It was the only way he could keep everything in place. There was a natural order to shit, and people needed to respect that.

Not go confuse the issue by messing up his own work. Fuck the nerve of this asshole. Just let him have five minutes alone with that killer. He'd teach him to not be a copycat.

CHAPTER 8

HOW COULD SOMEBODY reach the age of seventy and have less than a half-page history behind them? Connor Breaker had been an electrician, with his own business. As such he must've known a lot of people, had a lot of clients. Sure that might have ended eight years ago, but maybe he'd done some work for the killer. There were too many unanswered questions, but the one that really got to Tavika right now was the fact that she couldn't find out anything about him.

There had to be more. He owned the house and had for over twenty years. He cashed his social security checks every month and paid his bills on time. That was it. Nothing to suggest a connection to the girl or the killer.

There had to be one. Tavika turned her attention to the girl. There was no matching missing person's report anywhere in the last three to four years. How could anyone have a beautiful young girl in their life and not notice when she'd gone missing?

Not likely. Of course that instinctively made her think the girl's parents had something to do with this. And that was always a possibility, but, at the moment, Tavika wasn't interested in those. She was looking for something locked down. Her phone rang. It was the coroner. Awesome. "Hey, Shelby. Anything new?"

"Not sure it's the same killer."

"What did you find?"

"Breaker had a puncture wound on the right shoulder, likely a pressure syringe."

Tavika nodded, a big smile on her face. "So I was right. Some kind of sleeping drug was administered, so he couldn't fight back. What about the girl?"

"No pressure syringe wound."

"So why leave them both in the same house?"

"Any sign that a child lived there?" Shelby asked.

Tavika shook her head. "Not that we saw. No sign of anyone but the old man there."

"Unless she was a relatively new addition."

"No sign of personal belongings," Tavika noted cautiously. "I can check in with the neighbors. Maybe they saw a child around."

"It just occurred to me that both deaths involved throats. One was a slashed throat, the other a broken neck."

Tavika tapped her pencil on her notepad, as she contemplated somebody with a fixation on necks. "I'll check the other case histories and see if we come up with somebody using an MO that might be similar. Maybe run it through the database."

"I'll let you know when we get the tox screen back, but, at this point, I'm guessing we're looking at a simple knock-out drug."

"No other signs of injuries on either of them?"

"Too early to tell," replied the coroner. "I'm not done yet though. Just starting on the girl."

Tavika frowned. So one killer or two? And, if one, he could have a fixation for the neck area. There was a special database for modus operandi. She'd have to see what she could find. She checked her watch. Damn, it was already two in the morning. She should have done this at home. Then she could start the searches and crash, while the computer did its thing. Instead she set up a couple searches and sat back to wait. Very quickly they all came back negative.

Definitely bedtime. She logged off and shut down her computer. Mark may have had a viable reason for logging on and trying to use her system, but she didn't want him to succeed next time. No way in hell she would get blamed for any more computers having viruses. There had been a lot of them lately. They'd all been warned to make sure they stayed off social media and to keep office hours to business concerns.

That wasn't her problem. But she knew Mark had way too many girlfriends and was on multiple dating sites. She wouldn't put it past him to try to log on to her computer so he could play. Peters was another player. He better not be hooking up on her computer either.

With a headshake at their antics, she stood. All she wanted to do was go home and rest. She walked out of the station, realizing she was, once again, without wheels. The bus service had stopped for the night. Damn.

As tired as she was, walking was out of the question.

She was too far away to walk. She'd have to catch a cab.

"If you aren't too stubborn, you can catch a ride with me."

She turned to see Jericho, leaning against the front wall of the station. She came to an abrupt stop. "What are you doing here?"

"I wondered if you'd found a connection between the two victims yet."

"Even if I did, it's none of your business. You know I

can't share confidential information." She glared at him. She was too tired to fight him—or her hormones, down in the well where she'd shoved them. Particularly as her energy reserves were at an all-time low.

"Doesn't matter about the syringe. I already knew about that. I was wondering if anything in their history connected them to the Ghost."

"No," she snapped. "Nothing that came to the surface, and it will take days, if not weeks, to get to the bottom of this."

"If then …" He straightened and held up his keys. "You walking, or you want a ride?"

She stared out into the night, her mind whirling. Even if she walked home or took a cab, nothing would stop him from driving back to her place. She would have to deal with him one way or another. She was too damn tired. She glared at him. "I'll accept a ride home, thanks. You can grab your personal belongings when we get there and leave."

"You're half right." He laughed, nudging her around to the side where he'd parked. "I'll grab my bag, but I sure as hell won't be leaving."

HOW COULD JERICHO have possibly missed Tavika's open, friendly manner? He snorted. She was so damn prickly. He drove them home, enjoying the empty streets of the city. He pulled up out front of her apartment building, turned off the engine, exited his side, and waited while she got out of her side. He followed her up and asked, "Did you eat?"

"You know I did."

He'd actually forgotten about the Chinese food he'd seen upstairs. He was starving but knew he may have to forgo a meal. He'd love to order in pizza but didn't think this would be the time. Up at the apartment he was happy to see she didn't even protest his presence. He grabbed his bag, sauntered over to the couch, and lay down. The apartment was closer to being a studio, as it was an L-shaped room with the bedroom in the shorter side. The layout didn't provide much in the way of privacy.

Then again she didn't appear to need it, as she walked to the end of the bed and collapsed, fully dressed and face-first on the bedding. He knew within a few minutes that she'd succumbed to sleep.

Solomon took up residence on her butt. Jericho wondered if the cat watched over her or was just taking advantage of a soft, warm place to sleep. As Tavika spent little time here, it was also Solomon's chance for more human contact.

Damn. Jericho wished he could go out like that. His stomach growled. He wouldn't sleep until he had something to eat. Unlike Tavika, he burned through calories at an alarming rate when using his abilities. Today had been harder than most, as he tried to keep track of her and the Ghost.

Her half-eaten Chinese food container sat on the table. He walked over to check it out. It actually looked good, as it was meat, vegetables, and noodles. The other container was soup. He grabbed the noodles, sat back down on the corner of the couch, and proceeded to finish her dinner. Growing up in his household, ignoring food in one's dish meant losing it. With two older brothers, he couldn't keep food safe unless it was in his stomach.

He ate the last bite, ready to grab a few hours of sleep, when he heard an odd sniffling sound. He tossed the empty container into the garbage and looked toward the bed. Tavika lay, as he'd seen her last. She appeared almost comatose, as she slept so heavily. When he heard the sound again, he took a hesitant step forward. She was making the sound, but he had no idea why. Not sure what to do and hating to invade her privacy, he peeked around the corner so he saw her face.

What he saw was enough to break his own heart. This big, tough, independent cop—who'd kick his ass if she got a chance—slept, but huge tears rolled down her cheeks.

He knew her history. Hell, media around the world had picked up the story.

Psychic's daughter survives slaughter.

The headlines had been lurid and compelling. The pictures devastating. Tavika had been around eleven or twelve at the time. The details on what she'd gone through were a little sketchy, and that was a good thing. He knew she'd disappeared for a while. Presumably to heal and to wait for the sensationalism to die down.

Not that she needed any more reasons, but he wondered at the sadness and the grief on her face. Feeling like an intruder, he turned away, leaving her to her pain, knowing there was nothing he could do that she'd accept. At least not yet.

HE HAD AN easy name to cross off his list next. He'd take care of that tonight. It should add to Tavika's pain. After all, he'd watched her talk to this guy in the past.

Not that the victim deserved to die for that reason.

There were other reasons. Good ones. However, having lost credibility, maybe he didn't have to die, but he was still a loose cannon. No way could he be left to shoot off his mouth. Nope. Peace of mind in moving forward was everything.

And this guy should never have followed him way back then. But this guy had seen something he shouldn't, heard what he definitely shouldn't have. However, his mind had broken. Hell, it had fractured. Now he was more of a mess than ever.

It was too dangerous to leave this guy alive. He'd planned to at first, figuring no one would believe anything he had to say. But, over time, he'd gotten more nervous, and he couldn't leave it alone. Not now.

They'd been buddies once. Until he himself had been drummed out of the military. He didn't owe this guy anything now. Best he put him out of his misery for good.

Anything was better than this slow painful dying, inch by inch.

Honestly the guy should thank him for easing his suffering.

CHAPTER 9

S HE BOLTED UPRIGHT and stared out at her apartment. Tavika's nerves were on edge; tension vibrated her long frame. She couldn't see the danger. So what had woken her? She reached for her phone and checked the time. It was five-thirty in the morning.

Solomon hopped up on the bed and butted her chin gently. His huge engine kicked in, as soon as her hand stroked his back.

As much as she could use a few extra hours of sleep, she wouldn't get them. She spent another moment cuddling Solomon, before she hopped to her feet to find herself fully dressed from the night before. It would be easy to spend the rest of the day in these clothes, but she avoided that when she could. She'd spent enough time on cases in which she never got to sleep or a shower. She took several steps to the bathroom and stilled, awareness sliding over her system.

She wasn't alone.

She spun and froze. Her breath gushed out. Damn it. Jericho was still here. Lying on her couch, sound asleep. Enviously she watched the rise and fall of his chest. She'd love to be sleeping too. But, for her, the night was over, and the day had begun. Uncomfortable that he was still here but not sure what to do about it, her gaze swept through the kitchen and back around to her bedroom. Spinning back to the kitchen, she realized one of her Chinese food containers was missing. She glared at the empty package in the garbage. Damn.

She headed for the shower, stripped down, and stepped under the hot water as fast as she could. There, she leaned her hands against the wall and just let the hot water hit her. The bruises and scratches from yesterday were starting to ache in a deeply painful way. Nothing she couldn't handle, but it would be nice to get through a couple days without getting banged up.

She tilted her head back, letting the water pound down on her scalp. When done, she stepped out, wrapped up in a towel, and brushed her short hair back. She wrung out as much moisture as she could and walked back out to her bedroom. She made a quick check and was reassured when she saw Jericho was still sleeping. She grabbed clean clothes and dressed quickly, her movements economical and fast. Everything in her world was about efficiency. It seemed the only way to catch these assholes.

Mistakes would get her killed.

If she wasted as much time as her coworkers did, nothing would ever get done.

Dressed, bed made, dirty clothes tossed into the hamper, she headed for her miniature kitchen and put on a pot of coffee. She could've just grabbed one walking to the station, but she might need a cup before then. With the brew dripping, she checked out the rest of her kitchen to see if there was anything for breakfast and found a little bit of stale bread. She tossed it in the toaster. A suspicious package of sliced meat hit the garbage. The toast was done before the coffee. She sat down to eat, leaving a piece of crust for Solomon to lick on the table beside her.

Fueled, she walked to the front door and let herself out, without saying a word to the sleeping man. It was better this way. She had no intention of keeping her roommate around, but, at the moment, she didn't have the time or the energy to kick him out. He figured he needed to be here to save her. Good luck with that. She wouldn't be anywhere close to the couch for the rest of the day. With a grin on her face, she headed back to the station.

On a good day it was a fifteen-minute walk. In shitty weather, she could shave an extra five minutes by walking faster. The fact that the skies poured rain down on her head, well, maybe she could shave off more than that. She could have driven. But the walk was good for her.

Even if she hadn't been up for it just about four hours earlier.

Halfway to the station, she sensed the tendrils of energy.

She slowed her steps, letting the feelers find her. She didn't know who was looking. … Her mother would be screaming at her to run by now. But she had spent her life on the streets, and a lot of people knew her here. Not everyone hated her. Some even liked her.

Much to her surprise.

An alleyway was up ahead, which she passed every morning. Tavika often stopped to say hi to Gordon, a homeless man. He was a vet with PTSD and couldn't seem to fit into a normal life. Everything she'd seen about him confirmed he was harmless though. As she crossed the alleyway, she turned to look at him. It was early in the morning, and he should be sleeping, but his bedroll appeared empty.

She frowned. Instead of walking away, she turned and walked deeper into the alleyway. Her nose wrinkled at the smell. She knew that odor. Gordon wasn't old, just in his late forties.

But now he wouldn't get a day older. She studied the man, her heart aching for a system that did so little for him. Nothing anyone could do now either.

She called Dispatch. Putting away her phone, she straightened and looked around the alleyway. Often several of his friends huddled up close, but right now there was just Gordon. Had they left before or after their friend had died?

With his jacket pulled up tight against his neck, he looked huddled against the cold, as the temperatures did get chilly at night, even in summertime in Portland. But the massive amount of blood under his head said he hadn't taken very long to die. Pulling out her gloves, she squatted beside him and gently eased back the collar of his jacket.

She studied the slash across his throat. A second man with a sliced throat? In twenty-four hours?

That was too much of a coincidence. Staring at the empty alleyway, she considered the victimology of both males. Both men had lived alone, had vulnerable lifestyles, and were discards in society. One too old to be of use and pensioned off, the other too damaged to continue the good fight.

Both physically weak, alone. Neither had put up a struggle.

Gordon had been in prime physical shape at one time and fully capable of defending himself against an attack.

She glanced back down at the lack of defensive wounds on his hands. Just because he had been able to fight at one time didn't mean he was capable of doing so anymore. The bottle was his world now. There was a fine line between becoming drunk and *being* drunk in terms of motor control. Depending on his blood alcohol level, Gordon couldn't fight back at all.

Because he wore a long-sleeve shirt, she couldn't tell if he'd been given a pressure syringe of drugs or not. And maybe it would have been easier to administer it on his neck before slashing it. Still, why waste the drugs? Gordon wouldn't have offered much challenge.

None of the three victims would have—particularly if drugged first.

On that note, she tagged the coroner. She wanted Shelby on this. Calling her, knowing it was early but part of their lives, she waited for Shelby to pick up.

"Tavika?"

"Yeah, it's me."

"What have you got?"

"A second throat slashing. Another defenseless victim. This time a homeless vet."

There was silence for a moment, as Shelby digested the new information. "Where?"

Tavika gave her the address.

"That's only a couple blocks from the station."

"It is. I was walking to work, when I found him."

"I'll be there in ten minutes." Shelby hung up.

Thankfully Shelby hadn't asked about her detour to check on a homeless person. But then again, she probably already knew. Tavika looked down at the cup she'd brought with her. She often stopped by and filled up Gordon's cup, so it was there when he woke up. This morning, well, there was no point in leaving it behind.

Gordon would no longer care. Hearing footsteps off to the side, she turned to study the two cops arriving. Apparently her day would start earlier than she expected.

JERICHO HEARD THE door close behind her. No point following her physically. He could keep track of her from here. At least for a little while. He lay back on the couch, wishing he could chalk up a few more hours of sleep under his belt, but it wasn't to be. He sat up, put on his shoes, and walked to the coffeepot, smiling when he realized she'd left a little bit behind.

He snagged that up, then checked for more food, and realized the kitchen was totally empty. Even the cat was looking at him, hovering protectively over his bowl of kibble.

It was energy-burn time. He walked back to the couch and lay down. He might as well be comfortable when he took this spirit walk. Within seconds, he stepped outside of the apartment and downstairs. When he made it to the front door, the snap of the fresh morning air hit him. Unless there was an all-night coffeehouse around, he wasn't about to get anything sustaining soon.

It was too early for most of the businesses to be open in this part of town. Maybe closer to the station he'd find a place. Something else to keep his eye out for.

Jericho followed Tavika's footsteps easily, seeing the waft of energy that floated behind her. She never made any attempt to hide her trails. Something he always did. Given the type of work she did, such an oversight surprised him. Staying far enough behind that she wouldn't know he was there, he watched her walk steadily toward the station.

Just in case her sensitivity was ratcheted up, he kept his energy low and snug against his body. It was much harder for her to know if he *was* following. He wasn't sure what her shield allowed her to do when she trailed energy. Keep unwanted hunters from finding her? Or a specific one from finding her? Did she think it made her invisible to everyone?

Because, as far as he could tell, it didn't do anything but weaken her and blind her in many unexpected ways.

They'd traveled only a few blocks, when she stopped.

He watched in amazement as multiple threads of energy reached out across the block for her. What the hell? He didn't know if he should race forward or stay where he was. He couldn't remember seeing this before.

Unless in a fight, where several people were trying to tear apart his body.

Except there was no violence to this energy.

And no energetic response from her. She'd stilled, as if making a decision.

He knew that she'd been a beat cop for many years, before making detective, and that she'd been comfortable there, happy. So he revised his earlier guesses. What he was actually seeing were people checking that she was okay. As if they respected her. Liked her. Maybe ... missed her?

More energies stretched out toward her from all directions. Instead of walking faster, like most people would, her footsteps slowed, and she made her energy brighter, stronger, attracting those actual energies toward her.

He wanted to yell at her, "Wait! Stop! Don't do that."

But he didn't. He raced closer. He'd never met anybody who would actually attract all this energy. There was no malevolence that he saw, but that didn't make these energies safe for her. Why welcome danger? Maybe she was on a suicide mission. Hoping, one of these days, that somebody would take her out, so she could join the rest of her family? It certainly wasn't unheard of. Survivor's guilt was very real, but, for her, this should have occurred a long time ago.

Suicide made no sense after this long. She could have committed suicide anytime, had she wanted to. Then again that would have been an action on her part, whereas killed in the line of duty would be a different story.

He frowned, as she stopped at the end of an alleyway. Now what the hell was she doing?

He thought he heard her call out something, but he couldn't decipher the words. Then she disappeared into the alley, making his gut clench with fear.

Jesus. Had she no common sense? When she didn't return immediately, he picked up his pace, until he was close to the corner. He saw her energy milling at the entrance. It appeared normal but was filled with sadness and grief.

It was also mingled with a paler energy of death. Just as he was about to enter the alleyway to make sure she was okay, two cops walked up and headed her way. They didn't notice him. He grinned and slipped around the corner to see what was going on, then stopped abruptly at the pile of rags, bleeding red.

Off to one side, Tavika studied the crime scene, her professionalism plastered on tight. A defense mechanism to the horrors she saw on a daily basis.

Yet he saw the hurt. And, for that, he was sorry. She knew the victim. That was never easy. In front of the homeless guy was an empty take-out cup, as if waiting for the rain to fill it. Considering how he'd died, Jericho had to wonder if the killer hadn't placed it so it stood in plain view. Like a beggar's cup, waiting for something good to drop in. But instead Death had dropped by.

Jericho's gaze went from the cup to the huge mug in Tavika's hand. And he understood. This big tough cop was a bit of a softie. She'd brought coffee to dispense into the homeless guy's cup.

That was why she'd come to the alley. Not because she'd

sensed death but because she knew he needed his coffee as much as Jericho did.

Tavika wasn't quite as heartless as she'd like the rest of the world to believe.

Interesting. He walked closer to the man, his gaze taking in the pool of blood under the body, already mostly dried. He saw the dog tags showing inside the jacket, and he sighed. This was yet another war vet who had found it impossible to assimilate back into society after returning from active duty.

Jericho studied the rest of the crime scene, but there wasn't much to see, except other faded energies of times past, likely from the dead man's friends. Maybe their instincts had been better, and they'd chosen a different sleeping place for last night.

Moving off to the side, he turned to study Tavika, wondering how long she'd be here. He would need food and coffee soon. Neither of which he could get here.

What he couldn't see was the killer's energy. Not now. So he hadn't been here anytime in the last four hours.

Jericho might be good, but he couldn't see energy that had dissipated to nothing. There were some who could, but he wasn't one of them. Some he couldn't see at all. Like, he'd yet to see the Ghost's energy. But whether that was because it was impossible to read or he hadn't come across it early enough, Jericho didn't know.

As he raised his gaze, he found Tavika looking straight at him, her eyes wide with shock. Then she understood. And gasped in horror. He wanted to howl at her expression. Served her right for taking most of the coffee.

She went to say something and then stopped.

He grinned at her. What could she say that wouldn't

sound foolish?

Just then one of the cops stepped forward and walked right through Jericho.

CHAPTER 10

TAVIKA FROZE.

"Detective? Excuse me, Detective Bantrell?"

Finally the policeman's voice penetrated Tavika's mind. She tore her gaze from the grinning vision in front of her to study the cop. "Sorry, I was distracted."

Like hell she was. Spilling coffee was a distraction, as was seeing someone you knew.

Seeing a cop walk through another person—one she'd thought was real—that was a hell of a lot more than a distraction. Forcibly she tuned in to what the cop was telling her.

"We're going to canvass the neighborhood."

She looked down at Gordon's body and nodded. "He was murdered after four p.m. yesterday afternoon. So focus your questions after that time frame." She glanced up at him. "You have to wait for the coroner for a closer time of death."

Behind the policeman, Mark and Lawrence strolled toward them.

"And how can you know he died after four p.m.?" Mark laughed. "What, are you psychic?"

She shot him a dirty look, knowing his comment had more to do with Jericho's visit at the office, but still answered him good-naturedly. "Like hell. I saw Gordon around four p.m. yesterday. He was here with a couple of his friends."

"Then you can run down those friends to confirm when they left him." Mark grinned at her. "Better you than me. I know how much you love spending your time on the street."

It was always better to ignore Mark. But still she would have to see if she could find Gordon's buddies. They'd talk to her. She wasn't sure they would to Mark. He didn't speak their language and was trying to move up higher in the ranks.

"I'll follow up on it in a little bit." She glanced at her watch. Most of the homeless would be sleeping. Some got up early, but this was a bit too soon for even them.

"This case is tailored to you." Mark laughed and slapped her on the shoulders. "However, a couple other calls have been coming in." His grin flashed. "Only our prize detective hasn't been answering her phone."

"Shit." She pulled her phone from her left pocket and realized she had the wrong one in her hand. That was Travis's phone. She pocketed it quickly and grabbed her other one. There were several messages. With a note of humor threaded through her voice, she said, "I love how my pocket turns off this damn thing."

"If you got yourself one of the new ones, it wouldn't do that so easily." Mark lifted his phone in front of her face. "You can't keep going with those cheap phones you always kill. Get yourself a brand new one. It will last a whole lot better than the others. Time to join the new age of technology."

She ignored him, like she always did. Mark was okay. He was a good twenty years older than she was and could eventually end up being her boss. That might suck. She doubted he'd get that far though. Not that he didn't have ambition—because he did—but he lacked work ethic. Then again she wasn't sure how many of the people above her had it either. There were more corrupt politicians in the police department than she'd like. It wasn't something she was proud of.

Besides, she had no way to explain that watches and cell phones died quickly around her. Something to do with her energy load.

Just then Shelby arrived. She turned to greet Tavika with a smile. "There you are."

Mark snorted. "Wow, must be really busy in the city if you're actually dragged out to this case." He shook his head. "I haven't had coffee yet. I'll head over to the next block and grab some. You want one, Tavika?"

She still held the travel mug from home in her hand but said, "Sure."

Coffee was always a good icebreaker, and she had to find Gordon's friends. After Mark took off, Shelby turned to Tavika and shook her head. "He doesn't belong out here."

"I know," Tavika replied softly. "He's working on a promotion, then he'll never have to come out here again."

"What kind of an industry is this that we promote incompetency and bad attitude?"

Personally Tavika agreed, but they only spoke about such things among themselves. The two street cops were now at the alley entrance, making sure nobody else came in. In the distance she heard the ambulance. "Busy night for you guys?"

"You don't know the half of it," Shelby noted, fatigue in her voice. "Got a stabbing on the other side of town. Four dead in that incident alone."

"Oh, shit." Tavika winced.

"I trust your instincts. If there is a connection between

the recent victims and this one, then I want to be here." She did a quick examination, then sat back on her heels, studying the victim. "Did I hear Mark say something about you knowing the victim?"

"I saw Gordon here on the beat all the time. I delivered coffee every once in a while. He was a vet with PTSD and a whole lot of other problems. He didn't like walls. He felt much better in the open air, so that's where he lived. He was also young. Gordon was only about forty-seven maybe."

"Well, he deserved a hell of a lot better." Shelby turned to look at Tavika. "There could be a connection. Our seventy-year-old victim was in the military for several years too."

Tavika frowned and filed away the information. "Millions of people in this country served," she noted, "but I'll see what I can find."

The coroner went back to assessing the wound, before standing up and pulling off her gloves. "Nothing else I can do here. I'll need to get him on my table. I can tell you right now that the knife wound across the throat is the only visible injury and likely the cause of death. Also, as you suspected, it appears to be a single cut. with no hesitation."

"And he's wearing a long-sleeve shirt."

Shelby shot her a sharp look and asked, "What are you thinking?"

"I'm thinking that, if a pressure syringe was used, it'll be underneath the knife slice. These killings were targeted. The victims were killed in a quick, efficient, and painless manner."

"Yes, efficient." Shelby nodded. "Like he's ticking off boxes on his list and moving on."

Tavika caught back her breath at Shelby's words. Jericho

had mentioned something similar—that the Ghost was cleaning up. That the Ghost was coming after her soon.

Next chance she had, she'd ask Jericho more about that.

In the meantime, she had work to do. Gordon had been harmless. Innocent. He deserved better. She would ensure he got it.

NOW WHERE THE hell was she going? Once again, back in his normal physical form and wandering the street, Jericho headed over to the coffee shop, grabbed a large cup of coffee, and now sat outside the alleyway on the park bench one-quarter of a block away. Too far away to look interested in the scene going on around him. At least he hoped. There'd been a couple times in the past when the cops had approached him, asking what his business was. He'd so far managed to convince them that he was an innocent bystander, curious about what was going on. Only twice had he been required to pull out his identification.

Once he knew the ambulance and the coroner's vehicle had arrived, he figured Tavika would need another half hour or so, and then she'd be heading out.

He timed it.

He was off by four minutes. When Tavika finally exited the alleyway, she stopped for a moment, as if to reorient herself, then took a left. Someone called her name. She turned abruptly, and a second detective walked toward her, with a big coffee.

Jericho frowned. Another coffee?

She took it with a smile, then walked away. Jericho couldn't hear the conversation, but he noted the look on the other man's face. It was almost comical. And then, with a shoulder shrug, the detective turned and walked the opposite direction.

Tavika obviously didn't give a rat's ass about her relationship with this detective. Curious now about the double coffees, Jericho walked behind her at a far-enough distance that she shouldn't be able to sense him. He knew he had failed—once more—when she lifted her hand to shove her middle finger into the air, obvious even above the coffee.

He laughed. He should walk up beside her to keep her company. Just when he was ready to catch up, she disappeared into another alleyway. Swearing, he walked across the road, getting honked at for his troubles, and made it to where she'd turned. Another one of those really shady looking back alleyways, full of dumpsters. What the hell was she up to? Her energy was clear as day, as she walked down this path, a bloody beacon for anyone to follow.

She would get herself killed.

And why couldn't he leave her alone to whatever fate was ahead of her?

Walking quickly, he made it halfway down the alley, before he heard voices ahead.

He sped up, and, as he came around the corner, he heard her say, "Thomas, no need to be worried. This is just a friend of mine. His name's Jericho. If you ever see him around, he's okay. He's not here to give you any trouble."

Jericho frowned, as he cleared the last dumpster and saw yet another homeless man, his shopping cart and cardboard house hidden behind it. In fact, the dumpster itself didn't look like it had been emptied in a long time.

He gave the terrified man a small smile. "I'm not here to hurt you, Thomas." He nodded toward Tavika. "I'm with her."

Thomas's gaze ran from Tavika to Jericho. And finally he gave a heavy sigh and sank back into his jacket.

"Where's your coffee mug, Thomas?"

His face lit up hopefully, and he turned and scrabbled around in the cardboard box behind him. When he spun back again, he had it in his hand.

But, from the looks of it, it wasn't capable of holding any liquid anymore.

Tavika shook her head. "Where's the other cup? You should have a plastic one, Thomas."

He squinted up at her, as if a little confused. He turned back to the box and rummaged again, then he turned around a second time, with a plastic take-out cup.

She smiled. "That will do." She opened her cup and gently poured some of the coffee into his. Snapping the lid down tight, she carefully placed his cup against the edge of the dumpster, but within his reach. "Thomas, can you see this?"

Thomas nodded. In a broken voice he whispered, "Thanks." Then he curled up in a tight ball and tugged his blanket over his shoulders, the coffee mug close beside him.

Tavika motioned Jericho toward the street again. "Let's go."

When they were almost at the corner, daylight shining in from the street, Jericho asked her, "Does he know anything?"

"No. He left Gordon before dark. He was fine then."

Jericho nodded. He expected nothing else.

"But he did say he left Steve behind with Gordon."

He glanced at her sideways. "And who is Steve?"

"Steve is one of the missionary workers. We'll see him at the soup kitchen." She lengthened her stride. Not to walk with him or to leave him behind but because she was so focused. Her long, lean steps ate up the sidewalk. She passed everyone without seeming to recognize what was around her.

Until he saw her eyes dart. It wasn't that she didn't see anything around her. She was cataloging everything, but, with nothing out of the ordinary, she just kept on moving.

Fascinating. And then he watched her send out tendrils of energy, checking out spots she was uncertain of. All of this going on as she moved rapidly down the street.

Were her actions conscious or unconscious? Did she understand what she was doing? He wanted to ask, but something held him back. He was amazed at the efficiency in which she sent out these probes, analyzing the data that came back instantly and sending more off again.

Her face was neutral, as if she had no idea how much information she was processing in a millisecond. He was impressed. To hell with asking her if she knew what she was doing. Better he ask how she was doing it, so he could learn.

Not to mention how she'd squashed the sexual energy between them. Not that her resistance would do any good.

Then she did it. She turned to gaze at him, her footsteps not slowing, and asked, "How did you do that?"

Her question was the same one he'd been planning on asking her, so, for a moment, he was confused. Did she read minds too? But that dark hooded look of hers was intense and maybe a little worried, before it darted back to the world around them.

He wanted to ask her to clarify the question, then remembered her crime scene, where he'd shown up in spirit form. He frowned. "Do you mean what I did at the crime scene?"

She swung to look at him again, then gave a curt nod.

"Ah." He smiled. "I have to admit I was quite surprised

you saw me. Shows how strong your abilities are naturally."

She stayed silent, as she continued to walk down the street, never making a comment. Of course not. She would keep her own counsel, regardless of what he said.

He shrugged. "It's a trick Stefan taught me to control. I can leave my body at one place and travel to another, where I get to hear and to see what goes on."

Her features pinched a little tighter, but still she said nothing. If anything her footsteps gained speed, as if trying to pull away from the truth. Too bad. He could keep up with her anytime.

"Tavi!"

Her body made a slight jerk, as if from a blow. *Interesting.* So Tavi was a nickname. She stopped and turned, as the voice caught up with her. A young man who looked like he'd spent his lifetime on the streets walked up behind her. He held out a hand. Jericho watched as, instead of her filling his hand, he gave her something. With flashing urgency the young man bolted around the corner. The small piece of paper was well folded.

Tavika took a moment to carefully unfold and read a short message. Instead of trying to see it, Jericho watched her face. Only to be disappointed. Nothing moved. Her gaze went from one side to the other, as if reassessing her destination, then she shoved the piece of paper in her pocket and took a sharp right.

"I thought we were heading to the soup kitchen?"

"We are. In a few minutes."

Okay, so that note was about a meeting somewhere. She'd been a beat cop. She had informants, and obviously a lot of people knew her. Within a minute they came to yet another alleyway.

Was this where she spent all her time? But she bypassed it and ended up in a very small park. It was barely bigger than a residential lot, yet a couple trees were in the center, and, yes, in the background were more cardboard-looking houses. She walked over and stood in front of an old woman, who appeared to be asleep.

"Maggs?" Tavika asked softly. "You okay?"

The old woman opened her eyes and smiled. "I'm not dead yet, Tavi."

Tavika squatted beside her and reached out a hand. Jericho watched as she picked up the woman's coffee cup, then poured warm brew into it.

The old woman struggled to sit up, until Tavika gave her a hand. He studied Maggs. She was not on this earth for much longer. It appeared all three of them knew it.

With her shaking hands, she grabbed the coffee cup and took a sip. She gave a heartfelt sigh and patted Tavika's hands gently. "Don't be so upset, child. If the universe is generous, it will take me before next weekend."

He wouldn't have seen the movement if he hadn't been studying Tavika's face quite so intently, but, when she bit her bottom lip at the old woman's words, he realized she really did care. And those who didn't understand her or who saw her like this would get a completely different impression of who she was inside.

"You live as long as you're meant to live," Tavika replied neutrally. "It's all good." She straightened up and studied the cardboard shelter beside her. "Are you alone today?"

"Maybe." Maggs yawned and rubbed her shoulder. "I haven't seen anyone yet this morning." She studied the boxes. "They'll be back soon." She looked up at Tavika.

"You look like you're on a mission."

Tavika dropped her gaze to the old woman and smiled. "I am," she replied in a soft voice. "You and the others need to be careful." She motioned back toward the way they had come. "Gordon was killed last night."

There was no shock of surprise from Maggs. Just a heavier set to the multiple wrinkles on the woman's face. "How?"

Tavika took a step back and murmured, "He was murdered. Likely in his sleep."

Maggs stared off in the distance. "He was a young man."

"He was." Tavika took a quick walk around the park and returned to Maggs. "You take care."

Maggs gave her a toothless grin. "Don't you worry about me. Besides, if my maker comes, I'll give him a warm welcome."

Tavika nodded. "I know you will. Only everything has to happen in its own time frame."

With that cryptic sentence she turned, motioned to Jericho to move ahead of her, and they left. Just as they were almost out of sight, Maggs called out, "I saw him, you know. That's why I wanted you to come and talk to me."

Jericho froze. That explained the detour here.

Tavika turned to look back at her. "Who did you see?"

"Death. I passed him in the alleyway on my way home. I asked him to take me instead."

Tavika never said a word, she just waited.

Maggs shook her head.

Fondly Tavika asked, "Was he going to Gordon when you saw him?"

Maggs nodded. "He was." She made the sign of the cross across her chest. "It really would've been better if he'd taken me." And she sat back, sipping her coffee.

"Any description?" Tavika asked.

Maggs opened her eyes again and smiled. "He looks the way he always does. You know as well as I do that Death comes in many forms." And she sipped the last of her coffee, then lay down.

Tavika turned and walked away. Jericho raced to catch up. "Why don't you press for more description?"

"Maggs has seen a lot of murders in this town. To her, killers look the same. I've seen the description many times over, but it's always an avenging angel with a dark cloud around him, killing her friends."

"So she's not the most stable mentally?"

Tavika shot him a strange look. "Or she's more stable than most of us."

SO WHAT HAD he missed? Work had sucked today. But he wasn't independently wealthy, so he did what he had to do to keep his job. Besides, it paid well. And being there gave him some access to the information he'd needed all these years to stay safe from the police. Who were all too stupid to figure out what he was doing right under their noses. Of course he'd had to switch from one account to another to get what he needed. So far he'd managed just fine.

At least he was no longer traveling all across the countryside as part of his previous job as a drug rep. As much as his new hunting grounds had given his extracurricular activity some variety, he was a homebody at heart. Now he would have a real home. And he could stay where he belonged.

Now a full day had passed, and he needed to try and catch up. He logged in to his computer and quickly found the city police network and did the same. It was easy to travel to Tavika's files and get an update.

With a hot coffee at his side, an hour before his lover came over, he sat down to read the latest.

CHAPTER 11

"**A**RE YOU PLANNING on following me around all day?"

Jericho snorted. "As much as that would be fun, … no."

"Good." She motioned at the soup kitchen. "I'm going in here, then I'm heading back to the station. I have a lot of research to do."

"If you find anything, let me know."

She gave him a bark of a laugh. "Did you ever hear of confidentiality?"

"Don't be foolish. There has to be a connection between these three victims."

"Yeah, they were murdered," she noted in a dry tone, "but I'll need a whole lot more than that to take this killer to court."

"He'll never make it."

Jericho's tone of voice was so final that she stopped in her tracks to look at him. Carefully she asked, "Are you planning on doing something to ensure that comes about?"

He grinned at her. "Not happening, *Tavi*," he stressed her nickname. "I'm a precog. I see the future. And what I see is that he dies."

She raised her gaze to stare at the clouds above. "I can't find anything bad about that."

"We just have to be certain …" he added, "that he dies

alone." Jericho took a couple steps back, motioned at her to carry on. "I'll be around."

She didn't move. She studied him intently. "Around to watch my back? Around to find out information on the killer for your own purposes? Just what is your game, Jericho?"

"No game. A passion. Hunting a serial killer who has taken out a lot of people. He has to be stopped."

"Well, on that point we agree." She spun on her heels and walked into the soup kitchen. Only to find Steve knew nothing either. Damn.

Over an hour later she walked into the station. Again the noise hit her like a club to her head. Her stomach clenched, and her nerves tightened up like tensile wire. She should have worked from home.

She made her way to her desk and plunked down. Mark wasn't in, neither were several of the other men. Had another case come in while she'd been out?

She hoped not. She really wanted some computer time to see if she could find any links. Just then the captain walked into the room. "Tavika."

She lifted her head. When he made a hand motion toward the ceiling, meaning upstairs to his office, she stood. She didn't know what the hell this was about, but she hoped it wouldn't take long. They'd identified the teenage girl. And Tavi was just starting to delve into her history. She walked into his office. The captain nodded. "Take a seat."

She sat.

"You always look like you think you're in trouble." He glared at her. "Stop it."

"Am I?"

He sat back, with a half laugh. "Hell no. You're the best detective on the force."

Her head tilted to the side, as she studied him. It was unusual for him to give any compliments. It made her suspicious. "So why am I here?"

He leaned forward. "Bring me up-to-date on what you're working on."

She quickly ran through the three murders.

He barked out several questions. Then he stated, "You need to find that link."

"I know. There could be more victims," she admitted.

"There always are. Call Shelby only if you have to."

So this was what the meeting was about. "Did Shelby contact you?"

The captain shook his head. "No, she wouldn't. And, if the cases are connected, then you made the right call. But you know that not everybody appreciates your methodology."

She snorted. "I get results."

"Which is why you get into trouble."

She pondered that for a moment. "If we had more staff as good as Shelby, I'd be okay with calling them too."

He grinned. Big and beefy, a linebacker from way back when, the captain was a good man. She enjoyed working under him. "I'll be telling the coroner's office that."

She bounced to her feet, with a smile. "Not a good idea." She turned and walked back to the door, calling back, "I'll keep you updated."

As she went downstairs, she met Henry. Dressed in a suit, he looked good. "Wow, you moving up well above us?"

"Damn right." He grinned at her affectionately. "Hear you caught a hot one?"

She nodded.

"That's my girl."

"And I'll close it too." Then she remembered Henry had a meeting upstairs today. "Good luck." He waved in acknowledgment. He walked out the front door as C.J., another of her detective team, walked in.

"How did it go?" she asked C.J. He had caught the overnight knifing case that Shelby had mentioned earlier.

"Fine. Great actually." C.J. flashed her a big grin, then bent down to pull some stuff from his desk. "I'll be back in a couple hours." He strode from the room. And she knew his trip out this time had nothing to do with a case. He was a fit and sexy animal. With no wife, no kids. And even in his mid-fifties, he had a lot of appeal. He did a ton of volunteer work and was 100 percent a people person. He was one of those guys who would do well no matter where he was.

She envied that. She did well here. But take her out of this setting, and she was dying.

Now she had to find out if the three murders were connected. The last thing she needed was to be accused of hogging the coroner for her cases over somebody else's. In truth a lot of very capable people were in the coroner's office. But Tavika understood Shelby better than the others. And she liked to think Shelby understood her.

Since Shelby had already been tagged on the other cases, it only made sense that she be brought in on this one. But, as Tavika had yet to prove the connection, … that's what she would focus on for the next couple hours.

She sat down at her desk and logged on to her computer. Or rather she tried to. An alert came up, saying she had used up all her attempts and would need to contact the administrator. She sat back and under her breath said, "What the hell?"

She'd changed her password yesterday. And last week.

And the month before. She had more log-in issues than anyone in the station. She knew she was paranoid, but she couldn't help but wonder if someone wasn't just screwing with her. Or trying to make it look like she was a complete idiot.

Peters and Mark, who sat just slightly ahead of her, turned to look at her, their eyebrows raised.

She studied their faces for a moment, then asked quietly, "Did you see anybody sitting at my desk today?"

Mark frowned. "I only just got in, maybe fifteen minutes ago. Nobody was here then."

"Pretty much the same," Peters replied. "I came in maybe five minutes before that. The office was empty."

She nodded and kept her thoughts to herself. She picked up the phone and contacted the administrator. Then taking a picture of her screen with her cell, she got up from her desk and walked out of the room, with her jacket over her shoulder. She deliberately made it look like she was heading down to the coffee shop to grab something for lunch but raced to the stairwell to the captain's office instead. She walked into the general office. His admin was away from her desk. Tavika headed toward his personal office. She knocked on the door.

"Come in." The captain looked up at her and frowned. "What's the matter?"

She stepped in, closed the door behind her, and showed him her computer screen from the photo she'd just taken.

He read the error message then glanced up at her. "What does this mean?"

"I was up here with you. When I went back and tried to log in, that message came up."

He sat back and studied her. "You think somebody's

been trying to log in to your computer?"

"Yes, and for at least the second time." She sat down on the edge of her seat and explained about the problems she'd been having with her computer log-ins.

He listened quietly, his pencil tapping the notepad he'd been writing on. "Did you contact the administrator?"

She nodded. "Yes, several times." She took a deep breath. "I'm wondering if someone hasn't been gaining access to my account for a long time now. I've regularly changed my log-ins, and they are very complicated—more so every time just because … I think we need to take a closer look."

He leaned forward, his pencil snapping in his fingers. He frowned at the busted wood and tossed it into the garbage can beside him. "What do you suggest?"

"I was hoping I could get a little extra help?"

JERICHO TOOK A sip of his coffee. He sat in one of his favorite little cafés in the neighborhood. More for the location than anything else. They served good brew, but the food was just so-so. It had the added advantage that the house where the killer had taken Tavika hostage so long ago was visible from this window. But only if he sat in this space. Often when he came in, somebody else was there. And then he had to wait his turn.

Today the restaurant was empty. As he sat and studied the dilapidated house and the few on the other side, he wondered at the Ghost. Jericho had been hunting killers for a long time now. Although he didn't necessarily understand every act they made, he knew that, for the killer, those particular acts were not only something that made sense but they were often mandatory. Something to do with the twisted logic inside their heads.

"Do you want a refill?" The same middle-aged woman in her gingham apron stood in front of him, the coffeepot held in her hand.

"Sure." He smiled. "Thanks." He'd been here a lot over the years. He tried not to come so often that the staff would remember him though. And that was tough because it was also one of the few places where he could think and feel like he was accomplishing something. Of course that was a deception in itself. The longer the Ghost continued to operate under everybody's radar, the more uneasy they all felt.

In this case, Jericho knew Tavika would be one of the best chances they had to catch this Ghost guy. But, in the meantime, how many more people had to die? He'd spent the morning researching the cases that had been attributed to him, looking for any kind of connection between the old man and the Ghost. The trouble with serial killers was that what was logical to them wasn't to everyone else.

The problem with the Ghost was the sheer lack of evidence leading to a viable suspect. Jericho slouched down in his seat and pulled out his phone. Of course there was nothing from Tavika. Considering he had spent the night at her place, you'd think she'd at least have a modicum of good manners to stay in touch.

He almost grinned to himself at that thought. She'd more likely slug him in the face than say *thank you* for the night. Still, he was getting a sense of who she was inside. His initial impressions had proven to be quite wrong, and that bothered him. He had thought she was a hard, almost arrogant cop, who utilized her talents to close cases and to pat her ego. Probably lording it over everyone around her, without giving anyone an idea of how she was doing so well. Instead he found an introvert. Someone so reserved as to be considered cold. Which he now knew wasn't true.

He could sense the banked fire inside and the control she exerted over it. He'd seen visions of the two of them in bed, so he knew what was coming. The anticipation was killing him, but, at the same time, it appeared a hell of a long way away. The visions had also showed her dying, and that was something he wasn't willing to sit back and let happen. Even though he railed at the accuracy of his visions up until now, he kept the faint hope that maybe, this time, as the victim was also psychic, she could possibly influence the future herself.

As he enjoyed his coffee, snippets of images showed up and drifted away. A young boy crying, a man straightening a stapler on a desk, a group of teens sitting in a circle with candles lit, a young man in coveralls.

Nothing connected. Nothing clear. Typical. Just snap-shots of bits and pieces.

He picked up his coffee for a sip—and stilled. Tavika sat on the bench seat across from him.

Only in spirit form.

His gaze widened. He wanted to lean forward and to say something to her, but, in truth, he didn't dare. Someone could be watching. And he would look like a hell of a fool talking to an empty seat. The longer he looked, the more defined the bench seat showed through her faint form. Glancing around the restaurant, he leaned forward and asked in a hoarse whisper, "What are you doing here?"

A gay laugh rang across the restaurant, but he knew no one else heard. *I was just practicing what you said you could do.* She shrugged those shimmering shoulders and added, *It's interesting. Not sure there's much advantage to this. But at least it works. I haven't figured out how to just walk like this. All I did was think about you and found myself here. Pretty neat.*

Her humor died, and she leaned forward, glaring at him. *But, if I wanted to be in the circus, I could join anytime.* Her voice hardened, ringing as it did through his head, as she added, *Instead I think I'll stick to police work and actually find killers.*

Just like that, she disappeared.

He wanted to call out after her, but his mind was still reeling with the ease at which she'd picked up a new skill. Although it was quite possible she already knew how to do it and was just playing mind games.

He'd met people like that before, but it was not how he saw Tavika. So far she'd seemed genuine, with little patience or tolerance for such games.

Maybe Stefan knew about her abilities.

Stefan's voice popped into his head. *Don't bother questioning it. Tavika just learned that trick, and, as she went screaming through the divide, she woke me up. Her crossing was … powerful. Ungainly, like a teenager, but, with a little bit more practice, her control will be extraordinary.*

"So she is an unaware psychic?" Jericho glanced around to make sure nobody was listening in on a strange conversation because, in truth, he must really look like an idiot. But he sucked at telepathic communication. Stefan could jump into his mind, like he could anyone's at will, but that didn't mean Jericho had the same ability. He could do it—but not all the time or as easily as others could. He grabbed his cell, popped it to his ear, as if getting a call, all to make him not look like a loon. He still had to whisper, given the nature of their discussion. "Is it really possible that, on her first attempt, she managed something like that?"

Absolutely. And it's not that she's an unaware psychic because what you don't understand about Tavika is that, to her, these are not psychic skills. They are something she's been able to do for decades—just normal everyday abilities. Possibly since before her kidnapping. I suspect a lot of her skills developed at that point in time. And quite likely as a defense mechanism.

"Defense mechanism?"

In order to survive the horrors of what she saw and experienced.

Right. He could understand that.

HE HAD TO admit to feeling pressured. It wasn't normal for him to rush a job. But that sense of panic never quite went away these days. That need to look over his shoulder, as if he were being watched or the police were on his trail and getting closer. Of course they weren't. But having his crime scene used as a dump site for someone else? Yeah, that had been unnerving.

Unfortunately several names remained on his list yet.

And he was starting to feel like he needed to take care of them as soon as possible before … Only he didn't know how to finish that sentence. … Before *what?*

Still, the need to do something needled away at him. He chose a name off his list. She'd be easy. He'd get her done and out of the way—now.

CHAPTER 12

B Y THE TIME Tavika finished her research, she was more than a little tired. It had taken over an hour to get a new log-in from administration. Time she didn't have.

Sure, she'd asked for a little bit more than the usual, but that was what these people did. Right? Shaking her head, she plunked herself back down at her computer and logged back in. Finally it worked. Only to be effective, she would now have to log out every time she stood up for a cup of coffee or a bathroom break.

That would piss her off as well. Still, she'd found something. Although there was no connection to the Ghost, the old man and the teenage girl were connected.

The old man had done a bunch of work for the girl's family. And they'd identified her fairly easily because she was in the foster care system. Sarah Miller had gone missing off and on for the bulk of the last year. She was a regular runaway. In fact, several reports had been filed with the police, though none in the last few months. So, when she disappeared this time, they assumed she was just pulling one of her tricks again.

Unfortunately, in this case, the girl's time-out would now be permanent. Tavika patted the file she had at her side. She'd printed off a hard copy of everything she'd found. She still preferred paper over the digital world. Particularly when it came to her notes. Especially with someone trying hard—repetitively—to get into her system.

What she needed to do was set up a wall in one of the case rooms and see how all three of these victims were connected. Maybe tomorrow. Now that she had the old man doing electrical work at the foster home, Tavika was trying to figure out how Gordon fit in as well. So far he'd been a blank in that regard, but she knew there was a connection. She could sense it. In truth she saw a tenuous line from Gordon to the old man.

She'd seen those since she had first opened her third eye, about the time she turned into a teen. Mentioning a dotted highway through a classroom was enough to get her in trouble. But growing up and through school, she'd been warned to stop making up lies. Even her own mother had told her not to tell anyone. Who knew seeing colorful dots traveling from one point to another would upset people?

Even so, Tavika continued to see connections everywhere. She knew Peters was having an affair with someone who came into the building off and on. She'd seen the dotted lines. Seeing these connections was just another aspect that made her not want a permanent relationship.

Although to see most dotted pathways, she had to disappear into the abyss. Something she couldn't do at work. Better she went home with her files and took her trip there. To that end, she logged off, shut down her computer, stood up with her files, stuffed them into her bag, then walked out of the room without saying anything to anyone. Only Peters was left from her team in the office.

At least Peters and Mark didn't try to be anything other than the philanderers who they were. Still, they were good and steadfast cops. She could appreciate that. That Peters's love life was a mess was typical of many officers. Cops didn't do so well in that regard.

They needed more solid ones. Portland was no better or worse than any other major city across the US. But there had been several incidents in the last few years that had given them a bad name. Dirty cops were good for nobody.

She'd considered going into internal affairs to hunt down the corrupt cops herself but figured the best use of her skills was on the streets.

Outside, she stopped in confusion. Then saw her truck. She walked over and hopped in. She sat inside, the keys in her hand and she stopped.

When had she picked up the truck? She'd walked to work this morning. Or had that happened yesterday? She sat here, trying to figure it out, and realized that somehow her truck was here, but she hadn't brought it. She had the keys in her hand, but she had not driven it to work. So what the hell was going on? She went to start up the engine, uneasiness deep in her soul, and caught sight of something else. *Jericho.* Standing in front of her with a big grin on his face.

Goddammit.

She rolled down her window. "Did you drive my truck here?"

He laughed and, before she had a chance to lock the passenger door, he hopped in. Inside, he buckled up and replied, "Absolutely I did. And you are welcome by the way."

She stared at him, both in anger and relief. She'd had blackouts for months after she'd been rescued twenty years ago, but she had never told anybody. She'd kept that deep inside. But like all fears, it came to the surface every once in a while. And today, when she sat in her truck, not remembering where and how the truck had gotten here—so many fears about blackouts and more came rushing to the surface.

"I should arrest you for grand theft auto," she snapped.

He gave her a look of mocking innocence. "You should be happy. At least today you don't have to walk home."

There was so much outrage burning through her that she didn't know what to think. And she had to wonder, … when had he given her the keys? Bewildered, she looked from the keys to his face.

He gently cupped her cheek. His hand slid down her arm to her hand and squeezed her fingers. "I'll explain later. Let's just drive please. Being around cop shops makes me nervous."

"Not surprising, considering you just stole my truck."

"Actually I delivered your truck. I knew you were tired and having a tough day. I was just being nice."

But something in his tone of voice bothered her. She glanced over at him but couldn't read anything in his expression. Suspicious, she asked, "Or is it that you want to be driven somewhere? But why? You have your own truck."

He laughed. "You're a hard person to fool."

She withdrew the keys from the ignition and glared at him. "What the hell?"

"It's okay. You really want to go there too."

"And why do I want to go there?"

"Because there'll be another spirit in that electrician's nightmare of a house."

She sucked in a breath, too shocked to even stare, much less glare at him. In a hoarse voice she asked, "How do you know?"

She waited for him to answer, but he didn't. Her mind raced with the implications. It also explained why her vehicle should be driven. He didn't want anyone to notice his presence. Whereas, she went there all the time.

Out loud she said, "You told me that you are a precog, meaning you see things before they happen. Has this next victim actually died? Or is the Ghost about to kill this person?" Seeing the answer on his face, she turned on the engine, ripped it to life, and tore out of the parking lot, heading for her house of horrors. Damn. Maybe Jericho would be of some use after all.

Now maybe they could get there before the next victim died.

SHE PULLED ONTO the street in record time. He'd seen a lot of people drive fast, but she drove with almost a furious disconnection. A scary one. She parked down the block, where several vehicles filled the side of the street. He hopped out of the truck and waited for her. And again she surprised him.

He figured she'd run for the house. Instead she walked cautiously forward, her stride never slowing, but her energy sent out a ton of feelers. Very cool. Not only was she an incredibly good driver but she was cautious.

He was afraid she'd go half-cocked crazy, after realizing the killer was back in town. If she were to impede his investigation, he couldn't afford to let her in on the case. He still wasn't sure. He may end up shutting her out at one point.

Nothing and no one would stop him from taking down this asshole. Not this time.

Two steps behind Tavika, he watched as she approached the front door. She had her hand on her weapon, as she studied the front window. Or what should have been one.

Instead it was just broken glass lining a big hole in the wall. The place appeared deserted. Instead of going into the house, she slipped around to the back. He followed. Together they searched the outside to search for a sign of anyone around.

He couldn't see anything. His vision had been strong, so he knew another victim was arriving. He just didn't know when. She shot him a questioning glance. He shrugged. How did he explain precog half-truths to somebody who didn't understand them?

Around the back, where the kitchen door was already partially ajar, she slipped inside. He raced to keep up. She really didn't understand the concept of teamwork, did she?

Inside the house, it was cold, desolate, and dark. Empty. Tavika walked through quietly, searching the physical space. On her heels, he studied the area. It was empty. Back in the kitchen now, she asked, "Is the time frame still accurate?"

He nodded. "As much as I can see."

Interestingly she didn't question his ability. Of course that was an entirely different issue altogether.

"Then let's get out of sight." She stepped outside. "I'll keep watch from the neighbor's. I suggest you do your ghostly thing and hide out but keep watch from the front." She turned and walked toward the next property.

His eyebrows rose.

Interesting. Acceptance. And trust. He kind of liked it. But she was right. He could keep track in a far different way. Unless the killer was also psychic. If Tavika was watching the back, Jericho needed to watch the front. Contemplating his options, all he really needed was to be out of sight physically. His gaze caught on the long line of huge trees out front, lining the streets. They were in bad need of a trim, so they were heavy and lush. If he had enough time …

The words were barely through his mind, when he was already climbing up the tree. With a couple jumps and pulls, he was tucked up in the greenery on a large limb above the sidewalk. He was at least fifty feet from the front door, but he had good visibility.

Now to secure his position and then hunt for the Ghost.

He laughed. This time he'd be one himself.

NO. NO. *NO.* How did they know? They shouldn't know. He was happy to blame the guy she was with. He'd never seen her with a male before—other than the other detectives she worked with.

But this one was a different relationship.

If they weren't lovers already, they would be soon.

He sat in the car, the engine running, trying to figure out what to do. His plans had to be changed. But what was his plan B? He'd thought this one would be easy. The woman had been walking by when he'd left the damn electrician's house. One of those more impulsive moves that had caused him more trouble than it was worth.

He'd planned to dump her inside where the others had been. But that was out. So now what?

Plan B? Hell, there wasn't one because he'd never needed it.

His breath came in hard gasps, his black gloved hands squeezing the steering wheel so hard he couldn't feel his fingers.

Think, damn it. *Think!*

CHAPTER 13

T AVIKA SETTLED DOWN behind the huge busted window in the neighbor's sunroom. Luckily this house seemed deserted, so she wouldn't scare anyone or have someone come upon her. She had a great view of the back of the Breaker house. She expected the killer to show up, once night settled in. She didn't know how many deaths Jericho had attributed to this serial killer, but she knew of at least eleven that the Ghost looked good for. She wouldn't be surprised if the number were four times as high.

Too bad she hadn't brought food with her for the stake-out. This was not how she had planned to spend the rest of her night.

Although she was hungry, she was hungrier for this killer.

She closed her eyes and hunkered down for a long wait. The houses all around her had the same desolate look. The area had been nice at one time, then drugs had moved in. It was possible the Ghost actually lived in one of the other houses on the block. Which meant he may have seen them arrive. She frowned. That would suck. She leaned back and let her eyes drift closed. Her shield wavered with all the stress. Instinctively she plugged the drain by pouring more energy into it. Feeding energy to her shield would kill her one day. She knew that.

But she had no choice. Some secrets had to be kept.

They were just too precious not to. She had no idea if this killer had any abilities or not. She hadn't thought he did. She'd listened to her mom's broken cries back then, but she'd not made any sense. Tavika had been blessedly unconscious in the beginning. By the time she'd woken, her mother had been broken. During that week Tavika had been held, her mother hadn't mentioned anything that clarified who her killer was. And Tavika had had lots of time to listen, but she'd never recognized the voice.

Her phone rang. Damn it.

Then she realized it was Travis. Pulling out the phone from her left-hand pocket, she smiled and held it to her ear. "Hey, bro. How's life?"

"What have you done, Tavi? Talk to me," he said. His voice was sharp, angry.

Of course he was angry.

"Stop tracking the Ghost. Vengeance is no way to live."

He might be right, but she was hardly living. "Like you've moved on," she scoffed. "I'm surprised you're not here, trying to take him out yourself."

Until she put away this Ghost asshole, she knew it would dominate her world. Only after she took down this man and made him pay for all the things he'd done would she be able to move on.

"Tavika, that's not the way to handle this." Travis's voice sounded distant. "We've gone over this time and time again."

"And I never change my mind," she stated. "I understand where you're coming from, but it's different for me."

"It doesn't have to be. You can walk away. At least you get to live that way. To have a good life, not this half existence."

"If he doesn't kill me, it'll be somebody else. This is my job. My calling." She gave a partial ugly laugh. "Who knows? Maybe what happened had to happen to set me on this course."

"Don't think like that. It's over. It's been so for a long time."

"No," she argued. "It is over for you. I'm still reliving the nightmare."

Silence followed, but then what could he say? He knew what she'd been through. That she had any kind of a normal life was amazing. Things could've ended up so much worse.

She heard a sound outside. She froze and shifted her position and saw nothing but ... "I have to go," she whispered. "I'll talk to you later."

"Tavi ..."

She put away her phone, rather than listen to more. It had all been said many times over. In truth there was nothing more to say.

Footsteps? Did she hear footsteps? Her mind strained to focus on the sound more clearly. To figure out exactly what it meant. Why would anybody walk so loudly that she heard the footsteps? Or was it ...

She'd come here to this neighborhood hundreds of times over the last few years. This group of bungalows were just a couple blocks from her family home, and most of them were vacant deteriorating hulls. Only three times had she ever met anybody walking around outside this area, and one time she had found maybe a half-dozen people inside her childhood home. Other times it had just been one or two squatters. Regardless she didn't like it and shooed them all away.

Still, to hear footsteps in this neighborhood was rare

during the day, so at almost dark it was disturbing. Right now she couldn't see anything from where she sat. The window was busted and open, giving her access, if she needed to jump through to get to the Breaker house. But the footsteps came closer from the front. She stilled, scared to breathe.

The footsteps were young, with energy. Not an older person or anyone carrying a burden, like a dead body. Then they stopped. She sensed their hesitation.

"Hello. Anyone here?"

She frowned. What the hell?

Jericho whispered in her mind, *Don't move. It's a trick.*

The young voice called again, "Hello. I have a pizza delivery for someone named Tavika."

She closed her eyes in frustration. How the hell?

She didn't know if she should jump up to quiz the delivery boy or stay where she was. It had to be from the Ghost. But how could he know she was here? And how had Jericho not seen this? And had this event then made Jericho's vision defunct? Or was it still part of it? Damn. None of this made any sense. Like most psychic visions, it was as clear as mud.

Outside she heard the delivery boy talking on the phone.

"You're sure you have the right address? Are you sure she's living here? The house is really destroyed." A pause came, as he listened. "No, another house is on the right, but honestly it doesn't look like anybody's here at all. The windows are all smashed in, and the front doors are hanging off their hinges. I think you need to check the address again." He waited for a few minutes.

But she knew the address was correct.

The young man spoke again. "Okay, what about a phone number?" There was silence as he listened. "Okay I'll call. Thanks."

She strained to hear. Interesting.

He quickly dialed. When a voice answered, he spoke. "Hello, I'm trying to deliver the pizza, but the address appears to be wrong. … Okay, so it's 964 not 984?"

He turned to look at the house beside the hovel.

The house Tavika was hiding in.

"Okay. If you're sure she's in there," he noted doubtfully. He put away his phone and walked closer to her hiding spot.

Tavika was torn. Obviously the gig was up. She wanted to answer the door and question the delivery boy, maybe gather information of value.

I said don't move, Jericho snapped.

She went to stand up and found she couldn't. Her body was locked in this position, frozen to the floor. What the hell? She struggled harder, but there was no moving her legs. She could move her upper body, but her knees were frozen to her chest, the same position as she'd been hiding in under the window.

Jericho had to be behind this. She didn't know how he managed it, but it was pissing her right off.

She'd had more than enough of being any man's prisoner.

TAVIKA BETTER NOT fucking move. Jericho had been sending her warning messages for the last five minutes. Either she wasn't hearing him or she'd slammed the door so hard between them that she *couldn't* hear. And that worried him. He didn't know if the pizza guy was another errand boy and completely innocent in all this or if something else could be inside that box. Either way he didn't want her to move.

He'd heard the phone call the pizza delivery guy had made, checking on the address. The fact that the guy was now heading toward the house where Tavika sat was terrifying. Jericho shifted his position to study the street below. The only way this could be happening was if the Ghost had actually seen Tavika go into that house. And if he'd ordered that pizza. If so, he must have used a credit card. Jericho needed to know who had placed that order. And to trace the customer's phone number too.

He sent Hunter the request. The answer coming back was damn fast. The pizza order had been charged to Jericho's own credit card and had been called in on his own damn cell. Damn it. The Ghost had watched them arrive and had thereafter cloned Jericho's own phone number, plus hacked his credit card info.

Jericho cursed his decision to hide in the tree. He was stuck. If he had chosen any other damn place he might have had a better chance of seeing the Ghost.

Stefan's voice reached in through his mind. *No. He already knew.*

"Knew what?" Jericho whispered under his breath. "Stefan, what do you know?"

Know for sure? Stefan said in a low voice. *Nothing. This was too well-planned. The pizza was delivered so fast after Tavika walked into that house.*

Jericho sat back. Stefan was right. He'd known ahead of time—somehow. Shit.

HE SHOULD HAVE sent a double order of pizza for the cops because they were being so stupid. He saw them from his living room. It hadn't taken him long to come up with the plan, but it required he return to his apartment.

He'd stashed his victim for the moment. Hopefully Tavika would realize she'd been made and would promptly leave.

He'd chosen his apartment specifically for the view. When the high-end units went up, he had bought one right away. There weren't many of the larger ones with the layout he wanted on this side of the building, but it had to be this side. So he saw the house that started it all. He loved watching that place, and many others he had fond memories of. Just looking down on the roads and alleys he knew so well put a smile on his face. Particularly if he would shut down that part of his life.

He sighed. This place held a lot of fond memories. It also gave him a clear view of the comings and goings there now. And, if he needed to open up that house again, well, he would. Especially if Tavika really was psychic. He'd let himself be convinced she was innocent of all that evil, when she was a child.

But, if he found he was wrong, then she would have to be destroyed, like the rest of her family. He'd given her lots of time to prove herself. ... However, with his future plans, he couldn't afford to leave any threads to unravel—especially not if she found out the truth about him.

Besides, he needed to be sure.

And the only way she could know about him at this point was if she were using those nasty, evil ways of her mother's. A woman he could cheerfully kill a dozen times over.

There was no end to that kind of evil.

CHAPTER 14

NSTINCT TOLD TAVIKA to stay still, but it warred with the primal fear aching with her need to run. She couldn't do either. The fact was, she couldn't even move. She could barely breathe.

What the hell was this? She struggled to free herself from the invisible bonds, her panic increasing with each movement, which caused the bonds to tighten. Like she was fighting against herself.

And you are, came a gentleman's smooth voice. *You need to stay where you are right now. Stop fighting it. Relax.*

It wasn't Jericho's voice; she'd heard voices like that before. The shrinks had told her that she was making it up.

That they weren't real.

That they were all in her imagination.

She knew her family's voices weren't her imagination. She'd eventually learned to not tell the shrinks anything of the voices. And finally had learned to tell the shrinks to go away and to leave her alone. That's what she would tell this asshole too.

"I don't know who the hell you are," she replied in a hard voice, "but I'll kick your ass for doing this to me." She snorted, managing to raise her arm, even though it felt like lead, with a forty-pound weight attached to her wrist. "Don't think I won't."

Then you must just punch yourself in the face because this is your doing.

The note of humor in the man's voice made her pause. She snorted again. "Like hell. No way I'm doing this."

Maybe I should say, you're letting this happen to you. After a quick pause, his tone became sharper. *You don't have time for this. You have allowed power over you to someone in your space. Whether it's a belief or fear of a person, I don't know. All I can tell you is that it's keeping you immobilized on that floor.*

"What hocus-pocus bullshit is that?"

Tavika, this is Stefan. He released a heavy sigh. *It would make life so much easier if you weren't so goddamn stubborn.*

"I am the way I am."

We were all the way we were sometime, he shot back. *It's called free will. The ability to change, to grow, to learn. You don't have to sit there, refusing to acknowledge what happened to you way back when. You're using your abilities at a rate that is alarming, but now it's burning through your system. You have one goal, one vengeance, one purpose in your life right now, and achieving that will kill you.*

"And I care why?" she cried out in anger and frustration. "There is nothing else in my life but this asshole."

Because you've fed on that same theme over and over and over again. It's up to you, if you want to let it go. To walk past it. To move on and to actually have a life of joy.

"Joy? I don't even know what that is." Her laugh was bitter, flat. "He took everything from me."

Then in a much softer voice, Stefan added, *Not quite. Your brother is still there.*

Her heart froze. He couldn't know. No way. No one knew. Some secrets were never meant to come to light. As her fear and panic magnified, she doubled up her shield, as she tried to keep Stefan from learning her innermost secrets. It was too dangerous.

I don't want to intrude. I don't want to pry into your history, Stefan told her. *Your secret is safe with me.*

She shook her head. "No," she whispered. "No secrets are ever safe."

Then let me help.

She froze, her mind consumed with the fact that somebody wanted to help her, and her instinctive reaction was to let him. She hadn't had much of that in her world. Maybe some help had been offered, but she'd never been in a position of needing to take it. She'd been able to handle it.

Right now she needed help. But, when you let someone in, you opened yourself up. Things changed.

Stop. I'm not trying to take over your world. I'm not trying to control anything. I want you to calm down, so you can see that you're doing this to yourself.

"If I'm doing this, why is it I can't free myself?"

You can. He paused. *Take several deep breaths. Get your energy to a lower alert level. You've been using your energy shield for so long that you no longer recognize a real threat.*

She frowned. Did she even know what that meant? Then she realized she did. But less from knowledge than an intuitive sense. Following his instructions, she took several deep breaths. As she did, the constriction around her chest eased. Following that came the ability to move her hands. When she realized it was working, she quickly repeated the process, until the force paralyzing her eased back. "What started this?"

That's a little harder to explain. Likely someone in your circle thought you should be forced to stay in this position.

"Jericho?" she hissed in alarm. "How is that possible?"

I can see you, Stefan stated clearly. *It's possible that this person is also watching the house and could be psychic. And it could also be your own alarm systems preset to trigger this paralysis, whenever you come up against something that terrifies you.*

Tavika hopped to her feet and walked around the small room, shaking her hands and legs. She didn't understand what had just happened, but she understood Stefan's words even less. The fact that he was speaking to her, that she heard his voice, just as if speakers were in the room—which there weren't—was mind-blowing. Her mother had been able to do that, but Tavika had lived in the cocoon of belief that her mother was special and that nobody else could do what she did. It was a shock that Stefan had the same abilities. As did Jericho. As did … she. *Not only do I have the same abilities, but a lot us can do the same things.*

"Unbelievable." She glanced around the room, the setting sun casting shadows. And so much more. Had the pizza delivery guy left? She hoped he got paid, but no way in hell would she open the door and let whoever sent her the pizza then know she was actually in the house. Not now.

What if the Ghost had been responsible for her paralysis? If he'd seen her arrive, then he might have thought that's where she'd be, but she'd be dammed if she'd confirm it.

Then she stopped and frowned. The paralysis issue was so much bigger than the pizza delivery guy knowing exactly where she hid. How the hell could this person do this? And what would she do about it?

You'll keep the communications open because it could save your life, Stefan snapped. *I don't care if you don't think your life is worth saving. It is. And you can do so much more to help the world than what you're doing now.*

How dare he? She felt that old rage boiling up. It had haunted her since she had been a child. Knowing she would die young, knowing she wouldn't escape her family's killer. Not wanting to escape. Did Stefan understand how hard it was to do anything, knowing her life would end?

Convert that rage into something useful, Stefan snapped. *I don't have time for all this, and neither do you. That serial killer is out there, and he's on a mission right now.*

Her gaze narrowed, as she stared out to the sky. "It's bad enough that you're inside my head. That you can read my thoughts and mind. What do you know about the Ghost?"

I know everything you do and more.

She gave a shuddering breath, wondering what had happened to her world.

The Ghost happened. Are you really going to let the Ghost get away with it? Stefan's voice was determined, as he added, *You're no longer a child. What happened to you was horrific. You have carried forward the vestiges of all that guilt, that grief, that loneliness, from the death of your family members. And he's using it against you. But worse? … You're letting him.*

JERICHO WONDERED IF anyone other than a psychic saw the strong cloud of energy bubbling through the house, right where Tavika sat hidden from most of the world. She was so damn powerful that her thoughts and energy were just firing off, like a lightning storm. He knew Stefan had gone in to talk to her. Most of the time Stefan was a gentle soul, but, when he needed to be, he came down with Thor's hammer and made the world happen.

Tavika was caught in a time warp—so hung up on something she needed to do that she'd programmed her entire life to achieve it. Fear kept driving her forward. Jericho did not want to see her die. He knew she was on the Ghost's list. He just didn't understand why. Especially after all this time.

Stefan's voice slammed through his mind. *Something has changed in the Ghost's world.*

Jericho closed his mind and cried out, "Tone it down will you?"

Instantly Stefan softened his voice, as it rippled through his mind. *Sorry.*

"It's okay." Jericho gently massaged his temples. "What do you mean, something's changed?"

There has to be a reason why he's coming after her now.

"Maybe he's just found her again? Maybe he was looking for a long time and just came across her path now." Jericho liked that idea but knew it wouldn't fly. Tavika had an unusual name, and, although she was not in a high-profile position, she *was* in one that put her in the media spotlight every once in a while, and she'd been in it several times over the last few years.

Or ... Stefan's voice fell silent.

"Or?" Jericho waited, knowing Stefan was trying to get his thoughts clear.

Almost hearing a mental shrug, Jericho heard Stefan say, *We've seen it before. He's cleaning up.*

"Cleaning up?" Jericho rolled the idea around in his head. "That's along the same lines we were considering."

He could be moving on maybe? He could be afraid of getting caught for some reason all of a sudden. Stefan's voice turned humorous.

"Scary thought." Jericho shook his head. A lot of people out there were real psychics, and most of them were in hiding. Then there were those few who wanted the publicity, who wanted the media to know what they did. There was no shortage of people who were *not* psychics who handed out misinformation for a bit of money on a daily basis. Casual comments could have incredible results, when given to the wrong people. It would be just stupid enough for something like that to come into play here. "Any sign the Ghost is psychic himself?"

I wondered that, Stefan noted thoughtfully, *but I haven't got any reason to believe so.*

"And yet so many psychos are, especially the ones we haven't been able to capture yet." Jericho should know. He'd been involved in several big cases lately. The cops involved would not have wanted anything to do with psychic killers. They liked their serial killers vanilla style, just plain old bad guys. Jericho couldn't blame them.

As he straddled the tree branch, with the stars in the night sky settling heavier on the town, he heard a vehicle slowly approach. He froze. "Is that him?"

And heard Stefan's startled gasp. *Yes, it is.*

CASUAL. JUST BE casual. But the blood pumped through his veins and his adrenaline matched the panic roiling inside. Drive as if you have a place to go and a place to be. They should be gone. He'd thought they *were* gone. Surely after the pizza showed up, they'd have given up and walked away for tonight at least.

Surely?

He had to dump the body. He'd planned to leave it at her home, where she belonged, but then decided to throw the cops off by putting it at the same house as the old man.

Surely another body would muddy the waters even more.

But Tavika's appearance had blown that.

Now he had a new location, but he had to get there first.

Without being seen.

He drove past the electrician's house. He never turned his head, but he was watching. Was anyone still here? A tree branch shook, catching his eye. He thought he saw a face … in a tree?

Oh, hell no.

He hit the gas and took the first corner. He shook so badly he could hardly hold the steering wheel.

Damn. The new destination was just a couple blocks away. However, he kept taking corners, trying to throw off a tail. They didn't have time to get into a vehicle and to come after him. No way they'd see where he went, but fear rode him to take this erratic route.

Shit. What if she *was* a goddamned psychic, like her evil bitch of a mother?

If she was, he was fucked. Then he gave a hard laugh.

In which case, she was too.

CHAPTER 15

TAVIKA COULDN'T STOP shaking. Stefan's words still echoed in her head.

Are you really going to let the Ghost get away with it? You're no longer a child. What happened to you was horrific. You have carried forward the vestiges of all that guilt, that grief, that loneliness, from the death of your family members. And he's using it against you. But worse? ... You're letting him.

She understood *some* of what had just happened, leading up to her frozen in a crouch in an abandoned house. But, for all her efforts to focus forward, into the future, on catching—killing—the Ghost, it never seemed like she could put her past behind her. And she had tried. Damn, she had tried. It wasn't fair of Stefan to say she was hanging on to it because she'd been trying to slough that off her shoulders forever. What would he do if the spirits of his mother and his sister were stuck inside the house where they had been killed?

Tavika shook her head. She had listened, as they had died a horrible, painful death. Those cries, images, were stuck inside her. As if on a big color TV, stuck before her eyes. Just what the hell was she supposed to do about that?

Nothing. There was nothing she could do. Because she had tried. For twenty years.

Then her mind jumped up and, playing devil's advocate,

asked, *But what about Stefan? What if he could help? Maybe not your mother and your sister but maybe he could help you.*

Way back when, he'd said she was perfectly capable of helping her mother, her sister, both cross over. That had *not* been the answer she had wanted to hear years ago. It had been hard to realize so much more was out there in the field of energy work than she'd been aware of. And she knew plenty. Just because she chose not to tell anyone didn't change the fact that her mother and her sister had been extremely powerful in their own rights. And her mother had been insistent in training her children.

And then there was her brother. Her twin. Their mother's favorite. Their mother had initiated them into the psychic realm when young, but none of Tavika's abilities had shown up until later. When she didn't have anyone left to mentor her.

Tavika was the youngest—the last. And, in her mind, the stupidest. The least talented.

And she had paid the price for not having anybody there to help guide her through the changes, when they hit.

So she was untrained. She could control certain aspects of her psyche but not all of them. And nothing like her mother or her sister could. Her twin brother, Travis, had been a bit of a wild card. He hadn't wanted anything to do with their mother's world, but he'd been a strong telepath. That's the way he liked it. He had said he was *sleeping on his supposed gifts.* Tavika laughed. She presumed that was the term for *rebelling.* Like that was a choice for her.

According to some people it was; Tavika just didn't understand how it could become *her* choice. She shuddered, a chill settling on her soul. She could never lose track of the fact that a serial killer was out there. She could never forget what he'd done to her family.

Now he was tormenting other people.

Why? Why now and why so many?

Why so many victims, so fast?

He'd been dormant for years. At least from what she knew. What had changed? Something had triggered the shift. Some killers were predictable, until an event made them seriously unpredictable. She'd been hunting killers for ten years now, and something was horribly compelling about her job. She knew she could never do anything else. She figured, once she had killed the one she'd been hunting, she would have nothing left in her life to strive for. She no longer had the death wish that had tormented her teen years. Not really—yet, if it happened, she wouldn't mind.

In so many ways her life sucked.

Her phone in her left pocket rang. *Her brother.* Of course it would be him. She pulled it out. "I'm fine," she said into the phone.

"No, you're not. Stop talking about having a death wish."

"If you'd been paying closer attention," she protested, "you would've understood what I was thinking. I don't have a death wish."

"And yet, *if it happened,* you'd be okay with it. Do you understand that nobody else would be *okay with it?*"

She stared out at the abandoned house next door. "I hear you. You weren't meant to hear me."

"Too damn bad. It'll be a cold day in hell when I don't know what you're thinking." And he hung up.

With a heavy sigh, she shoved the phone back into her pocket. Such was her life. Apparently everybody could read her mind.

So why the hell couldn't she read Jericho's? He'd even managed to open some kind of corridor from his mind to hers. Could she duplicate that, like she had the spirit-walking, when she'd found him at the coffee shop? She thought about the serial killer, imagined his ghostly form in front of her, and drove a tunnel corridor wide enough for her to enter his mind.

As she stood here, in this abandoned house, glaring at the damaged wall in front of her, the house disappeared, and an office showed up. She gasped and stepped back, but the office overlooked the city.

She recognized the landmarks. The city skyline was Portland.

What the hell? She stepped forward, her hand instinctively trying to touch the wall of the house she knew she was still in. It was here, beneath her hand—solid. But, like a color TV that suddenly flashed on the screen in front of her, she no longer saw a plastered wall before her; she saw a glass floor-to-ceiling window from a high-rise office building.

Involuntarily her viewpoint changed, giving her a glimpse of the rest of the office, then she stared down. And she quaked. A janitor in blue coveralls lay dead on the floor. She couldn't tell how he had died, but blood seeped under his head. She tried to glance to the side, looking for more information, but couldn't. She had no control over what she saw. As if she were in someone else's mind, using their eyes, Tavika saw what he saw, and that was it.

And then she realized what she'd done. She'd connected to the killer's mind. At his movement, she glanced down at his gloved hands and noted the thin wire wrapped around one fist. Little pieces of wood were on either end, and she recognized it instantly.

The murder weapon. The killer had used a garrote.

Somehow the doorway into his mind slammed shut, and the office disappeared. Then she realized it wasn't just the office door that had disappeared but the doorway into that world had too.

That's when her shaking had begun again. And the doubt. Was she crazy? Had she just seen what she thought she'd seen? Or was it all a figment of her imagination? And where the hell was Stefan when she needed him?

The same place I've always been. Everywhere, he stated in a light voice. *Anytime you need me, you only have to call.*

She heard his words in her head. In a shaky voice, she asked, "Did you see what I just saw?"

No. What did you see?

She quickly explained, not giving herself a chance to question how absolutely absurd this conversation was. Or that she spoke aloud, while he spoke in her head. When she slipped from out loud to talking in her head, she didn't recognize her own transition.

Until Stefan pointed it out. *You do realize you are now communicating telepathically, the same as I was doing with you before? You've opened doorways into your world that you had kept closed before, and that vision was yet another glimpse of your gifts.*

But was it real? she cried out. *Was that really the killer's view I saw?*

Yes, quite likely. You've connected to a killer, the one you were thinking of.

In bewilderment she stared at the destroyed house surrounding her and asked, *How can I tell if it was the Ghost?*

That's for you to find out. You're the one who made that connection. You drove that connection into his head, whether he knew it or not, whether he was willing or not. You opened a window into the killer's world. You might be able to use that pathway again.

I don't think I can. She collapsed onto the floor, her knees no longer willing to hold her upright. *This was too unbelievable.*

It doesn't matter whether it's unbelievable or not. It's happened. Your mother had visions, right?

Tavika raised her gaze blankly to where she imagined Stefan would be standing, if he were actually here in physical form. And, for the first time, she admitted, *Yes, my mother had visions. She saw the future. But she was unwilling to share very much because it was all so horrible. She hated that she'd brought children into this world, children who would suffer.*

Stefan's voice was gentle with compassion. *Your mother saw much of the darkness of this world. Her attitude was understandable, but it does not have to be yours.*

And how is anything I've seen any different? How is it supposed to lead me to any kind of different conclusion than what she came to?

Slowly another truth filtered through her head—with all her mother had seen, no wonder she had become hard, abusive, living life with a frantic edge.

By choice, Stefan noted. *That was her choice. It doesn't make it your choice. You can see the other side of life—by taking the time to see the goodness in this world. By seeing the best parts of people, not just the worst. And, right now, you aren't doing much of that. You're actively hunting down the Ghost who killed your family. You're keeping him alive in your world. You're making him a party to your every breathing moment. You have no room in there for something bigger, better, happier. You need to make those changes, those choices. Or else you'll end up just like your mother.*

The neighbor's front door burst open then, and Jericho blasted through the house to the sunroom. "Tavika, the killer just raced down the road. He was driving an old Cadillac Seville, gold in color. I got part of the license plate." He gave her a fat smile. "And, for the first time, I got a chance to actually see his energy."

She took all of a split second to switch from Stefan's internal dialogue to Jericho's presence and the reality that maybe they finally had something concrete to go on. "Are you sure? How do you know it was him? Did you actually see him?"

"I didn't see anything else but the energy in the vehicle. It was him driving."

"Give me the license plate," she said, racing out to the front yard. "Any idea where he went?"

They both jumped into her truck, this time Jericho in the driver's seat. He held out his hand for her keys, and she dropped them into his palm, not taking time to argue. He said, "You call it in. I'll see if I can find this asshole."

"Can you track his energy?

"I can try."

JERICHO SAW VESTIGES of the energy racing down the road ahead of them. It was dissipating way too quickly for his comfort. He gunned the truck to go faster than was safe, as it rounded the corner. The truck rocked from side to side, and he felt Tavika's look, but she didn't say anything. He knew she wanted to catch this asshole as much as he did.

The energy shimmered weakly, getting fainter as they traveled deeper into the traffic. He heard Tavika on the phone beside him, as she called in for a trace on the license plate. He suspected the vehicle would be stolen, but maybe it would at least give them something to go on.

He turned a corner and then another and yet another. Did the killer know he was being followed? Or did he just presume he needed to hide his tracks to get as far away as possible?

Maybe he was being naturally cautious. And maybe he was completely lost in this part of town.

Jericho passed another block and realized the energy was gone. He spun the truck around in the middle of the street, thanking the good Lord this residential area was once again empty of traffic. He backtracked, picked up a little bit of energy to the left. This took them along a more rural area. He gunned it, knowing he was taking a chance of losing the energy if he went too slowly. Up ahead was a strip mall. He pulled into the parking area, his gaze flashing across the vehicles here for any sign of the one he was looking for.

Tavika pointed. "Stop." He slammed on the brakes and looked in the direction of her finger. Sure enough, there was the Cadillac he'd seen earlier, parked in the far corner of the mall. And, of course, no driver was visible. Jericho approached slowly and parked a few feet away.

HOW HAD THEY found the car so fast? He'd been counting on having more time. Fear struck his heart. It was too soon. He wasn't far enough away. He'd barely had time to run anywhere, before they turned into the lot.

He watched as Tavika and Jericho circled the Cadillac.

A shudder slipped down his back.

"Hey, sir, are you okay?" a young woman asked.

With a nod, he backed deeper into the shadows. Thankfully, after sending him an odd look, she had walked away. He critiqued the last few moments of their interchange, then decided she wouldn't tell anyone anything.

He was safe.

The mall was a good place to get lost. But this wasn't the way it was supposed to be. He narrowed his gaze at Tavika. Even from this distance he saw the look in her eyes.

She knew what was in the car.

Bitch.

CHAPTER 16

TAVIKA HOPPED OUT of her truck and walked quietly past the other vehicles parked in the mall lot. Nobody was in the driver's side or visible in the back seat of the Cadillac. In fact, nothing was suspicious about the car at all. Except she knew better. She turned to study the strip mall in front of her. A laundromat. A Chinese food take-out restaurant. What looked like a cold beer and wine store. A quickie mart took up the end spot. The trouble was, she had no idea who or what she was looking for. Making everyone a suspect.

Her phone rang, and she picked it up. It was Peters.

"The vehicle's stolen," he stated. "It went missing yesterday."

She smiled. *Perfect.* "Send a couple beat cops here." She read off the address of the mall. "The Cadillac's parked here. No idea who the driver is."

"You get out of the line of sight," Peters said. "There's a good chance he'll come back out, if he's shopping."

She laughed. "That's why I'm walking toward a corner store to see if I can buy a coffee to-go."

"You and that goddamn coffee. That shit will eat your insides. You know that, right?"

"It might," she admitted, with a smile. "For you, the alcohol and the lovers will ruin your health."

"Lovers?" Peters asked cautiously. "You know I'm married, right?"

"And I know you're not faithful." Like he was fooling anyone.

An odd silence came. In a strangled voice, Peters asked, "Have you mentioned anything to anyone about that?"

"No." She snorted. "Why would I? It's your suicide mission, not mine."

Peters gave a big sigh of relief. "Thanks. I'd really appreciate it if you don't mention anything."

"I have bigger and better things to take care of in my world than your screwed-up love life." She shook her head. "But you're a fool if you think the *other* people involved don't know." And she hung up on his shocked gasp.

She walked into the mini-mart, her gaze assessing the interior. One clerk was behind the counter, a second pouring some juice into their slushy machines on the far side. Two customers, men, were in the back, looking at sandwiches in one of the fridges, with a single guy—older—at the front counter, paying for his stuff. She didn't recognize anyone, but then nobody had a visual on the Ghost yet. He could be anybody, literally, in the world.

And that was just infuriating.

She did a quick walk through the store to see if she'd missed anything. She had no idea what Jericho was up to. Presumably his hunting thing, whatever the hell that was. She could only handle so much info as to what he did.

Supernatural woo-woo stuff was not her topic of choice. Brought back too many painful memories.

Yet she couldn't help herself from using her newfound skills, looking to see if she found any signs the killer might've been here. Now that she'd seen the getaway vehicle up close, she saw the shimmer of energy left behind from the Ghost. Jericho had mentioned an odd gray-black color. She saw dark, almost black, tendrils. *Seeing* it was new. Understanding how it worked was beyond her.

She walked back outside and found Jericho leaning against her truck, waiting for her. She hurried over. "Anything?"

He shook his head. "No. He's long gone."

"Damn it." She turned to study the Cadillac. "So what's the deal with this?"

"I think you've been through too much of a shock today to handle much more."

She shot him a shuttered look. She wanted to ask, *What shock?*—but was too afraid. From the knowing look in his gaze, she figured he knew exactly what she'd been through today. She turned back to the Cadillac and froze, as she made the connection between the black energy … and the trunk of the car. "Goddammit." Her voice was soft enough to be almost a prayer and yet loud enough that he heard her.

"Yes," he agreed softly, his voice pained. "The question now isn't what is in that trunk but who."

The black-and-white police car turned into the lot beside them and parked. The two cops confirmed the number on the plate and that the vehicle had been stolen earlier today, somewhere around dinnertime.

She motioned at the trunk. "We need to pop this."

One of the policemen returned to the cruiser and brought out a pry bar. In seconds he had it jammed underneath the trunk of the Cadillac and, with a hard push on the bar, came a resounding *pop*, releasing the latch, but the hood remained down.

She took a step back. The cops looked at her and asked,

"What are you expecting?"

She had one of the uniforms open the trunk wider, so they could take a look. Wrapped in plastic, presumably to keep the vehicle protected from the blood and the bodily fluids, was the body of what appeared to be a middle-aged woman. Not the victim Tavika had expected.

For some reason, in the back of her mind, Tavika had figured it would be the janitor she'd seen in her office vision.

With the driver's side door now open, one cop went to the front of the vehicle and checked the registration papers. "The vehicle is registered to a Valerie Vermont."

They had no picture ID yet or anything else to confirm the body might be Valerie, but it was a pretty damn good guess that's who she was.

Tavika walked over to Jericho and told him, "It's a good chance she's the owner of the vehicle."

Jericho's eyebrows rose in surprise. "I guess that makes sense. He needed a set of wheels and likely had to get rid of the owner."

"If that's the case, where did he go?" Her gaze never stopped scanning the mall. But since they'd first arrived, Tavika had seen no sign of anyone who looked like a viable suspect.

She'd always figured her kidnapper had been younger, just from the voice she'd heard that one day. He could have been much older, … but, if he had been younger twenty years ago, then now the suspect could be in his late thirties to forties at a bare minimum. Chances were, he was closer to fifty, if not sixty. She couldn't rely on her childhood memory to properly age an adult. Every adult seemed old to a kid.

THE GHOST HAD changed patterns. Again. When the Ghost killed, Jericho had always found him methodical, his actions smooth. This did not appear to be the same at all. This was almost an impulsive decision.

There could be a lot of reasons for that. Maybe he just needed the vehicle. Maybe the woman had pissed him off. Maybe she was his intended victim in the first place, and he just decided to take her car. There was no way to know. At least not yet. It would make sense eventually. A new victim gave them another whole set of variables to work with, and that was a good thing. Every little bit they could find was something they could use. Maybe next time they could save a life instead of analyzing a death.

Jericho watched from a distance, while the two policemen and Tavika went over the Cadillac. An ambulance was on its way. Of course he knew Tavika would bring in the same coroner.

He hadn't seen any energy trail from the Ghost since they had arrived. That bothered Jericho. Where could the man have gone? With a weird sensation in the back of his head, he turned and noted another small mall and a coffee shop were on the opposite side of the road, partially hidden by trees. Had they been looking in the wrong place from the beginning? He considered telling Tavika his plans, then realized she would be busy for a while. He'd be back before she was done.

Crossing the road, he saw a thin thread of silver ahead of him. Someone had crossed here and recently. *Had* the Ghost crossed over? Jericho had no way of deciphering who's energy it was, except that, when he was on the hunt, the only energy he generally saw was the killer's.

Stefan had said it was a quirk of his talent. Jericho wanted to be able to track anyone, anytime, anyhow, but apparently that wasn't to be. Once he was on the opposite side of the street, he let his senses open wider, so he saw the energy's pathway. He tracked it into a coffee shop, only to come back out, then to take a left, before disappearing around the corner of the building. The early evening sky helped the thread to shine.

Casually, in case he was being watched, Jericho followed the silvery trail.

BLOODY HELL. THAT was faster than he would have liked too. If he hadn't sprinted across the road, they'd have seen him. Now standing among the trees, coffee in hand, he watched as Tavika's friend crossed the road, coming right toward him.

Who was this man? What role did he play in these events?

Things were getting hot quickly.

Time to make a few changes.

The unknown pissed him off.

CHAPTER 17

WHEN TAVIKA HAD finally finished at the scene, she headed back to her truck to find it empty. She checked her pockets for the keys but didn't have them. To make sure, she opened the door and searched to see if they were anywhere inside. No, of course they weren't.

The ambulance had left; the coroner was long gone. The cops were almost done, and the tow truck was on its way. She couldn't do much more here. There was a hell of a lot more she could do at the office. *If* she could get there. Where the hell was Jericho anyway?

She pulled out her phone to check for messages from him. Nothing. Damn.

She turned and walked into the corner store, intent on grabbing a coffee. None of the food looked appetizing, though she hadn't eaten in so long that she'd forgotten when. But the coffee would hold her until she got home. She hoped. As she was paying, she asked if the clerk had seen anybody around the abandoned car. The older woman shook her head.

"No, I didn't. A lot of people were in here earlier, especially this morning, but not recently. You guys are bad for business."

Tavika nodded. "Sorry about that. It would've been well before all this happened anyway. Maybe an older man, late forties, early fifties, possibly sixties, well-dressed?"

The clerk frowned. "A couple guys in jeans were in here earlier. But I did see someone jaywalk across the street," she noted. "He might've been in that age category."

"When?" Tavika asked, her voice sharp.

The woman hesitated. Then she shrugged. "I'm not really sure. Seems like it was before you arrived."

Tavika had a few more questions, but the clerk didn't have more to offer. Tavika nodded. "Thanks." She turned and walked out the door, hot coffee in her hand. And, lo and behold, right in front of her was Jericho.

"Where the hell have you been?" She held out her hand for her keys. "I'll drive home. Feel free to take a walk in any other direction."

He laughed. "Long day and no food by any chance? I was tracking the Ghost's energy across the street, but he was long gone by the time I got there. I asked around, but no one seemed to remember him." Jericho shrugged, as he got into the passenger side. "You seem to be cranky whenever you don't eat."

"I'm cranky because I wanted to go home fifteen minutes ago, and not only weren't you here but you took off with my keys." She turned on the engine and headed toward home.

"If you're hungry, we could pick up something on the way, or we could order something when we get home." Jericho pointed out a grocery store up ahead. "If you pull in there, I'll buy groceries and cook dinner."

That was an offer too hard to refuse. She gave it all of two seconds' worth of thought, then changed lanes and pulled into the grocery store. Thankfully it was still open.

Besides, she wanted answers. At least that was the reason

she was willing to look at to keep him around.

With a sigh, she parked outside the entrance. Within seconds they both strode through the aisles. If it had been just her, she would have grabbed sandwich stuff. Who had time for anything else? But he appeared to be on a mission. He pushed the shopping cart ahead, quickly picking up fresh vegetables and even fruit. She studied the bagged apples in the section in front of her, wondering when she'd last had one. Such a simple thing. Now that she'd seen it, she really wanted one.

She glanced around the store, as if she'd never seen one before. In truth, it had been a long time. Meals had always been haphazard for her. She needed food to live, to keep her energy up, but it never mattered exactly what she ate. More often than not, it all tasted like cardboard anyway. She was either too exhausted or too busy to know what she ate.

Jericho arrived at the meat counter. She watched in amazement as he picked up steaks, ground meat, and ribs.

They were halfway to cash out, when it registered. She blamed her slow response on being so tired. She grabbed him by the shoulder and gave him a hard jerk. In a low voice she hissed, "And just how long are you planning on staying with me?" It was late. And she'd had a long day. She wasn't up for a fight, but she couldn't let him walk all over her either.

From the look on his face, he loved it. He smiled, smoothed a finger across her cheek, and said, "A couple days. Maybe longer, depending on the Ghost."

She came to a dead stop in the middle of the aisle. He leaned over and kissed her directly on the lips and then, with a whistle, walked toward the empty cashier stall.

Tavika stared at him in disbelief. How dare he? Not only had he walked into her life and all over her ... but he'd kissed her too.

"That wasn't a kiss," he called back. "That was nothing like a real kiss."

She raced to catch up with him. "It certainly was. And you can't do that anymore," she snapped. "I don't have time for that shit."

He slanted an amused gaze at her. "You don't have time for sex?"

She flushed and frowned at him. "A kiss and sex are two very different things."

"Oh, absolutely." That grin flashed again. "Glad you know the difference."

While she was still trying to figure out what he meant, he quickly emptied the cart of groceries onto the counter, as a cashier rang it up. Pushing the cart through to the far side, he then bagged the items and paid for the order.

Back at the truck, he took the keys from her and nudged her toward the passenger side, then placed the bags of groceries at her feet. He walked around and started up the truck. Tired, struggling to find the energy to fight, hating that he could so easily manipulate her into doing what he wanted, she found herself trying to come up with ways to get rid of him.

But he cut her plans short.

"Don't bother. I'm here to stay for a few days, and that's it. I know it'll disrupt your nice orderly life, but you'll deal with it."

That just made her sound like a bitch. He was helping, even though she wasn't sure she should be accepting that help. She couldn't do anything to compromise the evidence, and his methods could do that. She needed to put away the Ghost forever. She understood Jericho's perspective—that the Ghost would die at Jericho's hands or somebody else's. But, just in case that vision didn't turn out to be true, she had to make sure the Ghost didn't walk on a technicality.

Inside her apartment, he nudged her toward the bathroom. "Grab a shower. I'll get dinner started."

She shook her head. "Don't bother. It's too late. I'll have a shower and crash."

"No." His voice was adamant. "It will be ready when you come out."

She shot him a look of disbelief. "Like hell it will."

"Is that a challenge?" He gave her a snide smirk. "Accepted."

Muttering to herself, she walked into the bedroom—or what would've been the bedroom if there had actually been four walls and a door—grabbed some clean clothes, and headed into her shower. There she carefully undressed and hung up her holster. Today had been yet another day filled with shocks. Her body hurt in ways she hadn't expected.

And she had no idea why. She hadn't argued with anybody. Hadn't been beaten up, nor had she beaten anyone up. So what the hell was going on?

She turned on the hot water and stepped underneath. As it poured down over her head, she remembered the paralysis she'd experienced, along with the panic and fear. That train wreck of emotions would explain why she was such a mess inside but not the physical aches and pains. Maybe they just came along with it all. If so, that was hardly fair, considering her emotions were already bruised.

She'd done a lot today. Meeting Jericho in her own spirit form at the restaurant. She'd spoken telepathically with Stefan. And she'd learned how her own energy abilities could cause trouble, like paralysis. Then the tunnel vision through the Ghost's eyes. All in all, that alone was enough to deal with, but the loss of Gordon had hit her harder than she liked. She'd known him for years, and his plight was one she had seen often enough. His demise was also so very similar. There had to be another way for these people to live. A safer way. She just didn't have any answers.

She didn't want to stay in the shower too long because that would give Jericho a time advantage. But, at the same time, she was hungry. She could shove down her hunger, collapse on the bed, and sleep like she did every other night, but the thought of fresh home-cooked food waiting for her was enough to give him an extra few minutes.

She shampooed her hair a second time and then just leaned under the water, letting it pour down her aching body. When she was finally done, she turned off the shower and grabbed a towel. Drying quickly she put on a loose pair of slacks, bra, and T-shirt. She hated bras and could often get away without one since she was small breasted, but the material of her shirt clung to the gentle mounds in a way she didn't want to be suggestive.

Gathering her dirty clothes, she dumped them into the hamper, before walking into the kitchen. She put on her boots and snagged Solomon and cuddled him, as the aroma hit her. She moaned in delight. "What are you cooking?"

"Come and see."

As she walked into her small kitchen, she marveled at how much he'd accomplished in no time. The kitchen was actually clean, the table cleared. Sure the garbage was stacked high and would need to go out, but the area was actually functional. She said as much.

"Yeah, I had to clean it in order to cook," he noted drily. "Maybe you could give me a hand to get this garbage out."

"I can do that." Placing Solomon at his food dish, she straightened to snag the bag out of the can, and then, with the stack of pizza boxes, she headed to the garbage disposal chute in the hallway. When she walked back inside, her gaze swept over the small space of her apartment, and she realized how downright ugly it was. But she was never here. She was either at work or on a case in the streets. This was just a place where she rested for the night. Other than that, she didn't give a damn.

"Sit down. It's ready."

She sat down, not sure what to expect, but, when a thick juicy steak landed on her plate, followed by steamed vegetables and a big salad, she was astonished. "How did you get a meal like this ready so fast?"

"It's called *cooking*," he quipped. "It's not hard. You just have to make a little bit of effort."

She didn't say anything, but she was pretty damn sure no effort she could make would put all this on the table in the fifteen minutes it had taken him. She picked up a knife and cut the steak. The knife slipped through the meat, like it was butter. As she put the first bite in her mouth, she raised her gaze to his. The meat was so tender and flavorful. "It's wonderful," she mumbled around her mouthful.

He nodded. Forking up a piece of steak, he took a bite almost experimentally. As if analyzing how good a job he'd done.

She didn't know what he would consider this as, but, for her, it was perfect. She worked her way through the food on her plate in no time. When she put down her knife and fork, she was amazed to see all her food gone. "That was delicious," she said sincerely. "Thank you."

He waved a hand at her, his plate still half full. "Glad

you enjoyed it. Did you have enough?"

She nodded. "I'm stuffed."

"We can pick up wine for our next dinner."

Too happy with her full tummy and having enjoyed the meal so much, she couldn't wait for the next one. Yet she didn't make any comment about his assumption he would be here with her. Besides, she hadn't managed to kick him out of her place yet. She just wasn't sure how she felt about having a roommate. Although she loved having Solomon around. Somehow he filled the void of living alone.

She stood and carried her plate to the sink, already full of hot soapy water. She quickly washed up her plate and utensils, while Jericho finished eating. Then she washed the dishes left from the food preparation. She was fading quickly.

"Go," he urged. "You need sleep. I just wanted to make sure you had a full stomach before you dropped."

"It's definitely happy now. Thanks again." She walked the few feet to her bedroom and lay down on top of the bed. A few minutes later he called out, "Don't you get changed for bed anymore, or do you live with so much stress that you're ready to hop up at a moment's notice and go?"

She sat up and stared at him. "In a way, yes." She lay down flat again. No way had she wanted to discuss that issue. This time when she closed her eyes, sleep was reaching for her. She quickly and easily reached back and sank under.

JERICHO HAD NEVER seen anybody go to bed quite the same way. Fully dressed, as if expecting to get up in another two hours. If he was doing a security detail and hoping to sneak in a few hours of rest, that was fine. But this was her home, her bed. This was *not* normal. She had to have hit an emotional wall to do this. He prowled around the kitchen, cleaning off the counters and feeling more domesticated than he liked.

Inasmuch as he was tired, he wasn't quite ready to go to sleep. He envied her ability to just drop and nod off. He'd never been like that. Not since his friend's son had gone missing. That nightmare stopped at the conclusion of that case. That nightmare didn't reach for him in the middle of the night anymore. However, until he caught the asshole murderer, Jericho had been given no quarter. Jericho had been innocent of life before then. Trusting. Naive.

He lost it all that day.

That the killer had turned on Jericho next had helped him to deal with this horror. The fine line between right and wrong was never an issue in that case. Self-defense all the way.

But that day had changed the course of Jericho's future. And it had set him on this path to make the world a better place. Psychic-style. Abilities he'd thought of as jokes until then. He'd been busy building his real estate career, until his best friend's son had been kidnapped. Afterward, Jericho had walked away from that career without a thought.

He sat down on the couch and pulled out his phone. He needed to do more research, and this was a good time. He wanted his laptop, but he'd left it in his truck. He could slip outside and grab it, but he was afraid she'd wake up and lock him out. Leaving herself alone, unprotected. Why did he think she welcomed that? So far she was a mystery. An enigma.

She certainly stood for people in her world. Bending over backward to help them out. He was surprised by the little bits and pieces of her that he'd learned so far. They were good pieces. Also a lot of energy talent was in her. And he knew some of it was not new. A lot of old energy surrounded her. He didn't know what happened in that house decades ago, and he didn't want to, but her family's massacre had definitely made some impact on her abilities.

As he glanced over at the kitchen, he saw her bag sitting there. The folder within. Damn it. He really needed to look at that.

Would she be pissed? And, if so, was it worth it? Hell yes, it was. His whole goal here was to take down the Ghost. If that meant crossing the line and looking at her notes, then that was what he had to do. Besides, they'd already verbally gone over all the notes. There shouldn't be anything in there that was new, but he couldn't leave it alone, just in case there was. He needed every little bit of information. There was no way to know which tidbit was the nugget that would blow apart the case.

He quietly reached for her bag and pulled out the folder. It wasn't very thick. Maybe twenty-odd pages in it. He sat down with his notebook and carefully took notes, as he read from the first page right through to the last. When he got to the end, he went back to the first page and reread a few of the highlights. It was mostly her notes and bits and pieces from the case files. Nothing new but a good refresher. After packing the folder back in her bag, he took it to the front door. Then at least it would look different than the way it was when she'd last seen it. It was his way of getting permission after the fact.

With his notebook in hand, he returned to the couch and stretched out, his mind going over what he'd learned. The teenage girl had had a history of running away. That was why nobody had called in when she went missing. That was sad, but it wasn't news in itself. Every single day in America there were thousands of runaways. It just made things more complicated when they showed up dead. In this case she hadn't been sexually assaulted, as far as anybody saw, but they were waiting on the autopsy results.

Just as he dropped off to sleep, he realized he and Tavika were in bed, not very far from each other, and both of them were still fully dressed.

What a waste.

He smiled over that, when he heard a sound that sent a chill over his skin.

Tears. A female crying. But not Tavi. At least he didn't think it was her. He sat up and looked in the direction of Tavika's bed. From where he sat, she looked to be sleeping normally, Solomon once again on her back. But the sound came from the rear of the tiny apartment. He got to his feet and, in his socks, slowly walked toward the bathroom. The crying was definitely coming from the bedroom area.

He stopped and stared at the wall, shared by the apartment next door. Could it be coming from the neighbors?

Out of the corner of his eye, he caught movement. In blue.

Fascinated he watched what appeared to be the spirit of a young girl. Her energy was soft and wispy. And, yes, blue, but not a bright one, more like the blue of an early morning sky.

He couldn't place her age, as her features drifted in and out of focus. She was young though. Maybe eight or nine.

However, the tears, the tiny cries of anguish, yeah, they were too hard to walk away from. It could be Sarah's ghost. The runaway they'd found with her neck broken. But that girl was older, in her teens. Although spirits didn't show their age the same way.

He called out in a soft voice, "Hello, are you okay?"

It was a foolish question. If she had a problem, it wasn't likely to be one he could solve.

Was she even listening? She now curled up on the bed beside Tavika, her body shuddering, as she attempted to still the sobs. As if afraid someone would hear.

Well, he had heard. Now he wasn't sure what to do about it.

HE HUNCHED OVER his computer. Why hadn't she logged on to the main computer in the last while? He'd gone to great pains to track her system, but she was forever changing her damn log-in. It always took him a while to get back in. He didn't have time for this. It was as if the IT department had put an extra layer on her machine. Damn it. This was no good. It was like he'd gone blind in one area.

He couldn't have that.

It was bad enough she was lead on these cases, but somehow she also seemed to know he was looking at her digital files.

And that was seriously freaking him out.

And made his decision that much easier.

CHAPTER 18

TAVIKA WOKE REFRESHED on one level and exhausted on another. Her mother had spoken often about preserving different levels of existence. At the time Tavika hadn't understood. Part of her mother's lectures included always keeping one level as a backup in case she exhausted herself doing healing work. Her mother had been a great healer. And she had believed that it helped her other abilities develop a lot.

Bellamy, Tavika's sister, had been a precog, like Jericho. And Lord knew what else. Her sister had been beautiful, flawless looking. She'd had many guys hanging around her in high school, much to her mother's alarm. She had tried to keep Bellamy chaste and sweet, saying, the longer she remained pure, the stronger her powers would develop.

Her mother had been very strong. Without having children, would she have been even more so?

No way to know. Tavika could ask her mother, but she wouldn't tell her. The spirit left behind was only a single layer of the multiple personalities her mother had been. She hadn't been an easy woman to live with, but her heart had been good. Even if misplaced at times. At the end her anger and her fear had overwhelmed everything. When it was obvious her killer would give her no mercy, the goodness in her mother's heart had turned to screaming threats and curses at him.

Tavika had no idea if curses had any merit, but she understood her mother trying. Tavika hoped the Ghost had had a hellish life these last twenty years.

She swung her legs over the side of her bed. And stared, disgruntled, at the boots still on her feet. This was no way to live. She needed to get to bed at a decent hour, also actually strip the clothes off her body so her skin could breathe. Her feet ached already, and she had yet to stand. Holding her head in her hands, she lifted her gaze to the small space she called home.

It was clean. That was one thing. Not by her hand though. She looked toward the living room. Sure enough, Jericho was sprawled across her couch. Just his position alone made her wince. His spine had pretzeled into a shape to accommodate the couch. He would pay for that as soon as he woke up and tried to move. Then, as she stared down at her feet in her boots, she noted his were on the floor beside him. She forced herself upright, wincing as she took the weight on her soles, and headed for the kitchen.

With any luck she had ground coffee still. She should have picked some up at the grocery store yesterday. She made a pot, grateful to find a half-full pack. She searched to see if they had brought any groceries home for breakfast. The steak last night had been amazing, but it was long gone. Her system preferred to eat often, but, when she couldn't, she followed the trick her mother had shown her and just shoved down more energy into her poor stomach.

It would hold off hunger for hours, but she'd been doing that too much for too long, and she really needed food. In the freezer she found a loaf of bread. She pulled it out and popped two pieces into the toaster. She needed protein, but her cupboards were bare. Although she had lots of cat food. She'd never let Solomon suffer.

As she waited for the toaster to pop, she stared out the window. Instead of sunshine, gray clouds promised rain. Great. Feeling off and depressed, she turned to look around the small apartment, but, outside of Jericho's presence, nothing was amiss. She felt like something was going on, but she couldn't see anything. Another of her mother's tricks had been to look at something sideways and see the layers. Tavika tried that often but with no luck.

You're not trying hard enough, her mother's voice said, rolling through her head. *You can do it because you've done it once or twice before. You just have to figure out how to do it at will.*

Like many of her mother's techniques, they all had to be learned to be done at will. Why was nothing ever easy?

Being a rebellious misfit, Tavika had learned to do things her way. But it sure wasn't easy.

The coffeemaker behind her beeped, signaling it was done. After she ate her toast, she turned and poured herself a cup in her to-go mug, grabbed her jacket and keys, popped the lid on her mug, and strode to the door.

Jericho slept soundly. Relaxed. The dark curls of his hair made him look a decade younger. There was an innocence there in his sleep. Once he opened that laser gaze, however, there was nothing young about the man at all. In fact, her mother would've called him an ancient soul. Here on this Earth to learn a few more lessons before his last trip home.

Wouldn't Jericho love to hear that? Still, just looking at that relaxed lion of a man made her want to drag him into her bed for a few hours. She stuffed the need, the desire, way down deep. With everything else going on, it should have been easy to keep it there but now? Seeing him asleep like that, she was tempted to cross the room and stroke his soft cheek. Yet she knew, as soon as he opened his eyes, that face would firm up into hard lines again.

This gentleness was a gift.

She cast one long look at him and mindlessly grabbed her bag and opened her door to head out into the early morning of a new day. A fallen angel on her couch or not, she had work to do.

JERICHO WOULD HAVE loved to know what that look in her eyes had been about, as she had walked out the door. His eyes had been opened just enough to peek through his lashes. And there had been a softening of her face, something pointed in her glance, as she gazed at him. He had no idea why. It had been one of those brief glimmers into the inner dimensions of who Tavika was, that person she kept hidden from everyone else. He considered following her but realized it would be a repeat of yesterday. If that were the case, he could stay where he was and follow her in spirit.

Before she got into trouble again.

Then he remembered the little girl ghost. He bolted upright and walked to Tavika's bed. Solomon once again slept in the center of the bed. Tavika had smoothed out the wrinkles of the bedding. So it was ready for her to collapse on again tonight.

Except he had plans that didn't include her crashing in bed fully dressed.

He walked past the bed, searching for remnants of the ghost, but nothing was left. Either she'd dissipated so that he couldn't see her or she'd left a long time ago.

The energy around Tavika's bedroom was cold. Distant. But warm energy surrounded the cat.

Odd. Jericho didn't want to make too much of it, but something was weird about Tavika's sleeping spot. She oozed sex appeal in a raw, unbridled way. She brandished her power—physical power, power of her position—as she went about her day. But not her feminine power. He could never imagine her pulling out high heels and a short little black dress to charm any man.

If she wanted something, she would reach out and grab it.

Now what would it take to have her reach out and grab him? Jericho snorted; he'd have to blow the lid off the damn storage containers where she kept all those unwanted emotions. He'd had a lot of relationships in his life but had yet to come up against a woman who matched him in so many ways but who refused to acknowledge what was between them.

That thought put a smile on his face, as he had a quick shower. When he came out and dressed, he checked his phone to see he'd missed a call. He hit Redial.

"Jericho?"

"What's up, Tavika?"

"Did you go through all of my files?"

He sucked in his breath, having forgotten that. He admitted, "I did. I didn't think you'd mind. Still I know it was wrong because I should've asked you first, and I would have, but you were sleeping already. That's why I put your bag by the door, so you'd notice that I had moved it."

An awkward silence filled the line. He could almost see the steam shooting from her ears.

"Why?" he asked. "How did you know I actually read it

all?"

"Because you wrote across one of the pages," she snapped, her anger making her tone vibrate.

"Whoa, no, no, no. I did *not* write on any of those pages," he countered, not sure what she was talking about but knowing he'd never do that. Had he left one of his sheets of notes in the folder accidentally? "I have my own notebook and took my own notes."

"Are you sure?"

He heard the rustle of papers in the background and the confusion in her voice. "Of course I'm sure. I'd never do something like that to your working file."

"But there's a name written on one of these pages. Not neat and tidy in the top corner but scrawled across the whole page."

"What is the name?" he asked curiously.

"Anna. It's written across the entire page."

"No last name?" Anna? Jericho frowned. No way he would have altered one of Tavika's pages. But if he hadn't—who had?

Her voice faded, as she held the phone away to flip through the pages. "No, I don't see anything else. That's the only name and just on the one page."

"What page was it written on?"

"On the page I wrote up on Gordon."

"Did Gordon have a daughter named Anna?"

A sharp odd silence passed, as she digested his question. He should already know the answer. And he did, but he couldn't help asking.

"I'm not even sure I want to know where this is going, but I can tell you right now that Gordon had no children," she replied in low tones. "I have to go." And she ended the call.

Anna. He spun around to look at the bed. It looked the same, with the exception of Solomon having stretched out on his back. Could Anna have been the ghost Jericho had seen last night?

To the empty room he called out, "Anna, is that you?"

No answer. He frowned, and then another thought struck. Jesus. He grabbed his phone again and called Hunter. As soon as his buddy answered, Jericho asked, "Is her name Anna?"

Hunter snapped to attention. "Yes. Have you seen her?"

Whoa. Jericho took a deep breath. "Maybe."

"Maybe?" Hunter asked incredulously. "There is no maybe about this. She's been missing for seventeen days."

"I know. You've told me all this." Jericho didn't know what to say. "All I can tell you is that I saw a child last night, maybe ten years old or younger, but she was in spirit form." He took a deep breath. "Then this morning Tavika was looking through a file she'd brought home last night, and the name *Anna* was written across one of the sheets. Tavika didn't write it. I didn't write it. And nobody else here could have done it."

"Spirit form?"

"Yeah. Spirit form."

"So she's dead?" Hunter's voice fell in defeat.

"I have no idea. It's possible though but not necessarily true," Jericho rushed to reassure him.

"I guess that's a question to ask Stefan." Hunter rang off, leaving Jericho wondering if somehow Anna had been attracted to Tavika's energy.

He couldn't confirm Anna was a ghost, yet she had definitely appeared in spirit form. Still, Jericho could walk in the same form, so he knew that seeing her like that didn't have to mean the little girl was dead. But it did mean that Tavika, with her beacon of energy, was attracting more toward her than she knew.

And, if Anna had found Tavika here at her home, who else was Tavika attracting?

HE HAD TO go out of town for work. Shitty timing. And he wasn't in a mood to make the trip fun, like he had on different occasions.

He stood in front of the window, staring out at the world. Maybe not. Maybe a few days to cool off would help.

His phone rang. His heart rose in joy when he saw the number.

"Hi, sweetheart. I know. I don't want to go. Just for two days, I promise. I'll be back soon." After reassuring the love of his life that he would only be gone for as long as necessary, he rang off.

Damn, this love shit was hard.

But the thought of losing it was harder.

He had to make sure he was safe. He wanted this new life. He could almost taste the normalcy of it. It's something he'd craved all his life. And no way would he let Tavika ruin it for him.

CHAPTER 19

ANNA? SHE DIDN'T have any cases involving victims named Anna. She set up a search, but, with only a first name, it would be hard. As a secondary search, she set up one for Anne. Wouldn't it be nice if somebody would obligingly give her a last name? It would make life simpler. Still, this name was more a curiosity.

But anything in the spirit world of a psychic or a precog tended to be obscure. That just made it harder to deal with. Jericho could have written the name aimlessly, while he was studying something else. She'd been known to do a few things like that, but she would look at it later and remember what it was about. She shifted the papers in her file once again, studying Gordon's information.

Nothing new was here. As she'd suspected, he'd been killed with a single slice to the neck, same direction and pattern as old man Breaker. So likely the same killer. She was still waiting for the tox screens on all the victims. Outside of the fact that both men were single, lonely, and vulnerable to predators, she had found very little connection between them.

And cases involving a serial killer taking out strangers were the worst to solve. Essentially they were random targets murdered by the same killer but for no discernible reason that connected them. It was as if one day a man chose to kill a young girl sitting on a park bench. The next day he'd take out a young man in a bowling alley, and then the next day he would pick off a senior walking down the street.

Random occurrences brought about by random choices. Those types of killings gave the police nothing to go on. She slammed her file closed and tucked it back into her bag. She logged on to her computer, happy to see she managed to get in without any trouble. She had a huge amount of recent email messages, but what else was new?

She scanned through them but saw nothing urgent; she immediately closed the program. That was the last thing she needed right now. She checked on the searches she'd set up. The search for the name *Anna* popped up with three cases over the last ten years. One was a four-year-old, who she discounted as too young. Another was seventeen, which she discounted as too old. That left her with one possibility. She opened up the file and read the child had gone missing three weeks ago, but Tavika frowned, not remembering the case. There'd been no Amber Alert.

She read the details. The child had gone missing from her house, only the family hadn't known about it because she'd supposedly been picked up by a relative to get her out of the way while the family was in the middle of a move. Missed communications had the child missing for two days before anyone realized. Detectives were on that case, but, so far, they had no one who looked good for this.

The odds were too high that a family friend or relative had taken the little girl for some sexual fun and then dumped her body. She'd be found in a ditch somewhere.

Shaking her head, Tavika reached up and massaged her temples. Too many years on the job made it hard to keep looking at things without a bias. Of course no one in this business remained fully neutral. It was hard to look at these cases and to not see the damage, the pain. But it was what she did, and she was good at it.

The second search for *Anne* came up with more options. As Tavika scanned through them, none looked as good. No, Anna was likely Anna Hathaway. She would send Jericho a message and ask if he knew anything about her.

Only she didn't get that chance.

Stefan's voice boomed through her mind, making her shudder.

Instantly he toned down the volume. *Sorry,* he whispered. *I thought I'd have to pound to get through, so used to using a little more force than necessary when communicating with you. Instead,* he added, with a note of humor, *you opened the door. Good for you.*

Mentally she responded with, *And I might just shut it if you keep coming in unannounced like that.*

Am I limited to ringing the doorbell?

She threw down her pencil and sat back, glaring at the office in front of her. A couple other people were in residence, thankfully nobody looking at her. Good thing. She probably looked like an idiot. In her head she asked, *What's up?*

Anna?

She straightened. *Anna Hathaway?*

What do you know about her?

Maybe nothing. She related what she'd found on her search, starting with her name scribbled on her file. She didn't know if Stefan saw things or not when connected like this, but she pulled out the sheet and held it up in front of her, as if studying it. It felt so stupid. He was in her head; that didn't mean he was in her eyes.

Something shifted inside. Like a realignment. She blinked at the sensation. What was going on?

Stefan explained, *Actually I can see through your eyes, but only exactly what you see. And my eyesight isn't as good.*

Bemused, she pulled the sheet closer, holding it at eye level. *This is the page I found when I got to work this morning. Jericho says he did not write this, and I certainly didn't.*

Did you meet Anna Hathaway's ghost?

She gave a half snort. *No, the only ghosts I see are my family.*

Interesting.

What does that mean? she asked crossly. *I hate always feeling like somebody knows more than I do.*

In this case nobody knows more than you do. We're trying to understand how you figure into this.

Tell me about Anna Hathaway, she stated.

One of my men, Hunter, has been tracking her down for over two weeks. We suspected she was taken by an uncle. One with a little too much interest in the girl.

Hearing him echo what she'd already considered made her stomach sour. *Who's Hunter? And what has he learned so far?*

We're still hoping she's alive. However, if you've seen her in spirit form, that changes things potentially.

Have you spoken with Jericho? she asked.

I have. He's actually the one who saw her spirit—in your apartment.

Damn. Inside her stomach sank. *So she's dead?* she asked softly.

No, we don't know that. If I'd seen her, I might be able to tell. According to Jericho, something was very lifelike in her spirit. Only her time is dwindling.

Curious, Tavika asked, *If her spirit form has already separated, does that mean she's dying? Or does she has the same ability that Jericho and you have?*

She also may not know she's doing it. If the world little children find themselves in is too devastating, they can just go away inside. Sometimes they do it in spirit form. It's up to us to find her, before her spirit separates from her body. At that point it's death. If we find her before that, then maybe we can save her.

Tavika loved the idea of saving her. But she hadn't seen Anna. So there wasn't anything she could do.

Jericho told me that she laid down on the bed beside you.

That almost broke her heart. She hadn't known. If she had, she might've been able to offer some comfort. *But why me? Why would she come to me?*

Actually I was going to ask you that question, Stefan stated. *I think it has to do with your beacon.*

She gasped. How did he know about the beacon? And why would it bring the little girl to her?

At least you aren't disputing the fact that you have a beacon, he noted quietly. *Thank you for that much honesty.*

If that were the reason, then I should be inundated with spirit forms coming toward me, she replied. *And that hasn't happened.*

If you aren't actually seeing these entities, how do you know? Jericho saw Anna. Maybe your space is completely full of spirits, and you don't know it.

Is that even possible? She shook her head. This was beyond odd. *Or maybe I should say, what difference does it make?*

Maybe these people are trying to communicate with you, Stefan said. *It's not uncommon to have that happen.*

And they chose the wrong person to try to talk to, she

snapped, irritated at the sense of guilt she felt for not having sensed or seen anyone. *As I can't see them, I can't help.* She gave a half snort and an inelegant shrug of her shoulders. *It wouldn't matter if I saw them because, the bottom line is, I can't do anything for them.*

And what if you could? Stefan asked. *What if there was something you could do to help them? Would you?*

I don't know. She pinched the bridge of her nose. This was all too stupid. *We're talking about stuff that isn't real to most people. Even if it's real to a few, it's not to me. Because I can't see them.*

Her second phone rang. She refused to answer it. Last thing she wanted was to talk to her brother right now. She was inundated just having Stefan in her mind as it was. Having Travis read her mind right now would just be too much.

With that thought, Stefan disappeared, and her phone stopped ringing. The tension around the back of her neck and the pressure inside her head eased. Oh, happy day. Under her breath she whispered, "Thank God for that."

She stared down at her files but struggled to get her focus back. Just the idea that spirits were attracted to her and that she had no idea was bothersome. She'd always felt so alone. But, if she felt alone, and they were all hanging around her, how did *they* all feel when she didn't respond? Did they see each other? Could they communicate with one another? What were they talking about? And how often was one trying to talk to her? But why was it that Jericho saw Anna, and yet Tavika couldn't?

And did it matter?

JERICHO LEANED AGAINST the wall inside Tavika's apartment, his head bowed. He wafted out a gentle wave of energy. Energy that floated lightly on the air. He didn't want to scare Anna, but, if he could find a way to communicate, then maybe he could talk to her.

If he could talk, he could find out something about where she was.

And where she was being kept.

"If you can hear me, I mean you no harm. I'm here to help."

Silence.

"Anna, are you there?" He continued to send out a gentle healing energy throughout the space. He didn't know if the little girl had followed Tavika or had been attracted to come here to this apartment. Both were long shots. With ghosts, one just never knew. He sat down to wait, letting that energy shimmer lightly. "Anna?"

No answer.

He raised his head and turned to look around. He couldn't see anything to the side or in front. He closed his eyes, so his mind could pick up her energy on an intuitive level. Then, with a technique that Stefan had taught him, he opened his eyes, looking for an energetic position through the layers, and found the room completely overwhelmed with other energies. So many pressed in on him. He closed his eyes, trying to regulate his breathing. He had to appear controlled, otherwise the other energies would react negatively to his. He needed everybody calm. And what the hell? Was Tavika running a halfway house for spirits here?

And did she even know?

He could answer the last question on his own. No. She had no idea what was going on.

He'd seen no sign of her energy acknowledging the other entities. And yet they appeared to be on the same dimension. He'd seen her attract them, had seen her send out feelers, as if letting everybody know she was there. But she didn't seem to know what she was doing when she got them. But it all required energy—energy she didn't have.

As if there was a disconnect.

That wasn't unusual but was something she needed to change. Just as he was ready to give up, he thought he heard a tiny sniffle. Trying not to move, his gaze slid from one side of the apartment to the other, coming back to the bed. There the little girl was curled up in a ball, her head on the pillow. Her form curled up around Solomon. Was that by accident? Or was she gaining what comfort she could from the feline? As Jericho listened, the sniffle came again. In a low voice he reached out mentally and verbally. "Anna?"

The spirit bolted upright. She looked around fearfully. At one point she shoved her fist into her mouth, as if to stifle cries. His heart went out to her. She was obviously panicked, and that was not what he wanted.

"I'm sorry. I didn't mean to scare you. My name is Jericho. I'd like to help you."

Where are you? And how can you help? she asked. *Nobody came for me. I waited and waited, and nobody came.*

"Take it easy, little one. I'm trying to help you now. Lots of people are looking for you."

She raised her gaze hopefully.

He saw Tavika's bedding through her.

He was struggling to determine if this was a spirit form or a ghost. He didn't want to ask her. Reminders of traumatizing events often made the ghost run away. He couldn't see her silver cord from where he sat, but that didn't mean there wasn't one. And, in some cases, the silver cord itself was awfully hard to find.

It's too late, she said sadly.

"What's too late, honey?" he asked, his heart stalling at her pitiful response.

Nobody will find me.

"Why? Where are you?"

She gave an unhappy sigh. *I don't know. It's dark. I don't like it here. I'm scared.*

Pushing the issue and knowing he was in danger of having her disappear on him, he asked, "What kind of a place is it? Is it like a box or like an empty house with no lights?"

She raised her gaze and looked over at him. Her eyes were fathomless, deep and dark. She whispered, *You'll never find my body.*

His hope sank. "Body?"

She nodded. *He says I'm dying. And that no one cares. He says I'm nobody. Nothing.*

"He's wrong," Jericho stated urgently. "He's very wrong. You *are* somebody. Someone who matters. We will find you. We just need a little bit of your help. Can you tell us anything about where you are being held?"

But she looked at him with such sad eyes that he knew she had no idea.

He tried another trick. "Do you remember where he took you? Did you see any houses nearby? Any flowers?"

Her energy brightened. *There was a blue house. A bright blue one, with daisies all along the front of it. But I don't know where it is,* she wailed.

"Did he hurt you?" Jericho knew he shouldn't be asking these questions, but it was so hard not to.

She nodded, tears shimmering in the vicinity of her eyes.

Sometimes he says I'm his little princess. His little china doll.

"Oh. And did he dress you up in a pretty little dress?"

She nodded. *A really ugly dress. And he put makeup on my face. It's not the same kind of makeup Mommy uses on her face.*

"Right. Did he take pictures?"

The energy shimmered—little bits and pieces flickering off in the room—as she nodded. *He took lots of pictures. But he wouldn't show them to me,* she cried out. *He said they weren't for me. They were for him.*

"Does he have any pets? Did you see a veranda? Did you see any part of his house at all? Where were you when he took these pictures?"

In my room, she replied. *Then he brought me food.*

"And what about after he brought food?"

Her energy rippled. *He took his pictures and then left.*

And this was where the problem was. Jericho lowered his voice and asked, "And has he been back since?"

She shook her head. *No. I was so hungry for a while, but now I'm not.*

"What about water? Do you have water?"

I'm not thirsty, she whispered.

"When did you start walking?"

She looked at him, puzzled.

He clarified, "Without your body?"

I don't remember. After his pictures, I think. Her form shrugged. *I don't want to remember.*

What she'd done was in response to trauma, and the last thing he wanted to do was probe into that. He was afraid he already knew.

I did like the music though.

His gaze sharpened. "What kind of music was it?"

Christmas songs, she said, with a smile. Instantly the

room filled with a gentle noise, as she hummed the chorus of "Jingle Bells."

"Stefan, you getting this?" Jericho asked, hoping not to scare away Anna.

I'm here, Stefan responded in a very tired voice.

"Any idea what she means?" Jericho asked.

No. Not a bit. It's the middle of summer, Stefan murmured.

Jericho laughed. "I think I just heard something about a Christmas in July sale?"

There was a long silence from Stefan. Then he admitted, *Actually I don't know. I try to avoid most of the stores, and I definitely don't like to listen to ads. But I will get Hunter on it.*

"It could mean she was somewhere around the mall."

Or around somebody who loved Christmas songs, Stefan corrected. *We can't afford to assume anything at this point.*

"Maybe not but at least we have something to go on." Although Jericho admitted it was damn little.

CHAPTER 20

TAVIKA STARED INTO the phone. "What did you say?"

The coroner repeated slowly, "The teenage girl had a medical procedure done for a bone marrow transplant."

"She had leukemia?"

"I'm waiting on the tests, but it's quite possible," Shelby confirmed.

Tavika shook her head. How sad a life could any one girl have? Then she considered something else. "Any chance she was the donor of the bone marrow?"

"Not usually done in one so young. It would have to be extreme circumstances. Even then I'm not sure. I have to make a couple calls. We have her name, and now we know something, so maybe there is a possibility to learn more," the coroner noted abruptly. "I have to go. Leave this with me, and I'll see what I can find out." She hung up.

Bone marrow transplant, interesting. So difficult for anyone. Tavika tended to agree with the coroner that the girl had received the bone marrow. The question was from whom? There was a database for bone marrow transplants. If the coroner didn't get to it by the end of the day, Tavika thought she might be able to find more information. That didn't mean it would lead them to her killer, but who knew?

"Tavika?"

She lifted her head to find the captain standing nearby,

his legs in a wide stance and his hands on his hips. Someone was in trouble. He motioned upstairs. She immediately got up, taking an extra moment to log off, snatched her notebook, and followed. The office fell silent as she walked out, all eyes tracking her progress. Outside, she saw Henry, speaking with his partner, Charles. She gave them a quick smile, as she followed the captain to his office.

Henry raised an eyebrow at her in question. She shrugged. She didn't know what was up but somehow felt a reprimand coming, that she was in bigger trouble than usual.

In his office, he motioned her to the chair, while he shut the door. She sat and opened her mouth to speak, but he held up his hand to stop her. A knock came on the door. A man she didn't recognize entered. He took a seat beside her.

"Tavika, this is Marshall Henderson of the FBI."

She sat back. Goddammit. Why hadn't she seen this coming?

Henderson studied her carefully. She never said a word, just gave him a flat stare.

"Tavika Bantrell is lead detective on this case."

Tavika shot her captain a look and asked, "Which case?"

Neither of the men answered her. She sat back stone-faced. Like hell she'd speak first. This wasn't how it worked. Not if she wanted to keep everything to herself.

Henderson replied, "We have reason to believe one of your cases is the work of a serial killer known as the Ghost."

She stared back, barely stifling her gasp and deliberately kept her own counsel. How the hell did they figure that out? It wasn't like she'd registered any of the evidence that would point to the Ghost. She had accessed several data banks looking for information. But how did they know? All she said out loud was, "Interesting."

The captain stated impatiently, "Tavika, you already knew this. So let's just lay our cards on the table."

She shot him a cool look and asked, "The first card I'd like on the table is why the FBI is involved?" She crossed her arms over her chest and added, "We're quite capable of handling this."

"But this is not just *your* case. The Ghost has been attributed to forty-seven different killings across the country."

Her jaw dropped. "Forty-seven?"

That meant, with the three recent killings here, which she thought were connected, they were fifty strong. Possibly fifty-one, counting the woman in the trunk of the Cadillac. If Tavika were to add in the janitor she'd seen dead in the office building, she had to wonder just how many this asshole had truly killed. Jesus Christ. Maybe it was that thought, which had her feeling a little less antagonistic.

She couldn't resist murmuring, "And you still haven't caught him?"

The FBI agent smiled at her. In a low voice he stated, "Just imagine how well we could do if we actually had cooperation."

She snickered. "My understanding is that you need to be called into a case in order to have any kind of involvement."

He shook his head. "The FBI are not so easily pigeon-holed into what we can and cannot do."

Under her breath, she muttered, "Damn."

"Your full cooperation in this instance would be much appreciated," Henderson said, with an easy but firm smile.

Before she had a chance to answer, the captain stepped in and nodded. "Tavika will help you." The captain turned those laser eyes on her. "Won't you, Tavika?"

Like she had any choice. "Of course. Not much to tell

you at this point. Breaker was found alone in his house by a neighbor. He'd been killed approximately twelve hours earlier. No signs of resistance. Television was still on, a cold cup of tea sat on the table. No defensive wounds. We're waiting on the tox screens."

"Tox screens? Any reason beyond standard procedure?"

Her gaze shot up to his. "It appeared there was an injection site. Possibly a pressure syringe."

His eyebrows rose slowly. "Interesting."

"So maybe not one of your cases?" She tried really hard to tamp down the joy at the thought but knew she had failed when he gave her a short laugh.

"Unfortunately the pressure syringe confirms it, as we've seen an increase in the number of instances when the Ghost used them to keep his victims from crying out."

"That is opposite to what he was like years ago."

"You've been following the Ghost?" Henderson asked.

Tavika shot her captain a look. Damn her unruly tongue.

He shrugged.

She dropped her gaze, then stared at him and back at Henderson. He should know damn well who she was and what she knew about the Ghost from personal experience. If he didn't? That was his fault.

"Sure," she admitted. "The Ghost is notorious."

He nodded. "Unfortunately that's quite true. I hear criminologists are even singing his praises in the classroom," he noted in disgust.

She laughed. "I don't think they are singing his praises as much as using him as a case study on success stories. I've actually attended a couple of the night courses. They were quite interesting."

Henderson's lip curled downward. "It's not a good idea to look up to these individuals. They thrive on the notoriety."

She wondered at the certainty with which Henderson spoke about the Ghost. Many serial killers were full of themselves, but she wasn't sure the Ghost was the same. Then again he didn't fit into any stereotypical box. When she'd met him, he'd been a much younger man and yet seasoned to killing already, with lots of blood on his hands. He'd changed over the years, morphed.

She wanted to know why. And how. This was the field she planned to study for the rest of her life. The more real-life studies she solved, the better off everyone was. Her chances of killing more of these assholes went up with every new thing she learned.

But, in order to do that, she had to get out of these goddamn meetings and get something done.

She stood, turned to face her captain. "I can email Henderson the little bit we have on the file. If there's nothing else, maybe I'll get back to work?"

The captain studied her face, and she knew he was considering her other cases. She gave a tiny imperceptible shake of her head. He dropped his gaze, pursed his lips, then said, "You're good to go."

With a cheery smile, she turned and walked away, without saying goodbye to the FBI agent.

Taking the stairs two at a time, she stopped outside the bullpen door and took a couple deep breaths, then walked in to head to her desk. If she'd hoped to catch anybody on her computer, that was a faint hope because nobody was in her corner. Of course if anyone knew IT had been setting up a new system, they would take greater precautions.

She headed to her computer, sat down, and logged in again. No problem.

It was stupid to feel upset when things were actually going correctly, but, if she had somebody trying to access her computer, she really wanted to catch him, before he went and did it to somebody else.

She finished up a couple reports, checked the time, and realized only an hour had gone by. The office was closing in on her. She shut down her system again and walked out of the bullpen and headed to the main area of the station, where two cops were dragging in Stoner. Again. Damn, she knew him from the old days and some not so old, as he'd ripped her shirt during their last meeting a few days ago. She wore more than a few bruises from that asshole. She stepped off to the side and waited for them to pass. At the last minute Stoner saw her and lunged. She'd been prepared—only one was never prepared for Stoner.

The 360-pound man should've been a linebacker instead of selling drugs on the street corner, when he was cognizant enough not to get ripped off. The rest of the time he lived up to his name and spent his time drugged out in a back alley somewhere.

But, when in motion, he was almost impossible to stop. And he headed right for her.

The two cops yelled, "Look out! Stop him."

Yeah, right. Only one way to stop Stoner. And it hurt. She readied for the blow to come.

He was growling by the time he reached her. His hands were out in front, fingers curled into claws and his face twisted in a snarl. She'd won the last round, and he was looking to get even. And here she wondered if she'd get out with just a few bruises this time.

On the other hand she really could use a target for her own temper. She waited until he was almost upon her, then slugged him once in the belly.

As he bent forward, she leaped on his back, sending him forward into the wall. He smacked his head and fell to his knees. She hopped off, stood back, and waited. For Stoner, that was damn-near nothing. A love tap. But he didn't move.

What the hell was wrong with this guy? Just when she thought they were good, the cops approached him.

Still on his knees, Stoner twisted, reached out, snagged her leg, and pulled her down. And the fight was on. With the cops trying to grab his arms and pull him off her, Stoner was having none of it. He lashed out, his fists catching her on the shoulder. Her boot caught him in the jaw. Several rounds later she turned, jumped, and executed a double flying sidekick into his nose, which sent him sprawling to the floor on his back. This time he wouldn't move for a while. She landed on her feet, then lost her balance and fell to the floor. Stars swam in her eyes.

Like what the hell?

Only when she heard the applause around her did she realize the size of their audience. Once again the guys in the station had something to talk about.

She sat up, looked down at the big man, still out cold, and shook her head. "Why the hell did you guys bring him in here? Just take him right to the bloody jail."

One of the cops, who had lost his grip on Stoner, gave her a cheeky grin and said, "What's the fun in that? Managed to record that fight on my cell phone. Dammit, Tavika. You are one bad-ass fighter."

The admiration in his voice made her feel odd. She jumped to her feet and brushed off her clothes. She grinned, wiped the blood off her cheek, and added, "At least I managed to keep my clothes intact this time." With a salute to the guys, she walked to the front door and out into the sunshine.

She heard them all talking behind her. Whatever. She was used to being talked about. At least this time it had been good. Out in the fresh air she stopped and assessed the world, looking for a sense of direction. Her mother had always told her to reach out to see what she was supposed to be doing at any given time. That there was a job that everyone should be doing. It was up to her to understand what that was from moment to moment, hour to hour.

Her mother had life all worked out. So what the hell had gone wrong?

Tavika had so many questions that she wanted to ask her mother. Her mother's spirit refused to answer any of them. That really pissed off Tavika. Her sister wouldn't talk either. And that was just part of the ordinary sibling crap she'd grown up with. As the youngest by eleven minutes, Tavika had been blamed for a lot. The older two had always thought they were Mom's pet, but, in truth, that honor went to her sister at the end. Her mom had doted on her because her abilities were so much like her own and with the promise of being much stronger. Travis was very capable, but football had been his passion. Speaking of her brother, she reached into her left-had pocket and pulled out her phone. It was time to talk to him again.

Chances were, he'd be pissed for days.

Holding the phone to her ear, she asked, "Travis, you there?

"I'm here."

Instead of being angry, like she expected, he sounded

sad. She winced.

"Why do you always end up in trouble?" he asked.

"I wasn't in any trouble," she replied, hating the defensive note in her voice. Travis always knew when shit happened in her world.

That heavy sigh filtered through the phone.

He did that to her all the time. She groaned. "Look. What was I supposed to do? He attacked me. I had to defend myself."

"And *why* did he attack you? Because you were asking for it."

She glared out into the cloudy sky. "I did not. I was walking on the side of the hallway. I tried to step out of the way, and he came at me." She shrugged. "So I put him down."

"Like a dog?" Travis snapped.

"Hell no. But this guy knows me. I was forced to knock him down the last time we met, so he was looking for payback." She shook her head. "Do we have to talk about that? Surely there was something else?"

"Yeah, how about the Ghost?"

She winced. "How about something other than him?" If there was one thing Travis was fixated on, it was the Ghost. She understood, as she was afflicted with the same issue, but whereas she was hunting him, Travis was just looping over and over on the same issues, unable to help, so he also couldn't move on.

Reading her mind, as he'd always done, he snapped, "Sure, I've got another topic. How about the guy you're hanging around with?"

"Jericho?" How did Travis find out about him? Dammit, her twin could always read her mind. She just often forgot what was in there.

"Isn't he hunting the Ghost?"

"Yes, he is." That should make Travis happy. Her brother was in a hell of a mood. It was starting to put her in one too. "Look. If you don't have anything else to say, then I have to go and do something called a real job."

"Hunting killers is not a job," he growled. "It's a death wish."

Well, as a conversation killer, that was a good one—because she already knew how she would die, just not the final details. As her mother had often told her, there was no way to avoid fate. Tavika didn't really think there was any point in worrying about it. But it wasn't a pleasant end and getting murdered was almost a guarantee, given her line of work. She just hoped that was a long time in the future. At the Ghost's hand? She hoped not. Still, if she took him with her, she'd die happy.

"Stop that," Travis cried out. "Don't you know how much I hate hearing you talk about that?"

"And we all know some things can't be changed. Look, Travis. I have to check up on a couple people. I'll talk to you later." She didn't give him a chance to argue; she ended the call and put away her phone. Her brother had a lot of good qualities, but he was very narrow-minded and focused.

Unfortunately sometimes she fed into it because she was the same. They were both obsessed with finding the Ghost. But her twin brother didn't want Tavika to find the Ghost. She saw into her brother's world enough to know it wasn't the healthiest obsession for him. Her twin brother looking into her world also saw how detrimental her absorption was.

When they discussed this Ghost topic, it sent them both into a tailspin.

Originally she'd planned to go straight home. Take some time to sort out her notes. Today had been a wash. She hated that. Instead she decided to take a quick walk through the area and check up on some of the less fortunate people in the world. Maybe someone knew something.

At the first park, she checked to see if Maggs or her friends were around. This was one of their alternate locations. But no shopping carts, cardboard boxes, or even people were huddled in corners.

Maybe that was a good sign? She picked up the pace and carried on past a couple alleyways but didn't see anybody. She walked down to where she'd seen Maggs last and stopped when she saw her stuff but no sign of Maggs. Not liking the way her thoughts were taking her, she turned to study her surroundings. She had yet to make a trip into the abyss and to sort out these dots that she saw everywhere.

This place was full of those dotted pathways, but she couldn't see the big picture standing here. She pulled up the collar of her jacket against the sudden wind and hurried back to her truck. As soon as she got home, that would be her priority. Until she opened up the front door and walked in.

And remembered Jericho lived here now. She no longer had the privacy to do anything. Definitely not to walk into the abyss.

And how the hell did that happen?

"Good timing." Jericho smiled at her, as she stepped through the door. "Dinner is almost ready."

She stared from the doorway, her plans crumbling into dust. And yet she couldn't afford to let it go. She'd meant to visit the abyss last night, but it hadn't happened. Time was of the essence. This was important. Somehow she had to take that trip. But how? She glanced around at what had been her private space and didn't know what to do.

"WHAT'S THE MATTER?" Jericho stood in front of her, gently lifting her chin with his thumb to stare into her eyes. "Tavika? What's happened?"

She tried to shrug off the questions. But he wouldn't let her. "Nothing. Nothing's wrong. It's just …" She shook her head. "I made plans, forgetting you were here."

Plans? What the hell did that mean? And what difference did her plans make if he were here? Unless … her plans included another man. Shit. His research revealed that she didn't have a partner and hadn't in the last year. It was one of the reasons why he'd chosen to move into her physical space—to help keep her safe. And, if he were honest, to be closer to the Ghost, knowing that Tavika was his final target.

He stepped to the side, so she could enter and carefully place her bag on the floor.

"Dinner smells good," she noted.

"Glad to hear that. What plans?"

She gave him a hooded glance and said, "Private plans."

"A man?"

From her startled look he could tell she hadn't considered that option. Something inside of him settled. Good. This had nothing to do with the competition, and, therefore, he could afford to be magnanimous. "Obviously not. If you need space and privacy, that's fine. I can head out for a few hours."

Something lit up in her dark brown eyes, before she dropped her gaze, shutting him out. It just made him all the more curious. And he was plenty curious already. "Let's get you some food first. Then I can take off for a while."

Much more agreeable now, she nodded and went to the table. "Is there anything I can do to help?"

He hated that her voice was much happier now that she knew he would leave soon. That wasn't exactly what he'd hoped for in her reaction.

"No, it's ready." He brought out a big pan of ribs from the oven. At the table he quickly cut them into smaller portions for the two of them. He loved the way her face lit up at the sight of real food. "Do you know how to cook?"

She shrugged. "A little. Never taken the time to learn."

Right, with her family situation, he doubted domestic skills were at the top of her priority list.

They dug into the hot food. He watched as she devoured her plateful with the same single-minded purpose he'd come to see with her work. He knew right now that it was more a case of her wanting him to leave rather than the food. How depressing was that? He wasn't at all sure how to make a move on this woman. Not that she might rebuff him but that he wasn't even sure she had noticed him. It was as if she had shut down her initial attraction. Her body *had* been aware, but, in a way he'd never seen before, she'd managed to shut off her sexual attraction.

That's the last thing he wanted her to do.

As much as he admired that ability—because sexual energy was a huge resource that could be utilized when needed—it was also frustrating as hell because he didn't know how to do it himself. Besides, he had liked the buzz of their sexual attraction. It felt great, and he didn't want to let that go. Damn, the woman was someone he'd like to spend time with.

He finished eating, gathered up the empty dishes, and washed them. He'd had other plans for them tonight. But it was her space, and he'd moved in, without giving her much choice, so he felt obligated to follow through on granting her a few hours of privacy tonight. Still, he wouldn't go far. Turning, he snagged his jacket and said, "Okay, I'm off." And he walked right to the door, leaving her still sitting at the table, staring at him. He flashed her a quick grin and added, "Don't miss me too much."

Outside the apartment, standing in the downtrodden hallway, he couldn't help but wonder what she was up to. If he sat here, he would notice if anybody came or went. If he went down to the main entrance, he'd have to sort out visitors who were coming to her versus going to somebody else.

Maybe she was only trying to make a couple phone calls. He was a fool. He needed to let it go.

A coffee shop was across the street. Ten minutes later he was sitting down with a hot cup, his notepad open in front of him, as he sorted his own life. Seconds later, he grabbed his phone and punched a saved number. "Any news?"

Hunter's voice was tired, angry. "No, nothing yet. Not enough information. You know it's past daisy-flowering time, right? They are going to seed now."

"Sorry. I'll try to contact her again tonight."

"Try now," Hunter urged. "If Anna's attracted to that apartment, you know she'll be hanging around there."

"I'm not in the apartment right now. I'll give it a shot when I go back." He wouldn't go into details about why he was not at Tavika's apartment. Hunter would howl with laughter. That was one of the things almost impossible to keep private between psychics. If Hunter was close by, he'd have no problem pinpointing how much Jericho was interested in Tavika.

"Hell, I don't even have to be there," Hunter noted in disgust. "I can pick that up from half a county away. It would help us all if you would just take her to bed. Then maybe you could refocus on what's important here." And then he hung up.

Jericho slunk lower in his seat and sipped his coffee, his mind on Tavika. What the hell was she up to? He seriously contemplated popping into the apartment in ethereal form for a second just to see. Not to invade her privacy but to make sure she was safe. At least that was his argument. She was entitled to time alone. He didn't have to like it, but, if he had plans, and somebody crashed his party, he wouldn't be very happy either.

As he lifted the cup in front of him, a powerful blast of energy hit him. He slammed back into his seat. His hand that held the cup wobbled, spilling coffee all over the table.

"Shit." He jumped up and looked around, but the little café had no other customers at this hour.

The waitress ran over, a cloth in her hand. "Oh dear." Jericho stepped out of her way, as she cleaned up the mess and was soon gone.

His mind still tried to figure out what had happened. He couldn't sense any danger, but he knew something major had happened. He could only ask one person about something like this.

"Stefan?" Thankfully the door to his friend was open.

What?

"Shit. You didn't feel that?" How was that possible? Jericho had suffered a major shock wave.

No. But I've been painting. Give me a minute.

Jericho had seen Stefan do this many times, but it still unnerved him.

Stefan would sit down, close off his mind, and open up his senses at a damn-near universal level. He had a connection to the eighth planet, Neptune, ruler of psychics, like none other. Stefan would know if something deadly and evil were tearing in the fabric of their existence.

Hunter had seen Stefan do this as well. Hunter and Jericho had discussed this scary and amazing talent of Stefan's occasionally. Both of them were in awe, neither one jealous. Both of them were also wary of the risks involved—akin to delving into the Earth's core and meeting Satan himself—wishing Stefan the best, but knowing something like this could kill him.

Jericho paid for his coffee and stepped outside. He glanced at his fingers to see a fine tremor still working its way through them. The hairs on the back of his neck stood upright. He couldn't help but stare up at Tavika's apartment. And sucked in his breath. Where there'd been lights was now an odd glow. Where there'd been windows was now something that wavered and shimmered in the evening. "Stefan? What the hell is going on?"

Stefan came back instantly. *I have no idea, but it's centered around Tavika.*

"I'm standing outside her apartment right now, but her windows don't look normal. They are glowing with this weird light. I just got hit by a tremendous energy blast. And you tell me that it's all about her? How is that possible? I have no idea."

But somebody is … No, it can't be …

"Stefan, dammit. You're not making sense. Tell me what's going on."

It's like somebody—and I'm not saying it's Tavika—has blended layers, almost pinching things together, so she saw them better. In the process creating a mini–sonic boom.

Jericho stood on the street, staring at the building slowly coming into focus again. He didn't know if it was what Stefan had done that made seeing it difficult or if it was what she had done. It was most likely Stefan's reaction to whatever she'd done. Jericho struggled with the concept that she'd done anything on the scale Stefan was talking about.

I wasn't kidding when I said she was powerful.

"But we had also assumed she was untrained and unknowing."

No, never that. We didn't know to what level she'd been trained, nor how much she knew or accepted. Those are three different things.

Jericho was still shaky at the thought of what he'd just been through. And more so as the concept of this being something anyone could do. "Okay, say it is her. Say she did do this. How come nobody else was affected? I was just in the coffee shop with a server who had no clue this was going on."

I think the question is more to the point of how far is her reach? How many people who understand what might have just happened are in that field? And does she have the power to make that become even greater?

"You didn't feel it though?"

Stefan replied thoughtfully, *It's interesting because I was painting, and, at a point in time, my hand slashed across the canvas. As if I had no control over my hand. The painting's quite ruined,* he added, with a laugh. *Afterward I was almost cheering, thinking it was my subconscious telling me to stop painting and to take a break.* He laughed again. *It's really quite ugly, so I'm happy to toss it.*

Jericho shook his head. He didn't even know what to

say. "How is it that nobody was upset that some woman managed to send out a shock wave?"

It could be you were in the blast radius this time. Stefan's voice lowered. *I wonder how much power she can pack into that? Considering she's sitting on a pressure keg, what's the effect when she dies?*

Jericho shuddered. Jesus, he didn't want to find out. He raised his gaze once again to her windows to see a weird blue glow. Okay, enough of that shit.

He bolted toward the apartment building.

CHAPTER 21

T HIS WASN'T GOOD. This wasn't the way it was supposed to be. Tavika should have had more control. The
energy should feel more sustainable. She didn't understand
why it was causing her so much trouble this time, yet her
consciousness whistled through her mind and said, *Of course
you do.*

And, yes, she did.

She reached up to scrub her face. The pressure inside
was squeezing at her, tensing her muscles into concrete. The
problem was Jericho. She was afraid he'd rush in at any
moment and disrupt her. So she'd made the transition
harder, rather than gentle, more abrupt than smooth.

A foolish error.

What the hell? She had more skills than that.

That shock wave had been an amateur move. She could
only hope nobody noticed.

Her mother would be screaming at her right now for
being so undisciplined, for being so dangerous to the world
around her. That she should practice and practice and
practice, until she got it right.

Tavika opened her eyes and stared dry-eyed at the small
space.

How the hell did one practice something dangerous
without *being* dangerous? This was a difficult skill to learn.

Accidents were bound to happen. They had happened too often to make her mother happy.

But Tavika's excuses had fallen on deaf ears a long time ago. So Tavika had stopped developing. Well, she had stopped in any way that her mother would recognize.

Tavika closed her eyes and sank back into the abyss. Her mother had called this place something very different. But, for Tavika, after all she'd been through, the name *abyss* had stuck.

It was a space of everything—and of nothing. It was a space where she could get lost forever.

And sometimes she wondered if she shouldn't do just that. Let go and fall away. She didn't know what would happen, but she assumed it would be the end of her physical body too. The end of everything as she knew it.

She frowned. Dare she go in again?

The pattern of dots weren't making sense. Maybe because she hadn't been able to focus. She'd tried to track the blue dots and had found the trail, but it was faint, edgy. The dots faded, as if worn away or possibly not fully formed enough to follow. She didn't understand.

She had to try again.

She spread her hands out in front of her and started moving the clouds out of her way. They snarled but drifted obediently. A few of them clung to her fingers refusing to move. Gently she insisted. This was her domain. Everyone in the physical world might try to hide from her, but good luck trying to hide here.

Some could. Like the damn Ghost. That made no sense to her, but it wasn't something she could change. Then she had so much more to learn. She thought it had something to do with wanting something too much, ... and, therefore, the energy pushed it away.

There. … Blue wafted to the left. She reached out to touch it, and it disappeared again. She blinked several times, trying to see past the clouds. She had seen so many similar patterns in the midnight sky. Now the space in front of her was lit up like one million Christmas lights. And yet—as if she were caught in the middle—everything was obscured. Off to one side was a faint string of gold dots. Whose pathway was that? It wasn't Anna's though, and Tavika had to stay focused. Just as she went to snag more clouds and toss them away, she heard footsteps.

No. No. *No.* It couldn't be Jericho. She needed more time. She slammed out a warning and dove deeper and deeper into the cloud. If she could just get below the clouds, she could see what she needed. She pushed at the clouds and shoved them away, but, instead of moving back, they closed tighter and tighter, until she gasped for breath. Just enough panic coursed through her to make her realize she was causing some of this on her own.

Another amateur stunt.

Jesus, it had to be Jericho throwing her off. She knew better than this. She had to. This performance would get the Ghost.

She gasped for breath, trying to ignore the pain, determined to go deeper.

Hands reached out and snagged her up. She felt her soul being pulled up and away, and she cried out, "No, no, no."

"Yes." Jericho's voice snarled through the mess of confusion. "Come back, Tavika. Come back."

Her voice weak, her heart frantic, she called out, "No, I'm almost there. I'm almost done."

"No. You *are* done. That's enough." He did something,

and her world dissolved in front of her.

She slowly opened her eyes to realize, instead of sitting in the middle of her living room floor, she was now on the bed, Solomon crying softly beside her. Tavika's eyelids were so heavy that it was hard to raise them. Her body was so light that she couldn't feel the bed beneath her. She stared into Jericho's dark eyes and whispered, "What happened?"

"You tell me. I came racing in here, when I realized something was wrong." He glared down at her. "Can you see yourself? Can you feel how you are? How lax your body is? How absolutely ice-cold your skin is?"

Her eyelids drifted lower. "You should have left me. I was so close."

"So close to what?" he asked in frustration. "And why is whatever you're so close to *killing* you?"

"It's not me. It's you," she whispered. "I let you get to me. My mother would hate me for this." Her voice faded lower and lower.

"Tell me what you're trying to get close to?"

"Not what. Who. *Anna.*"

Shit.

"I was on Anna's trail." Then her head rolled to the side. "I saw one end. I was trying to track her to the other."

And she lost consciousness.

"TAVIKA?" JERICHO GAVE her shoulders a gentle shake. "Tavika? Wake up. Please wake up."

Her eyelids fluttered open, and a cloudy gaze stared back at him, only to slowly tumble closed again.

He gave her a harder shake. "Tavika, you need to wake up."

"Tired," she mumbled. "Can't stay awake."

"Damn it. You need to. You have to tell me what you're doing. Did you find Anna?"

Her eyelids opened up, and this time her gaze was confused. He saw her fatigue, the drain of whatever she'd been doing inside her system.

"You need to recharge," he snapped. "This is important."

"Recharge?" She frowned, as if she worked through such a concept.

He bowed his head, trying to hold back his frustration. He'd come up against this before. It was the missing gaps in education. The pieces psychics needed to learn, so they could continue to do what they were gifted to do but on an efficient level.

"You've drained your energy, doing whatever it was you were working on," he stated. "You need to grab ahold of whatever source you get your energy from and recharge." He lay his hand between her breasts. "Like this." And he sent a heavy dose of energy into her heart chakra.

She arched up above the bed, crying out.

He lifted his hand.

She collapsed back on the bed, her eyes opened wide. The color flowed back into her skin.

"There," he noted, with satisfaction. "You look much better."

She lifted up on one elbow, a cough wrenching from her chest.

"Well, I haven't seen that reaction before." He reached over and gently rubbed her back. "That shouldn't have hurt you." But, as he watched her struggle to recover from the energy-infused blow, he realized he'd dislodged something somehow. She was struggling to recover.

Stefan's voice whispered through his mind. *It's old energy. You hit her in the heart chakra, whether intentionally or on purpose, I don't know, but that shock wave disturbed a lot of old stuff. You can expect some repercussions from this.*

"Damn it. She was tracking Anna. Said she was close, but I didn't ask or listen. I just reacted."

It will be okay. But you know what happens when you stir up old stuff.

In front of them Tavika coughed and coughed, and then finally, when it seemed like she was done, she hacked up some more. She bolted from the bed and raced to the bathroom.

And retched.

Jericho sat on the bed and stared after her. "Jesus, Stefan, I didn't hit her hard. I never even thought that such a thing were possible."

She will adjust.

"You sure I didn't cause an injury? Maybe she needs to see a doctor."

No, she'll be fine. She just needs time. You've opened up a blockage. One she put in place to keep her history locked down. And a lot of difficult emotions ended up piled on top.

Jericho wasn't sure how that would go. Just the thought of it made him wince. Opening up her history, those old aches and pains would do more than hurt. He stood outside the bathroom, wanting to help but not knowing how. "Tavika, I'm so sorry, honey. I didn't know that would hurt you."

In a weak voice, still huddled over the toilet, she replied, "I'm fine."

He heard sounds that were distinctly not fine. But no

point trying to talk to her now, as it was very hard to reply when your stomach was emptying itself. He went back and sat down on the side of the bed and waited. What the hell had he done?

CHAPTER 22

T AVIKA TOOK A swallow of water and rinsed her mouth. She'd been awake all of five minutes and had bolted to the bathroom as soon as she could.

What the hell just happened? She leaned her hands on the bathroom sink and stared at herself in the mirror. She looked odd. Different. She recognized that Jericho had sent a lightning bolt of energy into her heart chakra. That accounted for the color in her cheeks and the brighter look in her eyes, but the pain on her face, the grief in her heart, and the ache so deep inside? She swore it penetrated through her bones. Where had all that come from? She wanted to cry, to scream. She wanted to do something. ... But, at the same time, she wanted to curl up into a tiny ball and to hide away from life. How was any of this fair? None of it made any sense. And was any of it even explainable?

She opened the bathroom door to see Jericho, sitting lost on her bed, Solomon in his arms. He was a good man. He'd been trying to help her. He didn't deserve to feel guilty. It was her fault for stuffing everything inside, basically brewing a cauldron of emotions.

A similar blow could have come from any number of directions. That it was from him just added to the nightmare. She made her way weakly to the bed and sat down beside him. He never said a word, but she felt his gaze drift over her face, searching for the truth of her condition.

"I'm fine." She flopped backward on the bed, needing the support beneath her back.

"I'm so sorry," he murmured. "It's not what I meant to do."

She gave a broken laugh. "Well, it *is* what you meant to do. That shot of energy was meant to stop me from what I was doing. In that sense it worked. You wouldn't know how much I had stuffed into that chakra with the hope of it never seeing the light of day."

"No, but I should've. I know what happened to you. I know what you went through. I opened up old wounds that I never intended to. And, for that, I'm really sorry." The sincerity in his voice rolled over her.

She believed him. "I'll be fine. I just didn't need this right now. The Ghost's return is enough of a trigger. In fact, that's likely why your bolt of energy did as much damage as it did. His arrival has already sent minor shocks through the parts of my psyche that were on lockdown, weakening them. You just popped the walls wide open."

A comfortable silence was shared between them. He flopped backward to lie beside her.

Solomon walked onto her tummy, his engine loud, as he curled up in a tight ball. She wrapped her arms around him and held him close.

After a long moment Jericho asked, "What exactly were you doing?"

She rolled her head sideways to look at him. "Connecting the dots." She hoped he'd allow that answer to fly by, but she knew, before the words were out of her mouth, he wouldn't.

"I was sitting in the restaurant across the street, having a cup of coffee." He stared up at the ceiling. "When a shock wave hit me. My hand shook so badly that I spilled coffee all over the table and me." He turned to look at her, their faces only inches from each other. "I had no idea what it was. It terrified me." He smiled crookedly. "I raced out of the café, petrified something had happened to you. Yet what I saw, when I looked up at the apartment, was out of this world."

"What did you see?" she asked curiously. "I've never seen or heard of anybody being affected by me connecting the dots before."

"When you say, *connecting the dots*, why is that? I don't think you mean drawing lines on a piece of paper, making connections within a case or something like that?"

She dropped her gaze and rolled back to stare up at the ceiling again. She took a deep breath and admitted, "That's exactly what I do. Only …" Her voice trailed off.

"Only?"

She winced. "I do it on the etheric level. I call it *going into the abyss.*"

The silence from Jericho was surprising.

Then again, what did she expect? He probably didn't know what that meant.

"Meaning?"

What to say? How could she explain something like that? He was psychic. But he had a lot of abilities she'd never heard of. Was it possible she could do something he couldn't? She contemplated that idea.

Her mother hadn't had anything to do with any other psychics, preferring to keep the family isolated. The circle of knowledge Tavika was familiar with had come from her family. That didn't mean it was all-inclusive. Neither did it mean her mother had shared everything she knew. It wasn't really part of her mother's makeup.

"It means, I search through the fabric of our world for colored dots that show me patterns that connect people, places, things—on the physical level."

More silence came.

She wanted to smile. She didn't dare.

"Colored dots?"

This time she laughed. He rolled over, so he could stare down at her. With a smirk on her lips, she asked, "Of everything I've said, you pick up on the color issue?"

He grinned. "Stefan works on the fabric-of-our-existence stuff too, but I don't think I've ever heard anybody talk about colored dots. And, although some people can see things at that level, I'm not sure I know someone who has been able to see or follow the patterns there."

"Oh." She frowned. "Stefan goes there?"

This time it was Jericho's turn to laugh. "Sounds like you and Stefan need to spend some time together."

Now her smile was natural, as she noted quietly, "And maybe I'd like that."

He reached down to entwine their fingers. "I think you've been alone for so long, on many different levels, that you've become afraid. A prisoner almost. Afraid of the world you didn't know. Afraid that nobody else could be like your mother, like you, your sister, or brother." He gently stroked his thumb across her hand, adding, "It's not like that. There is a group of us. It's only a life sentence if you're alone. When you have other people to help—those who are in the same boat, with the same challenges—then life is a lot easier."

"I was the youngest of a family of very strong and talent-ed psychics, some of them very aggressive." She squeezed his fingers, then added, "That didn't make it easy. They didn't make it comfortable. In many ways nothing was pleasant about it."

"I was raised with nobody around me having any kind of abilities. I came into mine late in life," Jericho shared. "I knew nothing about it, and I knew no one to ask. I had always assumed my life would've been so much better if I had been born into a family who already knew about these challenges and could help me to adapt."

"Do you have brothers and sisters?"

He nodded. "Two brothers. Lots of cousins, aunts, and uncles." He grinned. "And now one nephew and niece."

She rolled her head to the side, so she could study his features. "Did you fight lots? Have any arguments and disagreements with your family?"

"Absolutely. Some days it was like World War III."

"Exactly. Do you know what it means when everybody's a psychic, but they're all more developed than you are because you're the youngest? It means no privacy, no thoughts of your own. It means constant competitions in terms of abilities—who is better, bigger, or stronger. It means realizing you are the weakest, ugliest, youngest, and the worst off, being raised and formed by criticisms and judgments inside and outside your head, every waking moment."

She snickered. "Nothing was peaceful about my life at all. I was *raised* in the middle of a war. Among very aggressive people, who all knew more than I did. In a field where there was nobody to ask for help. In a field you can't even mention to other kids because they'll look at you like you were not only lying but off your rocker."

He dropped her hand to prop himself up on his elbow.

She studied the man that had somehow worked his way into her apartment, her life, and she feared he'd easily work his way into her heart—if she let him.

She wasn't sure how she felt about that. Everyone who'd been close to her was dead. And she didn't want anyone else to get hurt.

IT HAD NEVER occurred to Jericho that Tavika's childhood would have been anything other than wonderful—up to the point of the Ghost's arrival. But, as he listened to her and really understood what it had been like to be the least developed in a family of psychics like hers, … well, that would have been incredibly difficult. He couldn't imagine. He reached over and, with his thumb, gently stroked her cheek. "I'm so sorry. I didn't know."

She laughed, but the bitterness was obvious.

And the pain.

"How can anybody know? I think honestly I was so determined to not be like them that I shoved all my abilities down deep inside, so I wouldn't have to deal. So I didn't have to strive to be better than they were. I was the failure. I was the one born without any special gifts. I was the worst thing you could be in my family. I was *average*."

"But inside it didn't work for you. You just pretended to be."

Her gaze turned sad. "I don't know if I pretended to that keeping it secret made me feel superior." She stared at him. He saw the embarrassed honesty in her eyes. "I didn't like myself very much. I knew they liked me even less. I was just playing mind games, as children do."

He tapped her lightly on the chin. "Not mind games.

Survival. You did what you had to do to survive. Your family life, your childhood, couldn't have been easy."

"No, it wasn't, but that didn't excuse me from not making the best of it. I had so little time with any of them. The realization afterward that they were gone, that I would never see my mother again, that even my sister's cutting remarks were done because she was dead …" Tavika shook her head.

"I fell into a deep spiral of depression and anger. It was very hard to pull out of. Took years of growing up. Even now I feel guilty. Guilty that I lived, with so little to offer the world, when they, who were so gifted, died." Tears lit up her gaze, the drops slowly tracking down her cheeks.

He leaned forward and kissed her on the cheek. "It's okay. You couldn't have known what would happen. No child ever makes the best out of the situation they have. The point of being a child is to live in the moment. Not to look down the road at what's coming. You are *not* responsible for what happened to your family."

Her lips trembled. "That's the trouble with words. They hit at one level, yet emotion hits at a very deep one. And no amount of words would have convinced me that I wasn't responsible. That if I had just developed as I was supposed to—instead of trying to hide that part of me, keeping it secret—that maybe I'd have had abilities that could have saved us." Now the tears flowed steadily. "Do you know what it's like to have your family die at the hands of a madman, knowing you'd wasted the time you'd been given and could have saved them?"

"Of course I can't know what that's like. But I do know that guilt eats through your soul. You can't let it. You deserve a life. You survived that nightmare. All the things that happened before then don't matter because, from the moment it was over, you became reborn. You became somebody new. There was baggage you could never let go of."

He smiled at her tenderly. She was so damaged. So proud. So capable. "But you stood tall and you made it. You took those steps, and you walked forward. You survived. Nothing in this world is stronger than a survivor."

She was not to blame for what the Ghost had done. Jericho knew a lot more needed to come out, but this was a start. "Let me tell you how I came to do what I do."

She turned to look at him, a question in her eyes.

He told her about Darren's boy being kidnapped. The cop-turned-child-predator who had opened Jericho's eyes to the real evil of the world and how Jericho had met up with Hunter, who'd introduced him to Stefan.

And both had shown him the reality behind the polite face of society.

"So this is what I do now," he stated quietly. "Every day there's something new to learn. Something new to see." His smile deepened, turned lazy. "Like you. I had no idea who you were on the inside. What you were dealing with. How unique you are inside and out, … but I'm learning."

He had so many more questions he needed to ask her. Questions about her connecting the dots. And what the hell had that blast been all about? Because, wow, that was a weapon in itself. If she could learn to do that, nobody out there could touch her. Nobody could harm her ever again. Maybe, indeed, that was partly what she was so upset about. If she'd been able to trigger that while she'd been a captive …

Right now it didn't matter because that little girl inside Tavika desperately needed reassurance. To know she was not responsible for her family's demise. He took her in his arms, gently rubbing her back, until her tears dried up. There was still a lot of work to do. He didn't know when or how, but they needed to get to it as fast as they could. Anna was still out there.

And so was the Ghost.

HE WALKED THROUGH the station and headed for Tavika's desk. The office was empty as usual at this hour. He had clearance here but not in this particular area, but he came often anyway. No one ever checked.

The room, as always, was completely disorganized. With a sigh he moved her stapler to the corner of the desk. Everything had a place. A home.

Why couldn't she get that through her head?

It was early yet. He was safe for at least an hour. That should be plenty of time. He had a brunch to get ready for. And a lover to meet. Life was good; he wanted this future. He was trying to clean up, but it really was an addiction.

And so hard to walk away from. Still, it would be worth it in the end.

He pulled out his list. He needed to make a selection soon.

Time was running out.

CHAPTER 23

*T*AVIKA! TAVI! THE harsh whisper slammed into her brain, jolting her awake. She didn't know who had just spoken, but such insistence had filled the voice that she had no way to ignore it. She lay quietly, trying to figure out what was so different. First, she was held in a man's arms. Second, she knew it was Jericho, without even having to look. And third, a raw ache was inside her. As if she'd been to hell and back emotionally. Then she remembered last night's trip to the abyss and Jericho's subsequent assistance in getting her back on her feet.

Tavika, forget about that. You have to give up the hunt for the Ghost.

"Travis, I am too tired for this." She dismissed his words. She had heard them too many times before. … Then his tone, his urgency hit her as something new. She bolted upright, disentangling herself from Jericho's gentle attempt to tug her back into his arms. "Why, Travis? What's different?"

He's hunting.

She waved her hand in a dismissive motion. "He's always hunting. What's different *now*?"

Besides the fact that he's back in town and hunting in his own playground? Travis snapped.

She shook her head. "He's been here for the last several

days. What's changed?" She kept her voice low and insistent.

I saw a list, he admitted.

"A list?" She felt stupid for repeating it, but, for someone who'd woken her up, he wasn't being very forthcoming.

Yes, a list.

But he would not say more. She hopped to her feet and stared at her small apartment. "Dammit, Travis, what was on the list?

I couldn't read everything, but there were names. And your name was on it. You were in the middle. There was a whole pile of lines crossed off the top. For all I know, you're next. You can't let him get you. You have to leave town.

She came to a standstill in the middle of the room.

"Travis, I've never heard you like this. Why is this upsetting you?" She struggled to understand the panic. "You knew he was coming. You've been fixated on him since forever."

Yes, but I didn't know he was coming now. *I thought maybe he'd be coming when you were old and gray, for heaven's sake,* Travis shouted.

His voice drumming through her ears, she spun and stared at the front door. "Now? Is he on his way here now?"

Frustration rolled through Travis's voice. *You're being deliberately obtuse. He's in town. He's knocking names off the list, and your name is on it.*

"Okay," she said in a soothing voice. "See if you can get a picture of the man, so I can identify him. Or, if you see the list, try to read the names, so we can save a life next time."

You don't understand. I saw the list, he cried out. *A couple names are above yours. But he's also marked off a couple names below yours. So he's not doing this in sequence.*

"Oh, shit," she murmured out loud. "Well, that explains your panic. Maybe."

What were the chances that the Ghost was taking out other survivors, like her? She frowned. Or potential witnesses of previous crimes? *Potential* in his eyes. … That didn't mean the police knew about them. … That could explain why they all seemed so unrelated.

Maybe these people had been somebody the Ghost felt were a threat. Maybe they were connected in one way or another to him or to his crimes. That would make it all that much harder for the cops, the FBI, because they weren't even sure exactly how many people the Ghost had murdered. But this gave her a hell of a starting point. She was sure Henderson from the FBI would like to see that list too.

"Thank you, Travis." She looked down at her watch and checked the time. Six. She needed to be at her files. She brought up her computer, gave a quick glance to Jericho, making sure he was still asleep and logged on to her office computer. Somehow, somewhere, there was a connection from these people to the Ghost.

As they didn't have a name for the Ghost, she would have to search for a violent crime in each of these people's lives. Excitement rippled through her blood and nerves, knowing something was there. If she could only find more. She called out to the empty room, "Travis? You there? Did you see any other names? If you get a chance, try to find me another name on the list."

Only silence filled in the room, and then Jericho's sleepy voice murmured from the bed, "Tavika, you okay?"

She called back, "I'm fine. My brother just suggested something about the Ghost. I'm working the lead now."

Jericho stumbled to his feet, rubbing the sleep from the corners of his eyes, but his gaze was sharp. Hard. "What have you got?"

"A line to tug," she stated. "I was searching for connections between the victims. But what I needed to do was search for a violent crime in each of their lives. Travis saw a list. He suggested the killer was cleaning up, eliminating those people. And, although the Ghost isn't taking out the victims in order, Travis mentioned that many names had been crossed off. He thinks these potential victims are a danger to the Ghost, so he's cleaning up."

She sensed Jericho's unanswered questions, but she wanted him to just hold off. Her fingers danced on the keyboard, as she started searches. A thought occurred to her, and she asked, "Any chance Anna is related to the Ghost?"

Jericho shook his head. "No way to know at this point. But she's not his typical victim, and it appeared a relative was involved in this one."

She nodded. "I'm working Gordon's case. I know him the best."

"And yet, as a homeless man, he could have seen any number of things or even thought to be a threat, when he was actually not."

"Which would explain why it was hard to connect these people. It also explains why my name is on that list."

"In fact," Jericho replied smoothly, "you're the only witness any of us have."

She shot him a hard look. "The condition I was in didn't make me a witness. If anything, it left me barely capable of speaking for months."

He nodded in understanding. "But you do realize how unusual you are in that way."

"Only in that I lived through his torture. Whereas all these people may not even have a clue as to what they saw. But it doesn't matter to the Ghost. He's taking them out anyway."

TAVIKA'S THEORY WORKED. Jericho had seen it happen before. The Ghost was making sure nothing and nobody could tie him to his old crimes. That often happened if killers got married, moved up in life, or some other major change occurred, making them fearful of being exposed. And people who were safe at first were no longer, now that he was reassessing.

What they needed was proof. Not conjecture. And he wanted to ask her about her brother. Actually one thousand questions were bursting through his head.

She stood up abruptly. "I have to go to the office. I'm having trouble with my computer and log-in." She put on her holster and grabbed her jacket and badge. "I'll call you if I find out anything."

And she was gone just like that.

He sat down to read the screens that were still up. Solomon jumped up onto his lap. Absentmindedly Jericho scanned the information. She was looking for violent crimes in Gordon's past. And, of course, in Gordon's case, there were more than a few.

Gordon had had several confrontations with the police, a few complaints about and from him, and he'd been beaten up once. He'd had people steal from him and groups torment him. Although nothing appeared to be big enough and worth killing him over, even if he'd seen something. He wouldn't have been called as a witness because his testimony would've been deemed unreliable. The drugs and booze had taken so much of his mind already that nobody would trust him on the stand.

As he sat here, Jericho wondered if Maggs knew more. Would she talk to him? It was morning. The sun was rising, and it was still early. He put on a pot of coffee, filled the travel mug, and thought maybe it would be worth a try. He sent Hunter a quick update on last night, adding that he'd try to get Tavika to track Anna in a few hours. She was so focused on the Ghost that Jericho didn't think she could take her attention off that right now. It sucked, but everybody only had so much energy. Tavika's life was inundated with murder cases. How could one be deemed any more important over another?

Then he remembered the words she'd asked of Travis, while Jericho had pretended to be asleep, only to watch as she spoke to the empty room. She'd asked if there was a name on that list they could save, instead of finding them dead. Meaning, she would prioritize *a life* over death. So Anna was the priority. Or would be if they had any proof she was alive.

Walking briskly in the morning chill, Jericho made his way to Maggs's corner. He didn't want to scare her but was afraid that, given her age and health, anything could happen at any time. He stood in the corner of the park and called out gently, "Maggs, you there? I'm a friend of Tavika's. I have a couple questions about Gordon for you." Silence came first, but he heard a rustling of the underbrush next, as if she were moving.

"Maggs?" He took several steps forward, looking to see if any of her friends were around. Several slept off to the side. He didn't want to disturb them. Maggs was just off to the left. He approached slowly. "Maggs?" There was a tiny snuffle, almost a grunt. "Do you remember me?"

Her faint voice echoed, "I remember you."

There wasn't the same joy or trust in her voice. Who could blame her?

"I brought you some coffee."

She opened those ancient eyes to stare up at him. Then she nudged her cup toward him.

He crouched down, took off the lid to his travel mug, and filled Maggs's cup. In a quiet voice he said, "I didn't mean to disturb you. I was hoping you were awake. I wondered if you know anything about Gordon's history. Do you know if he ever witnessed a violent crime?"

Eyes black as the night blinked at him several times.

He rushed to clarify. "I don't mean his war days. I mean, since he's been on the streets. Or even before that."

"It's what sent him to the streets." She reached out a greedy hand and brushed at the steam wafting up from her cup.

He stepped back slightly. "What do you mean?"

"He came home from the war, disillusioned, hurting, and angry. Not long after his return, he was frustrated with the government, with not being able to find a job. His health issues were getting worse." She stopped and had several nasty chest-rattling coughs, before she hacked up a big plug of sputum.

He waited. No good pushing her. She would only say what she wanted to.

When she finally cleared her throat, she lay back down, gasping. "Gordon saw a murder. He said at the time a whole family was slaughtered. But then he changed his story, saying only some of the family were killed. Then he started talking about ghosts and the devil. The police didn't believe him, but it ate at him. He thought coming home would be different. He thought he'd be safe here. But instead he told me that the war had come home with him."

She sighed and reached for the cup. "I think he blamed himself. In his confusion with the drugs, the PTSD, and everything else going on, he felt like, if he'd stayed overseas, the family would still be alive. But because he came home, he brought the war with him, and the people dying were his fault."

At her mention of a family and then ghosts, Jericho nodded. "Any idea how long ago this was?"

She waved her hand. "A long time ago, ten, twenty years maybe. Gordon has been on the street as long as I've known him. We met not long after it happened. It's all he could talk about. He needed medical help. But, to the eyes of the world, he was nobody, just a washed-out, no-longer-useful man. And there was nothing and no one available to help him."

"Did Gordon know who the family was or where the murder happened? Do you know any details, so I could possibly track that murder?"

She sank down into a pile of rags, her body more bone than meat, her skin thin and translucent. Evidence she was not of this world for much longer. He figured she'd be happy to stay where she was, rather than go to a hospital and accept society's brand of geriatric care for the end of her life. She closed her eyes, and her breathing sank deeper and deeper.

"Maggs? Do you have any recollection of who the family was?"

And in the way of so many people who don't understand the meaning behind the knowledge they have, she shook her head. "Not much. It made the headlines because the mother was a psychic. That much I remember. I thought it was funny because, if she were, how come she couldn't protect herself and her family?"

She curled up, and, with her hands tucked under her cheek, she drifted off to sleep, the hot coffee cooling beside her.

CHAPTER 24

T AVIKA WALKED OUT of the captain's office, heading
back downstairs. She'd explained what had happened
with her log-in again. They had to wait for the IT department to show up, as it was way too early for them to be here.
It used to be they had someone on twenty-four hours a day,
but that was before all the budget cuts. Still, she had a spare
laptop. An unusual step but she needed to be working. At
her desk, she cleared a spot and logged in on the new
machine. As she sorted her emails, her phone rang. She
pulled it out of her pocket and answered absently, "Hello.

"Tavika? It's Jericho. I just spoke with Maggs. She said
Gordon witnessed a violent crime ten to twenty years ago,
and that was partly why he was on the streets. He was afraid
he was guilty for bringing the war home."

"What?" She leaned back, pinching the bridge of her
nose. It was one thing that Maggs actually spoke with
Jericho. It was another to think she held important information on Gordon. Why hadn't she thought to ask her
about that? "What else did she have to say?"

Jericho relayed the conversation. Then he added, "Psychic gets murdered ..."

And her stomach lurched. She clamped her hand over
her mouth. *Dear God.* She bent over quickly, dropping her
head between her knees, trying to calm the heaves rattling

her system. But her stomach wouldn't be still.

"Tavika, you okay?"

Was she okay? She would be. She was a pro at hiding shit. "I'm fine. It was a shock. That's all." No, that was too bland a word for the visceral reaction in her gut. As if there were a disconnect from her mind to her body. One making excuses and the other still recovering from it. "I'm fine. Interesting headline …" She was proud her voice was calm, even though her nerves were shot.

"I know, but it's also a connection."

That it was. She hung up from Jericho to study Gordon's files in front of her. Could he really have seen the Ghost? There was no mention of him being a witness anywhere. She brought out the old case files and statements, but Gordon's name wasn't listed. By protocol every call, complaint, and witness was checked out. Because no one ever really knew who had valuable information.

But she also knew lots of crazies were in the world. Regardless the statements should have been logged in and registered. That didn't mean that their statements were kept for twenty years. What was kept before the digital age was very different than what was saved now.

But even now some statements cops ignored, like those from psychics. There was a major stigma against them, except in her mother's case, where she'd done a lot of work for law enforcement. Needing to know for sure, she reopened the files and searched for Gordon's name. Then for the word *psychic*. Still not finding anything, she went through all the witnesses' statements. But nothing to show that the police had kept Gordon's.

She didn't know if it would have made any difference back then, but it had obviously traumatized him. Had he actually seen the Ghost? Had he known him? Did he recognize him?

Surely if he had, he'd have said something during all these years. But, as she looked back on the time she'd known Gordon, his downward spiral had been consistent. His mental stability more fragile by the month. If Gordon had seen something, the fear and guilt would have sent him further downhill.

What a life for a vet. Feeling guilty for a war he hadn't created. Feeling inadequate for the job he'd done. Feeling like there was nothing more for him …

She cast her mind back to the events twenty years ago, wondering if anyone in the neighborhood had known. At the time she hadn't understood how anybody could *not* have. Occupied houses were all around. Enough screaming had been going on at her house that she swore houses ten blocks over had heard. Only later did she realize that originally a sound engineer had lived there, and he'd built a recording studio in the basement. Where they'd all been kept. Where their screams had gone unheard.

New luxury high-rises were just a few blocks over, but they were new developments. Most of the old neighborhood houses on this side were now empty. A definite case of a wrong-side-of-the-tracks neighborhood. By accident or design, she didn't know, but it was good news for the Ghost. It had given him a playing field that would've been difficult to arrange on his own.

But she also understood serial killers. They were capable of adapting and making good use of circumstances. Some needed everything perfect to make their fantasy work. They had to follow developed rituals.

She'd been unconscious for a lot of the time during her

captivity—but not all of it. She hadn't seen any sign of repetitive or ritualistic OCD behavior with the Ghost. But she'd been young and traumatized. And in the dark. She didn't know there'd been set behaviors to look for. Even during her law enforcement training, she knew the Ghost didn't fit the boxes the psychologists had for guys like him.

She stared at her notes. This meant there was a connection from Gordon to the Ghost. And somehow the Ghost must have known.

So was there also a connection to the old man and the girl? Tavika wasn't willing to include the woman in the trunk of the stolen Cadillac into the bunch because she could have been at the wrong place at the wrong time. But Tavika wouldn't discount the possibility either.

They'd screwed up the Ghost's plans that night.

Maybe the woman in the Cadillac had died just because of that.

Making a note to herself, Tavika opened her files, looking for a connection from the old man to the Ghost and soon grabbed her phone and dialed his granddaughter's number.

After the woman answered, Tavika quickly identified herself and explained, "We are looking into your grandfather's death. I'm trying to see if there is a connection with a couple other murders." She winced at the woman's gasp of shock. "Did your grandfather have any exposure to another violent crime in the past?"

Silence came first, then the woman spoke. "Violent crime? You mean, like another murder?"

Interesting she choose that word. "Yes, something like that. But it could be a different type of crime."

"He was supposed to be a witness at a murder trial a few

years back. But the case fell through, and it never went to trial."

Tavika's pen moved quickly as she took down the details.

"My grandfather was really upset about the idea of going to trial. He was pretty sure it was the wrong person, but the prosecutor wouldn't listen. They were determined to convict this man."

"What man?"

"I'm not sure I remember who was involved," the woman replied in surprise. "It was a long time ago."

"If you can give me any information on what it was about, where it happened, or the names of people involved," Tavika noted, "then I could possibly track it down and see if there was a connection."

Tavika sat back and listened, as the woman described what her grandfather saw. "He was doing a small job for a woman who lived alone. He had to slip out and get some materials from the store. When he came back, he heard some arguing, but he needed to get the job done, so he headed back downstairs to finish the electrical work on the circuit panel. He heard an odd sound, so he put down his tools and snuck back upstairs. He saw a man, bending over the woman, strangling her. My grandfather jumped into the room to help, and the killer took off. Because he never saw the man's face, he couldn't ever identify the killer, until the police caught one guy and had enough evidence to take him to court. But that later fell through. Granddad had been adamant that they had the wrong man."

The woman stopped to take a shaky breath. When she regained control, she continued her story. "It was about fifteen years ago. Granddad was never the same after that. He stayed to himself and just did less and less work, until finally he became more of a recluse than anything. We used to go around once a month or so to say hi. … And he seemed happy to see us, … but it was almost as if, within a few minutes, he was itching for us to go. As if he were scared, not for himself, but for us."

A heavy, sad silence followed. When the granddaughter continued, she added, "My mother always said that Grand-dad was waiting for the killer to come back. Honestly, when I heard he'd been murdered, I figured that's who it was."

"Did you tell the police that?"

The granddaughter laughed, but it was a bitter, hard one. "No, I didn't. There didn't seem to be much point bringing up old cases that went nowhere. If they couldn't find the guy back then, I doubt they'd find him now."

"They might," Tavika noted quietly.

"I didn't want to get involved. And, if this guy came after Granddad, he'd likely come after me."

Thanking the woman for her cooperation, Tavika hung up and tried to organize her notes. The fact that the grandfa-ther had actually seen a murder was just too much of a coincidence in her mind.

What possible crime could the teenage girl have wit-nessed? If any, surely at her age, she wouldn't have known what she saw. But then she was close to the age of Tavika when she'd been captured. Inasmuch as the police tried back then to get information out of her, there'd been nothing worth getting. Her name on the list did, however, add some credence to both Travis's and Jericho's comments about the Ghost coming after Tavika. As if he were cleaning up. She was on the list because he'd let her live once. But maybe he'd changed his mind. She didn't know how long she had. Her brother told her that names below hers were crossed off as well. Why the hell could she never get a step in front of this asshole? Her phone rang. "Shelby, morning. What have you got?"

"She was dying," Shelby stated abruptly. "Results have been confirmed."

"Sorry?"

"Sarah was dying from a rare form of leukemia. She might have made it for another year or two. Aggressive treatment might've extended her chances, if she continued on the path she was on, but, without any treatment, she wouldn't have lived to the end of the year."

Tavika sank back in her chair, her mind whirling. "I'm trying to figure out if this changes anything."

"It changes everything and nothing," Shelby noted. "She died of an overdose. A heavy cocktail of opioid drugs, mixed with alcohol. Self-ingested. Honestly it looks like she was at a pharm party and took a crazy mix by the handfuls."

"*Uhm*. The broken neck was just for show?" They'd both seen cases of assisted deaths, where people were dying anyway, some in excruciating pain. Sometimes to help the person, other times to line the pockets of the helper. "Thanks for this. I will get back to you."

She ended the call, sat here, and let her mind spin. How? Or maybe why? She jotted down notes.

The case just got a whole lot more complicated. Could Sarah have taken the drugs on her own? Or been forced to take them? Had somebody seen an opportunity to dispose of her? Just dump her body at the same crime scene? Why would anybody do that? A lot of questions. No answers.

It was time to hit the streets. Somebody had to know more about this teenage girl. And, if she'd been taken out by a different killer, then they needed to know that now.

JERICHO WANDERED THROUGH the various parks and alleyways, talking to a few homeless people. Outside of Maggs, he couldn't come up with any more information regarding Gordon as a potential witness to anything criminal. Still, Jericho liked the idea of the killer cleaning up. They had to match the old electrician and the teenage girl to the Ghost too. Unfortunately the middle-aged woman in the back of the Cadillac would probably be seen as a crime of convenience.

Yet that was too easy. Jericho decided to focus on her. It had been his vision that had sent them to Tavika's prior crime scene that night. He'd seen a victim there, but the features were indistinct. From the body size and type, he couldn't tell if it was this woman in the Cadillac or somebody else. Therefore, he couldn't discount the fact that the killer may have killed this middle-aged woman with the intention of bringing her to that house.

He already knew her name was Valerie Vermont from the registration papers in the Cadillac at the time her body was discovered in the trunk. He then confirmed her facial match to her DL within the DMV records, which was where he also got her home address. He drove there and found out she lived only a couple blocks from both the electrician's house and Tavika's old home. But a couple blocks made a huge difference. One went from the poor neighborhood that was druggy town into upper-level elite high-rises. He drove past the woman's house to find it was a lovely well-kept bungalow.

Her records showed that she had lived alone and that her

husband had been dead for four years. The woman was fifty-four years old. Which put her in her early to mid-thirties way back when, if she'd seen the Ghost when he had first started his killing spree in town. But twenty years of crossing paths with a serial killer gave the Ghost lots of opportunity—whether finding his victims or later finding any potential witnesses. Still, Jericho was grasping at straws, looking for connections where there were none. He had to find proof to back up his conjecture. He parked down the block and walked up to her place and around to the back of the house. He knocked, just in case somebody lived here, but got no answer.

He pushed open the door to find it unlocked. Was this actually the original crime scene? The police had checked it over but hadn't found any sign of a struggle. The current theory suggested that she'd been killed in a parking lot, and her body dumped into the back of the vehicle, but, without a crime scene, there was no way to know.

The kitchen was clean and tidy. The house cold. Sterile. He made a quick trip through the main floor and realized there was nothing to see down here. He took the stairs two at a time and did a quick trip through the upstairs. But found nothing. He stood at the top of the stairs and considered the walls, holding lots of photos of family, trinkets, and little mementos. Surely she'd have kept anything as important as memories of her life. Maybe even horrible ones.

He wandered back into the master bedroom and stood in front of the big closet. Up on a shelf, far in the back, were a couple black cardboard boxes. The color appealed to him. With gloved hands, he reached out and tugged down the first one and set it on the bed, then went back for the second. He opened the first to find it was mostly mementos of her first marriage that had ended in divorce. Trips they'd taken, things they'd done, diaries, journals.

He opened up the second to find mementos of a child. Baby pictures, toddler photos, report cards. One report card noted the little girl's name was Carol. He tried to puzzle through the box, but the pictures ended when the girl was eight years old. Then he found medical reports. The trail ended abruptly there. No explanation. Being in a black box, he had to wonder if there weren't some negative connotations surrounding these memories within.

But it was obvious at the time that she'd loved the child because many of the baby photos showed the two of them cuddling. Why did it all stop? He laid things out on the bed and proceeded to take photos of what he'd found. He'd have to ask Tavika to get a search warrant to access any of this for legal use.

When he was done, he carefully replaced the boxes and took a quick look around the rest of the room. He opened the night table drawer to see if anything of value was there and found a journal.

A very old one. He picked it up and took a look. It went back fifteen years. He sat on the side of the bed, hating this glimpse into somebody else's life. Especially because the journal started on the first page with, *She's gone. My little girl is gone. I know he has her. That I should lose her to my ex … is so impossible.*

I'm dying inside.

He closed and replaced the diary. This wasn't anything to do with the Ghost. But somehow their paths had crossed with horrible consequences for her. He stood here for a long moment, hating the sense of wrongness. As if the place were being watched. Maybe *he* was being watched.

Was this in any way connected to the Ghost? Was this just the pain of a bad divorce and the husband who got custody? From her diary Jericho suspected that was likely the case. Then why kill Valerie? What possible connection could she have to the Ghost?

After the number of years he'd worked in this field, nothing surprised Jericho anymore. From fathers kidnapping their children for ransom, only to kill them and to take the money and run, to children, just babes, killing their parents, grandparents, siblings. Jericho shook his head. It was unfathomable.

He'd seen it all. Heard it all. And hated it all. Somewhere along the line humanity had taken a wrong turn. Now, as he stood in the morning light on the back steps, he felt energy reaching for him. Somebody searching for him. *Something* searching for him.

He immediately boosted his energy to shield him and to put guards in place. Using these, he kept his energy snug to his body, walked to the back fence, and, under the cover of the trees, jumped into the neighbor's yard. Out on the street he took a left and headed back around toward his vehicle.

He kept his eyes straightforward.

But, with all senses alert, he sent out feelers in every direction.

He wasn't sure what had just changed, but something had. Because now, instead of being the hunter, he'd become the prey.

WHAT THE HELL was he doing at her house? As he put on the teakettle, he kept an eye on what was going on below. He watched Jericho go around to the back of the house.

That he was there at all was unnerving. Sure they'd found her body, and the cops had come and checked out her house. All to be expected.

But this guy had come back.

He lifted his binoculars to take a closer look. Something about that asshole made him reassess. Jericho Sands looked like he was no one to cross.

Too bad. Jericho had already crossed him.

The question now was, did he add Jericho to his list, then cross him off permanently?

CHAPTER 25

TAVIKA WAS CROSSING the street, when the sneaky wrenching feeling hit her in the gut. She'd barely left the station, intent on checking on some of Sarah's friends. See if they knew more than they were letting on. Then this hit. She grasped her body, shuddering against the physical shock, and raced to the opposite side of the road, before she collapsed on a bench at a bus stop. She threw herself down on it, waiting until the foreign energy blasting through her could be stabilized.

She realized her shield was down. What the hell? Immediately she poured reinforcement energy into her system, shoring up her defenses to maximum protection. But it was draining out the hole. How had she allowed the energy barrier to go down so low? For decades she'd carried that energy up high, strong, and tight. And now, just after a few days with Jericho, she was falling apart. Stupid. Especially right now. It was also damn dangerous. And that couldn't be allowed.

An old woman with a kindly face sat down beside her. "Are you okay, dearie? You look a little peaked."

Tavika wanted to laugh … and cry. She patted the other woman's hand and stood. "I'll be fine."

She turned and walked away, wondering at the truth of that, as her steps were still unsteady, her gait weak. The speed of her attack and the damage? … It had been terrifying. A little park was around the corner, and she made her way there, one careful step at a time. Collapsing on the first bench, she felt so many energies reaching for her, and, with her shield straggling and the hole still open, they *could* reach her. It would take her a long time to repair that.

There was no time for that. She had to fix it now. If she got docked for hours of work, well, that was just what it was.

This was way too important to let slide and actually took less time than she expected, as she poured energy in to heal and to reinforce her protective guard.

She didn't recognize the original energy that had blasted at her. That was another troubling thought. The barrier was there for the Ghost and other killers like him. Something she had yet to explain to anybody. But that the minute her guard went down, someone else had blasted her …

That was scary.

Stefan's voice filled her mind. *Sorry, that was me. I didn't mean to hit you so hard. But I was trying to show you the shield was down.*

She froze. *You knew?*

I popped in to make sure you were okay, and I saw that the energy bands were low. I was curious as to why, so I sent out a blast to see if you had a new way of hiding that shield and yet keeping it as strong as possible. But your shield was down, and I hurt you. I'm so sorry. His voice was apologetic and sad.

She was still too stunned to realize the extent of what just happened. Too many things going on. Not only had her shield gone down—and she hadn't even been aware of it— but somebody had penetrated that shield, and she hadn't even noticed until she took the hit.

Why is your shield down? he asked curiously.

No idea. I didn't even notice it was, until you hit me, she said in a hoarse voice. How could it sound so odd to her own ears when she wasn't actually speaking?

Hmm. Maybe from the shock wave you sent out? Or from Jericho's attempt to bring you back?

"Oh," she replied. Relief washed through her. *That makes sense.*

Whenever we deal with heavy emotions and old energy, it causes ripples. In this case, it's the old energy you've kept locked in your heart chakra that you've been using to keep up your shield. As you drained one, you drained the other. His voice turned serious, as he added, *That is something you need to be aware of when you meet the Ghost. Because old energy will still be fueling your shield. You haven't drained it all. You have a lot in there from that time he held you. However, if you go into shock, if you become numbed by fear, if anything happens that causes you to lose control on an emotional level, the energy from your shield will shrink. And it'll make you more vulnerable than ever.*

She went numb just as she processed this.

And that's something you do not want to happen.

Not only was it something she didn't want to happen, it was something she couldn't allow to. No one knew better than she did just how dangerous the Ghost was. And, if he were coming for a second round, … she needed every available defense she could muster.

In her mind she tried to track the process of removing the old energy from her defense shield and replacing it with new, but it seemed like a complicated process that would knock her off her feet for days. Days she didn't have. What she needed was a simpler, faster method.

And even though Stefan was there, potentially willing to

help, she hesitated.

Are you always so stubborn? Stefan asked. *You only have to ask.*

She almost growled. In her head she knew it was stupid. She didn't understand why she was having such a hard time. Unless it was because he reminded her of her mother.

And that is not *a compliment,* Stefan snapped. *Just because she was your birth mother does not make her a warm, cuddly person. And just because she was psychic does not make her a generous, caring soul. I did not know your mother. I knew of her. And not a whole lot that I can read on the energy levels or in the papers say that she was like me.*

A long shuddering breath escaped Tavika's chest. Then a second. And then a third.

Take it easy. Keep letting that old air out. Get rid of all that old energy. It's coming up from way down deep. And it needs to be gone.

What about the emotions? The pain? The memories? What do I do with all those? she cried out in anguish. *I don't want to relive them. I don't want to see, to hear, or to remember any of that.*

In the softest voice she'd ever heard, Stefan asked, *And is that why you can't remember what the Ghost looks like? Because you've blocked it all out? Because you're afraid that to bring up his face is to bring up those of who passed?*

His questions ripped at her soul, tearing apart her safely confined world. He was doing just as much damage as Jericho. And he wasn't even here. How fair was that?

It's not fair. None of it is. But you can do something about this. Stefan's voice turned brisk. *I know somebody who can help. She can assist you in releasing all this and in replacing the energy in your defense shield, without having to relive all these memories. Or at least she should be able to help blank out the worst parts.*

Tavika stared dry-eyed at the park, until she felt something drip onto her hand. She reached up to touch her cheeks. Tears flowed from her eyes in a never-ending stream, yet inside she wasn't crying. Not a sound escaped her lips. It was as if her soul were crying.

And she knew she needed help. She could no longer go on. But she didn't trust anyone with this. Nor could she let anybody close enough to help her. What if they died too? For all of their difficulties, her mother had died, trying to save Tavika.

And, to her guilty shame, Tavika had let her.

JERICHO QUICKLY REACHED the safety of his truck and hopped inside. He turned on the engine and sat quietly, studying the world outside. He felt the dark energy coming, but instead of it coming from one direction, it was almost as if he were surrounded. He didn't understand. And what he didn't understand, he had a healthy respect for. He'd called out to Stefan once already, but Stefan was busy. For Stefan to ignore him meant he was helping someone else in greater need.

Given the case he was working on, he had to wonder if this darkness was the Ghost's handiwork. They had considered the Ghost might be psychic, but there'd been no reason to assume so.

It was almost a *go to* excuse when it came to cases they couldn't solve. As if the killer had some abilities that kept him out of reach of the law. Jericho had seen a few who were psychics. One who hadn't even known that's what he was.

But there'd never been signs to lead them to believe the Ghost had similar abilities.

He didn't understand this blackness that pursued him. An odd sensation wrapped around him, threatening to choke him.

He pulled up at the traffic light, then drove around the block, curious to see if he could find the source of the darkness. And found nothing. Driving carefully he headed back toward Tavika's place. It was still afternoon. She shouldn't be home from work yet.

As he drove around the park, he saw something that made him hit the brakes. Tavika sat on the bench, not twenty feet from him. He pulled in quickly and shut off the engine. The darkness, the sense of danger eased. Confused and wary, he got out and quietly closed the truck door.

Wait, Stefan ordered.

That explained why Stefan hadn't answered. He was here, working with Tavika. Jericho stopped and studied her energy. *She* was the source of the darkness.

He shook his head. Jesus, what the hell was she up to that she could transmit with so much power?

This letting-go stage will be very difficult for Tavika. I'm trying to contact Maddy to get her help.

Almost absentmindedly Jericho nodded. "That would be very good."

So far, Tavika is refusing to go to Maddy's place.

"Of course she is." Jericho motioned to the park around them. "She doesn't like closed-in spaces at the best of times." That also explains why she spent so little time in her apartment. "How about Maddy coming in spirit form? I could get Tavika back to her apartment, and the healing could happen there."

Stefan seemed to consider the matter, then said, *I just got hold of Maddy. Back in five.*

And he blinked out of Jericho's mind. No matter how often Stefan popped in and out, there was always an odd sensation; his leaving always left a void.

Jericho sat down on the bench, close enough for Tavika to know he was there but far enough to give her space.

"Go away," she muttered.

"No. I don't think that's a good idea right now."

"It doesn't matter what you think. I want to be alone."

"Too bad." He stretched out his legs, crossed them at the ankles, and dropped his head back, his arms over his chest. To anyone observing, it would look like he was taking a nap. With his eyes closed, he let the darkness emanating from her swirl around him. It wasn't dangerous. Not to him. There was so much pain, anger, and frustration that he knew she had no control over the flow. It was just spewing forth.

He sympathized. There was nothing gentle, kind, or easy about this process. Plus it was also dangerous as hell.

She was attracting energetic beings from all over the planet. Both good and bad.

He'd never seen anything so loud, so huge, and so powerful.

That she was caught in the midst of her own pain, blind to what she was actually doing, what was happening, was itself amazing. He wished she could learn to direct it, but he knew all of this had to be expunged regardless.

Nothing was comfortable about the bits and pieces he saw and heard. Voices, yelling and screaming, always voices, loud strident ones. Harsh critical voices. Complaining angry voices. He recognized her mother's voice. And then the mocking disdainful voice of her older sister. Some comments from the twin brother but not as much. As if the brother had distanced himself from all this mess. Smart boy. But these old memories, old wounds, were like tiny knife cuts—only thousands of them at once. And when mounded together in the millions, he saw the child she'd been, bleeding from every one of those voices and their words of hate.

He was relieved she was no longer struggling to send him away. All he could do was send her calm loving energy, as she went through the process.

He wasn't sure she was capable of doing anything at this point. It hurt him to hear and to see the bits and pieces of memories. And, if it hurt him, he could just imagine what it was doing to her. In the center of the storm was a huge black hole. He knew that would be the week she'd been held captive. He hoped she didn't open that here. It would be good for her to let it go but better in a safe place with someone like Dr. Maddy to help. Here Tavika had no privacy, and he wasn't sure what the effect would be on her physical body.

From where he sat, he could feel Tavika's fear. Her guilt. Such hopelessness from her.

From the faint child energy, there was a sense of desolation. As if she knew what she was unlocking was so ugly and so bad that nobody would ever love her. As he watched the pieces fly around, he wondered if Tavika knew what love was. Every child had the right to be loved. Every child or adult should know somebody cared for them. Even if it was just for an occasional hug, a smile to brighten up the day.

Everybody needed somebody.

Did Tavika know what love was? Had she ever experienced it? Only as he pondered the issue did he understand he'd taken the wrong route with her.

He should have treated her like one does a newborn, a puppy, a kitten. Someone fragile, without protection—despite all her special energy skills.

Good thing she couldn't read his mind. *Yet.* She'd hate to hear that he found her defenseless and would probably dropkick him unconscious.

He had gone about this all wrong. Instead he'd treated her like he had treated all other women, working out their particular relationships, in light of past ones, both good and bad behind them, including the dynamics of the families, both good and bad. But Tavika didn't have all that experience of working through relationships. She'd been verbally abused continually as a child, to an unbelievable degree, for the first twelve years of her life—by her own damn family. Then she'd been further verbally abused and terrorized by the Ghost.

Tavika had never experienced a healthy relationship, one of give and take, trial and error. She had never known what it meant to belong, to be accepted, to be loved—even to be loved if she happened to do something wrong or even hurtful. He shook his head. He seriously doubted this poor woman had been hugged—genuinely, with no strings attached—even ten times in her thirty-two years. Sex was great, but sex was not love. Two different things. Sex without love was meaningless, unfulfilling in the long term. He was pretty damn sure she had never experienced love—not as a friend, not as a family member, not as a sexual partner, not on any higher level of some universal love either.

Jericho felt certain that Tavika had experienced sex, as they had clearly been attracted to each other from the start. Plus he had read her thoughts that day as well. However, he had been trying not to intrude on them again, unless if needed to protect her.

Jericho was amazed that she could withstand that staggering amount of lack of sweet loving physical touch, atop a lack of any genuine emotion nearing love, all while battling that barrage of verbal abuse he had just witnessed within the evil blackness she was purging from her system.

It's a wonder she hadn't poisoned herself with all that negativity locked inside her.

It's a wonder she didn't become just like her horrid family.

It's a wonder she didn't break down mentally under all this hate, rejection, criticism, and judgment.

Tavika stood as an island. She let no man in. She let no part of herself out. She was, as always, alone.

In a way, she had been defending herself from further abuse, from further terror.

It all made so much sense now.

And she was no longer a case to him. Or a person to help or someone who could help him. She was someone he truly cared about. Someone he wanted so much more with. He'd been alone a long time. And somehow, in the last few days, she'd gone from being someone "out there" to someone "inside"—held deep within his heart.

He thought he'd been alone. Until he'd met her and understood what that really meant.

And it broke his heart.

Now he wanted to make sure that neither of them would be alone again. Not when they could be with each other.

CHAPTER 26

HOW DID SHE go on from here? It was like somebody had pulled the plug on all the emotions and pain Tavika had stuffed way down, and, instead of draining away, here she was reliving it all again.

Caught up in her chaos, she barely noticed when Jericho grabbed her gently by the arm and tugged her to her feet. "Let's go home."

She stared down at his hand. Weird colors sparked from their point of contact. She'd never seen it before. It was both amazing and terrifying. Not sure she had any strength left to fight, she stood.

He reached out his other hand to steady her. And she realized she was swaying on her feet, the world around her shaking. Barely cognizant of where he was taking her, she walked toward his truck. Yet her apartment was barely one block away. At least she thought it was. The world around her didn't look normal, not with the darkness of the stale air, the flares of heat and color.

"We'll take the truck. I know home is close, but it's too far for you right now."

Like a child, she followed his lead. When he put her in the truck, buckled her in, and shut the door, she never said a word.

At her building he nudged her to the elevator, then led

her carefully down to her apartment. Once the door was open, she stepped inside and walked straight to her bed. She still hadn't said anything but closed her eyes and let her body fall face forward. The welcome softness of the blankets reached up to meet her.

Instantly Solomon greeted her with a series of yowls and howls, before jumping up to lie on the small of her back.

In the background she heard Jericho calling out to Stefan. How was it that Stefan had nothing better to do than come when called? Like a genie. She didn't think he had any wishes that could make her life better though. Right now she'd fallen into an abyss like no other.

Interesting term came a beautiful melodious voice through her head.

Tavika smiled. She didn't know whose voice that was, but it was not hard to listen to. She rolled onto her side and curled up in the fetal position. Maybe, if the world were just, it would let her sleep this lifetime away. She closed her eyes, willing herself into unconsciousness. The woman's voice, not quite so soft or perfect now, snapped, *Not yet.*

Tavika's eyes popped open. Jericho crouched in front of her, worry lines creasing his face.

She reached out a shaky hand and stroked the wrinkles at the corners of his eyes. "So worried," Tavika whispered. "Don't be. I'm fine."

Jericho gave a half laugh. "Sweetheart, you're anything but fine. You will be though, but right now you're in crisis."

Considering the word *crisis,* she stared into his deep dark eyes. That was actually accurate. She felt like she'd been in crisis for twenty years. All she'd ever done was shove everything inside. It had been necessary to get up and to move on.

I'm Dr. Maddy. And I'll help you deal with this crisis, said the woman with the melodious voice.

Tavika smiled and let her eyelids close. Solomon slipped off her back and disappeared. This was too strange, even for him. Tavika had heard of Dr. Maddy. She was supposed to be really good. Why were all these exceptional people here helping her? She was nothing.

You need to stop thinking like that, Dr. Maddy stated. *You are exceptional.*

Too tired to argue, Tavika gave a tiny shrug, muttering, "Whatever."

I need you to lie there and to rest but do not fall asleep. Can you do that for me?

Tavika managed a tiny nod and relaxed. She wasn't even sure what was consciousness or unconsciousness at the moment. Because her mind was just … everywhere. She didn't like it. It wasn't her. It wasn't as she knew herself to be, but, at the moment, she floated—tossed and turned by whatever emotions buffeted her system. Who knew emotions had such power?

Dr. Maddy's voice rolled through her head, as she explained a few basics. *Emotions are the essential building blocks of our world. We all have them, abuse them. We rarely look after them. In your case they were so painful that they limited what you could do. You blocked them out and ignored them. That has worked on a basic survival level up until now, but it can't continue.*

Tavika stayed quiet, listening.

First, we'll do a complete scan to make sure nothing else is going on that I don't know about. Then I'll start cleaning the old dark energy. I'll try to work at such a level as to keep the actual events at bay, but some will slip through. Do you understand?

"Yes," she whispered. "I just don't understand how."

It's not necessary that you do so right now. You can always ask questions later. Right now we need to get to work.

When Dr. Maddy said *get to work*, she meant it. Tavika lay here, as somebody came with a massive vacuum that grabbed ribbons of energy and pulled them from deep in her gut. Her body twisted and turned, pulled up by the harder tugs, before crashing back onto the bed.

Somewhere in the deep recesses of her mind, she heard Jericho whisper, "Jesus. Maddy, really?"

And she realized he knew Dr. Maddy as well. Of course he did. It seemed like they were all in the know. She was out in the cold. Again.

You will never be out in the cold alone again, Dr. Maddy said. *There's no way for that to happen after this.*

There was a distant sound to Dr. Maddy's voice. A distant feeling to the events going on around Tavika. As if she'd taken that one final step of separation that she'd always been trying to achieve. It had started in childhood, then had crystallized during her nightmare week. She'd managed a major step at that time—which had allowed her to move forward in life.

Don't try to disassociate. Not right now. Your energy is too frail. You've been keeping this cauldron of emotions tightly held within you. It could blow up at some point. And most of the stuff in here is very *dark.*

Tavika found herself lying on her back, facing the ceiling, so overwhelmed by the scenario going on around her, through her, inside her, that she barely heard Dr. Maddy's last words.

But she did. And now she couldn't stop wondering what she meant. Then Dr. Maddy added, *It's* very *dangerous.*

Just what was she doing that was so dangerous?

JERICHO WATCHED FROM a safe distance. Dr. Maddy had asked him to step back a little to give her some space. He saw the darkness fill the room. He didn't understand why there was so much of it, but he could feel a lifetime of pain stuffed inside the apartment.

Neither could he disrupt Dr. Maddy long enough to ask. Jericho settled in the living room and just let her work. He knew her from years ago. The skills she had, well, they were nothing short of magical.

Catching the shimmer of another presence in the room, Jericho turned to see Stefan standing beside him in spirit form. He didn't say that very often. "Stefan, you okay?"

I'm fine, he murmured. *Tavika on the other hand is dealing with some major traumas.*

"Why is it so black? Why is there so much of it?"

The darkness speaks to the age of the energy. And there's so much of it because it was not just one little bit of trauma in her life. There was a lot of it. Whenever we have experienced trauma, other emotions go with it. We're not even talking about the Ghost yet. Her mother wasn't the easiest to live with. Neither was her sister. So this goes way back.

To Jericho there still seemed to be too much energy for something like that, but he kept his own counsel. "What will she be like when this is over?"

Stefan shot him a curious look. *It's hard to say. She spent a lifetime pretending to be this other person. Once we clean out all this damaging energy that's been poisoning her system, she should be more peaceful. But no guarantees are here, as she's also been among a lot of murderers in the past ten years. And, more than that, she's taken on bits of each victim's energy. That's why there's so much blackness. And, with all that trauma and pain came her own reaction to each event. It's kind of like a tornado, that just grows and grows and picks up more and more debris. At some point it just overwhelms.*

Now that made sense. Jericho had seen that with the homeless people Tavika had interacted with. That hard edge of hers had everybody believing she was uncaring and cold. They were wrong. She cared too much, took on too much. He didn't understand how her defense shield kept out the bad guys but could allow the hurting people to feed in and out of it. He just didn't understand what the point of the defense shield was if certain energy continued to travel through it.

And where in the hell did she get the energy to power all this energy she seemed to so easily generate?

He also had one question he needed to ask.

He hated to but knew he had to, for the sake of Hunter and Anna, not to mention for the capture of the Ghost. "How long will this take? And will Tavika lose any of her abilities or forget any of the conversations up until now?"

No way to know. Stefan shook his head. *It will take as long as it takes. She should not lose any of her memories. I also understand the time factor. But we can't have Tavika be yet another victim. If we can do anything to help her, then we need to do it. If she, in turn, can help the others, then that's a good thing all around. But this cannot be rushed.*

Damn. Jericho had really hoped for a different answer.

As he sat here on Tavika's couch, wondering what his options were, the black energy changed to an odd gray color. And, damn, if that fogginess didn't appear to morph before him. "What the hell, Stefan?" Jericho rose.

I am not sure, Stefan murmured in a low voice. *I've never seen this before.*

With the two of them standing side by side, one in physical form and one in spirit form, they watched in amazement as the gray energy softened and separated into dozens upon dozens of other spirit entities, all walking through the apartment. But so many of them. … How could she have so many people in her world?

Not just in her world—in her energy, Stefan noted in shock, reading Jericho's mind. *Dear God, no wonder she was always worn down.*

"Are these people who have passed over? Is she communicating with them? Or are they spirit entities of people in physical form but …" He let his voice trail off. This was crazy. He'd never seen anything like it.

You haven't? Hell, I haven't either. Stefan snorted. *I can't answer that question because I don't understand it myself.*

Jericho turned to stare at Stefan. "She mentioned something about going *into the abyss.* She would take these trips, where she saw through layers to find these dots, so she could follow them and see the connections of that person to other people."

Into the abyss? That's a really good way to describe it. Stefan smiled, his gaze returning once again to Tavika. *She's stronger than I thought. I don't know anybody who's managed to travel through the layers and not lose themselves forever.*

"What do you mean by *layers?*" Jericho asked.

Think of the universe around us as more than just dimensions. It's almost worlds upon worlds in layers—or bubbles. Your world atop someone else's world. All of this functions in one dimension, so people can go about their day in happy ignorance, living in their own layer. Other people function in other layers.

And so on and so on. The problems occur when people cross through the layers and connect with somebody else's.

Stefan motioned at Tavika. *The Ghost might function on one layer completely different than the one Tavika is on. But, because of one meeting, a dotted pathway exists between them now. Say, she's tracking somebody and sees a dotted highway. She'll go through the different layers to see where each person intersects with another.*

Stefan's smile widened. *I can track somebody in an instant, but I can't go back into their history. We know those who can go back for a few minutes to read the energy of time. But to actually take a person's pathway and track it through the layers to where it intersected with other people? Now* that *is a talent.*

Jericho stared at Tavika with new respect. "And can she still do that after all this?"

Stefan spun to stare at him, his eyebrows raised almost to his hairline. *I hope so. We need her skills. We need what she can offer those of us who work in this field. Not only that, she needs us. She's been alone for a long time. That's why all these people surround her. She's collected bits and pieces of everybody she's ever touched, so as to not be alone. But—because they're all in different layers, different levels, different forms of existence, from ghost to spirit entities to some of us able to cross the divides— Tavika is essentially still alone.* Stefan's smile flashed his way.

"No." Jericho gave a hard shake of his head. "She is no longer alone. She has me."

Jericho didn't know why he had declared that out loud, but it felt right. If nothing else, he'd stand by her side and be her friend. He knew full well that more was going on between them, but he didn't know how far or how deep the relationship would go. One thing he did know—she didn't have to walk alone anymore.

HE SAT BACK in his big comfy recliner and let out a huge sigh. Things were calm. Almost too calm. No one had been around for a while. Days, it seemed. He knew the cops were working the crimes in the background.

He'd planned for that.

Yet he hadn't expected the unnerving sensation of waiting. He'd committed many murders but not as many or as fast as now.

He wanted to pick up and to continue but found his normal self-confidence shaken.

He didn't like it. He'd never come close to getting caught. And, of course, he wasn't now either. But, for his lover, he had to remain calm and to appear to be in control. That was the thing about love. He loved but was also loved by others. And sometimes their form of love was stifling, as they watched and hovered over him.

He couldn't let them know.

No unraveling was allowed here. He couldn't afford to let it.

CHAPTER 27

H OW WAS IT possible to have all these feelings washing through the center of her in broken snippets? She was buffeted from side to side, as they shook the foundation of her being, yet the details were obscure. She recognized voices, places, names, faces. Cases, acquaintances, childhood friends. But so much of this had been lost to time. She didn't understand why all this was familiar but, at the same time, didn't come from that one particular place of her life that she knew was so very damaging.

We'll get there, Dr. Maddy noted, her voice soothing. *You're doing great. Just keep letting this go. These time bombs were ready to go off, so I'm opening a hole in that block to reduce the pressure, letting the emotions flow. Releasing these can have the effect of them being new again. Raw. And that's what we're trying to avoid, but it's almost impossible. I'm doing my best though. Just let the river flow.*

I don't want to look at the memories of that time, Tavika stated abruptly, then paused, as she realized she was communicating in her mind—with Dr. Maddy—in such a way that was natural, normal.

Dr. Maddy smiled. *Of course you don't want to see those. And, if I weren't here right now, and if Jericho hadn't done what he'd done, and if you hadn't been doing whatever it was you were doing at the time, then that would be an option. We wouldn't look at any of this, but, at some point in the near future, you'd be in deep trouble. And that is not something you want. Let's deal with everything we can right now, and maybe, over the next few weeks or months, we can slowly ease out some more.*

Tavika felt such a sense of relief to know Dr. Maddy wouldn't insist on all this happening today.

A light tinkling laughter filled the room, as Tavika realized Dr. Maddy was reading Tavika's thoughts. Psychics saw too much. With no privacy she was ripped wide open—raw. Everything bare for everybody to see and to laugh at again. That brought up another barrage of horrible feelings.

No one is laughing at you, Dr. Maddy corrected. *That's the first thing you need to understand. Mothers are supposed to be warm, cuddly, and supportive. But they aren't all that way. And you won the loser's lottery when it came to yours. She wanted you to be bigger, better, brighter. She wanted to take pride in your accomplishments, and, because she couldn't, she kept driving at you to be better. But her methods were questionable, at best. The end result was, she made you feel demeaned, minimized, as if you had no value. But you don't have to continue to feel that way. Your mother is long gone. You cannot give away your power to her anymore.*

She's not, you know? Tavika didn't understand where all this honesty was coming from, but she'd never told anybody this before.

Dr. Maddy paused, a gentle hum in the air as she processed Tavika's words. *You mean, she's not gone?*

Tavika shook her head. *No, her ghost is tied to the house, where it all happened.*

In a way that makes sense. And what about your sister?

Tavika nodded. *Bellamy is there too.*

And are they still the same personalities?

Tavika winced. *Yes, very much so. But more focused, as if they're locked into the actual event. I've tried to talk to them until I was blue in the face, but they are convinced I want to die, and, if they stay, maybe they can help me out. My mother and I both know my end is near.*

Dr. Maddy's movements turned jerky, as she understood what Tavika was saying.

And maybe they can, she replied in a calm voice. *Fate says, this is what'll happen, but we do have free will. We can change the outcome.*

I told Jericho that, Tavika stated, *but he says, most of the time, his visions are deadly accurate.*

Then we'll have to do whatever we can to make sure he's wrong this time.

Tavika smiled. *Can't say I've cared either way, up to now.*

That's because of all this weighing you down. You've been living under a dark, ugly cloud, Dr. Maddy explained quietly. *It will be different from now on.*

I hope not too different. I still need to take down the asshole who killed my family. Growing up and knowing that was my one purpose in this short life? Well, that's a lot of pressure, but it gave me a reason to go on.

Maybe now you'll be able to recognize him—or you might once we open up that time.

Tavika wasn't sure anything was worth going back there. Even if it meant being able to find him faster. Some things were just too hard to face.

However, if you don't face it, it will kill you one way or the other. At least if you open up that nightmare in your heart, you can clear it out and come out as a fighter, versus someone paralyzed in victim mode.

JERICHO DIDN'T KNOW if he should tell Tavika that he knew what she and Dr. Maddy were saying. He doubted it. Tavika would not appreciate the fact that he heard most of the conversation going on in her head.

Stefan had long since disappeared, but he had Celina, his partner, to return to. Maddy had Drew too. Jericho figured Drew must have the patience of a saint to be okay with her bopping off all over the globe at a moment's notice. She was often gone for hours and hours on end. Then there were her patients. Dr. Maddy poured her heart into her project, Maddy's Floor. Now she'd started teaching and was flying between Norway and the US, as she consulted on their version of her center. There was talk of one in England, but Jericho hadn't heard the details to know if it was going through yet. Often she could do her energy work from anywhere in the world.

Sometimes she had to be there for hands-on work.

The real detriment in setting up centers like Maddy's Floor was they needed to have people like Maddy—powerful healers to be the heart and center of the projects. They could train support staff in the different healing modalities, but Dr. Maddy was gifted in so many ways that one couldn't train as her replacement.

Either the healers were gifted naturally and could be trained to do more or they weren't, and their training needed to be for support activities. Maddy had spent a fair bit of time looking for other people like herself to take on a second or third center, much like Stefan was involved in the new children's wing at the hospital. But that was the extent of Stefan's involvement, as his time was at a premium too.

Jericho's phone rang. "Hunter, any news?"

"False trails, missed ones, and diverting directions. Everything but what I need, which is a solid lead on this little girl. If she's been left alone as much as Anna says she has, there's a good chance she's dead. I'd really like to find her alive, but, in order to do that, we need to make this happen now."

Jericho looked at Tavika, lying on the bed. Solomon slept at her feet. Close, but not touching. He wondered what the cat felt with all the energy work going on. Tavika looked better and worse at the same time. As if she'd been to hell and back. Still, Dr. Maddy didn't appear to be done.

"Let me call you back in a couple hours. I might have something for you by then."

"You sure you can't make that half an hour instead?" Hunter rang off, but the anger and frustration were evident in his voice.

Jericho got up and walked to the bedroom portion of the apartment. He knew he had no business approaching with a request at this time, but, considering a little girl's life was hanging in danger, maybe they would forgive him.

What little girl? Talk to me, Maddy said. *I thought it had been determined she was already dead?*

"Tavika told me that she had caught sight of connecting dots, when she was doing her interdimensional traveling." He shrugged his shoulders. "I know that's not how she phrased it, but she was doing something in between the etheric layers. She has some weird system to see patterns and to then connect the dots between people, places, and things. She thought she saw Anna's trail. Unfortunately that's also where I tried to help by pulling her out of that world and back into ours by giving her that blast that caused all this."

Interesting, Dr. Maddy replied. *I do like the idea of some-*

body being able to do that.

Jericho reached up and rubbed his temples. "I do too. But, if that little girl is alive, we need to find out where she is. And we need to find out fast."

What would you like me to do?

"Any chance Tavika is strong enough to journey back into her layer of shit and see where that pattern led to?" he asked. "Or will that hurt her? We're frustrated because we have no leads, and Tavika held out this tantalizing tidbit of hope."

Right. Dr. Maddy's tone was brusque, as she added, *I'll check it out.*

And she disappeared from his mind.

Jericho didn't know what that meant. Was she checking out Tavika's abilities? Or what Tavika had in her mind? Or if Tavika was capable of doing her little into-the-abyss stunt again?

The thing about psychics was, some were too flaky to be useful; others felt they should be on all the time. Some people with abilities were unstable and couldn't talk about this at all. Everyone was different. Many were gemstones, like Tavika, who only knew half of what they thought they did. When she had developed her skills, she had done it solo, all in her own unique way. She had no teachers or trainers to show her to do it this way. And that meant she had created something nobody else had ever seen before. That was a gift in itself.

"Jericho?"

He spun to see Tavika, sitting on the edge of the bed. Her face was pale, and her body looked frail, shaky. He rushed to her side. "I'm so sorry, Tavika. I didn't mean to disturb what you're doing."

She waved off his concern. "A little girl is in trouble. We have to do everything we can to help her."

"And is there anything you can do?" he asked.

Using his arm, she stood up and took a few experimental steps. "Honestly I have no idea. Everything's changed. I don't feel the same inside or out. I like to think my methods and the tools I utilized are still available to me, but I don't know if my intuitive ability to use them is still there."

Shit. He hadn't considered that aspect.

Dr. Maddy's voice spoke out through the room. *No place like now to try. I will stay here for another few minutes to make sure she gets through this, but, after that, I'm gone.*

Taking a few more steps Tavika walked to the kitchen table, where she sat down. "Normally I would work from the couch, but I'm not sure I have the strength. This might be better for the moment."

He sat down opposite her. "Is there anything I can do to help?"

She shook her head. "No. But, as I'm a little out of touch, feeling a bit rough around the edges, not to mention raw, I can't say the transition will be terribly easy. There could be a mini boom or, as you called it, shock wave coming your way. You need to protect yourself. I'd like to think I have the skill to not make such an amateur mistake again, but I'm not on my game tonight. So it's possible." She gave him an apologetic look, then bowed her head and rested her hands flat on the table.

He stepped back, mindful of what had happened last time. She was right; she wasn't in the best shape for this, ... but he was desperate.

She took several deep breaths, which he recognized as a normal prelude for any kind of psychic trip. And suddenly she raised her head. The light in her eyes held an unworldly glow. Something seemed foreign about her right now. If he were being truthful, he'd say it was magical.

Then her hand started to move, as if she saw something nobody else could. She was pushing gently, flicking stuff sideways. He wanted to ask questions, to have some running tour-guide commentary, telling him exactly what was going on. Of course anything like that would cause a disruption for her, making it that much harder to work. So far, there had been no shock waves. He was very grateful.

He sat back down and watched. And waited. At one point in time she seemed to suck in her breath, and her back stiffened, as if she'd seen something that scared her. He leaned forward, questions on his tongue, but he bit them back and waited.

After a moment she leaned forward again and started to clean the air in front of her. When she reached down and picked up something out of the air that he couldn't see, he still knew that she saw something there. And he was hooked.

This was something he'd never expected to see. He had no idea if any of this would provide solid results, when plain old detective work hadn't done anything for them. But, for some reason, Tavika had picked up on the blue dots that supposedly signified Anna. He was willing to go with that.

If she found anything.

When she turned her head to stare directly at him, he rose and walked around the table to stand beside her. "Tavika?" he asked gently. "Did you find something?"

She tapped the table at the far end. He looked down, wondering what it meant.

"She lives at 427 Rhue Street."

His eyebrows shot upward. "Yes, she did. Do you know

where she is now?"

She stared at him. "No, you don't understand. She's at 427 Rhue Street."

"No. She *was* there. That's where she was kidnapped. We've been tracking her, but we've found no sign of her."

"It's like she never left the house," Tavika whispered. "None of this is logical."

He left that for the moment. In a low voice, he asked, "Is Anna okay?"

Tavika gave him a half smile. "Define *okay*."

He waved his arm impatiently. "Is she alive?" he snapped.

"She's alive, but she's dying. I don't know if you can make it in time."

"Is she injured, bleeding?"

"No. But she's alone, she's crawled inside. She knows he's coming back. And, if she's still alive, he will kill her then."

"Do you know when he's coming back?"

She whispered in a soft voice, "Yes. He's coming back tonight."

CHAPTER 28

S HE DIDN'T UNDERSTAND the pathway in front of her. It was as if the little girl had never left the house. Surely the place had been thoroughly searched? She knew the police wouldn't leave anything untouched if a little girl had been kidnapped. What the hell was going on?

Tavika stared down at the universe below, with its millions of lights shining. She tried to defocus to let the pattern show up. It helped her to see which ones she could access. This world looked different every time she came here. And, if she didn't follow a pattern at the time, she had no guarantee she could pick it up again on her next trip.

It was frustrating as hell.

Her mother didn't even know she could do this. But, if she had, she might've had some words of wisdom to show her the way. Although chances were her mother would've just told her to figure it out on her own.

As Tavika defocused, the blue stood out strong in a series of circles. It was Anna. Relieved, knowing it could have been anyone, she searched the pattern for an end, where Tavika could lock down and say where the little girl was, but everything kept coming back to the same place. She had no choice but to assume the little girl was still there—although that wasn't an assumption she could make from this far away.

Maybe that was the problem.

She stepped into another layer, a lower one, closer. She'd been this close before, trying to hunt the Ghost, but without any luck, as he somehow was untraceable. She couldn't afford to lose Anna. Several more steps down, she slipped through another cloud to see the bright and shiny dots off to the left. She stopped and studied the tiny little jagged line from one house to the other. And understood. Anna was very close to her home but was *not* at the same house.

No. She's in one of the neighboring houses, she told Jericho urgently. *Now that I'm closer, I can see her energy has been circling the area. And it keeps coming back to the same place, but that's because she's been there before. She's been there many times. She's at a house where she's been before. And it's close to her home.*

How close? Jericho asked. *Can you get close enough to see if it's next door or are we still talking one mile away?*

Good question. She closed her eyes and sank deeper and deeper and deeper. *I'm going closer.*

She felt the chill air on her skin. She didn't understand why there were physical changes, when all this was in the nonphysical realm. But there were sensations. She opened her eyes to see how she was doing in terms of distance.

And gasped. She was high above the city. Instead of dots, a new ribbon led her right down to a single house. Almost a ribbon highway. On a whim, she mentally stepped out onto the road and let go.

And she slipped all the way down to the end of it, land-ing with a hard *bump*, the physical jolt a shock to her senses—like tiny razor blade cuts all over her flesh. She wanted to cry out but knew that silence, for whatever reason, was paramount. She sucked back her breath, holding still, until her body adjusted. After a moment, she took a careful look around. She'd never traveled so deep, so far before. She wasn't sure if she ever wanted to again.

This was some scary shit.

Wherever she'd landed was a place of darkness. She wasn't sure what happened to the town or the bubble of lights that had been all around her. Slowly she climbed to her feet, looking down to actually see what appeared to be shoes at the end of wispy legs. She knew when she went into the abyss, she was in an etheric form. She started in the physical, and, as she sank deeper and deeper, she lightened the load of her existence, until she was basically only in spirit.

Apparently her spirit had feet.

And that made no sense. Perturbed and confused, she took a few experimental steps, brushing her hands down over her pants, feeling the smooth material, but at the same time her fingers slid through the material.

This energy stuff was unbelievable. No way she could explain it to anyone. They couldn't begin to understand.

Jericho, Stefan, and potentially Dr. Maddy would understand though. Tavika gave her head a shake, wondering at the differing sensations of weight and weightlessness all at the same time.

She turned to look around her. Was she alone?

Was Anna here?

The darkness was all-encompassing. She literally couldn't see anything. It was dark, like when she was in the middle of the clouds. She needed to move all this away, so she saw behind it. She quickly started shifting the dark energy. She assumed she was inside some sort of space. The clouds were resistant. She tried to force them, and they glued together tighter than ever. Frowning, she stepped back and reassessed. When she did this kind of work from above, she had to go in with peace and love in her heart. The minute she tried to force something, it didn't work.

She sank back down into a sitting position and closed her eyes. Willing the darkness to subside and to show her what was on the other side, she opened up a little bit of her own energy, as if shining a light on the problem. She wasn't sure what the effect was, but, in the face of light, the darkness moved away. More things she didn't understand. More things to ponder later in life.

She added more energy at a slower pace, so the light built up brighter and brighter. Then she could look around the darkness and see what was here. She stood up and walked four feet in one direction and found a wall. She turned slowly to look how far it went. To the right it only went about forty feet. And everything in the radius of her light was empty.

She turned to the left and did the same thing. Also empty. Twisting, she looked behind her at the place where she'd landed. It seemed important that she understood where she'd entered. She looked up, knowing there wouldn't be a shaft above her but unable to stop considering the possibility that maybe it was some kind of a sign.

But found nothing. Staring straight ahead, she added more light to see what was in front of her. It took a lot of light to see the eight-foot-long wall. She walked slowly, counting her steps. One. Two. Three. By the time she hit eight, she was up against the concrete. Trying to be systematic, she searched out the darkness on the right.

Nothing.

She spun to the left, wondering for what possible purpose Tavika was here, if this room was empty. She tilted her head to the side, and instincts had her up the wattage of energy. And there, just in the shadows, was a curled-up bundle of cloth. She slowly walked over and reached down to find a child. A small delicate-looking little girl with blond braids. Her heart breaking, Tavika reached out a hand, afraid to feel the chilled skin of death, but found her skin clammy and cold, yet blood still flowed through it.

And she realized she'd found Anna. Tavika tried to pick up the child only to have her arms go through the child's body. She was in spirit form. The child was of flesh. Tavika needed help. She didn't know how to get anybody here to this place.

She sent out a panicked alert.

Then she heard footsteps.

Dear God. She crouched down beside the child and gave her a shake, but she appeared to be unconscious. Or actually she had a different appearance—as if she'd gone away. A common event when someone's life became too difficult, when the pain became too much. Tavika knew how that worked. She'd been there once.

Stefan, can you hear me? She's here. I found Anna.

Stefan's strong, calm voice centered her. *Where is she? What kind of condition is she in?*

I don't know. I stepped on a highway of blue ribbons and landed beside her. We're in a dark room. But I hear footsteps. She's in bad shape, Stefan. Please help.

Stay calm. Can you tell me a general location? Tell me any-thing about the house? Can you look out of the window?

It's one of the neighboring houses to her home. I can't see the other ones, but I can sense she knows where she is—only she's gone away in her mind.

If she's alive, her soul is there. And we need to find her now. Hurry, please, dear God, someone's coming.

Tavika, I'm tracking you. I'll drag Jericho along with us. And Dr. Maddy. Think of us as the emergency response team.

She froze. Was that possible? She turned to look at the center of the room, to look where she'd landed here. And, sure enough, it filled with light. She could identify them. Dr. Maddy's energy was the pale cream. Jericho's was green. And Stefan was the golden light. Their combined energies glowed strongly in the room. Stefan raced to Anna's side. So much energy filled the room that it was well lit now, and Tavika saw the door, as Jericho bolted toward it. Dr. Maddy crouched beside Anna.

Her soul cord is intact, Maddy noted. *I need to call her home.*

Tavika felt like she'd suddenly walked into an emergency room, only one on an alien planet. … Dr. Maddy reached out and put her hand on the faint silver cord and gave it a shake.

In stunned amazement, Tavika watched as the little girl snuffled. Wait. … What? Then Anna moaned in pain, as if her body had been sitting for way too long in the one spot.

Stefan, Tavika asked, *how do we get her physical help?*

It's already on the way.

And the footsteps? Tavika asked. *How do we catch him?* They were only here in spirit form. She needed her kick-ass fighting skills to take down this asshole. Right here, right now. Except she was no more than a cloud of dust, one with feet.

None of that made any sense to her. But it was what it was.

Tavika? It was Jericho's voice. *Come with me.*

She turned to see the green energy at the doorway. She drifted over toward him. In a low voice she asked, *What are we doing?*

Going to set a trap for him.

She liked that idea. *How?*

First, let's see if you can go through the door.

She frowned and approached it. She reached out a hand for the doorknob, and it went right through.

Keep going through, he urged. *See if you get through to the other side.*

She shot him a startled look, but, already off balance, she just let herself fall through the door. On the other side she saw a basement. But this section was almost like an old root cellar. Walled off with no lights.

Anyone there? he asked.

No. She tilted her head, then added in a soft whisper, *Someone is coming.*

Try to open the door.

She hopped to her feet and reached out once again, but her hand went through the knob.

I can't. She frowned. *Just come through the way I did.*

I can't.

She frowned at the note of change in his voice. She reached a hand through the door and held it out to him. *Grab my hand.*

She felt the energy flare at her fingertips. She smiled and said, *Now walk through the door.*

And, sure enough, there he was beside her. He grinned. *I like that trick.*

Still doesn't help us catch the kidnapper. He's in solid physical form. We're not.

True. His voice was too cheerful.

She eyed him, warily startled to see his eyes really clearly in the center of the green energy. *And that means you have a trick to show me?*

Maybe. He went to the bottom of the stairs, and they heard the footsteps moving around calm, steady, almost unconcerned. But, in the distance, she heard sirens.

The footsteps froze.

What if he runs away?

Jericho was already racing up the stairs. At the top he turned to look at her. She peered around to realize the door was closed. She grabbed his hand and walked through, dragging him with her. In the kitchen they watched a man stare through the kitchen window down the street. As if wondering whether the police were coming toward him.

Do you know this man? she asked.

Oh, yeah. I sure do. Jericho turned to look at her. *It's Anna's uncle.*

HOW MANY TIMES had Jericho seen that uncle in the news? Pretending to be grieving, sorrow in his eyes because his niece was missing. He'd been sure that some pedophile in the neighborhood had snatched her. And here he'd held her captive all along.

How sick and twisted was that?

Something was just so damn wrong about this that Jericho wanted to rip the man's head off his shoulders. How could he just let Anna suffer like that? Leave her alone until she died, now that he was done with her?

Get me outside the house, he told Tavika.

It was so damn odd what she was doing, but it was also incredibly convenient. He needed this skill. Stefan had long told Jericho that he could learn so much more, but, so far, there hadn't been much he'd found lacking.

Today was an entirely different day.

Tavika grabbed his hand and walked to the outside of the front door. There he turned to look at the front of the house.

It wasn't Anna's house. It wasn't even her uncle's, but it was one not very far away. It was 247 Rhue Street.

So close.

It was an old house, fifty, sixty years at least. How many still had root cellars in them anymore? In the distance he heard the sirens, as the police cars turned the corner, racing toward them.

Take me back inside, he said urgently. Tavika grabbed his hand, and together they walked through the front door. He bolted into the kitchen, but the room was empty. They heard noises overhead. Jericho raced upstairs to find the uncle packing, panic on his face, his movements erratic, unsure.

An overnight bag stood open on the bed. A small stack of what looked like some business papers sat beside it.

The uncle snatched up clothes from the dresser, dropped several pieces, picked them up, and threw everything into the bag. And went back for more. When Jericho saw the Santa suit hanging in the closet, he remembered the faint sounds of Christmas carols playing in the background.

The sirens parked outside the house.

The uncle froze, then swore and finally just shoved all the papers into the overnight bag to race back down to the kitchen, taking the stairs two at a time.

Jericho, on his heels, passed Tavika trying to stop the man, but, of course, her hands went right through him.

The uncle grabbed his keys and bolted out the kitchen door.

And raced right into Hunter's arms.

OKAY, SO MAYBE he was unraveling a little bit. He stared at the medication in his hands. He'd taken various shit off and on for years. Damn army doctors put him on something a long time ago.

Sometimes he took it, and sometimes he didn't.

When he got nervous, these pills were great to stave off a panic attack. He put the pills back in the cupboard.

Not today. It wasn't that bad. He just had to clean up more. Then he'd be fine.

CHAPTER 29

S ITTING ON THE couch, cuddling Solomon, Tavika contemplated recent events. As days went, this was one of the most exciting and satisfying conclusions to any trip she'd taken into the abyss.

Before, whenever she'd gone into the abyss, she had been looking for information to help her find a criminal or a piece of evidence that would allow her to nail their ass to the wall. But this was the first time she'd gone directly into a scene.

And saved a child.

Being part of the team had been exhilarating, and she admitted privately, it was addictive.

The sense of satisfaction, the relief of knowing she'd helped save a child? … Well, that was pretty spectacular too.

She dealt with murder all the time. There were other cases she handled too, but generally murder ended up on her desk. And she appreciated the challenge. She hated the injustice. It angered her the way so many tossed a life to the side, as if it had no value. But, in all those cases, those people were dead already. All Tavika could do was bring closure to the families, bring criminals to justice.

She followed Jericho into the kitchen, then paused to fill Solomon's bowl. Poor kitty. Her life had been crazier than usual these last few days. At least the apartment was empty of ghosts and people. She didn't understand a lot of what had gone on earlier, but she felt better, lighter. Dr. Maddy had told her to get up and to walk around on a regular basis. That she needed to move old energy and sluggish muscles. She'd almost been affronted at the idea that her muscles were sluggish. Then she understood that meant old energy moved through the tendons, muscles, and bones of her body. And that, for a while, her legs would feel heavy and sore, as if she'd run one hundred miles the day before. And, as usual, Dr. Maddy was right.

The pain was excruciating.

Jericho pulled out a chair and spun it around for her. "Sit."

She sat, moaning slightly as her joints shifted. He put on the kettle, intent on making her some tea.

"Coffee would be good too, if you prefer," she noted quietly.

"Maybe. But I need food now," Jericho replied, fatigue eating at his voice. "I'm starving. I don't know about you, but I've burned through most of my reserves."

Tavika reassessed her body and realized she was hungry too. "I'm starving. I don't know why. I didn't do anything."

He snorted. "It's amazing you can function at all. You did a ton of energy work that burned so much fuel that I now understand why you stay so thin. But you need to eat more. Your body needs sustenance. You have to feed it in order to keep doing this kind of stuff."

She studied him carefully. "Will I keep doing more of this stuff?"

He shot her a quick smile, followed by a wink, and added, "I hope so. You're very good at it."

Tavika raised her eyebrows. "How would you know if I'm any good?"

"*Anna.* You found her."

Tavika settled back. Disgruntled, she replied, "But that was just one case."

"But, as a test case goes, you showed up in a pretty spectacular fashion."

"It never occurred to me that I could do what I did. I might have saved Anna earlier," she noted, shamefaced.

"There's been no time."

He had said it so simply that she had to cast her mind back, trying to figure out when she could've saved her. They'd had no idea Anna was even around here, until last night. Technically, putting her name to her spirit didn't happen until this morning. That made Tavika feel a little better.

She saw how, with a certain amount of experience with this energy work, other skills would be much easier to acquire. Now that she had found a certain appetite for this work, she wanted to learn more, to do more. Her mother would say, *Finally.* Maybe Tavika could get some help from the people in this group. She had no idea how many others there were. She'd love to meet more people like her. After a lifetime of avoiding them, she now was encircled by them.

"You need to learn control. Did your mother teach you?"

"Not so much." Disgruntled, Tavika stared off into space. Why did everything come back around to that woman? Her mother had loved Tavika in her own way, but damn, her mother hadn't been easy to live with.

"Did you ever wonder if your mother had anything to do with the Ghost?"

"What?" Startled, she turned to look at him. "Why are you asking that?"

"I just wondered," Jericho replied, shrugging his shoulders. "I remembered the headlines. Did she help the police often?"

"Yes," Tavika noted shortly. "She didn't go out of her way to help many, but she loved publicity. So she picked the cases she could do easily." She knew that sounded harsh, and she didn't mean it that way, but her mother was not a Good Samaritan.

Her mother worked very hard in creating her skills, so they were honed to perfection, but they were not for free for anybody. Maybe that was part of the mystery of her mother. And Jericho had brought up a good point. Tavika had often wondered why and how her mother or even her family had crossed paths with the Ghost. But Tavika had no answers.

"Jericho, do *you* have any information on this? My family does not fit his pattern. And neither do we have any cases linked to the Ghost from before my family was targeted." She frowned, as he shook his head. "And why don't I remember?"

He reached out and brushed her cheek. "Maybe you do, just not in any way you were willing to believe in. And, by not believing, you didn't look any deeper. Think about what you've gone through the last couple hours, days, and see how much everything you thought you knew maybe isn't the truth. All the information you had inside, you had locked down and had refused to examine in order to keep functioning. Now that some has surfaced and been released, you may very well find memories weren't the truth at all."

She gave him a startled look. "You're saying that I made this up? No way. Those nightmares were too damn real. Those memories are locked in stone."

"No." His voice was solid and reassuring. "It's not that

you made it up. A young mind often glosses over a lot of the details and creates fabrications to make it easier to live with. You may not have made anything up, but you may have allowed your mind to ignore a few truths because that saved some pain."

She remained on the chair, tired but energized. Something to his words she didn't understand. How could she? So much was going on. Her energy seemed to zap any unwanted blackness out of her with these little sparks.

"You may find all this easier to deal with in a day or two, when things calm down within your system. When your body and your psyche have a chance to smooth the rough edges, so it's not so raw."

"And yet it's because of all this that I managed to find Anna."

He gave her a gentle smile. "Exactly." He turned to the kitchen and said, "We did not buy enough groceries for too many more meals."

She barely heard, her mind locked into the maelstrom of emotions inside her. She had developed her skills in a major direction to help Anna. It could also be because a lid got ripped off her memories. Emotions flowed through her. Good emotions and bad—childhood ones ripping at her. She heard insults from other children. Cutting remarks from her sister. Laughing, teasing from her brother. Just memories. Old memories. And yet nowhere were there any of her father. Apparently he had not been happy when her mother got pregnant with twins. He'd taken off soon afterward.

Tavika would like to know if her mother got colder and angrier from that point or if she'd always been that way. Maybe she was only that way with Tavika. Given how messed up people felt after a trauma, maybe her mother had blamed Tavika for her father leaving. Yet her mother had never blamed Travis. *No.* He, with Bellamy, were the golden children. Tavika on the other hand …

She sat, content to watch Jericho once again take command of the kitchen and produce something that smelled absolutely lovely from the hamburger he'd bought.

She realized that, not at any point in all these years, did she consider tracking down her father. Maybe she should. Maybe he was just sitting off to the side, waiting, hoping that, when she grew up, she'd contact him.

Her gaze fell to her hands in her lap. But she hadn't.

She took a deep breath, easing more tension from her shoulders. Old injuries, wounds on so many levels, all came to the surface to be released. All she had to do was let them go. A cup of coffee was placed in front of her. She stared at it, wondering where her love of coffee came from. She'd loved it, even as a young child. And ignored those who tried to stop her from drinking coffee. Her brother hated it. Her sister said it was poison. Her mother never touched the stuff. Maybe Tavika loved coffee because, once again, the rebellious child was trying to make a place for herself in a family she didn't fit into.

"Ease up on the heavy thoughts," Jericho suggested. "Lots of old stuff's gonna come up. See it. Observe it. Don't get caught up in it. Just let it go. Keep taking lots of deep breaths, and let all this stuff fly away."

She studied him, loving the lean, efficient movements as he worked in the kitchen. A man who knew what he was up to. A man who understood. He was so very capable.

She really appreciated that minimum of expended movement. No wasted effort in any area. It was fascinating to watch.

She considered all the men she worked with. Some were good. Some lousy. Most of them in between. They probably thought she was in the middle too. But she never gave more of herself to them than she had to. Because she gave all of herself to her work.

She winced. That probably didn't say anything good about her either.

Jericho turned to study her. "It's getting awfully dark in here. Depressing. Can you get rid of it all and bring in something light and easy?"

"Sorry?" she asked in surprise. "Not sure what you're actually asking me to do."

He turned around a large beautiful tomato in his hand, studying it intently. "Find a way in your mind to visualize all the darkness in this room and then imagine a filtration system sucking out the old and piping in good clean energy. That's the fastest way to change the air in a room. Right now so much stuff is going on that the atmosphere is dark. It's your old stuff, sitting here. Just let go. Not just from your body but get rid of it from the area around you. Blast it out into space."

That startled a laugh out of her. Obediently she closed her eyes and imagined an air filtration system completely exchanging the air. Happy to play along, she turned up the knob on the imaginary system and blasted it throughout the small apartment.

"Whoa," Jericho said in surprise. "That's a powerful vacuum."

She opened her eyes and stared around the room. It looked the same. But he was right—it was fresher smelling and lighter feeling. She shook her head in wonderment. "How is it everyone doesn't know to do this?"

"That's one of the travesties of our world right now. There's so much the public could learn to use to make their lives easier, but none of it's taught. And then when people do find out, it all comes under the category of woo-woo stuff that should be avoided."

How sad was that? She picked up her coffee and had a sip. She loved the taste. Had he bought a fancy coffee when he'd been out? "Okay, what coffee is this?"

He laughed and brought over a plate of sliced tomatoes, onions, and pickles. He quickly returned with hamburger buns and patties. "It's the same old coffee that you have. Once again the benefit of letting go of all that old garbage is it's cleaning out your system and making you feel fresher. And that includes your taste buds. So if the coffee tastes much better imagine what these burgers will taste like."

"I can't wait." With an easy atmosphere and lots of laughter, she quickly built a massive burger and dug in. After taking the first bite she just sat back and chewed in joy.

"See? Everything must have its time. But when it's past its time, it has to be released. When you release it, you make room for something new, fresh. Doing this on a regular basis keeps your eyesight bright, your hearing strong, your taste buds excited."

She quickly finished off her burger. As she wiped her fingers on the napkin, her phone buzzed. She knew it was going to be Dispatch, but she wasn't sure how much more she could do tonight. Jericho reached across and covered her hand with his. "Another truth. Everything happens for a reason in the time it's meant to."

Watching his face, she picked up her phone. She wasn't sure what he meant, but when she considered all the things that had happened and that she knew were still to come, it wasn't reassuring.

"Bantrell here."

"We have a report of a deceased male in an office build-ing on Main Street. Seventh floor."

Tavika pinched the bridge of her nose. "I'm on my way."

She put her phone down and stared at the table. She'd wondered if this moment would come. Then she raised her gaze to Jericho. "I didn't tell you but somewhere in the last couple crazy days I had a vision." She winced at the look on his face. "Although as I don't see visions, maybe it was something else."

She stood, reached for her weapon holster. And then her jacket. Jericho followed her to the door. Silent at her side.

At the doorway she turned to face him. "In that vision I was looking out from somebody's eyes. I was in the room, staring down, but I was inside a body and could only see what this person saw. He was studying a dead man in an office building. The dead man wore a janitor's outfit."

She picked up her phone, shook it in front of him. "That was Dispatch calling. They just found a body in an office building downtown."

"I'm coming with you."

For the first time she wouldn't mind his presence there. Now that she understood he could do so much. Then she frowned. "I can't let you into the crime scene." Then she tilted her head. "You could come in spirit form though."

And his smile, when it came, was breathtaking.

As if an olive branch of friendship had been offered and accepted, she could almost see the shift in the energy between them.

Acceptance was a powerful thing.

Still uncomfortable with what was happening between them, to the newness of it all, she picked up her keys and walked out the door.

JERICHO WATCHED TAVIKA go, loving her smooth long strides, as she shifted from a woman dealing with a personal healing crisis to this no-nonsense professional, heading out to do a job so few in the world could do.

He really admired her. What she'd done for Anna was unbelievable. His phone rang, making him laugh. He was so consumed with Tavika that he'd ignored his early warning system. He pulled out his phone and answered it. "Hello, Hunter. How is Anna?"

"Alive, thanks to you and Tavika."

"Will she make it?" Jericho worried about that. Although her cord was still attached, and physically her body was alive, he knew what the physical and emotional and psychological trauma could do to a young girl like that. Hell, even to us adults.

"We have to trust the doctors are working on it, on her. There's definitely some physical injuries. Looks like she was sexually assaulted many times." Hunter's voice was carefully devoid of emotion. It was the only way he could discuss Anna's injuries.

A defense mechanism which Jericho understood. "Did you ask Dr. Maddy to help?"

"Yes. She did some work at the hospital. She's worried Anna hasn't returned yet. Dr. Maddy says she'll try to make that transition on her own."

Jericho winced. So often death happened for reasons other than physical injury. This was a prime example. "At least she's in the best hands possible. And she's safe."

"So now that Anna has been found, I thought I would help you with the Ghost," Hunter offered.

"Sounds good to me. Particularly since it seems we're not getting far."

"Tavika?"

Jericho was already shaking his head, before Hunter got the word out. "She's going through a lot right now. Not sure she can handle another trip to find him. Way too personal."

"Right. So how about a ghost talk?"

"A what?"

"Sometimes, as you know, I can talk to spirits. Which is why I prefer to try and find people before they are dead. Because talking to ghosts really sucks."

"That was just one case. You can't let that woman's anger stop you from doing something really cool."

"Yeah, that wasn't cool." Hunter's voice was light, but still the pain of that failure was inside.

It hadn't been his fault in any way. Hunter had only heard about the case twelve hours earlier. He'd led the police to the right location. But not in time. The woman had died a few hours prior. And, in a very unusual move, her spirit had stayed and then managed to turn her anger and temper on Hunter, once she realized he understood her. He'd been carrying that guilt ever since.

"I was wondering about speaking with some of the Ghost's victims," Hunter suggested abruptly.

"That would be good," Jericho agreed slowly. "Do you have one in mind?"

"One's been nudging me. I don't know who he is though, as he isn't talking very much."

"Interesting that he's talking to you. What's the connection?"

"He was in the military and somehow knows I was also."

"Gordon. He was a homeless man. We suspect he saw the Ghost murder a family twenty years ago. Likely Tavika's family. Gordon's throat was sliced open the day before yesterday." Jesus, was that just the other day or two? Regardless Jericho loved the fact that Hunter was on the same wavelength. Jericho didn't waste any time bringing Hunter up to speed.

"So what should I ask him?"

"After twenty years," Jericho asked, "why would the Ghost kill him after all this time? And how did the Ghost find Gordon?"

"Let me try to talk to him." Just as Hunter was about to ring off, he asked, "Where was his body found?"

Jericho described the alleyway.

"Good enough. Let's see if he'll talk to another military man." And, with that, Hunter was gone.

As Jericho put away his phone, he contemplated the other ghosts. He put out a couple feelers, but he wasn't much of a ghost talker. He hadn't gotten any nudges of ghosts wanting to talk to him either. That brought his thoughts back to another victim. The teenager with the broken neck. That didn't make any sense to him.

Maybe he could do some more tracking and find out if she really was one of the Ghost's victims.

Where was Tavika now? She was just approaching the office building per the call from Dispatch. Jericho sat on the couch in Tavika's apartment, then jumped free of his body. He thought himself to her side, as she walked into the building. He slipped in with her and tapped her on the shoulder. She turned in wide-eyed shock, then grinned.

Another connection was forged between them. Joined by a common cause, by shared skills. Soon he hoped joined in all ways. And yet there was no longer the physical need to mate. He was content with this process. This melding of the minds and motives. He knew it would just make the end result that much sweeter. And yet his prior relationships had made it very difficult for him in another way.

Given his profession, he'd avoided serious relationships because his job was dangerous work and hard to explain to anyone not intimately involved. He'd tried to find someone special, someone psychic, so she'd understand that part of his world. And would be better able to handle the type of work he did.

And … he'd just done that.

He'd found that someone. And she was psychic. Now he had to convince her that he was special and that they needed time together to see what they might have.

HUNTER DROVE DOWN the block toward the alleyway. Supposedly this was the spot where Gordon Denton had been murdered. Hunter parked a few storefronts away. After locking up his truck, he walked the neighborhood and noted it was a typical commercial street.

There were a few stores, but mostly offices and a couple lunch places were on both sides of the street. The block was small, with no traffic lights. Also the energy here was low-key. A little bit fraught. But nothing major. In fact, not very much in the way of energy surrounded the alleyway. He stuffed his hands into his pockets and approached the entrance. He stood here for a long moment.

All senses jacked up, he looked for signs of other entities.

Ghost-talking was a skill he'd slowly been building this last year. He'd managed to speak to several successfully, but there was never any guarantee. The trouble was often, when you went to talk to a specific ghost, others were around. Since ghost-talkers, like Hunter, were rare, once he showed up, these other ghosts grew louder, clamoring for attention—more so than the one ghost Hunter needed to speak to. And some ghosts just didn't know when to shut up. Hunter almost cracked a smile at that. The place to practice was the hospital because it was full of them, but almost *too many* ghosts were in there. He'd tried the cemetery too, with dismal results.

Sometimes nobody was around. He just didn't get it. He often wondered if ghosts had some kind of society on their side. He had no idea what and who Gordon would be in his ghostly form. Also ghosts fragmented into bits and pieces of who they'd originally been, but Gordon had been poking Hunter insistently.

According to what Jericho had told Hunter, Gordon had been fragmented on this side too. Hunter walked a few steps inside the alleyway, his senses not detecting any danger. But he also wasn't detecting any entity. Halfway into the alleyway he saw the dried blood on the concrete.

He walked to the far end to make sure nobody else was around, before slowly walking back. Whatever possessions Gordon had owned were already gone. Dumpsters were to the right of where he'd been sitting. It was possible somebody had cleaned up the crime scene area of his possessions, and it was also plausible that his friends helped themselves to whatever Gordon had left behind. And knowing several homeless people himself, Hunter doubted Gordon would have cared.

Hunter leaned against the opposite wall and studied the space. He noted a certain amount of energy disruption, but it wasn't bad. That surprised him. Often there was a tumultuous surge of energy left behind after someone had been murdered. But whatever had been here had dissipated.

Hunter's presence as he walked along places like this sometimes did that as well. Something about psychics being around that helped disperse violent energy.

As if, once acknowledged, it was free to move on.

He didn't see any remnants of violent energy that would hold Gordon here, but that didn't mean a whole lot. He waited a few minutes to see if anybody was around—to understand that Hunter would not hurt them. Then he called out in a low tone, "Gordon, are you here?"

At the same time he sent out a ray of healing energy over where Gordon had died. "I mean you no harm. I'm here to talk with you, … if you'd like to have someone to talk with."

He should've brought Stefan, but his buddy had one zillion other things to do than talk to a ghost. Stefan did a certain amount of rescue work, and, as part of this band of merry psychics, everyone was required to do some as well.

Just so many souls needed help crossing over that it was too big a job for any one person and, in fact, for any one group.

Hunter waited and rested against the wall, happy it wasn't raining. What would it be like to live homeless, like Gordon had? Having a shopping cart and a few cardboard pieces to create a shelter. He couldn't imagine it was the easiest lifestyle.

But it would be freeing. No bills to pay, no maintenance. No responsibilities to anything or anyone but filling your stomach. He didn't think he could survive in the city though. If he were homeless, he'd rather camp out some-where; except then essentially he would no longer be homeless, as he would have created a home in the woods—already failing his first duty of the experience.

Camping is nice. But food isn't as plentiful.

The voice whispered through his mind so softly and gravely that, in the beginning, Hunter didn't realize who was speaking. He used his peripheral vision to see his ghostly visitor. And, sure enough, the air to the side warbled and shifted. Being a new ghost, it was often hard to come and go. But he figured Gordon had already had one foot in the grave for a long time. He lived with his ghosts. Maybe that made the transition a little easier for him. "Did you have a hard time finding food in the city?"

There was a slight shimmer again from the side. The voice whispered, *No, people are always throwing away perfectly good food. One just has to stay close to restaurants.*

Hunter had never considered that. Since several lunch spots were right here on this block, he could imagine they threw out a ton on a daily basis. It was kinda disgusting actually. Not that Gordon would've gone looking for it, but more that the restaurants threw it out at all. Hunter hoped that some places were kind and left the food out for him. "Do you miss the good old days?"

Hunter knew bringing up any reference to those days could trigger a response other than the one he wanted, but that depended on what kind of military man Gordon was. For many, they enjoyed a sense of camaraderie with others in the military. A sense of acceptance. Of belonging. Many men would say those were the best days of their lives. For some it was the opposite. But society expected them to say it was horrible. To say it was the worst thing you could ever experience. Within that experience though, even within a war, there was also a sense of bonding.

Never had that. I went to war and came back to find I had never left the war.

Hunter nodded. "Sorry to hear that. It's tough when you return from war to find people killing each other."

Especially women and children. We were supposed to save them. Not kill them.

Gordon's voice had dropped even lower. He was hard to hear, as his words were coming more as impressions now, not actual enhanced sounds.

"And when you see women and children dying, it's hard to stop it?"

Then came an ugly silence. Gordon whispered, *Yes. I couldn't stop him. Them.*

Hunter straightened. *Them?* "Why was that, by the way?" Hunter asked, deliberately keeping his voice calm, curious. "It was a long time ago, so it's okay to talk about it, but just wondering why it wasn't possible to stop them."

Because he was my friend.

Back to a single pronoun. And a man he knew?

"If soldiers did something wrong when you were around, would you have done something about it?"

I'd report them. Then there was a heavy sigh. *Unless he was part of my unit. Then I'd have done everything I could to protect him and to make him stop. It's so confusing now.*

Interesting. Brotherhood over ethics. "Gordon, are you saying this man was in your unit?"

A heavy silence filled the air once more. Hunter wasn't sure whether Gordon had left or was just unwilling to answer the question. Hunter had never considered a military man to be the Ghost. And yet why not? So many came home and couldn't stop killing. He changed the question. "Had you known him long?"

But still no response came from Gordon.

Realizing he was likely losing his connection, Hunter said, "It's okay, Gordon. If you don't want to talk about it, that's fine. I just wondered if maybe the victims were his wife and kids? Or if they were strangers?"

Silence.

Shit. He'd lost Gordon that time. He tried to ease back the pressure. "It doesn't really matter. It's just kind of odd."

Then that same faint voice asked, *Why is it odd?*

"Because he killed a family, but he left one little girl alive."

That's not right. If he left anyone alive, he had a reason. Gordon's voice faded into the distance. *And it won't be good.*

And he blinked out.

Hunter called out a couple more times. But even the air felt empty, like Gordon had long gone.

Hopefully, now that he'd passed on something important, his spirit would be free to cross over to where it belonged. The last thing Hunter wanted was to have Gordon tied to this dirty alley for the rest of eternity.

Hunter pulled out his phone and quickly called Jericho. Now he had something important to tell him.

CHAPTER 30

I T WAS THE same scenario Tavika had seen in her vision. She positioned herself in exactly the same place as she had been the first time. A sense of déjà vu took over. She hadn't had time initially for more than a quick glance around the office because someone else controlled her view back then. She'd barely seen the wall, windows, and table. Her gaze had focused on the body on the floor. As she stood now, the only difference was the forensic team working in the room.

The janitor still lay with his head to the side, both arms up. What was different was a large pool of blood underneath. When she'd first seen him, he'd recently died. Now, with his life force drained, the pool of blood was rather substantial.

Since the forensic team and several of her team were here already, there was barely enough room to walk, let alone think.

Lawrence came up behind her and joked, "I guess somebody didn't like the cleaning job he did?"

She shoved her hands into her jeans pockets at the bad joke. "Or he interrupted somebody who shouldn't have been here? He could've interrupted somebody who was allowed to be here but was doing something he shouldn't be? Alternatively our janitor was doing something *he* shouldn't have been doing." She turned slightly to see Lawrence's face. "Too early to tell."

He nodded, his gaze on the sweepers to the side. "Couple good theories in there though." He motioned at the body. "Hard not to link this to the others. That's three now with their throats slit."

"All males."

"We still need a connection to the teenage girl."

"I don't think they are connected," Tavika stated calmly. "I think someone used Breaker's crime scene as a dump site, hoping it would turn the police off his trail." She shrugged. "Who knows?"

"Pretty stupid though," Peters said, coming up beside them. "It'll just make us look harder."

"As good a theory as any," Lawrence noted. "Still, until we get more information, it's just that—a theory."

"Which means, it has thrown us in the dark," Tavika added quietly. "If we'd found her somewhere else, we'd have treated her case differently."

"But because of where she was found, we're wasting our time trying to connect her to the old man." Peters nodded. "I like it."

Lawrence asked, "So then, we should treat the teenager as a completely unrelated case?"

Tavika nodded. She thought back to the golden dots she had seen when following the blue-dot connection to Anna. "I'd look at home or close to it for the teenager's cause of death."

She sensed more than saw when the two men glanced her way because her gaze was locked on the janitor on the floor. That's where her focus would be. She didn't know what the deal was with the teenage girl, and Tavika would certainly give her time and attention, but right now this janitor took top priority.

The Ghost had to be stopped. Before he killed again.

"What do we know about the victim?" she asked.

Peters answered, "His name is Eric Proteus. He was from South Africa originally. Lived in the US for the last fifteen years. For the last three he worked for the cleaning company contracted for this office. They've never had any trouble with him. They didn't know what happened, until the rest of his crew came looking." Peters brought out his notebook and checked it, then added, "We have the names of the rest of his crew."

She nodded. "Maybe the killer took the stairs or a different elevator, not the service elevator, to avoid the cleaning crew."

"And the killer could just as easily have been surprised by another member of the cleaning crew," Peters noted. "When I spoke with their manager, he said each were assigned a different floor of this building."

Tavika nodded. "The killer wouldn't have any way to know exactly where the other cleaners would have been at any point in time."

Lawrence added, "Then I guess we can safely assume he didn't run into anyone, as no one else is missing."

She raised an eyebrow at Lawrence. "You can confirm all the rest of the crew is accounted for?"

Lawrence nodded. "Yes, they have all checked in. And I agree. Had he seen anybody else, he likely would've killed them too."

She also happened to agree with them. In her line of duty she'd been forced to kill twice. She wasn't sure how many it would take for killing to get easier, but she was more than willing to write the Ghost's name on bullet number three.

After that, she ran through the basics, did a quick examination of the office, collected as much detailed information that she could get off the victim, and would later run it through her computer.

"I can wait for the coroner to get here," Lawrence offered.

She turned and smiled at him. "Who did you call?"

He shrugged. "I called the office. They said they'd send somebody."

She winced. "I would've called Shelby."

"Not for something like this," he protested. "She's the big cheese down there. Any junior would do for this case."

"No. This case is connected to several others she's working on. You call Shelby exactly for something like this." And because her friend would be absolutely pissed at having missed out, Tavika sent a text to Shelby to let her know a third male body with his throat slit had been found. As for Tavika, all she could think about was getting home. That would be hours out.

She couldn't wait. And, if she were honest, she really wanted to see Jericho.

Speaking of which, where was he right now? She looked around. He'd been with her when she had walked into the office building, but she'd lost him soon afterward. Where had he gone?

JERICHO COULD SENSE probing energy looking for him. Nice to know Tavika was reaching out to see where he was. He'd gone into the building with her and had made his way into the crime scene. But, when she started talking with the other detectives, Jericho had done a quick sweep and had gone back out to the hallway. He'd managed to get through doors by following the forensics team as they moved up and down the building, allowing Jericho to track the strange energy to the front door. He assumed it belonged to the Ghost. Jericho wallowed around in the entranceway for a while, before turning and heading to the elevator at the back. Except he couldn't open the damn doors. He caught her just as she was about to step outside. *Come this way.*

She turned, and a smile lit up her face. "There you are."

The Ghost went here. And he raced ahead of her.

She picked up the pace and ran to the rear elevator. They went down to the parking level.

He walked outside and studied the energy hanging around. He saw where some had traveled to the reserved parking spots in the front. He tracked the energy to an empty one with a number on it. He motioned with his hand. *He was here.*

She quickly wrote down the parking space number and then grabbed her phone. It didn't take long to get a name and an occupation. "Robert Greene. He's a consultant."

What kind of consultant? Jericho asked.

"Civil engineering. Specializes in houses." She frowned. "That might give him access to places and families."

Where does this guy live?

"I got the address. Let's find out." They quickly back-tracked to her truck. She got in the driver's side, then laughed because she had forgotten to open the passenger door for him to get in. Once he was inside, she asked, "Really, can you *not* open any doors?"

Sometimes I can. Others I can't. It's odd and frustrating as hell. Lots of times I can just go through glass, but doors are harder.

"Ha," she said, with a laugh. "Chances are it's all in your mind. You were probably punished for opening a door without permission."

He started to laugh. *You could be right.*

She entered the address into her GPS and pulled her vehicle out into traffic. "Greene doesn't live too far away. Let's go take a look."

Makes sense. He lives close to where he works.

They drove to the man's house and found a vehicle parked in the driveway. On instinct he told her, *Keep driving.*

"What's the matter?" she muttered.

An awful lot of dark energy is collected at the back of the car.

She studied the trunk. "Are you thinking we've found Greene in the trunk of his own car? Would the Ghost do that a second time?"

He didn't answer. She drove slowly past the house then pulled a U-turn and drove in the direction of the address. She parked on the opposite side of the street, two houses away.

They were close enough to see a light on in the house. "Do you think the Ghost might be in there?"

I doubt it. It could be Greene's wife and family. They may not have heard the vehicle return. It would be completely out of character for the Ghost to go into the house.

"Actually not really. We were all home when he entered our house."

He turned to look at her. *Are you starting to remember some things?*

Grim faced, she nodded. "And none of it's nice. First things first." She pulled out her phone. "I need a reason to examine the car."

Jericho watched a man walking a large Doberman on a leash. Jericho cupped his hands around his mouth and sent out a whisper of energy. The dog stopped, looked in his direction; then his ears went up, and he bolted forward, ripping the leash from the man's hand. Instantly there were cries of, "Bruno, Bruno, come back. Bruno, come back."

But the Doberman wasn't having any of it. He raced to the suspect's car and barked like a madman.

As the man got closer to the car and tried to pull away the dog, the Doberman just resisted. He snarled and howled at the back of the car.

It was obvious the dog's owner was nervous.

Open the window for me, will you?

She opened the window on his side, letting him out. He headed toward the vehicle and dog. The dog's owner was frantically trying to pull Bruno back. Other neighbors turned lights on, and various people ran outside to the commotion. A neighbor asked, "What's going on?"

Bruno's owner said, "I'm sorry, but my dog is going crazy over this vehicle."

The neighbor joined them. Eventually Bruno managed to calm down, but he wouldn't move away from the trunk, short of being dragged.

The neighbor suggested, "We should call the cops."

Bruno started to howl. Instantly other dogs within the vicinity joined in.

The neighbor got really nervous. "I'll call the cops. This is just way too weird." He raced inside his home.

Jericho watched and smiled. That should do it.

NO, NO. THAT goddamn dog. He wanted to slice its throat.

He'd bolted around the side of the neighbor's hedge, when he'd seen the man and his dog approach. They should have walked right on by.

Not stopped and raised the entire neighborhood.

Hadn't he had a bad-enough day already without this? He just needed to catch a break. Those were thin on the ground today.

The damn janitor shouldn't have been there. Not in that sector of the building. But, no, the janitor was going through every desk in the office. Looking for something to steal. He'd watched the janitor take a slug from a bottle found in one drawer. So gross.

Then he'd moved on to another drawer and had found some cash. He'd pocketed that damn fast.

Thief.

Scumbag.

Even then he'd have left the janitor alone.

Until he walked into the wrong office.

CHAPTER 31

T AVIKA CALLED INTO Dispatch. "I'm on the scene of a disturbance." She rattled off the address.

"Acknowledged. Reports indicate a suspicious vehicle ..." The dispatcher's voice droned on.

Tavika already knew what was suspicious. "I'll take it. I believe it's connected to my other cases."

She rang off, stepped out of her truck. She pulled out her ID and motioned at the other two officers now on the scene to move the gathering crowd back.

Once done, one of the officers returned with a pry bar and popped the trunk. They all stepped back at the gruesome sight of a blood-stained blanket wrapped around a male.

With a heavy heart she made the calls. Within minutes the crime scene tape went up, and the investigation process was in motion. She heard the murmur of the crowd behind her. Well, they'd have a lot more to talk about soon.

She pulled back the corner of the blanket and studied the man's face. It was Robert Greene. She dropped the blanket back over him and walked up to the front door of the house. Nobody answered. After a few minutes she walked around to the back, two officers with her. She knocked on the kitchen door. The door popped open. She stepped inside quietly, with the others at her side, and did a quick sweep of the downstairs. The kitchen light was on, but the room was empty, as if nobody cooked. That led credence to the fact that Greene had been on his way home from work and potentially lived alone. Although they'd seen the light on inside, they hadn't seen anybody. Maybe he always left that light on.

They moved through the house. Even in the bedroom were no signs of someone else cohabitating in the space. By the time they were done, a crowd had gathered outside. Several more units arrived, as the coroner pulled up.

Tavika walked out to greet Shelby with a smile. "Glad you made it."

Shelby snorted. "What's this about another victim with a sliced throat? Why was I not called to that scene?"

"Because I wasn't primary," Tavika explained.

"You should've been. They are all connected." With a disgusted shake of her head, Shelby walked to the car.

Tavika stood off to one side and watched the coroner examine the victim.

"He's in full rigor," she announced. "And, in this position, we're likely not looking at the crime scene."

"No, I believe he was killed in the office where the janitor was and loaded into his trunk and driven here." Tavika motioned at the house behind them. "This is where he lived."

The coroner's sharp gaze took in the two-story brick house, then it slid back to Tavika. "So the killer drove him home?" she asked incredulously.

"Apparently. I'm waiting for the sweepers to arrive. Maybe the killer went inside."

Shelby shook her head. "He's too damn clever for a mistake like that. This makes no sense."

"No, but I think this is the second time he's done this," Tavika suggested. "Only last time we found the vehicle before he could take her home—if he intended on doing that. I don't know," she admitted.

"Damn. He's on a hell of a spree." Shelby straightened up and turned to look around. "I have enough to do without some madman killing people, then delivering them home."

Tavika ran her fingers through her hair. It would be a long night. She was still feeling pretty shaky, but the last thing she wanted was to be taken off the case. She stepped back a few feet and studied the crowd. She doubted she'd find the killer there, but more than one criminal had stopped to watch the results of his handiwork. They got a thrill from seeing what they had instigated.

She found Jericho standing and watching. With an imperceptible head nod, she motioned to the house, turned, and walked back inside.

Before the forensic team arrived, she had a few minutes. She checked, but they were alone. "Did you find anything?"

Not much, Jericho replied. *The Ghost's energy came out of the vehicle, then walked down around the block.*

"He didn't go in the house?" she asked in surprise.

Not that I saw.

She turned to study the big empty space, wondering how many man-hours would be wasted checking to make sure no evidence was here. But it was a step they couldn't afford to miss. Just because psychics had information didn't mean they didn't miss it too. "How far did you track the energy?"

A good block away before it disappeared. He seemed to be on foot the whole time.

"Strange." She called her team members who were still at the office building's crime scene. "You need to find a second crime scene. A Robert Greene was killed there, dumped into the trunk of his car. The killer then drove the car to Greene's house."

"Cold. That's so cold," Lawrence stated. "If the crime scene is here, we'll find it."

She didn't understand what the Ghost was up to. If the teenage girl wasn't part of the string of his cases, then maybe he was returning his victim's bodies to their homes.

She stopped and pondered. The old man Breaker had died in his house. Gordon had died in what passed as his home. She didn't know what was happening with the woman in the trunk of the Cadillac. But certainly in terms of their latest victim, Greene, he'd been returned home. As if he were in the wrong place at the wrong time, and he should've been at home where he belonged. Which, considering the after-hours janitor had been killed while he was at work, if this man Greene had been killed around the same time, it would imply that he'd been working late—and not at home where he should've been.

Then why not take the janitor home?

With her mind trying to grapple with this new theory, she realized Jericho stood close, a curious look on his face. She quickly explained the connections. "For all I know, it's just a stupid theory," she admitted. "But we have links to home and to being in the wrong place at the wrong time, when they should've been home."

What about the electrician?

"Originally—with the crime he saw—he wasn't supposed to be there. He had left to get tools or supplies or something, came back, and went downstairs, working without saying anything to the homeowner. The killer didn't know that," she explained. "Gordon wasn't supposed to see the murders because he wasn't supposed to be at the house." She waved her hand. "We may never know why he was there—if he was just passing by or intended to go into the house." She refrained from saying, *my house.* "And, no, I don't remember ever seeing him there."

She motioned at the house around her. "This Greene guy was at the office, likely working late. Depending on his time of death, we'll probably find he was alone and a bit of a workaholic. He should've been at home, where he belonged. So what I'm thinking now is, maybe the killer took out the janitor first. Our victim here saw it happen, and he had to be dealt with. The killer didn't have a chance to go back for the janitor, so left him where he was."

But that has nothing to do with being at home. And he was exactly where he belonged.

"And maybe that's why he left him. Maybe the janitor was working that shift, and that's where he should've been. Whereas this Greene guy should've been home."

Jericho looked at her. *So he's putting people back where they belong?*

"Maybe? It's a stupid theory, isn't it?"

And the woman in the trunk?

She stared at him. And her shoulders fell. "Maybe we interrupted him bringing her home? I don't know. At least not yet."

Sounds like our killer has OCD. He can't leave his victims in the wrong place, but he's taking a hell of a chance moving the bodies.

"Like many OCD people, he feels he has no choice."

Do you know anybody like that? he asked curiously. *I've known some people who were anal about stuff but not like this.*

"My mother was pretty bad—except she wasn't *this*

bad."

How old was your mother when she died? he asked so absentmindedly that Tavika took no offense.

"She was coming up on her fifty-third birthday."

Older than I expected.

"Yeah, she had me and Travis just past her fortieth, I think." She shook her head. "Believe me. It's not something I ever focused on. Travis and I were the youngest by a good seven years. I'm sure we were quite a surprise at that time in her life."

IT HAPPENS THOUGH. Jericho had more questions about her family but knew it would still be a trigger point for her.

"Don't worry about it. I'm getting better at talking about them."

Good. He studied her face. She looked better. Stronger, younger. Happier. *It looks like the energy shifts in your system were a good thing for you.*

Her laugh was harsh, difficult.

He winced. *Or you are just really good at hiding the bad stuff.*

At that, she snickered. "Both, but the process isn't done. I'm still feeling pretty raw on the inside. And I'm seriously exhausted. If I wasn't running on so much energy right now, I'd be comatose."

I have to ask. Do you think there is anything locked away in the memory of what you went through that would help you to find the killer now? He kept his voice low, soft, gentle.

She shook her head. "No. I've thought about it a lot over the last couple decades. If there was, I'd have done anything to unlock it. At least I'd like to think so. Chances are, I don't know anything anyway. You have to remember. I was only twelve. I was traumatized. And I never really got to see who it was doing this to us."

Why is that?

"Because I wasn't in the same room as the others."

He stopped and stared at her. *What? You weren't?*

She shook her head. "No. For whatever reason I was in a small dark room, similar to where I found Anna, but I heard everything going on in the other one. Anytime he came into my room brought more pain and fear. But it was always in the dark. I never did really understand that or why I was separated, when everybody else was together."

There has to be some reason why you were segregated.

In a voice so soft he could barely hear her, she whispered, "I know. I've thought of nothing else over the last twenty years. But I don't know what the reason is."

You do realize, if you can ever figure that out, we'd have a good chance of catching this asshole.

She raised her gaze to him, tears brimming in the corners of her eyes. "I know. I'm so terrified it's somebody I know. That I was locked up because of it."

He shook his head. *No, you would've been killed, like your mother and sister.*

"My mother, sister, *and* brother," she whispered.

No. Wait. I've heard you talk to your brother. I figured I read the report wrong, and he survived.

With a sad smile she reached into her left-hand pocket and pulled up the phone and showed it to him.

Not understanding exactly what was going on, but realizing it was important, he studied the phone. It was an older model. Like one of the earliest small pocket-size phones with a flip-top.

When she turned it over and removed the small back panel, his nonexistent eyebrows rose.

There were no batteries.

The phone doesn't work? He studied her features, the tears slowly tracking down her cheeks. And then he understood. *You talk to his ghost, don't you?* And that made a crazy kind of sense. He'd met Travis—the twelve-year-old version—in the park but hadn't managed to put two and two together until now. Even then Travis was looking out for his sister—Tavika.

Her bottom lip trembled, as she nodded. "He was killed the first day. He talked to me right away. As if he knew ahead of time what was happening. He was so angry and devastated. And because we were connected like always, I never really lost the connection. But I learned very quickly that people don't like it when you talk to ghosts."

She gave a bitter laugh. "I saw shrinks, counselors, and psychologists. I saw every professional in the book. And finally I learned to watch my tongue. No, I don't see my brother. No, I can't talk to my brother. No, I have no idea why anybody would imagine that I could do such a thing. Yes, I understand my family is dead and buried."

With a flick of her wrist she gave the phone a shake. "I found this on the ground one day. And I realized I had the answer. It gave me an outlet to talk to Travis without anybody knowing. Without people thinking I was crazy. It's a habit now. He talks in my head sometimes too, like you and Stefan can, but, a lot of the time, when I'm with people, you will see me pull out the phone and talk to him."

As he stared at the dead phone in her hand, it started to ring. And ring.

CHAPTER 32

T AVIKA WALKED INTO her apartment an hour later. More dead than alive. Normally she wouldn't have left before all the work at the crime scene was done, but she was finished physically and mentally.

Jericho stood in the middle of the room, waiting for her. He frowned when he saw the fatigue on her face. "This has got to stop."

She dropped her jacket and holster on the table, kicked off her boots, and walked to her bed. "I'd love for this to stop, but, until we catch the Ghost, there's no rest for any of us."

She crashed, once again, face down. She wanted to just nod off and be done with it. Wake up tomorrow and have it all be over with, but she knew it wouldn't be that easy. She rolled over to her back and stared up at the ceiling. "This is no life."

"I'm so glad to hear you say that," Jericho snapped, stepping closer. "Get up and into the shower. I'll have a hot bowl of soup for you, when you get back out. Then you can crash and burn."

She stared at him. "So not happening."

"You do it, or I'll do it for you," he threatened.

She narrowed her gaze, feeling her temper spike. "Oh, I wouldn't go that direction."

He stared at her, hands on his hips. "You have been running wild for way too long. Burning the candle at both ends, until you're ready to drop, and you do this to yourself day after day after day. How long do you think you can live like this?"

Just because he was right didn't mean she wanted to listen to it. But instead of anger, confusion washed over her. She didn't know whether she cared or not. She was hungry. Yes. Tired. Yes. But her mind wouldn't shut down.

Did she want that hot shower? Hell yes. Maybe to confuse them both as much as anything, she swung her legs over the bed, stood, and walked into the bathroom and shut the door.

There she stripped down and stepped under the hot water. But, like everything else today, the shower felt different. The feel of the water hitting her skin, … the warmth, … were both odd and different. Unique. Refreshing. Soothing. She took her time shampooing her hair, letting her fingers massage her scalp, loving the feeling as her body became reacquainted with nerve endings she'd ignored for so long. She didn't know how much of this was from Dr. Maddy's work and how much was just from releasing all the old energy. But it was like she was living in a whole new space. It wasn't that it was uncomfortable but it wasn't yet *comfortable.* Like she was a visitor in her body now.

That would improve with time, she knew, but, at the moment, there was such a weird disconnect. She turned off the water and stepped out. Wrapping herself in a towel, she used a second one to dry her hair and feet. She should've brought something to sleep in. Then realized she probably didn't have anything. Walking back out, she headed to her dresser to pull out clean underwear and a large T-shirt.

With her back to Jericho she pulled the T-shirt over her head. He was in the kitchen doing whatever magical things he did in there. She had used the kitchen in the years she'd lived here, but it had never produced anything for her like what it did for him.

"Come and sit," Jericho called out. "The soup is ready."

She sat down obediently to a hot bowl of chicken noodle soup. It smelled heavenly. When he popped a few pieces of hot buttered toast in front of her, she shamelessly moaned in delight.

"Glad to hear you're enjoying this."

"It's wonderful. I could feel something changing, sharpening inside, but everything has been so chaotic that I haven't had time to analyze how or what."

"And it'll likely take you several more days to figure it out."

She nodded, not wanting to waste time or effort on words. Her energy was fading, and she wanted to get through the soup and toast before she completely collapsed.

That was something else she was struggling with—she couldn't judge her energy reserves. It was as if she expected to have more than there was and came up empty. She didn't like that.

She just needed to make it through this. She did not want to get caught short again.

Finally she pushed away the empty bowl and looked up at him. In a heavy voice she asked, "*Now* can I go to sleep?" Not waiting for an answer, she stumbled to her feet and, still in her T-shirt and underwear, walked back to her bed and collapsed. She barely had enough time to notice he'd pulled back the bedcovers, so she landed on the sheets, not on top of the bedding.

She appreciated the gesture. At another point in time, when her brain was actually functioning, she'd tell him so. She closed her eyes and drifted off to sleep, with Solomon comfortable on her belly. When a heavy weight joined her on the bed, she barely murmured. When an arm crept around her and tucked her up against a warm solid chest, she just snuggled deeper.

She woke several hours later to find a furnace at her back. One of the reasons she slept on top of the bed fully dressed—besides exhaustion—was because she didn't get hot or cold that way. Her body had found a comfortable level of temperature and just maintained it. But tucked under the covers in minimal clothing with Jericho beside her, her body had overheated to the point of waking her up.

Solomon must have gotten hot too, as he'd retreated to find somewhere else to sleep.

She rolled to her back and studied the sleeping man at her side. Who knew the sexy man who had walked into her office several days ago was a big marshmallow? He did nothing but look after her. She didn't understand how that worked because she'd never had anybody take care of her. Especially when she'd done nothing for him. She hadn't even thanked him for putting on soup. She'd just accepted it, eaten, and then gone to bed.

"I didn't do it to get thanks," his deep gravelly voice whispered close to her ear. "I sure hope I misheard that nickname. You did *not* just call me a *marshmallow*, did you?"

She laughed and rolled to her side so they faced each other. "You've done nothing but be a caregiver to this lost soul. That makes you a pretty big marshmallow in here." She poked his chest. Instantly his hand reached up and covered her fingers, flattening them against his smooth, warm skin.

Remembering his words upon their initial meeting, about them going to bed together, she understood she'd taken her sexual reaction and had stuffed it down deep inside. She hadn't known or trusted him then. It was as if she walked in some kind of dead zone at the time.

Had that energy been released with all the rest? Because it felt different now; she felt different now. There was something so very attractive about all that power and control of his. But to know he had a softer side, … that was seriously sexy.

Instead of that initial urge to jump his bones was a wish for something more tender, gentler. Like a shoot of a fresh flower in spring. Hopeful, as it opened to the sun for the first time. Trusting that this move would take her someplace she needed to go. To fulfillment, to joy. To a life best lived.

His eyes were closed, and he lay here just breathing gently. She knew he wasn't asleep, but neither was he pushing her.

As always he was accepting of her choices.

She let her fingers wander across his large chest up to his shoulders, finding tiny little scars there. They whispered up to the five-o'clock shadow on his chin. She smoothed over the rough texture, smiling at the rasping sandpaper sound.

He growled lightly. She let her fingers slide down across his shoulders, to his massive bicep and forearm. His hand was curled up on the bed between them.

She slid her fingers between his. He squeezed her fingers gently and then released them. She let her head rest on the pillow beside his, a smile at the corner of her mouth. This was special. She'd jumped plenty of men's bones. But that had been an animal mating. A ritual giving way to a physical need. She didn't know what *this* was.

But she wanted it.

And she knew he wouldn't push either way. He'd let her make the decision. With a cheeky grin she smiled, closed her eyes, and jumped into his mind.

And found him waiting for her. A blending of minds like no other.

Have you ever made love with another psychic? she asked.

When it came, his answer was like a warm wind, brushing down her spine from the inside out—heartfelt. *No, you will be the first.*

He slid his hands up to the side of her face and tugged her close for a kiss. But it wasn't just a kiss; it was … something new. Like all the old energy had disappeared and had taken the old experiences away with it. The impressions, the judgments, the criticisms—were all gone. She was starting anew.

And the touch of his lips, the warmth of his tongue, … the sexy slide of those long fingers against her scalp, … the heat coursing through her, … the shivers all over her skin …

It was almost too much. He rolled her over to lie on her back and smiled down into her eyes.

In her mind, he whispered, *And yet it's not enough.* He lowered his head and kissed her.

Loving, caring, it was like being enveloped in a warm hug. Tenderness and passion rolled into one. Inside and out. The kiss started at her lips and went to her toes, leaving her barely capable of thinking. He deepened the kiss, a gentle stroke of his finger wiping away the tears rolling down her cheeks.

Tears she had no idea were even there. She opened her eyes. "Everything feels so different."

He smiled. *Perfect then that I am the first. The one person you'll remember after sharing this.*

Her eyes drifted closed, more than willing to let this be her first time all over again.

He was both gentle and demanding, rough and frustrating, as he teased and tormented them both. His lips and hands were busy, and all she could do was whimper in joy, as nerve endings fired to life. Her body shuddered under his ministrations.

She wanted to touch him.

She wanted to stroke him, as he was stroking her.

She wanted to taste him.

And yet her body couldn't do anything, as she was caught in his web of desire. Mindless jelly for him to mold as he would. She'd never believed this was possible. She'd never trusted to this level.

In her mind, he said, *You can trust me. Just relax and let go.*

But ...

A kiss landed on her lips, a whisper in her mind. *No buts. This time is just for us.*

When he rose up over her, she was warm, wet, and lost to the rising storm clamoring for release. He surged deep inside her.

She let out a cry and burst into tears.

He stilled. *Tavi, did I hurt you?*

Blubbering like an idiot, she shook her head and wailed, *No.*

He slid his hands up to cup her cheeks, so he could look into her eyes and could see the truth for himself. *You sure?*

She lifted her long legs and wrapped them around his hips, forcing him in deeper.

I'm sure, she whispered. *You didn't hurt me.*

She pulled his head down and kissed him with all the longing she held deep inside. It seemed like forever that she'd been alone. She needed this. This sense of oneness with somebody else.

But not oneness with anybody, just me, he whispered in her head. *This is what happens when two psychics are perfectly aligned.*

And he started to move, his words already her undoing, as her body raced straight for the peak, his body driving her up higher and higher.

Her mind was consumed with the concept of love. The concept of where they were going. What they were doing. How quickly they would reach it.

Was this real?

Oh, yes, this is real. This is your future. When you let go of the past, only good things are ahead for you, for me, for both of us together. You are not alone anymore. I am here with you. For you. … One with you.

At his words, she exploded into the maelstrom of glory.

He cried out as he reached his peak to collapse beside her.

Emotions, fear, desire, frustration, hunger, fulfillment, and, yes, … love, circled around her, tantalizingly close.

Just accept it. Let it be. Don't try to think. Don't try to analyze. Open a big well into your heart, and let it all fall in.

She tried to comprehend, but her brain was on fire, … and her body hungered for more.

He added, *Experience it, and only hang on to that which you want. Let the rest fall away. Just sink into the place of well-being and peace.*

Tavika stepped inside herself and found that now it was a comfortable fit.

She was home.

JERICHO KNEW THE moment when Tavika had stepped into her body fully. He'd sensed her disconnection from her own being before. So much had been going on, so much old and new. But it was also a dangerous place for her to be. That disconnection allowed other people to step in and to take over. She never really did disconnect to the extent that it became a problem, but he had worried about that. Now it was like, instead of wearing a suit, she'd become it.

He couldn't be happier.

And although this wasn't exactly the lovemaking vision he had had previously in his mind, it was way better. And it proved that, no matter what his visions were, they were still just visions. And fate could take a hand and could change things. For the first time he felt emboldened about what was to come. Because he knew it was coming. That dark wave of death was approaching rapidly.

In less than twenty-four hours, she'd be dead.

That truth flashed through his mind.

He clutched her, instinctively pulling her closer. Events were moving too fast. He needed more time with her.

He *had* to make sure she survived the encounter with the Ghost.

They were linked. A link that would hurt him too, if she went down. But he could do nothing about it. She had taken this path, and he would do the best he could.

And hope they both had a future.

With her tucked up against his chest, gently resting, he stared at the ceiling, wondering.

About the people in her life, around her life.

One thought crept into the back of his mind. *Somebody who moved a ruler, until it sat at the right spot. Where it belonged.* Like a stapler, as Jericho had seen in the snippet visions. Making sure everything was just so on the desk. *Tavika's* desk.

His gaze flew open. Could it be? Was it so simple? At the same time so damn convoluted?

This person was in the perfect position. And had stuck close—damn close to his victim.

So why change it now?

And, if it were him, she really *hadn't* seen him back then. She wasn't blocking out the man's face. She wasn't blocking out his identity.

She really hadn't seen him.

Otherwise she wouldn't be able to speak with him almost every day now.

Dear God. She really had no idea.

Jericho had to be wrong.

CHAPTER 33

TAVIKA WOKE UP calm and rested, Solomon snuggled up beside her. Her body was warm, relaxed, almost glowing. Her mind alert. Her muscles felt fluid. Just think about that. Always before, she'd come home, exhausted, and had dropped on her bed. In the morning she woke up, ate, and left. As if there was no time for herself because she hadn't made time. She had that horrible driving sense of guilt that she didn't deserve self-care.

Rationally she knew that was stupid. She'd been a child back then. The fact that she'd tried to fit in and hadn't succeeded, so she'd gone the opposite route, was a common-enough story. And, if they hadn't encountered the Ghost, then life would have been incredibly different. Although she couldn't imagine what it would've been like growing up with her mother and her sister.

Tavika would have moved out at a very young age, as she'd already found it impossible to coexist within that family. Just too much psychic ability in one confined space. One without boundaries. Her mother had been lacking in boundaries. She had no filters. And that was why Tavika was so strict with herself. She kept herself locked down.

That didn't mean she didn't love her mother. Because she had. She loved all her family. But they were gone, and Tavika had been living for them. Not herself. Until Jericho had blasted open that buried cauldron of emotion of hers. There was a parallel here that she was just now understanding. Having locked up so much inside, she'd taken all those different layers of herself, all those different ones of her past, and had compressed them into this single space. As that space opened, the layers eased back, giving more space around her.

When she went into the abyss, she went through layers. She opened them up and explored the spaces between. But, within her own psyche, she'd refused to do that. She crushed it all down so there was nothing between them. And, of course, there was always something; she just hadn't taken a closer look. She hadn't seen the kidnapper's face. She'd heard his voice, but it was intermingled with the screams of the dying around her. She didn't want to remember the words.

She remembered the terror, the horror. Her mother pleading. Her sister crying. Her brother never said a word. Then he couldn't—the killer had cut out his tongue. But Travis had been unconscious from the beginning. A blow to the head while he'd been on the computer, and he never woke up. Never knew who his killer was. She'd asked Travis, but he was never able to tell her.

But always one thing defied explanation. She'd been separated. Tied up, gagged, and tossed into another room.

Why? What had made her so different? What made her not be the same as them? Why were they victims to be killed, and she wasn't? They were all well-known psychics. Her mom famous. Her sister a rising psychic. Her twin brother, much younger than his older sister, much less capable, but showing promise. Friends, family, even police knew Travis had budding capabilities.

Tavika had been the ugly duckling. Her mother had told

everyone that. That somehow she had had two children who were extremely gifted, and then there was Tavika. Her mother never brought up Tavika in public. And almost never with the family.

Tavika rolled over onto her back.

Was that why her family had been targeted?

Did the Ghost hate psychics?

Was he trying to take out a threat, before they came after him? Was that why Tavika had been saved? Because she was no threat?

Did the Ghost not know what to do with her? She had always been in the background. Not many people even knew she was part of the family. Although she was a twin, she didn't look like her brother, who did look like their sister Bellamy.

Jericho's big hand stroked up her hip, her side, sliding up to her shoulders and down her arm to clasp her fingers. "Heavy thoughts?"

"Heavy thoughts," she affirmed. "I think I know why I was allowed to live. At least at the time." She turned her head to stare into his now wide-awake eyes.

"Tell me."

"I was the only one who wasn't psychic," she admitted.

His eyebrows shot up.

"In the eyes of the world at least." She sighed. "I defied my mother's training, defied her wish to embrace that part of my heritage. So she retaliated—to the point of even publicly telling the world I had none of the skills of my family. I walked away from that side of her life. Even though, behind the scenes, my mother and sister were screaming at me to step up."

Jericho stroked the side of her cheek, his energy calm

and accepting.

She smiled. "Being a public circus monkey was not my idea of a good time. I wanted friends."

"Didn't your mom have friends? As I recall, something was in the case files about your mom being surrounded by men all the time. That had actually been part of the problem. There were too many men, too many suspects."

"Mom had a lot of men around, but I don't know how many were actual friends. Honestly, as I look back on the stream of men, I think they were more interested in the thrill of having sex with a psychic than they were in the family or a permanent relationship. Lots came looking for answers to their own problems, and then there were the professionals seeking her help on cases. There was talk of a TV show at one time."

"A television show?" He looked startled. "I don't remember anything about that."

"There was no one left to mention it," she replied shortly. "The thing is, she was likely targeted because of the publicity she loved." Tavika groaned. "And I was saved because no one knew what I could do. Hell, neither did I. The thing was, all kinds of men showed up—from cops to private investigators, even the FBI was on our doorstep. The Ghost could have been one or none of them."

That was one of the things about Jericho that Tavika loved. There was no judgment on his face, no censorship in his eyes. No criticism in the words coming out of his mouth. He was very accepting. "If she was any good, then I'm not surprised. And your sister, did she have a lot of boyfriends?"

"Mom wanted to keep the men at bay until Bellamy was nineteen. Said it was important for her skills to develop." Tavika's smile was sad, as she added, "But Bellamy's power shone in her sexuality. She loved playing with the men. They circled her as if she were a bitch about to come into her first heat. Each man vying to be the first one. The others all lining up to be next."

His eyebrows shot up.

"That's a mean thing to say," Tavika admitted in shame. "It's just my house was more like a bordello. It wasn't comfortable."

"Don't be ashamed. It's the cards that were dealt you. Life happens, and all we can do sometimes is play the hand we were given." He paused and studied her face. "Did any of the men come on to you?"

"No one saw me with Bellamy around," Tavika said. "She was gorgeous, confident, disdainful of me even. And, of course, I was a kid, seven years younger, when she was ripe on the edge of womanhood."

"And in hindsight, maybe that—"

"—was a good thing." She nodded. "It was for me."

"Maybe they were targeted because they were so beautiful, and you were spared because, as young as you were, your beauty had yet to shine."

She snorted. "Like it ever did." She shook her head. "No, I think it was more likely my lack of psychic abilities. I wonder if there was a connection to a case my mother had worked on. Maybe she'd come close to catching him back then ..." Jericho cleared his throat awkwardly. She turned to look at him, then narrowed her gaze at the ill look on his face. "What?"

"Did you ever consider the Ghost might be ... a cop?"

She stared at him. Then opened her mouth ready to blast him.

"Wait." He held up his hand. "Let me explain."

"Not if you are going to blame my profession and those I work with. You don't get to blame all cops because of what you went through," she snapped. "One bad cop is terrible for everyone."

"And yet we questioned if he was military, a psychic, and any number of other professions. So perhaps a cop. How did he know where to find Gordon? Answer that. If it weren't for having access to the database, how could he have known?"

"I have notes about Gordon on my own personal laptop," she explained. "Not in the computer at work. And he couldn't access that one."

"Unless he was a computer specialist."

"So now he's a cop *and* computer specialist?" She snorted. "Maybe he's been following me around and saw me with Gordon."

"Maybe. Look," Jericho said in a conciliatory tone. "We just have to keep our eyes open. He has access to information I don't think he should be able to. He's been a step ahead of us all the way. That would be a hell of a lot easier to do if he has access to the official case files." He shrugged. "Maybe he's a friend of a cop. The cop doesn't realize that all the questions he's getting from this man are because he's more involved than anybody could believe."

She was suddenly really tired again. Just the thought was so defeating. It would destroy her if she found out the Ghost was somebody she knew personally.

"Of course it could be somebody you know," he added, picking up her thoughts again. "Because what do predators like to do? Get close to their victims." He hesitated, then told her about Hunter going to talk to Gordon and what he'd found out.

She shook her head. "That's a help, but again that's not

making sense because I was already his victim. There is no point staying close to me now."

"Unless he was trying to make sure you didn't develop psychic abilities, in which case he'd have to correct his mistake."

That was harsh and cold and just a little too close to being a possibility. She wrapped her arms around herself, a chill setting inside. "That sounds so ... horrible."

He pursed his lips. "I'm not saying this so you look at all your friends and coworkers sideways, yet I don't want you to dismiss them out of turn just because they are cops and friends. The ideal person to keep track of this would be a cop. They'd have access to the files. And that's huge. He'd know what the police know and what they don't. He could change his MO if needed. In fact, he could change all kinds of things, based on what he found there."

"The FBI say he's been connected to forty-seven cases so far," she stated abruptly. "I only had eleven to his name."

"The FBI?" Jericho asked in surprise. "If so many, why has he not been caught?"

"I was called into the captain's office to find the FBI asking about the Breaker case. Apparently, in a few recent cases, the Ghost has used pressure syringes."

"So did you tell him about Gordon?"

She shook her head. "Not at the time. I should though." She glanced over at the phone but didn't make any effort to move. Her mind was still consumed with the possibility of the Ghost being a cop. "It would make more sense if he were an FBI agent," she noted. "He'd hayve access to even more."

"You don't know that he doesn't already. Lots of cops have friends in the FBI, and any cop working on a case can ask for information on other files, once connected."

She reached up to rub her face. She hated to think of a trail so close to her but so far away. "I know the guys I work with really well. I trust them. Some are good cops. Others are better. There are only a couple who are just so-so. That's typical of what you'd find in any station."

He had to be wrong. She'd never really considered this killer could be a cop. Why would she? Cops in half-a-dozen states were looking for this man. No. It didn't feel right.

"It wouldn't be a cop. They are all dedicated. Look at Henry. I have known him since I was a little girl. He's moving up the ladder of life, hoping to make the captain's desk and looking to do something more political." She waved her hand. "I don't know exactly what it is. I try to keep out of it because it's not my stuff. I just wanted to be a cop. Take bad guys off the street. Henry can do that political stuff. I can't."

"And who's Henry? You never mentioned him before."

She frowned. "I think you've seen him. Maybe when in spirit form." She stood and walked over to a picture on the coffee table, brought it back to Jericho, still in bed. She tapped the image of Henry. He took it from her and studied it. "I saw him the day I was at the station."

She smiled. "Yeah, he's all over the place." She replaced the photo and returned to stretch out on the bed. "Henry's been there for me all these years. Close but not tight in a confining way. But just kind of there, the odd phone call every once in a while to make sure I'm doing okay. He showed up at my graduation from high school. And he's the one who helped me get into the academy. Without him, I might not have made detective. He's been like a benevolent uncle."

"I guess he was one of the people to hang around the

house all the time with your mother?"

She looked up at him and frowned. "You know what? I'm not too sure about that. I don't know when I first started seeing him. I know he was there at the crime scene. I remember him holding me and telling me that I would be okay. And that he'd keep me safe. I wasn't in very good shape, but I do remember he's the one who took me out to the ambulance."

"He took you out to the ambulance? They didn't bring in a stretcher to collect you?"

She shook her head. "I don't think so. It was a long time ago, and I know I wasn't in my right mind, but I'm pretty damn sure he picked me up and carried me out. I was a mess though …"

"So you know for sure it was him?"

"Henry? Yes, it was him." She gave Jericho a hard look. "Where are you going with this?"

He shrugged. "I'm trying to look in places where we haven't looked before." He waited a beat, then asked, "Did Henry arrive with all the other detectives or did he come first?"

"I have no idea," she replied. "I wouldn't know."

He nodded, as if that was what he had expected. Then, in that voice she was getting very suspicious of, he said, "Maybe you should ask him."

"Why are you zeroing in on Henry?" She wouldn't let him back away on this one. But his answer surprised her.

"Who reorganizes your desk, even when everything is already neat and tidy?" he asked.

"How do you know anybody does?" She shrugged. "My desk is a mess all the time."

"And yet I saw a vision of somebody rearranging your

stapler, so it was perfectly aligned."

"Oh, Henry does that. But then I think a couple other guys might as well."

"Do you see Henry at work often?"

She wasn't liking this. She knew what it was to have a thought in one's head and to need to keep following the trail, but he was way off here. "Sometimes. I just saw him the other day. But I can go weeks and months without seeing him. I hardly see Charles either." She turned her head to stare at her jacket. "Henry just gave me an invitation to his and Charles's engagement party. I remember the oddly embarrassed look on his face." She smiled at the memory. "I forgot all about it. Henry and Charles got engaged."

"Does he work full-time? Or part-time?"

"Good Lord, you're really on about Henry." She shook her head. Better to satisfy his curiosity now and put the issue to rest. "I don't know. He's in more of a liaison position now, so he has flexible hours."

She watched suspiciously as Jericho studied her face. When she thought he may have finally put it to rest, he asked in a soft voice, "What does Charles do for a living?"

"He runs an IT company. He used to be a cop like Henry, but he burned out. His son runs it now."

BINGO. SHIT. NO, surely not. They were just guessing here. Pulling at straws. Yet so far this straw kept pulling back. Jericho would make some discreet inquiries of his own. "So someone to consider as we move forward but not necessarily the right person."

"Ha, Charles is not a suspect either. Go look somewhere else." She turned her back to him.

He could tell she was miffed, but, in a way, Henry was a perfect suspect. Nothing she'd told him made him less suspicious. In his mind he was already comparing what he knew and what he'd need to confirm. She might hate him forever afterward, but at least she'd be alive. He could work on healing the gap later. But he knew time was running out. *Less than twenty-four hours …*

"Speaking of which," she murmured, flipping over to face him again, "I caught sight of something when I was in the abyss last time. I need to go back there. I'd been chasing Anna's trail but caught a faint line on Sarah." The gold-dotted pathway Tavika had caught a glimpse of was hers. She was sure of it.

"Sarah? Really?"

"Yeah. I wanted to catch up and question her friends. She spent a lot of time on the street. I'm even more convinced her death had nothing to do with the Ghost. But, so far, no one will talk."

"That's fairly normal. Most people don't want to get involved."

"Especially when she had nothing to do with adults. She was known to hang around with kids her age and slightly older."

"She's fairly young for that."

"Young, but probably already very sick of the world and the adults in it." She explained the little bit of Sarah's background that Tavika knew. "And given that she died from a drug overdose, I'm wondering something completely different."

He caught his breath as the vision hit. A young girl smiling and laughing with other kids. A pile of drugs in front of her. Pills. Booze. A party-like atmosphere. "I'm not liking what I'm seeing, but, as I'm a precog, it could mean many things. Chances are some of the other kids are about to die," he said in a self-deprecating voice. "I see a young girl, laughing and joking with friends, as they piled up pills in front of her."

Tavika stared up at him. "Actually that's exactly what I think happened. She was dying of leukemia," Tavika stated simply. "Her various foster parents had done everything she'd let them do. The disease would have taken its toll on her system in its own good time. According to the foster families, one of the reasons she got moved from house to house was the medical care issue. She'd had enough."

"And you think her friends provided the drugs, so she could take her own life?" He thought about a young girl determined to take such a step but surrounded by friends and family. It said a lot about who she was. He saw that. Especially if she had been traumatized by adults who seemed to do things to her that never helped and always hurt. Who made decisions for her and wouldn't listen to her wishes.

Tavika nodded. "Taking her own life put the control back in her hands, whether the rest of the world agreed or not. That would appeal to the teens. They were on the streets, looking for validation in this world, while thumbing their nose at the authority they'd had so much difficulty with."

"Damn." His voice reflected how he felt. Both sad and yet happy.

"That's how I feel." Tavika stared up at him, the corner of her lips turned down. "But I haven't had a chance to get out and to prove my theory yet."

"And the kids will deny it to their graves. Because it's just as important to them that they helped her as it was to her that she did this on her own."

"Exactly."

He thought about the way she'd been found. "Why do you think her body was moved to the electrician's house?"

He watched her thoughts tumble and churn behind those huge chocolate-colored eyes. She had a brain he admired. Her way of working out a problem, of coming up with answers, was amazing.

"If we think about this from a child's point of view, I'm thinking she knew the electrician. Maybe even heard about his death or found out something bad had happened to him. Maybe she really liked him. And maybe it was the kids' way of taking care of their friend. Or maybe they were so afraid of authority that they didn't have a clue what to do with her."

He thought about that and realized there were any number of reasons for the kids to think such a thing. "But getting her there would've been a chore for a bunch of young teenagers."

"One of the kids likely had a driver's license. They may even be from the wealthy sector and in their own vehicles. If they were mobile, they could've taken her there."

"And the broken neck?" he asked cautiously. That was a little bit more bizarre. He wasn't exactly sure how or why somebody would do that.

"To throw us off," she stated simply. "Knowing kids, they may have thought we'd look at the broken neck, see that as a cause of death, and not look any further."

"If the cops thought she committed suicide or had drugs in her system, they'd go looking for the source," he noted in understanding.

"Putting her friends in danger of getting caught," she

added, with a small smile.

"True. What will you do about it?"

She sat up, grabbed a sweatshirt to throw over her shoulders, and walked to the kitchen table. She pulled out the chair and sat down. "I'm going into the abyss to find out where they are."

She bowed her head.

Just like that, she was gone.

HE STARED OUT the window. He hoped he was doing the right thing. That his plan would work. To take these names off his list was his way of letting go. Moving on.

Achieving the life he wanted.

The family he wanted.

This had to work …

There was one person in his way. And he had to stop her.

She was a distraction that he couldn't afford. He knew now she was to blame for all the things going wrong. And he knew why.

She was shit out of luck if she thought that would save her now. He didn't know how he would go after her, but he'd taken a few days' personal leave. That would let him follow her and pick the perfect opportunity.

The place he planned to take her was already there and waiting.

Hell, it had been sitting empty for twenty years.

Now it was time.

Only then could he achieve what he wanted.

He had to take her back home, where she belonged.

CHAPTER 34

TAVIKA WALKED INTO the abandoned warehouse on the corner of First Street and Wicker Avenue. Part of one of the many deserted areas of town that had seen better days at least twenty years ago. Now, with the new highways rerouting the arteries through the city, some of the streets had been totally abandoned. This was one of those. But she also knew now this was one of the main meeting places for the kids.

Jericho had wanted to come in. And she'd chosen to let him, in spirit form only. The kids would feel intimidated if too many adults, much less authority figures, showed up. From Jericho's point of view, she was putting herself in danger—because she didn't know if there were four or forty kids at any one time. And he was right. But, as long as she could keep this low-key, he could stay under the radar. If the teens got aggressive, then she would call in backup.

Her footsteps echoing hollowly in the large building, she walked over to the single door in the far corner. On the other side she expected there to be the series of offices that had at one point kept this mill working.

She didn't give anyone a warning as she approached. She opened the door and stepped inside.

"Hey." One young male stood and glared at her.

"Who is she?" called out someone else.

"Lady, what do you want? You aren't allowed in here."

She let her gaze drift from one to the other, then got sidetracked to the middle of the room. Photos and lit candles were in the center of a large beat-up old table. And Tavika recognized the girl in the photos. *Sarah*.

And Tavika understood what they were doing.

She let her gaze drift back over the faces of the two dozen kids collected here. She saw a monster of a boy in the back. He had tears in his eyes, but the look on his face was rapidly turning to outrage. Looking like he was fourteen, he had to weigh in at 250 pounds and stood over six feet. But he also appeared childlike. Somebody who didn't know his own strength. Someone who hadn't grown mentally into those size fourteen shoes.

She nodded. Just as she suspected. "It's a nice thing you are doing for your friend right now."

Silence.

A young girl with blue hair in front of her stood now, an apprehensive look on her face. "What the hell do you know?"

Another girl stepped up, with so much anger and hardness on her face that Tavika knew the girl had had a tough time in her short years too. "Get the hell out of here, bitch."

Tavika shook her head. "No."

Several of the young men now stood. She judged the power among them all and realized the odds were really not in her favor.

Beside her, Jericho snorted, adding, *Ya think?*

She ignored him and kept her attention on the tall, arrogant male in the center of the room, with several other young men lined up on either side.

"If I leave now, I'll be forced to come back with a lot of cops as backup. I don't think you want that." She turned to the girls in front, who were looking at each other. It would always be a mistake to turn her back on one of them. These girls had been raised in the streets and had earned hard-knock status in life already. They'd attack as soon as Tavika tried to walk away.

In a calm voice she added, "I'm not here to cause you any trouble. But, if you cause *me* any, I'll come back for you." Several sneers appeared. She smiled. "Sure you can find another place to hang out and to feel cool for a while, but I will find you, like I did this time."

A few kids snorted.

"Or we can have a nice talk, and I can leave." Her words vibrated in the air. She caught sight of tears in the girls' eyes, as they did their best to not panic.

For the males, well, their aggression was growing. Energy sparked and fired up from several of their systems. They were at a dangerous level—wanting to protect the females and themselves and having a natural hatred of cops. She was not in a great position.

From the corner of her eye, she watched and waited as Jericho sent out a blanket of calm and peace over everyone. *Nice. You need to show me how to do that. It would be great for riot control.*

That makes my blood freeze to think of you in the middle of a riot.

One of the girls in front, her hair a dirty blonde, asked, "Talk about what?"

Tavika studied her face, which had been battered and healed—badly. The cheek and eye socket were wonky, as if it had been broken once too often and not received any medical care. She could get it fixed. But she had no trust in anyone, and, at her age, it was hard to get anything done without involving the authorities or the adults at home. And it was obvious she'd chosen to go the opposite direction.

Not sure what to say, Tavika opened her mouth, and the words that came out surprised her—and them. "I want to thank you."

"For what?" asked the young man in the center, a confused look on his face, as well as distrust.

He had just enough arrogance to get himself in trouble. All these kids were living on bravado and street smarts. A dangerous combination. At the moment they still weren't sure why she was here.

"I understand why Sarah felt she had to do what she did, and I understand how she did it. Nice to know that the people closest to her in her life cared enough to help her out. To get hold of the meds so she could do it ..." She stopped talking, seeing several furtive looks among the kids. Nobody quite knew what to say or do.

"I don't know what meds you're talking about," said the big guy in the back.

"Prescription drugs, usually for pain relief, also in cough medicine. Harmless on their own but—in large proportions and when mixed with alcohol or other medications—deadly. Easy to steal from families and foster homes. Easy to break into houses and raid medicine cabinets."

More gazes stared at the ground. But many of these kids stared at her belligerently. She understood. They had done what they had to do to help out one of their own. She turned her gaze to the big guy. "At least she was dead before you broke her neck."

He gasped and straightened to his full height, panic rising across his face. "I didn't kill her. I didn't have anything to do with that."

Tavika nodded. "I know that. You hoped we wouldn't find the drugs in her system this way, I suppose?"

"She took them herself. But no way you guys would believe us," stated the blue-haired girl.

"Sometimes that would be true. You kids like to lie, cheat, and steal and think there are never going to be repercussions, so it makes it difficult to know when you're telling the truth."

One of the shorter males in the middle of the room laughed. "No way you or any other cop would have believed us if we had told you that Sarah took them willingly."

Tavika studied him. "Actually I probably would've, once I realized she was dying, and there was nothing the medical profession could do to help her, and she'd shifted from foster home to foster home to avoid getting more treatments. At that point it all made sense."

She let her gaze continue to drift around the room. "Of course we can also tell when someone was force-fed those pills. There's always bruising, damage to the lining of the mouth and throat. In this case, there was nothing. So we knew Sarah took the bulk of the pills on her own. Choosing to do so at her time and place, surrounded by her friends."

At those words, one of the girls on the side burst into tears. Another girl wrapped her arms around her and held her close.

"I do, however, have questions. And I do need to get the answers." She studied the girl with the broken cheek and said quietly, "If you want to get that fixed, I'll give you my support."

The girl sneered. "And what do you want in return?"

"I can see there's a hard-luck story behind this." The girl tossed her locks in disdain, but Tavika persisted. "What you don't realize is you're not alone. Many people have hard-luck stories. You can stay as you are, or you can fix them, so you make something of your life. It's up to you."

She turned her attention back to the big guy in the back of the room. He was already blubbering. "Why did you turn her head all the way around?" she asked.

The big kid went from blubbering to bawling. He shook his head wildly, and, in a harsh whisper, punctuated by sobs, he replied, "I didn't mean to. It just went all the way around. Like it was nothing …" And he broke down completely.

Right. As she expected to happen with a young girl who suffered from leukemia.

She glanced over at Mr. Cocky. "And you? Where did you get the vehicle to move her to Connor Breaker's house, and why take her there?"

"She really liked him. Every once in a while she'd slip over and visit him," he told her, with much of his bravado gone. "When she heard what happened to him, she was pretty upset. She didn't want him to die alone. That's when she made the decision to go."

"Ah. That explains it. She swallowed the pills at Breaker's house, didn't she?"

They all nodded.

Jesus, Jericho whispered. *This is unbelievable. They are something else.*

Yeah they are. They lost one of their own.

She pulled out a notebook and pen and handed it to the blue-haired girl. "Your name. And the name of everyone else here, please."

Silence. Miss Blue Hair turned to look at the others, then shrugged. She started writing.

"Don't make me come back for your correct names. I

will not be alone."

Miss Blue Hair shot Tavika a dirty look and scratched off what she'd started to write. She wrote down a name and handed it to the next girl. The process continued until everybody in the room had written on Tavika's notepad. Tavika knew chances were good that she'd get a series of Mickey Mouse, Donald Duck, and any number of superhero names on that list. But there would also be a number of real ones. And she was content to take this one step at a time. She didn't want these kids to end up like Gordon had. Unfortunately it was just too damn likely they might.

When the notebook and pen were handed back to her, she gave a nod, "I'm glad you're celebrating her life here. She died surrounded by people who cared, and that's more than many of us get." She turned and walked out. Back outside in the fresh air, she stood still for a moment and stared up at the sky. She whispered out loud, "No way law enforcement training ever prepared me for shit like this."

She heard the rumble of laughter from Jericho somewhere in the vicinity on her right. *Maybe not, but you did great.*

She shook her head and pulled out her phone. The call came through seconds later. "What do you want, Travis?"

I want you to stop hunting him, he snapped abruptly.

She closed her eyes and pinched the bridge of her nose. "Travis, we've been over this. You know I have to. It's the only way for this to be over. Most of the time you're on board with the plan," she added humorously.

Don't. It's not funny anymore. I think the list of names are people he's considering killing—but hasn't made a definite decision. In your case, I think he just made one. And just like that, Travis disappeared.

"Dammit, Travis, get back here. You can't just drop a bomb like that and disappear."

But apparently he could because he was no longer around. There wasn't even a sense of him being here.

What did he say? Jericho asked.

She quickly relayed the new information, adding, "But he didn't back up his comment with any proof. If he had any, he didn't tell me."

Stefan's voice ripped through her mind, making her gasp in shock. She bent over and almost fell to her knees. *Jesus, Stefan, stop that,* she cried out.

Well, if you'd open the damn door, I wouldn't have to do it this way, Stefan replied, anxiety in his voice. *You saved Anna once. We need you to help her again. Etheric form is fine.*

Tavika stumbled to her feet. "What's wrong with Anna? She's in the hospital safe and sound. Right?"

Not quite. We need you at the hospital. Now!

THEY RACED BACK to her truck, parked across from the warehouse. They'd head to the hospital from there. In spirit form.

Somehow Jericho beat her to the hospital and strode into the private children's wing ahead of her. Obviously something was going on. He also knew neither Stefan nor Dr. Maddy would be here in person. Then again he and Tavika weren't either.

At least not all the time. He was stopped by a nurse wearing a name tag. Carmen. He quickly identified himself. Her face cleared, and a big smile lit up her eyes. She led him over to the room in the far corner, where Anna lay still, sleeping. He leaned closer. No, not sleeping. Damn. He turned to the nurse. *Stefan didn't give us much in the way of details. What's wrong with her?* He was relieved she heard him. Only in one of Stefan's and Dr. Maddy's facilities would telepathy be normal in any way.

"Her silver cord is getting fainter. She's gone away and come back. Stefan and Dr. Maddy don't think she's got more than a day. And then she'll disconnect."

Jericho winced. It happened. At this point there was very little he could do to help her. *Any idea why Stefan thinks Tavika can help?*

The nurse shook her head. "No, but I trust both Dr. Maddy and Stefan. They said Tavika was required to bring Anna home."

Long clipped strides walked toward them. Even in spirit form he smiled. It was hard to miss her approach.

Well, I'm here, but I have no idea what I'm supposed to do. Why would you guys think I can help?

Stefan's voice echoed gently between the three adults as he explained, *Because you need to go into the abyss and follow her to find out where she's hiding and coax her back home.*

If the situation weren't so serious, Jericho would have laughed at the look of shock on her face. Her jaw actually dropped open.

But …

No, Stefan said sternly. *You have the capability. You do this all the time. The only difference here is you need to follow her deeper. In fact, this will likely be easier than what you are currently doing.*

That's not exactly the same thing. She shook her head. *I can't do it.* She turned to walk away.

Jericho raced behind her. *What's the matter, Tavika? You go into the abyss all the time.*

She refused to look at him. This woman who had just faced down dozens of angry teens and had single-handedly got them all on her side was now scared of going into a place where she'd already been many times.

He grasped her chin gently and tilted her head, so he could look at her face. And saw the terror inside. His heart ached. He might not understand this struggle, but it was obviously major for her.

Tavika? Why is this so difficult?

WHEN OPPORTUNITY STRUCK, one had to act.

Hell, it wasn't his fault they'd driven way the hell out here and had parked close to the river. He'd put a tracker on her truck. It was imperative he find her when he was ready. Of course his mind was immediately working on possible scenarios.

But when they came racing back, as if about to tear out of the lot—only to have the truck just sit there—he'd been stunned. He'd even gone for a walk to see what the hell was going on.

It was like they were sleeping.

Or maybe drugged?

Still, it was a gift.

One he had no intention of turning down.

CHAPTER 35

TAVIKA KNEW SHE should've gone home instead of jumping free while sitting in her truck. They hadn't thought that through. She'd never done this stuff from anywhere but home.

Leaving her body to come here in spirit form was already hard enough, but these requests, they were like blows to her system.

She took an unsteady breath and said, *I don't know if I can. You're asking me to go into her psyche. I could kill her. Don't you see that? To go in there? … That's where I went twenty years ago. No, it's impossible.*

He'd hate her after this. No way he wouldn't. It was hard to live up to the admiration and respect she'd seen growing in his eyes. She had wanted those badly. After a lifetime of scorn and derision, they were music to her soul.

But to ask this of her? … Besides, there was no way to do what they were asking. Even if she went deeper, it didn't mean she could go inside the poor girl and find her soul.

Hell, no one would have been able to find Tavika back then. She'd had to come out alone. And she almost hadn't. No way she could help Anna at this stage.

Dr. Maddy's voice whispered through her mind. *Yes, you can. I'll help. We have to save Anna. And, if that means you have to greet that little girl, who is still hiding in her own little locked-away space, then that's what we need to do. You knew this time was coming. No, we didn't expect it to be today, but, for the sake of another little girl, who has already been through enough, please try.*

Not fair. Dr. Maddy had already done so much to help Tavika. How could she now turn away from a request to help someone else? She bowed her head, raised both hands to cover her eyes. She should be out hunting killers. Not trying to track down silver cords in the abyss.

Have you ever seen cords in the abyss? Dr. Maddy asked.

Tavika opened her eyes and lifted her head. Maybe that's what those lines had been that she'd seen. *I have no idea. I see a lot in there. Most I haven't understood.*

It would be nice if we could talk later. I'd like to learn more, Dr. Maddy requested simply.

Tavika turned back to where Carmen stood at Anna's bedside. It was impossible to think Tavika could do something the famous Dr. Maddy couldn't.

Oh, it happens all the time, Dr. Maddy quipped, a note of humor in her voice. *We can't all know everything. Inasmuch as we would like to try.*

Her feet dragging, Tavika slowly turned her attention to Anna's bedside. And her feet as she walked closer.

Carmen's face glowed with happiness. "Thank you so much for trying."

And if I fail?

"Then we still thank you for trying," Carmen stated firmly. "Life isn't always about succeeding. We often learn more through failure."

And Carmen stepped back, giving Tavika room, while she sat down on the side of Anna's bed. She wasn't sure how to begin.

Did she need to go home first? Normally she was in her body when she started these trips.

A hell of an audience was here, something she wasn't terribly comfortable with. She was used to moving her hands as needed, and her actions would look comical to those watching. Not to mention impacting her ability to do what she needed to.

Forget about them, Dr. Maddy said. *They will have questions as to what you are doing, but they can wait until afterward or not at all, if you aren't up to answering them. It's not about you or them. It's about—*

—Anna. Right.

Tavika took a deep breath, released it on an exhale, and entered into the abyss. She tried hard to use minimal hand motions and to shrug off the sense of being watched. Dr. Maddy was right. This was about Anna. But the child was also out of time.

To make this as fast as possible, Tavika waved away the clouds and dove straight downward. Wind brushed past her face, blowing her hair, lifting the strands, as she dove deeper and deeper. She heard the faint gasps of those who watched her, knowing they were seeing something freakish. It didn't matter.

Focused now, she kept going. When she thought she was far enough, she opened her eyes, looking for and finding the blue dots. She had to make sure she didn't slip into the same place she'd been taken to last time. She had no wish to see that dark, cold room ever again.

A faint outline was to her right. She closed her eyes and chased after it. The clouds moved in between, but, with gentle firmness, she moved them away. She'd never done this so fast. The descent was almost headache-forming. She took several more deep breaths, trying to acclimate to the altitude in this weird space, as she fell through levels.

She tried hard to control the *boom* but knew the people around her were still feeling the shock waves, as she dove deeper and deeper and deeper.

She dared not go looking around. Dared not lose focus. She opened her eyes again and took a second to find loose strands. For a moment she thought she'd gone past where she needed to be. Having done that once and gotten lost, she knew getting back safely was one hell of a nightmare.

But, no, it was here. She twisted slightly and followed the blue strand. She slipped continually lower. Finally she was above the city, looking down. And froze because right below her was the hospital.

Where Anna lay. Where Tavika sat.

Surely that couldn't be right?

Stefan's voice surrounded her inside and out, the essence of his words sliding through her. *It's right. Keep going.*

She'd trusted everyone so far, so no point in stopping now. She closed her eyes and shot like a beam down the blue line, as far as it would go. There was an odd sensation of going through something cold and hot. She opened her eyes to see herself hovering right above Anna's body. Her own sat in front of her. Shocked, she didn't know what to do.

She'd never seen anything like this.

Once again warmth surrounded her. She heard Stefan urging, *Keep going.*

Shuddering, hating the fear rippling at the edges of her energy and the shock of this bizarre scene, she closed her eyes and let her soul fall all the way down. As far as it could.

When she opened her eyes again, it was to feel warmth, like a cozy hug surrounding her, except she was once again in total darkness. She looked around, grateful it wasn't the same room. It smelled different. The shadows a different form, color. But where was she?

It was like dark cotton balls were everywhere. She blasted energy out so she saw, and all the cotton balls moved back out of the way.

Anna was curled in a tiny ball, her form thin and indistinct. More spirit than body. More faded than substantial. Not like the first time she'd seen her. Why would she choose to be here?

It took a moment to assess the differences between the two spaces, the room where Anna had been found and this one, and Tavika realized that this room was warm, and the other had been cold. The other full of fear and pain. Here was a sense of comfort.

And it felt safe.

That's why Anna was here. She felt safe. Protected from all the horrors of the world.

Tavika sat down and lifted Anna into her arms and just held her. This time, instead of her arms going through the child, Tavika's energy blended with Anna's, and the hug became a two-way energy exchange.

Anna snuggled in closer.

If she'd had someone come to her in this form when she'd been held captive, Tavika knew she'd have stayed there too. It was too difficult to return to the land of the living. There was so much pain that anything was better than remembering it. Which was why Tavika hadn't opened up to live her own life. She'd locked down her memories and had refused to open them.

But she had grown up and had made something of herself. And now maybe, with Jericho, she could make something *with* him.

She wanted that for Anna.

First, she had to get the child to come back out of this space. *Anna, you can't stay here.*

Anna shook her head, little bits of energy flaring off her as she did. *Why?*

Because people who love you are waiting for you. There's a much better life than you've been able to have so far ahead of you. If you stay here, you'll die. You'll fade away and never come back. You'll never see your mom or dad again. Or have a puppy. You'll never dance, sing, or swim.

Doesn't matter.

What does matter? Laughter? Ice cream? Cookies? Your mother's hug?

She sent me to him. It's her fault.

Tavika winced. *And she's very sorry. She didn't know he was a bad man. She feels horribly guilty. It's breaking her heart to see you lying in your bed like this.*

He's a bad man.

Yes. He is a bad man, but he's been picked up by the police, and he's in jail. He will never get out. This bad man will have a very bad time in jail. It still doesn't stop your mom from hurting so badly, by losing her little girl who she loves very much. She felt more than saw Anna's response. *You love your mom, don't you?*

Anna nodded.

Do you want to see your mom cry for the rest of her life too?

This time Anna's headshake was even stronger.

Good. *Then let me take you home. When you wake up, your mom will be there to hold you. And she'll always hold you whenever you need a hug.*

Anna's small arms creeped up around Tavika's neck, and

she whispered, *Okay.*

Tavika wrapped her up tight in her arms and blended her energy as much as she could with the little girl's, and, in her mind, she wished Anna back into her body.

There was a soft *whoosh*, followed by an odd landing.

With her arms suddenly empty, Tavika opened her eyes, wondering why the hell anybody would trust her to do something like this. She had no idea what she was doing and could do irreparable harm.

She could inadvertently kill this little girl.

And, just like that, Anna's body appeared below Tavika. She watched in shocked joy as Anna's body shifted on the bed, as her soul realigned. Her mother rushed across the room, tears streaming down her face, joy breaking across her features. Instantly she sat down and snatched up Anna's hand.

Carmen stood at her side, tears in her eyes.

Beside them stood a beautiful man, who radiated a strong golden energy.

Stefan?

He turned to look at Tavika directly and smiled.

It *was* him. Tavika slowly lowered down, so she stood at Stefan's side.

In her mind he said, *You did a great job, Tavika. Never doubt yourself.*

She snorted. *You have any idea how badly I could have messed that up?*

He smiled. *A heart with pure intention will always rise to the top.*

She shook her head. *You live in a golden world, Stefan. Reality is a lot different.* She turned to look for Jericho. There was no sign of him. *Where is Jericho?*

Stefan frowned. *No idea. He was here.*

Just then a twisting, grinding pain took a hold of her. *Jesus.* Tavika arched, her spirit spinning out of control but consumed by pain. She didn't know what was happening. *Dear God, Stefan, what's going on? Something is wrong. Help.*

She screamed, a sound that seemed to go on forever—until a blow to the side of her head stopped it instantly.

And she went unconscious.

TAVIKA'S SCREAM WAS a sound Jericho never wanted to hear again. He couldn't even begin to recognize it. But the tone was one he knew well. That was Tavika's voice. He struggled to reach for her. Only to realize the scream had ripped through his mind.

She was no longer beside him.

What the hell happened? He cast his mind, trying to figure out where he was versus where he'd been. They'd been speaking with the group of kids, Sarah's friends. And then Stefan needed them to help Anna. They had raced out to the truck, and, given the urgency, they stayed and jumped free from there.

Tavika had been worried she wouldn't be able to go into the abyss, if she weren't in her natural surroundings, but he'd reassured her several times this was something they could do from anywhere.

Something clamored for attention. He was moving. The truck was moving. Rolling downward.

What the hell? The truck slammed into something hard, and he heard splashing water. With a horrible knowing, he watched as the truck sank in the river with him in it. His hands and ankles were tight. He sent out a warning to

Stefan.

Stefan, I'm in trouble. Tavika is missing. I just woke from spirit-walking at the hospital with you. I'm in the truck where we left our bodies, but she's not here, and the truck's sinking into the river. I'm not even sure what river. We were parked around ... He struggled to remember the address. Then it came to him—the warehouse district at First and Wicker. *She's been kidnapped. While we were helping Anna, somebody was helping himself to us.*

That was any psychic's worst fear.

Stefan's voice slammed into his mind. *Easy. We'll look for Tavika. Can you get out of the vehicle?*

I'm trying, but I'm tied up. He shifted in the truck, so he could slip two fingers into his pocket and pull out his knife. The water was rising to his knees. Within seconds he had his hands free and was working on his feet.

Done. I've cut the ties. Now I have to get the hell out of here. The doors wouldn't open. The windows didn't have cranks. That was the problem with power locks and windows. The water inside still rose.

Shit.

He turned and saw the rear window, a slider. He had it open in seconds, and water gushed in. Taking a huge breath, he squeezed his big frame through, panic helping him make it. Free, he kicked hard to the surface.

Breaking through the water, he gasped for breath. Where the hell was he?

He saw where the truck had gone over. He swam to the side and pulled himself out of the water. He sat here for a brief moment to catch his breath, then bolted to the top of the bank. *Tavika, if you can hear me, I'm coming for you, honey. Stefan, I'm free. Climbing up to where the truck went over. If Hunter is around, I sure could use a ride.*

He's tracking you. Should be there soon. I'm tracking Tavika. No sign of her.

Shit. Shit. If he's got her, he'll take her back to her old house, where he thinks she belongs. Jericho stood, swaying at the top of the bank, as a large Jeep Cherokee pulled up. *Hunter.*

Opening the door, Jericho hopped in and said, "We need to go to the same house where Tavika was held captive the last time."

"You sure?"

"As sure as I can be, considering Stefan can't find her either."

"So she's unconscious?" Hunter asked cautiously, as he pulled the Jeep around and ripped out of the parking lot, heading in the direction of Kinsman Park.

"No," he replied bleakly. "I suspect she's trapped in that damn soundproofed room she was in before."

"But wouldn't everyone know to look for her there?"

He hoped not. Dear God, he hoped not. Because that would mean the killer had taken her somewhere else.

And Jericho would have no way to find her.

NOW SHE WAS home where she belonged. He smiled, feeling a sense of satisfaction twenty years coming. He knew he shouldn't have let her live all those years ago. Stupid of him.

It was time to rectify the mistake.

He'd calmed down a lot over the years, and now he was more settled. Comfortable. Secure. Because he was in love now. He beamed. He just had to tie up a few loose threads. And grieve over the loss of an activity that he'd devoted a lot of time and energy to perfecting. That was the hardest part. He wondered if he could treat himself to one a year—or maybe two. Something to keep the fun alive.

But then that wasn't a fresh start, was it? He'd promised himself that. Promised the love of his life that.

He'd promised someone else a long time ago. And he hadn't kept that promise either.

He was a bad boy.

But a happy bad boy. Sometimes. Sometimes he was so conflicted. Then he'd see something that would piss him off, and he'd allow himself that treat.

Obviously that wasn't his fault.

All these people deserved to die. The victims were responsible because of whatever he'd seen them do wrong at the time.

He was busy correcting the wrongs of the world, and the people were just bent on creating more. Hell, he could spend a lifetime killing the bastards who deserved to die and still not get even close to a proper cleanup.

Not his fault.

On that note, he laughed and walked out. Almost nothing to walk back out of. This place was a hell of a mess.

Perfect.

She didn't deserve any better.

And, after this, she'd never get anything ever again.

CHAPTER 36

"TAVIKA! OH, TAVIKA ..."

She shuddered. No matter how old she became, that voice could still drive her to panic in two seconds flat. It wasn't fair. She should be past the stage of being controlled by destructive nightmares.

Tavika?

She frowned at a different voice. Stefan? Was she having a nightmare?

This is no nightmare. Wake up, Tavika. Now. You're in danger. So is Jericho.

Danger? She slowly woke up to find her body screaming in agony. Her muscles cramped, her bones aching—everything hurt. As if she'd had some kind of major trauma. Her mind was moving sluggishly, her thoughts cloudy, as she asked, *What the hell happened, Stefan?*

You've been kidnapped. You were in the hospital with Jericho, helping Anna, then you turned around and asked where Jericho was. Before I had a chance to answer, your physical body was attacked. The killer ran your truck into the river to try to drown Jericho, but he escaped. You hear me? He's okay.

Jericho? She tried to shake the cobwebs from her brain, get up to speed. Somebody tried to drown her Jericho?

Tavika, can you get out, can you move, are you tied up, are you hurt?

I don't know. My brain. She reached a hand up to her head and felt the stickiness on her temple. *I'm hurt,* she whispered. *I've got a head injury. There's blood.*

Is it bad? Stefan asked sharply. *Come on, Tavika. Get it together.*

I'm here, she protested. *Give me a second.* She took a deep breath and tried to assess where she was and what was going on. She could barely see the room. It was so dark. *The room reminds me of Anna's cell.*

Tavika tried to move her arms and realized her hands were tied together in front of her. She could still reach up and touch her head, but she couldn't separate one arm from the other. She tried to move her feet and found the same thing but not as tight. First things first.

Stefan, my hands and feet are tied up.

Are you tied to something, or can you stand up and walk around?

Just a minute. Using her teeth, she worked on the nylon knots holding her wrists. Finally she loosened one, then the other. With a cry of relief, she reached down and quickly undid the knots around her ankles.

The wall behind her offered support, as she managed to hop to her feet. Then she realized just how much her body hurt. She could barely hold back the gasp of pain. Tears burned her eyes. She wanted to bend over and to collapse on the ground. But that wouldn't do her any good. She studied her surroundings instead.

She'd been here before. Dear God, she knew where she was.

Are you sure? You just said it looked like Anna's cell.

No, her cell looked like my old one. I could be in my old house, but I don't know that. There are no windows here. But there was in my old house. Unless they've been painted black. I can't see any light shining in. The room is so dark.

Light up the room, Tavika. Pour out energy and light it up.

She did as instructed, feeling immediately better when she saw the four walls of her cell and the door. And she saw something else. Windows.

They'd been covered up with boards, then painted black.

And she saw something else on the wall beside her.

Her name.

A name she'd scratched into concrete when she'd been held here long ago.

Her stomach heaved. She bent over and puked on the floor. Oh, dear God. She'd known this time was coming, but she'd thought she'd have some warning.

Not to be caught in this nightmare all over again.

She took several deep breaths and said, *Stefan, I'm at my old house. My name is scratched in the wall. I did that the last time I was here.*

We're on our way. Jericho and Hunter are coming too.

Good. You need to bring in the police, she added. *He won't go out without a fight. He'll also make sure I don't survive.* She took a deep breath and added, *So watch for booby traps.*

Will do.

She almost laughed. What she would have done to have had Stefan with her in her last incarceration. In her mind she whispered, *Dear God, please let me survive. And, if I can't, then please save the others. Except the Ghost. I'd die happy if I took him with me.*

Stefan snapped at her. *Don't think like that. And don't let revenge drive you. Remember my warning about your old energy? It powers your shield.*

So how did he find me? she asked bitterly. *What was the*

point in having a shield if he got around it anyway?

Except for one thing …

Stefan's voice was faint and getting fainter. It was hard to hear.

If you didn't plan on having the Ghost find you, why did you send out the beacon so he could?

Sure, that was to lure him in, but the shield was to protect me from him. She frowned. *So how did he get in then?*

You have to answer that question. I don't know.

When her shield went down, had she let him in then? Or had he never needed the beacon to find her in the first place?

Just as she wanted to argue, knowing something else was there to understand, she heard a sound that made her heart freeze and her soul start crying.

Her mother was screaming, as if she were being killed all over again.

Tavika closed her eyes and whimpered. How were those screams happening all over again?

Just when she thought she couldn't handle it anymore, her sister started to cry and plead. The pain and fear her sister went through tore Tavika apart. She curled up on the floor in a tiny ball, trying to block off the sounds she'd heard once before. She didn't know whether the ghost of her sister and mother were here or not, but this was just too damn much.

Tavika couldn't do this.

She couldn't listen to them die—not again.

JERICHO AND HUNTER parked the Jeep half-a-block away, and both approached on foot on opposite sides of the house.

Stefan had set up communications with the police. Jericho knew he shouldn't go racing in, but it was so damn hard to hold back. Tavika was a prisoner in there; he just knew it.

Yes, she is in there. Tied up and working to free herself. Also something very strange is going on. Just before I blinked out, I heard the screams of her mother and sister, as if they were dying.

Jericho frowned. "But they're dead, right?"

As far as I know, Stefan said, *but it's not as if I've spoken to their ghosts.*

Interesting. Was something going on?

Tavika also warned about a booby trap, Stefan added. *She's afraid the place will be rigged to blow or something similar.*

Shit. Jericho hadn't considered that, but it made sense.

What he didn't want was to have the cops come in with their sirens screaming and scaring the Ghost off again. No way that asshole was getting away this time. A dark sedan pulled up and parked down the street.

Jericho watched as one man got out, talking on his phone. He put it away and walked closer to the house. He looked around furtively and then slipped into the back.

The problem was, Jericho recognized him.

Jericho narrowed his gaze. Was he going in alone or had he been setting up backup on the phone? Or did he have a different reason for being here? Jericho checked out his energy, but it was different from the Ghost's. Jericho raced behind him.

He caught him at the far corner and dragged him back and away from the house to the large stand of trees on the side. He shoved his face into the newcomer's. "What the hell are you doing here?"

"I'm Henry, a friend of Tavika's," he said urgently.

"She's in trouble."

"So you came alone?" Jericho asked in astonishment, letting him go. Surely this wasn't the backup.

"I am a cop," Henry snapped. "It's what I do. Besides, who the hell are you?"

Jericho snorted. "Then you also know she's been kidnapped and likely being held here." As Henry's face paled, Jericho added, "It's the same damn place she was held twenty years ago." He gave Henry a shake. "Did you know that too?"

"I do know that." He shook his head, then nodded in confusion. "But that was a long time ago. A different time. The Ghost went to sleep. He's not been active in years," Henry protested. "So it won't be him now."

"According to the FBI, the Ghost is responsible for over forty-seven murders in the last twenty years. Tavika has three on her desk that she's trying to prove—and that's just last week." Jericho sneered. "It sure as hell is him. And this time the bastard isn't getting away."

Henry gasped. "Dear God, how could we have missed this? I haven't been working cases in over ten years myself," he replied in a strangled voice. "Let me go in. I'll see if anybody is in there."

Jericho frowned. "I should be the one to go in."

"If she's retreated to the little girl she was last time, then she'll recognize me. I'm the one who saved her." He broke free from Jericho and ordered, "Stay here."

Henry bolted to the side of the house and slipped around the corner.

Shit. Jericho shouldn't have let him go. Suspicious, Jericho followed Henry. He might have rescued Tavika last time, but he'd also shown up damn quickly now. Nothing

Tavika had said had cleared this guy either. Even though his energy was different from the Ghost's.

He heard sounds of other vehicles arriving. Hopefully more cops.

He peered around at the back porch. It was empty. Henry must have made it inside. Hunter was on the other side of the house somewhere.

Jericho slipped up to the porch and listened. He heard voices but couldn't identify the speakers. Slipping free of his body so the men couldn't see him, he slipped along the porch to the door.

Once again he was stopped from entering. *Tavika? Can you hear me?*

Jericho? Be careful. The place could be booby-trapped.

Yeah, it's possible. Do you know any reason why Henry would be here? He felt her jerk of shock. *Can you come help me get through the door?*

I'm here. Tavika stood in front of him in ghost form. *We have to hurry. Are the cops on the way?*

I think that's why Henry is here.

She frowned. *He doesn't work the streets anymore. Neither does Charles.*

Jericho took a deep breath, his chest constricting in pain. *Please let me be wrong.* It did, however, explain something that had puzzled him after Hunter's conversation with Gordon's ghost. He'd used the term, *them.*

Help me inside. She reached out a hand and grasped his. Together they stood in the kitchen and stared.

Three men were in that room. Henry was one of them.

Jericho turned to face her, only to see tears clogging her eyes. *Tavika, was your mother married to Charles? Is he your father?*

She shook her head. *No. I don't think so. I don't know who my father was. He left before I was born. But Charles has been with Henry since forever. They both came to visit sometimes.*

Sometimes?

She nodded. *I don't remember when or why or how often. There were too many men. Remember?*

He remembered.

And the other man? he asked softly. *Do you recognize him?*

She shook her head, … then nodded. Tears flowed over her cheeks. *I don't know him,* she whispered, *but I think I know of him.*

A hard shudder racked her soul. *It's my older half brother, Barton.*

And her energy splintered into a million pieces.

CHAPTER 37

TAVIKA SLAMMED BACK into her body. Once again in the same damn basement. She opened her eyes, not surprised to feel the tears dripping down her cheeks. She'd hoped and prayed it wouldn't be somebody she knew personally, but that it was a family member, albeit one she didn't know, somehow made it even worse. She'd heard about Barton from her mother. Mostly laughing, mocking comments. About how nonpsychic he was. He'd taken after his father. But even now, as Tavika sat here in the darkness, she had no idea who Barton's father was. It might be Charles. But then why wouldn't her mother have said something?

I did. Why wouldn't you listen when I told you to stay away? Now you'll die too, her mother snapped in a waspish tone.

"Why didn't you tell me about Barton?"

Her mother's ghost shook her head. *I told you many times. You just don't remember. Hell, I wasn't cut out for motherhood. It was a good thing he went to live with Charles.*

Tavika couldn't understand. How did one let go of a child? "That's not what I mean. Why didn't you tell me that Barton was the killer?"

Because you'd have gone after him. I was trying to save you, but you wouldn't listen. Her mother's voice faded into the background, her form flickering in front of Tavika. *Barton hated me. More every day. He didn't want anything to do with the family, after I remarried. Besides, he was ten years older than Bellamy, and by the time you and Travis came along he actively hated all of us.*

"And you didn't tell me this earlier. Why?" Tavika was outraged. How the hell could her mother sit on this information all these years and not say anything? "You knew who was responsible, and yet you never told me?"

Tavika paced the small room. The ropes that had been used to tie her up were wrapped around her fists. She knew she had to get the hell out of here, but answers were here. For the first time her mother was talking.

He didn't just hate us, he hated what we stood for. He had no abilities when all of us had so many. I don't know if he was jealous or if, to him, we were evil. But something inside him snapped. Charles, Henry, and Barton came by to tell me Charles and Henry were getting married. I laughed at them. Said they were fools. That the law wouldn't let them. You have to remember that was twenty years ago, and the world wasn't as accepting.

Her voice thickened. *Barton came back that night. He told me what a horrible person I was. How lacking in love. How much I'd hurt Charles, and maybe it was the abilities inside me that made me so evil. He loved his father, and he didn't care about his alternative lifestyle.*

Oh, dear God. Tavika knew how harsh and overbearing her mother could be. And Tavika could easily see how angry she would have made Barton and how her insults and mockery would have hurt Charles and Henry. Tavika bowed her head. Everyone had suffered from her mother's nasty tongue at some time. They'd all wanted to shut her up. But only Barton had actually succeeded.

Then again he'll kill you anyway, and this is my chance to clear the air.

Tavika was shocked. "Did you ever care about me? Even now this isn't about saving me as much as it's about clearing the guilt off your shoulders."

I have nothing to feel guilty about, her mother yelled. *Barton's twisted. Something is wrong inside him.*

"Maybe so but he's killed over fifty people! People who had as much right to live a normal life as any of us."

Well, I couldn't have a normal life anymore, so why should I care?

Dumbfounded, Tavika stared at her mother's ghost. And she realized another truth. Her mother was nothing but an insecure woman, who'd used her abilities and the fame that came with it to stroke her ego, so she could gain some sense of self-worth.

She was a sad, empty person, who'd failed in every aspect of life. She was to be pitied. "Poor Bellamy and Travis," Tavika said quietly. "They didn't have to die. That's the really sad part in all of this."

I tried to save them. I tried to get him to kill you instead.

Her mother had said it in such a matter-of-fact voice that it took Tavika a moment to digest it. Then came a physical jolt to her heart. Her stomach twisted, as her mother continued her tirade.

But Barton wouldn't listen. Said you were the only one worth saving. But even then, he tortured you, so he must have hated you too. Her mother shrugged. *I should've listened to my gut in the first place.*

The blows just kept coming. What was Tavika to do with that statement?

Accept it and let it wash through you. Jericho's warm voice caressed inside her heart chakra. *She's a lonely, misguided ghost. Let her be. Don't listen to anything she has to say. You might want to consider that she's as twisted as Barton is. That she manifested her evil in a completely different direction than he did. Maybe that's where he got it from.*

Certainly nothing she'd confessed here and now was usable. Tavika walked over to the window. Reaching up, she pulled down the plywood, letting light in. The window was broken. It was easy enough to get out. Why would Barton make it that easy?

I don't think it was something he planned. I think he was so focused on doing what he needed to capture you that he couldn't think of all the details, like you escaping. Think of everything we know him to have done. It's all very simple. No elaborate plans. He leaves the bodies if they are home, or he takes them back home where they belong. Why? Jericho asked.

Maybe because he didn't have one. I'm going to find out. She ran her fingers through her hair. *I'm going upstairs.*

No. Wait.

Ignoring his protest, she walked to the basement door and popped it open. The lock was old and broken. She studied the rest of the basement for a moment and saw a tape recorder on the table. She popped the tape and read the label. It was dated the day her family had been taken hostage. Those screams she'd heard were real.

Barton had taped his handiwork.

Dear God. Shoving all thoughts to the back of her head, she pocketed the tape, and, with her weapon ready, slipped up the stairs to the main floor—and entered the argument raging in the living room now.

JERICHO SLAMMED INTO his body and raced to the rear kitchen door. Damn Tavika. Would she ever learn?

I'm learning exactly what I need to in order to finish this. Forever.

He crept through the kitchen to the living room. He could probably have screamed and shouted, and no one would have cared.

"Barton, you said you'd never do this again," Charles yelled in a horrified voice.

Barton sneered. "Sorry, Dad. You've always only listened to what you wanted to hear."

"But Jesus, Barton, the FBI said they have connected you to something horrible, like fifty cases," Henry cried out, wringing his hands in distress.

Jericho studied Tavika's half brother. Barton appeared to have no weapon on him. Was that possible? Both Henry and Charles, as former cops, were quite likely carrying. Tavika definitely was. And he saw her at the edge of the hallway.

Damn, she looked good.

She stepped into the room, her weapon trained on Barton. "Put your hands up," she ordered.

Barton turned on her and, in an instant, his smirk turned to fury. "How did you get out of the ropes?" he cried out, like a child upset when she hadn't played the game fairly.

"It wasn't hard," she noted calmly, her gaze never leaving him. "Charles and Henry, move to his side."

"No, you don't understand," Henry explained. "We didn't know."

"You might not have known about the bulk of those fifty cases, but you sure as hell knew he slaughtered my family."

Charles, his voice tremulous, pleaded, "But he had a psychotic episode. He's not responsible for that. He just snapped. Your mother …" And he stopped.

"I know exactly who and what my mother was. I also now know exactly what my half brother is. A murderer. He might have snapped that one day in my house, but killing someone in a fit of rage is not the same thing as keeping them captive for days to torture them at will."

She glanced at Henry. "Were you the one trying to use my computer?"

"No, that was me." Barton laughed. "I used Henry's log-in to access the cases early on, then switched to using yours."

A sick look washed over Henry's face.

Jericho stepped into the room, several cops behind him now. They quickly surrounded the group in the living room.

"And I know you were both here that day. That's why you rescued me, isn't it, Henry? You knew I was here because you and Charles had arrived at the scene first. Why was that?"

"Barton called us. Told us that he'd made your mother pay." Charles was sobbing now, as he held his hands out in front of him. "We didn't know until we got here what he'd done."

Jericho didn't trust any of them.

"I had to help him," Charles cried out. "He is my son. My only child."

"And Travis? Did he not have a right to live? What about Bellamy?"

Barton laughed. "They were spawns of the devil. They had to die. Only because you were normal did I let you live. The rest of those people? Nasty."

"And all the other people you killed?" Jericho asked. "Were they nasty too?"

"Some were. By then I had a taste for killing." A crooked smile appeared on his face. "I couldn't stop. I didn't want to. Then I was given the gift of love and an opportunity at a new life. A new beginning and I would have to stop killing. But the thing is, I was okay with that. Love does that to you."

"You're in love?" Tavika asked, her voice detached, calm.

Too calm, Jericho thought.

Barton beamed, and his whole face transformed. "I am. He's married, but he's leaving her for me. And we'll be a family. He has twin daughters who will be mine. We'll have a home of our own. And I'll have a place to belong. Finally."

Charles started to cry; Henry wrapped an arm around him.

A place to belong. Home. There it was. Everyone had one, and, in his mind, that was where everyone needed to be—in their own homes.

Jericho was stunned. Tavika was right—in such a horribly wrong way.

Charles stared at Barton in horror. "Does he know?"

"*He?*" Jericho asked. "Who is he?"

"Peters," Tavika said in a broken voice. "One of the detectives on my team and a friend."

Barton beamed. "Isn't he lovely?"

At the odd sound behind him, Jericho turned to see a man holding a weapon in front of him. It was aimed at the three men in the center of the room, but that stunned look on his face gave away his identity.

"Peters?" Jericho asked, hazarding a guess.

And Peters fired his gun.

Slowly Barton dropped to the ground, the bullet hole a macabre addition to his still smiling face.

CHAPTER 38

IN THE WEE hours of the morning, Tavika, Jericho on her heels, arrived back at her apartment.

They were exhausted.

Jericho opened his mouth to speak. She gently placed her finger across his lips and shook her head. "Tomorrow," she whispered. "Come to bed."

She dropped her jacket, unhooked her holster and weapon, and placed them carefully on top of her dresser. She stared at the weapon for a long moment, then turned her back on it. It took her less than a minute to shuck her clothes.

Jericho turned back the bedding and watched her collapse.

Solomon jumped up onto her back, his paws kneading her. And she didn't care.

"Let's cover her up first, big guy," Jericho said. Tavika smiled, as Solomon was lifted, blankets were thrown across her exhausted body, and then the cat gently replaced.

Solomon didn't give a damn; he lay down on her back and never moved.

Hell, neither did she.

Not until a good six hours later.

When she woke up, she was still tired and worn out, with sadness in her soul, yet peace in her heart.

And a nudge of her consciousness.

That little girl's blue energy she'd thought was new at her childhood home. That her mother had told her to forget about, as she'd been there forever.

She should have listened to her mother. She'd been right all along.

And Tavika was stunned to realize how.

That energy was a young girl.

But it wasn't a full spirit. It was bright because of the energy feeding it. It was, however, a partial spirit. From someone who'd been disconnected from her childhood.

Now she understood why she'd fought to not open that time of her life. Why she didn't have access to it. She'd disconnected from it.

That little girl was her.

And I'll love her as much as I love you. We just have to help you reconnect, Jericho murmured.

Tavika shuddered, as the incredible concept fluttered through her. *How was such a thing possible?*

Just like Anna, you went away. But, when you came back, you could only handle part of your experience, so, in a desperate move, you left part of you behind.

She closed her eyes, tears burning at the corners. She couldn't even begin to contemplate how cold and alone that part of her felt all these years.

Yet you can welcome her back to the fold, and you'll never feel separated from life again.

And she realized it really was that simple. She'd been actually separated. Disconnected at the most elemental levels possible.

Unbelievable.

And yet fixable.

It was so damn terrible and such a waste of what could have been glorious lives. All for what? A sense of revenge? She didn't even know what set Barton off originally—except her mother's wicked tongue.

And that had been bad enough.

As for Charles and Henry?… It wouldn't be good. They'd known what Barton had done and had covered it up and had enabled him to avoid paying for his crimes. Forced him into joining the military. That didn't last as he was given a dishonorable discharge within two years. They'd had him put on medication, even hospitalizing him at one point. They'd constantly monitored the case of the murder of Tavika's family, probably having a heart attack this last week as things blew up.

But the bottom line was, Charles and Henry had harbored a criminal, had obstructed a case, and who knew what else they'd be charged with. And through it all Barton had kept killing.

And Peters? That was tough yet again.

No way to hide what he'd done. He'd shot Barton in cold blood in front of many witnesses. Barton had been unarmed and standing as part of a group. Peters—shocked by what he'd heard—had put Barton down in a fit of his own rage.

That would not end well either.

As for Tavika? Well, she'd laid her ghosts to rest. She hoped to have Stefan's help to get her mother and sister to cross over. She had mixed feelings about the woman who gave birth to her, but the fact remained that her mother was stuck on this side, and she shouldn't be.

Then there was Travis …

He hadn't called. She didn't know if he was still here or

not. She'd be happy for his sake if he could finally move on, but she'd miss him.

Jericho's arm tightened around her belly, his fingers sliding up to cup her breast. She smiled and covered his hand with her own.

"You should be sleeping, not worrying about these heavy thoughts," he murmured.

"Lots to think about." She snuggled closer to him. She had no idea what brought Jericho into her life, but she was damn grateful. She'd do anything to stop him from disappearing as suddenly as he'd appeared in her life.

I'm not planning on going anywhere, he whispered in her mind. *Although we really could use a bigger apartment. Unless you didn't hear me earlier.*

She gasped, remembering what he'd said a few moments ago. *Did you mean it?*

Unless you don't want me to.

She heard the note of vulnerability in his voice. A matching note she held in her heart. *I want you to love me. As I am falling in love with you,* she admitted. *I just didn't recognize the emotion for what it was.*

We're a hell of a pair, aren't we?

You just want me to help you get through doors, she teased, with a smirk.

Actually I'd like you to teach me how to do that. And, if possible, I'd love to take a trip with you into the abyss.

Oh, I might be able to do that. And, in exchange, you can teach me how to cook, she noted wistfully. *I've been in that kitchen many times and never did it offer me anything as good tasting as you did.*

He froze, then he chuckled. He brushed the back of her neck with his lips. *Done. Does that mean we're going to live together?*

I wasn't planning on changing the living arrangements right now. Were you? she asked cautiously.

Nope. I'm right where I want to be.

She rolled over onto her back, so she saw the truth in his eyes. And she smiled. *Me too.*

Heat flared into life in the back of his eyes. *So maybe we should seal that deal with a kiss?*

And he lowered his head.

Just as his lips touched hers, she whispered, *I can get behind that.*

He laughed and kissed her.

There was no need for words now. Not at this point. With their minds already in sync, their hearts open to possibilities neither had ever thought to have, they let their bodies do the talking.

After all, they did it so well …

This concludes Book 10 of Psychic Visions: Into the Abyss.
Read the first Chapter of Seeds of Malice: Psychic Visions, Book 11

Seeds of Malice: Psychic Visions (Book #11)

Shunned by her friends, betrayed by her lover, charged with murder. Rinse, repeat...

After being acquitted of murder, botanist Fern Geller tells herself she's turning her back on the past. She intends to learn everything she can about poisonous plants by completing a six-month contract at the Garden of Death. Only then does she find the answer she seeks. But, when she returns to the conservatory where the first murder took place, she discovers the new boss is missing and several others are dead. Fern is once again the chief suspect.

FBI agent London Behring should know best that appearances can be deceptive...and deadly. Fern is as beautiful as an angel, and just as gentle. He can hardly believe someone would accuse her of murder. The first set of murder charges against her had been dismissed. The question is, why would she come back to the scene of the crime – at the very moment she would fall under suspicion a second time? Does she possess the seeds of malice that would be required to walk away after committing so many crimes?

The one thing London knows he needs to do is keep his guard up at all times while he finds out the truth. Fern's charm could prove to be the very lure that's impossible for him to resist.

Book 11 is available now!
To find out more visit Dale Mayer's website.
https://geni.us/dmmalice

PSYCHIC VISIONS: SEEDS OF MALICE (BOOK #11)
CHAPTER 1

BOTANIST FERN GELLER pushed open the door to the Milton Conservatory, one of Portland's brightest tourist spots, and took a deep breath of fresh humid air. She preferred to work outside when given a chance, but, if not an option, she enjoyed working here. She used to come on a regular basis, but that was before …

There was a slight nip to the spring air. In contrast, inside it resembled the moist tropics. She loved them both, but going directly from one to the other was a little rough. She took her long braid and twisted it atop her head, as she stood in place and took several more inhales, letting her lungs adjust to the shift in humidity. Also calming herself, shoving back the worry.

Loosening the top two buttons of her jacket, she strode through the main pathway toward the tour group ahead of her. The last thing she wanted was to get embroiled in a multitude of questions, if she met the wrong people here, but she needed to know where the head of the department had hidden himself. It was a bit of a joke, but Reginald Drover preferred to be where no one could find him. A fascinating man to talk to—incredibly intelligent and extremely knowledgeable about his specialties—but the dispensing of his knowledge or the offering of any assistance was just not his forte.

How he maintained his position here was a mystery.

At least everyone else in the place was responsible.

The tour had stopped to look at the orchids, and Fern caught sight of the tour guide.

Brittany. Good. She'd help. Fern stood in the back of the group and waited until Brittany's glance landed on her. She smiled as Brittany's face lit up. Brittany was a good kid, in her second year at the university, working on her own botany degree, while helping at the conservatory on a part-time basis.

Excusing herself from the group for a moment, Brittany walked toward Fern. "Hey, I didn't realize you were back in town." Brittany opened her arms and hugged Fern. Stepping back, Brittany studied Fern's face. "You don't look too bad for someone who's been working in the Garden of Death."

Fern shook her head. "And I'm trying not to let anybody know I've returned," she noted drily. "I'm looking for Reggie. Any idea where he is?"

"No, today is my first shift in a couple days. I haven't seen him yet. I suppose you checked all the usual places?" Brittany asked, with a big smile. "It's early enough that he won't have skipped out for the day yet."

"Or so you'd assume," Fern murmured. "In the months I've been gone, has he found any new hiding spots?"

Brittany shook her head. "I don't think so, but then I'm only here a few hours a week now, so anything's possible."

"Why only a few hours?" That wasn't good.

Brittany shrugged, her eyes downcast. "I almost lost my

job. Reggie said I could stay for four hours maximum. I know the budget costs have overrun, and, with the latest news, the donations and grants have almost dried up. I'm lucky to get even this much."

"Interesting. Last I heard, the conservatory was doing well."

"Oh, it was," Brittany stated earnestly. "But, since you've been gone, you may not have heard all the rumors."

"Rumors?" Fern shoved her hands in her pockets to keep her fists hidden away. Rumors were deadly. They could destroy anybody and everything in their vicinity, often created without a grain of truth.

"Two deaths in the last couple months. One was a maintenance man, the other a visitor. Apparently unrelated. Now people are saying the place is haunted," Brittany added, with avid horror. "Everyone is saying they've been murdered."

Fern's eyes widened in shock. That couldn't be good. "Haunted? Murders?"

That was the last thing she'd expected Brittany to say. Fern knew a little too much fraternizing went on between the staff employees, causing some rumor trouble, and—although they happened everywhere, when it came to grant money—nobody could afford to have the faintest whisper of wrongdoing.

"Yes." Brittany leaned forward, so none of the tour participants heard. "And nobody knows what killed either of them." She took a step back, hurriedly twisting around to look at her group, as if to ensure they weren't listening in. "Be careful," she told Fern. Brittany glanced again at the gathering of tour guests, shifting restlessly. "I have to go. Bye." With a little finger wave, Brittany returned to the front of the tour group and announced in a loud voice, "Okay, everyone, let's move on to the cactus gardens."

With happy murmurs, they followed along.

Fern watched for several moments. This conservatory was one of the largest in the world, split up into multiple themes. It had always been a favorite of the public, even housed a special plant that only bloomed once every twenty years. People flocked in to see that rare occurrence. All these efforts brought in a lot of extra funding.

Like any grant-run institute, keeping the money flowing was always a difficult job. Any suspicious deaths would dry up the funding quickly. And that couldn't be allowed to happen.

With a frown, Fern retreated the way she'd entered.

Why two deaths now? Unless they were connected. Yet Brittany said they weren't. But then Brittany was a student, not a detective.

Surely somebody would have more information. That somebody should be Reggie. Something else to ask him about. If Fern could find him … His admin should know his whereabouts.

Fern hurried toward the office building, and, pulling out her ID card, swiped it to gain entrance. Only it wouldn't open the doors. She swiped a second time, and it still didn't work.

Through the double glass entryway doors, she saw someone inside, walking toward the exit. She stepped out of the way, waiting until he opened the door. She flashed her card, and he held the door for her to enter.

Inside she headed down the long hallway to the stairwell. She took the stairs over an elevator any day. She studied her card, wondering if it had been damaged. Or had enough change occurred in her absence that her rights and access had been revoked, and yet no one had told her?

But then why would anyone do that? She was on the board, an active member in good standing. Sure, she'd been gone for six months. That was likely the cause of the problem. Maybe they'd been forced to upgrade the security system, and, as she hadn't been around, her access may not have been sorted out.

Feeling better with that explanation, she picked up the pace and almost ran up the last set of stairs. A lot of research was done here. Although they were listed as office buildings, the main offices were at the back, behind a separate locked entryway altogether. She'd phoned Reggie's office earlier this morning and had left a message, telling him that she'd be coming to see him. It was foolish in that she doubted he ever listened to those voice mail messages.

Rebecca Ferguson wasn't at her desk out front, like she normally was.

Finally reaching Reggie's office, Fern knocked gently on the wooden door. She gazed through the window beside the door, and it appeared dark inside, empty. Getting no answer, she knocked harder, then reached for the doorknob and turned it. It was unlocked. She pushed open the door.

She could tell it was empty with one glance. Exactly as she had figured. Damn.

She walked through the larger outer office and into the inner one in the back. If he was here, he'd be in the back corner. But it was empty too. His desk was cleaned off. Walking back out, she closed both doors and headed to the little coffee room at the end of the hall.

There she found two people, both strangers in official-looking business suits, their backs to her, as they faced the huge wall-to-ceiling window.

"Have either of you seen Reggie?"

The two men pivoted her way.

She gave them a casual nod.

She couldn't see the second man, as he now stood slightly behind the first, who stepped toward her and spoke. "No. Why do you want to see him?" The other man straightened but remained silent.

She gave the first guy a startled look. Not what she'd been expecting. She followed up with a noncommittal answer. "I was hoping to talk with him this morning." She shrugged. "Only he's not in his office."

She turned to leave, but the first man called back, "Why would you expect him to be?"

She froze. Then very slowly she turned around to stare at the two men studying her. She still couldn't see the second man. "Why wouldn't I? It's his office."

The first man's lips tilted in a sneer.

She studied him, then asked, "Who are you? And just what the hell is going on here?"

"Maybe we should be asking you that question. Dr. Death, isn't it?"

Her heart froze. That name. Dear God. When would she ever be able to discard it? She kept her face blank, as her spine stiffened and her blood pumped through her veins at triple the normal rate. If she could just get one breath out …

The first man stepped closer and pulled out a badge that he held up for her to see.

FBI. She stared at it with a horrible sense of déjà vu. Like hell she wanted anything to do with these two. Ripples snaked down her spine, but at least her chest moved properly. And she breathed.

She shook her head and took a step back. "Why is the FBI at the conservatory?"

"We'd like to see your ID," the first man stated, with a hard smile. "A nickname is not the same as proper identification. If you don't mind …"

"And, if I do, particularly as you seem to think you know who I am," she snapped, "what then?"

He took one more step toward her, conveniently in front of the second man, blocking her view again. "Then we'll have to insist."

She snorted in disgust. "Of course you will. After all, that's how you deal with people, isn't it? Manhandle your way into places where you're not welcome and through situations without any finesse or care for someone else. Especially not for the truth. Typical," she stated in a waspish tone.

She was instantly sorry for spouting out her wrath, but she had no love for the FBI—or any law enforcement. The FBI just topped the list. It was hard to forgive them for the treatment she'd received at their hands. At least London wasn't here in his FBI capacity. London, brother to Derek. Derek, her ex-fiancé, who had betrayed her in the worst way. That would just be the icing on the cake. She'd be running like hell back to England and the proffered extension on her contract at Alnwick Garden.

Still, antagonizing these men right off the bat wasn't the smartest move. "Look. I'm just trying to find Reggie. Do you know where he is?" She pulled her card from her pocket and handed it over. The agent took it and read her name. Instantly a frown whispered across his face. And she knew he'd heard her name before. At least the family name. Damn, she didn't need this. "So where is he?" she asked quietly.

"We don't know. He's gone missing."

She raised both hands. "Why not just say that from the beginning? He loves to do that. It's what he does. We spend half our days looking for him, just so we can get a few problems solved around this place." She turned back to the door. "Thanks for nothing but wasting more of my time."

As she walked through the door, the first man called out, "We mean, he's gone missing, not just unavailable for a few hours or a day."

She froze.

"That is, of course, one of the reasons we wanted to speak with you."

She bowed her head. Of course it was.

She pivoted, her emotions carefully removed from her expression. "And why would there be an 'of course' in there?" She waited a long moment for one of the two men to speak. When they stayed silent, she gave a gentle sniff. "I thought so."

With a hard spin, she headed out the door once again.

And heard the first man ask in a low tone, "Did you kill him?"

The pain ricocheted inside through her gut and bounced off her bones, before shooting a rod up her spine. "No. I didn't." And she took another step, the ache deep inside almost too much to bear.

"How can we believe you? You killed the previous head of the department."

She stood stock-still and closed her eyes, shaking her head. This would never go away. It didn't matter how many times she denied it or held up the acquittal for all to see. As far as anyone else was concerned, she'd killed Ben Kimball, the former head of the conservatory—the man Reginald

Drover had replaced. It didn't matter to anyone that Ben needed killing in the worst way.

She kept her eyes closed, even when she heard movement. One of the men stood before her now.

When she lifted her eyelids, her body jolted with the shock of recognition. Her heart? Well, it knew her mate—and the pain of losing him. No, it wasn't Derek—it was someone much worse.

It was London Behring, Derek's hard-ass and way-too-sexy brother.

Shit.

Book 11 is available now!

To find out more visit Dale Mayer's website.

https://geni.us/dmmalice

Simon Says... Hide: Kate Morgan (Book #1)

Welcome to a new thriller series from *USA Today* Best-Selling Author Dale Mayer. Set in Vancouver, BC, the team of Detective Kate Morgan and Simon St. Laurant, an unwilling psychic, marries all the elements of Dale's work that you've come to love, plus so much more.

Detective Kate Morgan, newly promoted to the Vancouver PD Homicide Department, stands for the victims in her world. She was once a victim herself, just as her mother had been a victim, and then her brother—an unsolved missing child's case—was yet another victim. She can't stand those who take advantage of others, and the worst ones are those who prey on the hopes of desperate people to line their own pockets.

So, when she finds a connection between more than a half-dozen cold cases to a current case, where a child's life hangs in the balance, Kate would make a deal with the devil himself to find the culprit and to save the child.

Simon St. Laurant's grandmother had the Sight and had warned him that, once he used it, he could never walk away. Until now, her caution had made it easy to avoid that first step. But, when nightmares of his own past are triggered, Simon can't stand back and watch child after child be abused. Not without offering his help to those chasing the monsters.

Even if it means dealing with the cranky and critical Detective Kate Morgan …

Find Simon Says… Hide here!
To find out more visit Dale Mayer's website.
https://geni.us/DMSSHideUniversal

Author's Note

Thank you for reading Into the Abyss: Psychic Visions, Book 10! If you enjoyed the book, please take a moment and leave a short review.

Dear reader,

I love to hear from readers, and you can contact me at my website: www.dalemayer.com or at my Facebook author page. To be informed of new releases and special offers, sign up for my newsletter or follow me on BookBub. And if you are interested in joining Dale Mayer's Reader Group, here is the Facebook sign up page.
http://geni.us/DaleMayerFBGroup

Cheers,
Dale Mayer

About the Author

Dale Mayer is a *USA Today* best-selling author, best known for her SEALs military romances, her Psychic Visions series, and her Lovely Lethal Garden cozy series. Her contemporary romances are raw and full of passion and emotion (Broken But … Mending, Hathaway House series). Her thrillers will keep you guessing (Kate Morgan, By Death series), and her romantic comedies will keep you giggling (*It's a Dog's Life*, a stand-alone novella; and the Broken Protocols series, starring Charming Marvin, the cat).

Dale honors the stories that come to her—and some of them are crazy, break all the rules and cross multiple genres!

To go with her fiction, she also writes nonfiction in many different fields, with books available on résumé writing, companion gardening, and the US mortgage system. All her books are available in print and ebook format.

Connect with Dale Mayer Online

Dale's Website – www.dalemayer.com
Twitter – @DaleMayer
Facebook Page – geni.us/DaleMayerFBFanPage
Facebook Group – geni.us/DaleMayerFBGroup
BookBub – geni.us/DaleMayerBookbub
Instagram – geni.us/DaleMayerInstagram
Goodreads – geni.us/DaleMayerGoodreads
Newsletter – geni.us/DaleNews

Also by Dale Mayer

Published Adult Books:

Shadow Recon

Magnus, Book 1

Bullard's Battle

Ryland's Reach, Book 1

Cain's Cross, Book 2

Eton's Escape, Book 3

Garret's Gambit, Book 4

Kano's Keep, Book 5

Fallon's Flaw, Book 6

Quinn's Quest, Book 7

Bullard's Beauty, Book 8

Bullard's Best, Book 9

Bullard's Battle, Books 1–2

Bullard's Battle, Books 3–4

Bullard's Battle, Books 5–6

Bullard's Battle, Books 7–8

Terkel's Team

Damon's Deal, Book 1

Wade's War, Book 2

Gage's Goal, Book 3

Calum's Contact, Book 4

Rick's Road, Book 5

Kate Morgan

Simon Says… Hide, Book 1

Simon Says… Jump, Book 2

Simon Says… Ride, Book 3

Simon Says… Scream, Book 4

Simon Says… Run, Book 5

Hathaway House

Aaron, Book 1

Brock, Book 2

Cole, Book 3

Denton, Book 4

Elliot, Book 5

Finn, Book 6

Gregory, Book 7

Heath, Book 8

Iain, Book 9

Jaden, Book 10

Keith, Book 11

Lance, Book 12

Melissa, Book 13

Nash, Book 14

Owen, Book 15

Percy, Book 16

Quinton, Book 17

Hathaway House, Books 1–3

Hathaway House, Books 4–6

Hathaway House, Books 7–9

The K9 Files

Ethan, Book 1

Pierce, Book 2

Zane, Book 3

Blaze, Book 4

Lucas, Book 5

Parker, Book 6

Carter, Book 7

Weston, Book 8

Greyson, Book 9

Rowan, Book 10

Caleb, Book 11

Kurt, Book 12

Tucker, Book 13

Harley, Book 14

Kyron, Book 15

Jenner, Book 16

The K9 Files, Books 1–2

The K9 Files, Books 3–4

The K9 Files, Books 5–6

The K9 Files, Books 7–8

The K9 Files, Books 9–10

The K9 Files, Books 11–12

Lovely Lethal Gardens

Arsenic in the Azaleas, Book 1

Bones in the Begonias, Book 2

Corpse in the Carnations, Book 3

Daggers in the Dahlias, Book 4

Evidence in the Echinacea, Book 5

Footprints in the Ferns, Book 6

Gun in the Gardenias, Book 7

Handcuffs in the Heather, Book 8

Ice Pick in the Ivy, Book 9

Jewels in the Juniper, Book 10

Killer in the Kiwis, Book 11

Lifeless in the Lilies, Book 12

Murder in the Marigolds, Book 13

Nabbed in the Nasturtiums, Book 14

Offed in the Orchids, Book 15

Poison in the Pansies, Book 16

Quarry in the Quince, Book 17

Revenge in the Roses, Book 18

Lovely Lethal Gardens, Books 1–2

Lovely Lethal Gardens, Books 3–4

Lovely Lethal Gardens, Books 5–6

Lovely Lethal Gardens, Books 7–8

Lovely Lethal Gardens, Books 9–10

Psychic Vision Series

Tuesday's Child

Hide 'n Go Seek

Maddy's Floor

Garden of Sorrow

Knock Knock…

Rare Find

Eyes to the Soul

Now You See Her

Shattered

Into the Abyss

Seeds of Malice

Eye of the Falcon

Itsy-Bitsy Spider

Unmasked

Deep Beneath

From the Ashes

Stroke of Death

Ice Maiden

Snap, Crackle…

What If…

Talking Bones

Psychic Visions Books 1–3

Psychic Visions Books 4–6

Psychic Visions Books 7–9

By Death Series

Touched by Death

Haunted by Death

Chilled by Death

By Death Books 1–3

Broken Protocols – Romantic Comedy Series

Cat's Meow

Cat's Pajamas

Cat's Cradle

Cat's Claus

Broken Protocols 1-4

Broken and… Mending

Skin

Scars

Scales (of Justice)

Broken but… Mending 1-3

Glory

Genesis

Tori

Celeste

Glory Trilogy

Biker Blues

Morgan: Biker Blues, Volume 1

Cash: Biker Blues, Volume 2

SEALs of Honor

Mason: SEALs of Honor, Book 1

Hawk: SEALs of Honor, Book 2

Dane: SEALs of Honor, Book 3

Swede: SEALs of Honor, Book 4

Shadow: SEALs of Honor, Book 5

Cooper: SEALs of Honor, Book 6

Markus: SEALs of Honor, Book 7

Evan: SEALs of Honor, Book 8

Mason's Wish: SEALs of Honor, Book 9

Heroes for Hire

Heroes for Hire, Books 4–6

Heroes for Hire, Books 7–9

Heroes for Hire, Books 10–12

Heroes for Hire, Books 13–15

Heroes for Hire, Books 16–18

Heroes for Hire, Books 19–21

Heroes for Hire, Books 22–24

SEALs of Steel

Badger: SEALs of Steel, Book 1

Erick: SEALs of Steel, Book 2

Cade: SEALs of Steel, Book 3

Talon: SEALs of Steel, Book 4

Laszlo: SEALs of Steel, Book 5

Geir: SEALs of Steel, Book 6

Jager: SEALs of Steel, Book 7

The Final Reveal: SEALs of Steel, Book 8

SEALs of Steel, Books 1–4

SEALs of Steel, Books 5–8

SEALs of Steel, Books 1–8

The Mavericks

Kerrick, Book 1

Griffin, Book 2

Jax, Book 3

Beau, Book 4

Asher, Book 5

Ryker, Book 6

Miles, Book 7

Nico, Book 8

Keane, Book 9

Lennox, Book 10

Gavin, Book 11

Shane, Book 12

Diesel, Book 13

Jerricho, Book 14

Killian, Book 15

Hatch, Book 16

Corbin, Book 17

The Mavericks, Books 1–2

The Mavericks, Books 3–4

The Mavericks, Books 5–6

The Mavericks, Books 7–8

The Mavericks, Books 9–10

The Mavericks, Books 11–12

Collections

Dare to Be You…

Dare to Love…

Dare to be Strong…

RomanceX3

Standalone Novellas

It's a Dog's Life

Riana's Revenge

Second Chances

Published Young Adult Books:

Family Blood Ties Series

Vampire in Denial

Vampire in Distress

Vampire in Design

Vampire in Deceit

Vampire in Defiance

Vampire in Conflict

Vampire in Chaos

Vampire in Crisis

Vampire in Control

Vampire in Charge

Family Blood Ties Set 1–3

Family Blood Ties Set 1–5

Family Blood Ties Set 4–6

Family Blood Ties Set 7–9

Sian's Solution, A Family Blood Ties Series Prequel
 Novelette

Design series

Dangerous Designs

Deadly Designs

Darkest Designs

Design Series Trilogy

Standalone

In Cassie's Corner

Gem Stone (a Gemma Stone Mystery)

Published Non-Fiction Books:

Career Essentials

Career Essentials: The Résumé

Career Essentials: The Cover Letter

Career Essentials: The Interview

Career Essentials: 3 in 1

9 781988 315256